HORACE McCOY'S

KISS TOMORROW GOODBYE

**MIDNIGHT
CLASSICS**

LONDON / NEW YORK

Library of Congress Catalog Card Number: 96-68817

A complete catalogue record for this book is available
from the British Library on request

First published in the USA in 1948 by Random House
First published in the UK in 1949 by Barker

This edition published in 1996 in the USA by
Serpent's Tail, 180 Varick Street, 10th floor, New York, NY
10014, and in 1997 by Serpent's Tail, 4 Blackstock Mews,
London N4

Cover design by Rex Ray
Set in Bodoni BE Regular by Avon Dataset,
Bidford-on-Avon, Warks
Printed in Great Britain by Cox & Wyman Ltd., Reading,
Berkshire

*. . . part
one*

. . . chapter one

This is how it is when you wake up in the morning of the morning you have waited a lifetime for: there is no waking state. You are all at once wide awake, so wide awake that it seems you have slipped all the opiatic degrees of waking, that you have had none of the sense-impressions as your soul again returns to your body from wherever it has been; you open your eyes and you are completely awake, as if you had not been asleep at all. That is how it was with me. This was the morning it was going to happen, and I lay there trembling with accumulated excitement and wishing it would happen now and be done with, this instant, consuming nervous energy that I should have been saving for the climax, knowing full well that it could not possibly happen for another hour, maybe another hour and a half, till around five-thirty. It was now only a little after four. It was still so dark I could not see anything distinctly, but I could tell by the little of the morning that I could smell that it was only a little after four. Not much of the morning could get into the place where I was, and the portions that did were always pretty well mauled and no wonder: they had to fight their way in through a single window at the same time a solid shaft of stink was going out. This was a prison barracks where seventy-two unwashed men slept chained to their bunks, and when the individual odors of seventy-two unwashed men finally gather into one pillar of stink you have got a pillar of stink the like of which you cannot conceive; majestic, nonpareil, transcendental, K.

But it never intimidated that early morning. Ever indomitable, it always came back, and always a little of it got through to me. I was always awake to greet these fragments, hungrily smelling what little freshness they had left by the time they got back to me, smelling them frugally, in careful precious sniffs, letting them dig in the vaults of my memory, letting them uncover early morning sounds of a lifetime ago: bluejays and woodpeckers and countless other birds met like medieval knights and thrusting at each other with long sharp lances of song, the crowings of roosters, the brassy bleats of hungry sheep and the mooing of cows, saying, 'No-o-o hay, No-o-o milk', that is what my grandfather said they were saying and my grandfather knew. He knew everything there was to know about everything that was completely unimportant. He knew the names of all Hadrian's mistresses and the real reason, hushed-up by the historians, why Richard took the Third Crusade off to the Holy Land and the week the Alaskan reindeers would mate and the hours of the high tides of Nova Scotia; my grandfather knew everything except how to run the farm, lying there deep in the feather-bed in the side room where Longstreet once spent the night, buried under the quilts that hid me from old John Brown of Osawatomie, dead and gone these many years, but who, they said, still clumped the foothills of the Gap gathering up disobedient little boys; smelling the morning and hearing the sounds, smelling and hearing, hiding from old John Brown (but hiding from something else too, although I did not then know what it was), frightened with little-boy fright (which, I also was to find out, was not so annihilative as grown-man fright), waiting for the daylight ...

The darkness began to fade slowly at the window, and a few men turned over, rattling their chains, waking up; but you did not need these noises to tell you that there was movement any

4

more than any other wild animal needs noises to tell him there is movement; the pillar of stink which had been lying in laminae like the coats of an onion was now being peeled and a little of everybody was everywhere. There was coughing and grunting and hawking and much spitting, and then the man in the next bunk, Budlong, a skinny sickly sodomist, turned on his side facing me and said in a ruttish voice: 'I had another dream about you last night, sugar.'

It will be your last, you Caresser of Calves, I thought. 'Was it as nice as the others?' I asked.

'Nicer . . .' he said.

'You're sweet. I adore you,' I said, feeling a fine fast exhilaration that today was the day that I was going to kill him, that I was finally going to kill him – as soon as I got my hands on those pistols I was going to kill him. I hope Holiday knows what the hell about those pistols, I thought; I hope they're where they're supposed to be, I hope Cobbett doesn't let us down. Cobbett was the clerk of the farm who doubled on Sundays as the guard in the visitors' cage, an old man who had spent his life as a chain-gang and prison-farm guard, now too feeble to have a squad of his own, and pensioned off to sinecures. He had taken a shine to Holiday the first time she had come to visit us, and from then on he had been less and less strict in the matter of her visiting hours, and now she had gotten him to help us make the break. He was to have met her last night and got the pistols and stashed them for us. They were to be sealed in an inner tube and hidden in the irrigation ditch that ran along the upper end of the cantaloupe patch where we were working. The exact spot of their submergence was to be marked with a rock the size of a human head, on which there would be a dab of white paint, placed in line with the pistols but on the other side of the ditch where it would be less likely to attract attention. This was all that Cobbett had to do. I hoped he had done it. If he had, if the pistols were there I was going to kill this swine Budlong, as sure as God made little apples I was going to kill him. . . .

All of a sudden the door banged open and there was Harris, the sergeant, standing in the gloom – no eyes, no nose, no mouth, just a great big hunk of obscene flesh standing there in the doorway with his arm hooked under a Winchester, yelling for us to hit the deck. Always he stood there in the same way and always he yelled the same thing and always the prisoners in the rear of the barracks called him the same names. But I never called him names. I was too busy being glad that the door was finally open. I lay there waiting for him to come and take the manacles off my ankles, and the fresh morning rushed through the door like children coming into the living-room on Christmas morning. . . .

On the way to the mess-shack I lagged behind, trying to let Toko catch up with me. He was going out with me and I wanted to see what kind of a night he had had, whether he had gotten any sleep. Probably not. He was just far enough removed from imbecility to have lain awake all night worrying, he had just enough imagination to worry. He was the last guy I would have picked as a partner in a crash-out; he was very young, this would be his first break, and Christ alone knew how his reflexes would work if something went wrong. But I had had nothing to do with picking him. Holiday had wanted him out and she had included me for the sake of whatever insurance my experience could promise; and that was fine because I did not know this country and had no friends around, and no money with which to buy friends, the only kind of friends I needed. Breaking out with Toko was risky business, but that was the way it had to be, I had no choice and that was fine. A hell of a lot of good my intellect was doing me locked up in this nidus of stink with offal like these, a hell of a lot of good, and hearing for month after month after month of the achievements of bums like Floyd and Karpis and Nelson and Dillinger, who were getting rich off cracker-box banks, bums who had no talent at all, bums who could hardly get in out of the rain. It was fine that I had this chance, however risky. Jesus, just wait till I got outside again. . . . Toko was so far back that I couldn't get to him without obviously trying to get to him, and this was no time for that. Once or twice during breakfast I caught his eye and smiled a little and winked very carefully, telling him not to worry, that this was going to be a breeze. He winked back and I hoped he knew what I was talking about. . . .

When we came out of the mess-shack it was almost full-up daylight. The sun had not risen yet from behind the mountains, but it had poked up a couple of playful fingers, goosing the last thin remnant of night, and the grey was scattering fast. Harris blew a short sharp blast on his tarnished silver whistle and the prisoners started racing for the water-closet. Thirteen stools, first come, first served and happy evacuations to the fleet of foot. If it was Number Two you had to do you had to rush because come hell or high water, you had only five minutes. Looking at the lump of men wriggling to get through the small door I could believe the stories some of the old-timers handed down about the bitter bloody feuds this had started; and I could believe some of the funny stories they told too, for, after all, five minutes are not very many for an operation like this unless you have your bowels under impeccable control.

I lighted a cigarette and looked around for Toko and in a moment I saw him coming towards me in what he patently thought was a casual saunter, but which was much more of an excited waddle. There was furtiveness in his face and furtiveness in his manner. The one morning of all the mornings that had for our purpose to look like just another day of ceaseless drudgery and here he was, advertising that something was up. It was risky enough without this.

7

'Please, please, relax,' I said quietly. 'Take it easy. Stop acting like everybody was in on this. Nobody knows about this but you and I and Cobbett. You got to remember that.'

'What about Cobbett?' he asked. 'Can we count on him?'

'This is a fine time to worry about that,' I said.

'I got to get out of here. I got to,' he said desperately.

'Relax,' I said. 'You'll get out. Relax.'

'You think there'll be a slip-up?'

'Not if the guns are where they're supposed to be.'

'After we get the guns. You think it'll go the way we figured?'

'It's up to us to make it go that way.'

'You think there'll be any shooting?'

How am I going to kill Budlong without some shooting? I wanted to ask. 'Take it easy,' I said. 'Relax. Please. This is just another day. Stop advertising.'

He licked his lips and looked around and sucked in the air through his nostrils.

'Goddamn it,' I said, 'I'm in on this to see that it goes all right. That's why Holiday took me in, isn't it? Isn't it?'

'Yeah . . .'

'Well, then, relax.'

This seemed to unloosen him a little. 'Ain't you supposed to be in the crapper?' he asked.

'I know what I'm doing,' I said. 'Relax. I'm going now. . . .'

He held out his hand for the cigarette I was smoking and I gave it to him and walked off towards the water-closet. One of the guards, Byers, was standing just outside the door. He had a heft of gut hanging from under his vest and the front of his cheap coat was shiny from the rubbing of the Winchester he always had cradled in his arms. He looked at me derisively as I approached. 'You're that dainty son-of-a-bitch, ain't you?' he said. 'You got to wait until you got the whole place all to yourself, ain't you?'

'I don't feel so good,' I said. 'I got the runners. They came on all of a sudden,' I said, going inside, pushing past the men who were coming out. Seven or eight were still in there, grimacing and grunting, straining against time, racing the whistle that soon would blow. I walked down to the end of the row, to the last open, unpartitioned stool and eased myself over it and put on my face what I hoped was the proper expression of distress. One by one the others finished and went out and I was left all alone. Hardly had the last man gone through the door before I heard the two short blasts from Harris's whistle.

Byers poked his head inside. 'Come on!' he shouted at me.

I spread my hands helplessly. He hauled himself through the door and stomped to me. This was his favorite part of the job as a guard. I knew what was coming, but I had to take it in order to set up the escape.

'You heard me!' he bellowed. 'Get off there!'

'I'm sick,' I said, putting agony into my face. 'I'm sick as hell, Mister Byers. I got the runners. . . .'

He slapped me hard across the face with the palm of his horny hand.

'Please, Mister Byers. I'm sick. . . .'

He hit me with the back of his hand, knocking-sweeping me off the stool.

'Fall in!' he roared.

'Yes sir, my liege, my master,' I said.

I picked myself up off the floor and started out, pulling up my pants as I went, with him stomping along behind, banging me in the rump with his Winchester at every step.

Oh, yes, indeed, there'll be a bit of shooting, I was thinking . . .

I fell in line directly behind Toko and when Harris right-faced us and started us for the cantaloupe patch we were then side by side. There were six guards on horseback, and fifty prisoners in

9

this detail. The path we took was through a dry-wash to the irrigation ditch, across the bridge of the irrigation ditch, and then northward towards the mountains to the patch. The patch was only half a mile from the barracks, a short half mile in the morning, but a very long half mile in the late afternoon. That I didn't have to worry about any more – I hoped. I had dragged my butt down this long endless half mile for the very last time – I hoped.

The short limbs of my favorite eucalyptus tree bowed good-bye to me as I marched by. It's been nice knowing you too, I thought. Well, good-bye and good luck. I won't be coming this way again – I hope. And wait a little while before you let your children out to play. I wouldn't want any of them getting hurt. It's just possible, just barely possible that there *might* be a bit of shooting. . . .

We swung out of the wash, up the back into the open, into the old alfalfa field we worked in season. The sun was coming up now, bright and brassy, an honest sun, not throwing out a lot of beautiful colors to fool you into thinking the day would be beautiful too, but hanging there, with no color at all, for everybody to look upon and realize that its only mission was to burn and scorch. It was not quite five-thirty, but already a lot of automobiles were rolling along Highway 67. You could see a few and hear more, so stethosopic was the quality of that fragile morning air that you could hear every beat of the motors. Those people were in a hurry, trying to get where they were going before the sun really levelled off; by ten-thirty or eleven the valley would be a furnace.

Harris started dropping back, and I knew we were coming to the bridge across the irrigation ditch. He was always the last one over because he was in charge of this detail.

I rubbed elbows with Toko on the bridge.

'Keep an eye open for that rock,' I whispered.

10

He did not say anything. I looked at him out of the corner of my eye. His upper lip was twitching.

Oh, God, I thought, he's going to screw this up for sure. 'Take it easy,' I whispered. 'The bus will be along pretty soon. . . .'

That part of the plan also was my idea. Since we did not have watches, and since perfect timing was absolutely necessary, I had suggested to Holiday that we use the air horn of the Greyhound bus as the signal for the break. The mountain highway was full of dangerous curves, and the driver of the northbound bus always sounded the horn at these spots. The bus came along the highway early every morning around seven-fifteen; it hit the grades, its diesel purring the way Satchmo blows his trumpet, until the first close turn, the bottom of a tight S, when it cut loose its horn in two blasts that rocked every living thing in the valley. In a few more minutes it made the turn at the top of the S, cutting loose with that horn again. This blast, the third one, was the signal for the kick-off. It would mean that Holiday and Jinx would be waiting on the dirt road, half a mile from the highway, beside a thicket of eucalypti. It was up to Toko and me to have the guns by then and when the third blast was heard we were to make a run for the thicket, a hundred yards from the cantaloupe patch. Once in there we would be safe, for the trees were so close together the guards couldn't get through on horseback. These were not the eucalypti with the thick trunks, these were the small ones, with trunks no bigger than your leg, and so numerous that you had to walk through them sidewise.

After we had finally crossed the bridge and were strung out northward again I kept my eyes on the irrigation ditch, looking for the rock Holiday had said would be daubed with white paint. Toko was on my left, between me and the ditch, but he was no help at all.

He kept his face and his eyes straight to the front. We were only a few feet apart, but it was too far for me to say anything without being overheard, too far for me to try to close the space without attracting attention. which would have been highly suspicious: these bastards would sell a guy out for an extra spoon of sugar, and I was too busy looking for the rock to waste time trying to catch his eye. We were getting closer and closer to the patch where we would be broken up and put to work, and I had to locate that rock before then. No rock, no break and we would have to start all over. I had set my heart on crashing out of here today. Jesus, I didn't want to have to go through the waiting again. This was what came of dealing with a senile old bastard like Cobbett, this was what came of not having any money. Jesus, that was the answer – money. You got just what you paid for – be it a handkerchief or a prison-farm guard. Money. That was the answer to Nelson's success, and the success of all the other bums – money. Jesus, would I *ever* have any money? Get me out of here, God, I thought, and I'll get the money. I'll endow a church. . . .

'. . . Halt!' Harris shouted.

The detail stopped.

'The first eight men with Burton!'

Burton was another guard. He counted off eight men and started leading them off across the field.

'Forward – march!' Harris yelled at the rest of us.

We started moving again and I glanced at Toko and saw that his face was paling beneath the tan, and that began to worry me all the more. Jesus, didn't he have sense enough to know that if the rock wasn't there, it just wasn't there and there was nothing we could do about it but start all over! I winked at him a few times and looked away – and then I saw it.

The rock.

It was the size of a baby's head and it had a daub of white paint on the top. The corners of my heart were caught and pinched with joy. The rock was only about twenty feet from the iron-wheeled chemical privy that always rolled with us to the different fields we worked. Holiday had put the guns as close to the privy as she could. A hell of a girl, that Holiday. A hell of a buy, that Cobbett. She really must have given him something to remember her by. I looked at Toko. He hadn't even seen it. . . .

'. . . Halt!' Harris yelled.

The detail stopped.

'You next ten men with Byers!'

Byers came up on his horse and counted off ten of us and we started following him across the patch.

'Forward – march!' Harris yelled at the others, and what remained of the detail moved off behind us.

Still side by side. Toko and I picked our way carefully across the patch so as not to bruise the melons or the vines. The cantaloupe patch, like the other fields we worked, was leased to a civilian contractor and he was very particular about his melons and vines. They must not be bruised. It was a very serious offence. But so far as anybody knew, he had never complained about the guards riding their horses through the patch.

'I didn't see it. . . .' Toko whispered.

'Did you look?'

'Sure. Whaddya suppose happened?'

'Take it easy.'

'I got to make it, I got to . . .' he whispered tensely.

'I saw it,' I whispered.

'You did?'

'Relax . . .'

'It had me worried. . . .'

Your worries are not over by a long shot, I was thinking. . . .

...*chapter two*

The part of the field where we were working was halfway between the irrigation ditch and the eucalypti thicket we were to head for when we had heard the signal. We were picking the cantaloupes, stacking them in little pyramids for the contractor's trucks to collect later, working towards the thicket. Byers had tied his horse to a small oak tree near by and was standing in the shade, a corn-cob pipe in his mouth, watching his squad like a padrone. The only difference was that Byers had the Winchester cradled across his stomach.

Toko and I were working close together, a little apart from the others, which included Budlong. This was delightful. This was a happy augury. Now I would not have to worry about my marksmanship. Now I had him at almost pointblank range.

'It's getting late, ain't it?' Toko said to me.

'We've got plenty of time,' I said. I was not nervous any more. I had all the confidence in the world. I had the feel of this thing now.

'Seems pretty late to me. . . .'

'Sun fools you this time of the year,' I said. 'Climbs fast. It's only seven. . . .'

I picked another armful of melons and stacked them, and took another look at the sun. You would think that at seven o'clock in the morning the sun would hardly be above the horizon, but here it was well up in the sky. When I got back to

14

Toko, I said, 'Well, here I go. And for God's sake, relax. You hear?'

'I'm relaxed,' he said.

'Stay that way,' I said. 'Falling out!' I yelled at Byers.

'Falling out, second squad!' Byers yelled, warning the guard of the next squad that he would be absent for a few minutes. He came over to me and stopped. 'You?' he asked.

'Feels like I got the runners again,' I said.

'He oughtn't to be working,' Toko said. 'He's sick. . . .'

Byers smiled at him lewdly. 'If he could only cook, heh?'

'He's got the runners,' Toko said.

'Something I ate, no doubt,' I said.

'All right, go ahead. . . .' Byers said, gesturing with the Winchester.

I started across the patch to the chemical privy, careful not to step on any of the vines, knowing that Byers was watching me, a pace behind.

'I'm sorry about this, Imperator,' I said over my shoulder.

'You know what I think?' he said. 'I don't think you got the runners. I don't think that's your trouble. I think you're constipated, be damned if I don't. . . .'

He kicked me hard in the rump, almost knocking me down.

'I wish you wouldn't do that, Majesty,' I said.

'That's the trouble. Sure,' he said. 'You're constipated. You need loosening up.'

He kicked me again. I fell against the wagon.

'Now, you make it snappy,' he said.

'Yes, sir, Mister Byers,' I said, going inside the wagon, behind the canvas flap.

I quickly slipped my pants down and sat on the hole looking through the crack at Byers. He was standing at the side of the wagon, fifteen or twenty feet away, and I knew that it was now or never. I got up off the seat and buttoned my pants and dropped to the floor, crawling to the opening, to the canvas flap. I looked out. Everything was just as it should be. I crawled out on the ground and lay motionless, face down and inert, the side of my face pressed flat against the earth, smelling the richness of the loam and the dampness of the dew that had now retreated from the sun to the sheltered side of the furrow, child-bound again for a moment, remembering the smell of earth and dew from a lifetime ago, but remembering in scraps and not the whole, remembering from the outside inward instead of from the inside outward . . . I started crawling up the furrow to the irrigation ditch, having no sense of motion at all. The only way I could tell I was moving was in the feel of the earth scraping against my belly. I finally reached the mass of cantaloupe vines where three days ago Toko and I had been plucking, and which was now dried-brown and brittle-dead. This gave me good concealment, allowing me to raise myself a little on my hands and knees and crawl instead of wiggle. When I reached the end of the furrow near the rock marker I hurtled for the edge of the ditch, wanting to get those guns as quickly as possible. The ditch was wide but not deep, not more than two feet, and was used principally by the truck farms farther down the valley. I reached into the water, feeling for the package, groping for it with both hands. Then I touched it and yanked it up. It was a red inner tube that had been doubled and redoubled and then vulcanized, and tied to it was a pocket knife. I opened the knife and hacked at the tube and finally split it. There were two loaded pistols and two boxes of ammunition. The pistols were thirty-eight caliber revolvers, not my favorite gun, but favorite enough for right now. I stuck the guns and the boxes of ammunition inside my denim jumper and turned around and started crawling back.

How much time had elapsed, I did not know; not much, perhaps two minutes, but certainly no more than three. This part of the plan there had never been any doubt about; I knew that I could bring this off, but from now on every passing second increased the danger and pulled tauter and tauter the thread of risk. Still, I had no impulse of panic. I had the feel of this thing now; I had myself under perfect control. This was what I had been waiting for. I had told myself a thousand times that if the pistols were there I would no longer worry about Toko... I crawled back down the furrow and reached the canvas curtain of the wagon and crawled inside, dropping my pants and sitting down again, trying to make a noise with my bowels to prove that I had been there all the time. I looked through the crack at Byers. He was still standing there, but he was staring at the wagon impatiently. There was no uneasiness in his manner, just impatience. I grunted and groaned a few times and then reached for a piece of newspaper on the stack, and tore it noisily, but did not dispel any of his impatience. He was still glaring at the wagon. I stood up and brushed myself off, using another piece of newspaper to dry my forearms and rub off some of the mud, and adjusted the guns and boxes of ammunition inside my jumper so they would not be noticed, buttoned my pants and stepped out.

'I thought maybe you had fell in,' Byers said.

You're a bowel-watcher, I thought. You're reviving a lost art. 'It was that supper last night,' I said. 'I have a very delicate stomach.'

'Everything about you is delicate, ain't it?' he said.

Including my trigger finger, you peasant bastard, I thought. 'I'm sorry, me-lord,' I said.

'For God's sake, stop whining!' he said. 'Move along.'

'I'm sorry, sire,' I said, moving along....

When I got back to Toko he was stooped over, digging into a cluster of vines. He paused, not moving his body, looking up at me past his elbow. With my thumb I indicated that I had the pistols inside my jumper. He straightened up, holding in both

17

hands a cantaloupe almost as big as a watermelon.

'Ain't that a beauty?' he said.

He moved over and stacked it with the others, and then came back to me and started digging in the same cluster.

'How many was there?' he asked.

'Two,' I said. I did not say anything about the boxes of ammunition. If anything went wrong, if he happened to get hit, it would be bad enough for them to find the pistol on him without also finding a box of ammunition. A box of ammunition is a hell of a lot easier to back-track than a pistol.

I leaned over and started digging in the cluster with him. I switched my eyes around and made certain nobody was watching us and then slipped him one of the pistols. He stuck it inside his jumper.

'Is it loaded?' he asked.

'Yeah,' I said. 'Now, take it easy. This is in the bag.'

From the north from the mountains, the strong vibrant music of a diesel motor reached our ears. We looked at each other. 'You see how these things get done when they get done by an expert?' I said. 'It's just like pushing a button. Now, start inching down towards the eucalypti thicket. Less distance we have to cover, less dangerous it'll be.'

'You think there'll be any shooting?'

Did I think there'd be any shooting? . . . 'It won't matter if you zig-zag,' I said. 'Remember that. Zig-zag.'

His face was paling again.

'It won't be long now,' I said. 'Go on, start inching down. And follow my lead.'

I followed him as he moved along the vines, stooped over, pretending that we were looking for melons. In a minute or two we had come close to the group that contained Budlong. He looked up grinning.

'Hello, sugar,' he said to me. 'Now, Toko, you treat this pretty

18

thing nice,' he said to Toko. 'Like to get myself a little of that,' he said to the others.

The others laughed.

'Dear old Budlong,' I said. 'Dear, dear Budlong. The Satyr of the Stable. Is it really true that you dream about me of a lonely night? You're not just saying that, are you?'

He smirked but said nothing, and Byers came up, stopping a few feet away.

'Looks like a goddamn Easter egg hunt,' he said. 'You guys stop jawing and scatter out. . . .'

We started scattering out, and then the two blasts of the bus horn came, so close together they almost overlapped. This was only the signal to get ready, not the signal to act, but with Byers so near and Toko shaking with nerves, I knew this had to be the moment, ready or not. Byers had suddenly sensed something, too. He took a step backward, uncradling his Winchester in a vague, instinctive sort of way, and I shot him in the stomach. He had the Winchester and I wasn't taking any chances with him. You can shoot a man in the head or in the heart and he may live long enough to kill you, it is possible; but if you hit him in the stomach, just above the belt buckle you paralyse him instantaneously. He may be conscious of what is happening, but there is not a goddamn thing he can do about it. I saw the bullet go into the little island of white shirt that showed between his vest and his trousers. The Winchester spilled out of his arms and he went down to the ground, sprawled in a heavy heap like a melted snow-man.

'Run!' I shouted to Toko.

Budlong was utterly dumbfounded. He didn't move a muscle.

'Here's a little dream I've been dreaming about you, sugar...' I said.

He still didn't move. When I extended my arm he just looked at the gun. It was no more than eighteen inches from his face. I squeezed the trigger and the bullet hit him in the left eye and a drop of fluid squirted and the eyelid fell over the hole as a window shade falls over a pane of darkness. There was no blood at all.

I turned and started running hard over the furrows, over the uneven ground, following Toko, zig-zagging, doubled over as far as I could lean and still get the maximum speed from my legs. All the guards were shooting now and the mountains were throwing back the thin quivering echoes of the Winchesters, but I was not worried even for the length of a half-formed thought. They hadn't done any shooting since God knew when. . . .

Toko's legs pumping up and down soon came into my line of vision and as I pulled beside him he stopped abruptly and straightened up and the look in his face was a distillation of all the nightmares that have been dreamed by everybody since time began.

'I'm scared. . . .' he said.

I kept on running for a few feet and then I turned, slowing up, looking back. Harris was on his horse, coming across the patch towards me, but the ground was uneven for the horse too, and his gait was jerky and cautious Toko was standing ten feet away, between me and Harris. I aimed at Harris but when I shot I shot at Toko. The bullet him him in the temple and a big saliva bubble formed on his lips and he fell forward in the dirt.

I started running again. The Winchesters were still shooting but I never heard the sound of a single bullet, only the crack of rifle fire and the thin echoes from the mountains. As long as these bastards could reach you with a club or a knotted rawhide strap their marksmanship was magnificent, but when it came to shooting . . .

I reached the edge of the patch and hurdled a small irrigation ditch, another irrigation ditch, a small one, a secondary one, diving into the eucalypti thicket. In here, in this thicket, I now actually heard the bullets for the first time. They were striking

20

the leaves and limbs with whispering laps and then, lightningly, there were new sounds close by, loud and harsh, and I looked up, startled and a little shaken, and saw that it was a machine gun. It was spitting jagged streaks of flame a foot long, and it was being held in the hands of a man I had never seen before.

The shock of seeing a man there instead of Holiday froze me. I felt as if someone had hit me in the navel with a blizzard. He wore a cap and a bow tie and a blue suit, and he was left standing at the edge of the thicket, full in the open, his left forearm against a sapling so young and slender that it trembled with the recoils, moving the machine gun from side to side in a short, straight line, like a man patiently watering a strip of lawn. I just lay there. . . .

'Go around to the other side!' he shouted at me, and then I realized that it wasn't a man at all, it was Holiday.

I got up, moving around to the other side, and looked out at the cantaloupe patch. Neither Harris nor his horse was to be seen. Some of the prisoners were stretched out flat beside the irrigation ditch, and to one side a group of guards were firing from kneeling positions, but not hitting anything. They were a good two hundred yards away. Holiday gave them another burst from the machine gun and then lowered it.

'This way,' she said, running off through the thicket. The bullets from the guards' Winchester were still slapping around among the trees, but no more harmful than spring rain on a slate roof. A new sedan was parked on the dirt road ahead, a good-looking one. The motor was running and Jinx was at the wheel. He had the rear door open as Holiday and I got there, and we dived in. The door slammed and the sedan lurched. Holiday pulled herself up on the seat and started putting a new drum of ammunition on the gun.

'That's a hell of a thing there,' I said. 'Jesus Christ, that's a *hell* of a thing!'

21

'I borrowed it from a friend of mine,' she said. She looked at me. 'That's the second brother I've had killed by the cops,' she said slowly,

'Poor old Toko,' I said. 'He straightened up at the wrong time. I tried to get him to keep going . . .'

She nodded to two cardboard suit boxes that were standing on end on the floor. 'Better put those on. I'm sorry about the shoes.'

'Didn't you get 'em?'

'Nine-C. I couldn't get eight and a half-D.'

'That's all right,' I said. I picked up one of the boxes opening it. Inside there was a complete outfit, shirt, socks, shoes and suit. They were cheap and shoddy, but what the hell . . .

'That's Toko's,' she said. 'The other one's yours.'

'He had the gun on him when he fell,' I said. 'I didn't have time to get it.'

'They can't trace it,' she said, laying the machine gun on the floor, propping it against the door, muzzle down.

'I'm glad of that,' I said.

I had my denim jumper half off when Jinx made the turn from the dirt road on to the highway. The sharp swerve threw me off balance on to the floor, across her feet. As I got back into the seat I felt the car flatten out and pick up speed.

'I'm sure glad Cobbett came through,' I said. 'That was the only thing that worried me.'

'I knew he'd work his end all right,' she said.

'We ought to give him a bonus,' I said.

'He's had his bonus,' she said, 'and I got plenty left. . . .'

You certainly have, I thought. You got more of that left than any dame in the world.

She reached over the front seat and got another suit box from beside Jinx. She lifted the top and took out a neatly folded dress. She took off the cap she was wearing and dropped it to the floor, and then fluffed her hair with her hands.

'That was pretty good,' I said. 'Wearing a man's suit . . .'

She smiled at me, unbuckling her trousers but not unbuttoning the fly, slipping them off, arching her shoulders against the back seat to raise her buttocks out of the way. Her legs were slim and white. I could see the skin in minutest detail, the pigments and pores and numberless valley-cracks that crisscrossed above her knees, forming patterns that were as lovely and intricate as snow crystals. And there was something else I saw too out of the corner of my left eye, and I tried not to look, not because I didn't want to, not because of modesty, but only because when you had waited as long as I had to see one of these you want it to reveal itself at full length, *sostenuto*. I tried not to look, but I did look and there it was, the Atlantis, the Route to Cathay, the Seven Cities of Cibola . . .

. . . *chapter*
three

We rolled right through the heart of town to a garage in the wholesale district. MASON'S GARAGE, a sign over the door said. It was a small place, one-story, a little on the shabby side with the entrance in the middle of the building across the sidewalk. Jinx drove the car almost to the rear near the alley exit and then swung into a stall between two cars and stopped. As we got out I saw two men coming towards us. One was trotting. He couldn't have been more than twenty-three years old, bareheaded and big-boned and wearing clean white coveralls. Above the upper left pocket was the name NELSE in red stitching. In one hand he held a pair of license brackets with the numbers already in them, and in the other he held two small wrenches, and without a word to us he started taking the brackets off the sedan. The second man was still coming towards us, bouncing up and down, and in a moment I could see that this bounce was caused by a club foot. He was about forty years old and wore greasy coveralls on which no name was stitched, and a black canvas beanie that advertised a lubricating oil. He had blue eyes and a ruddy face and a worried look.

'So they got Toko,' he said.

Holiday and I looked at each other in surprise. It had only happened two hours ago. Before she could say anything he spun on his club foot and moved around the car, inspecting it carefully. He opened each door as he came to it, poking his head

24

in, inspecting the inside too.

'They must've had the news on the radio,' Jinx said.

'I didn't hear it,' Holiday said.

'You were too busy,' Jinx said, looking at me.

'Who's this bird?' I asked Holiday, nodding at the clubfooted man who was still looking at the inside of the sedan.

'Mason. I got all the stuff from him,' she said.

Mason came back to where we were standing and he was a different man. The worried look was gone from his face and he was almost pleasant.

'From what they said on the radio I expected to find the Zephyr full of holes,' he said.

'Once we got started we were all right,' Holiday said.

'What did it say on the radio?' I asked.

He began looking me up and down.

'This is Ralph Cotter,' she said. 'Vic Mason . . .'

I nodded to him and he said: 'You shot up everything in sight, didn't you?'

'Is that what they said on the radio?' I asked.

'Yeah.' He turned to Holiday. 'You should've ditched them suit boxes and that prison uniform. You took a hell of a chance. Cops stop you . . .'

'I had to bring back the machine gun. Get stopped with that in the car we'd still been in a hell of a fix. . . .'

'They think you had six or seven men in your mob,' Mason said, the suggestion of a smile on his face.

'They put out any descriptions?' I asked.

'The usual crap. Only you're better-looking than they said.'

'You ought to see me in clothes that fit,' I said.

'I'll see you. I got an interest in you,' Mason said.

'What does he mean by that?' I asked Holiday.

Jinx spread his hands in a small gesture of impatience. All this time he had been standing there looking at me, just standing there looking at me. Once or twice I had the feeling that he was curious about me in a clinical sort of way and didn't quite know how to ease the itch. That is a very aggravating situation.

'Look,' he said finally, 'I got to get back to the shop. I'll see you later, huh?'

'You better call first,' Holiday said.

'Sure. Okay,' he said, moving away towards the alley exit.

'Shop?' I said to Holiday and Mason. 'What shop?'

'He works in a radio shop,' Holiday said. 'He's a radio man.'

'He's in the wrong business, way he can drive a car,' I said, looking at Holiday. 'He can handle a hell of an automobile.'

'You don't think I let everybody drive that Zephyr, do you?' Mason said. 'You said it, Cotter. That Jinx is some jockey. Yes sir.' He was so pleased at getting his car back in good shape that I knew the announcer on the police radio had given him a good scare with all that big talk about a gunfight. 'You'll be needing him again, won't you?' he asked Holiday. 'Real soon?'

'I suppose so. . . .' she said.

'Got anything lined up?'

'I'll have to talk with Ralph first.'

'You do that right away. . . .'

'I will. Stash him away for an hour or so . . .'

'I'll stash him good. I got an interest in him,' Mason said.

I did not know what they were talking about. They were speaking across me, bouncing their words off my shoulders, but it was as if I had not been there. Then Holiday put her hand on my shoulder and said, 'We better not be seen together. I don't think they're expecting us to hole up here, but we better not be seen together. I'll call you as soon as I can.'

'I'll stick around. . . .' I said.

The boy who had been changing the license brackets, Nelse, came to the edge of the group. His right forefinger was bleeding and he flung the blood off, looking at Mason.

'Is that all?' he asked.

'Needn't even have done that,' Mason said. 'This was clean. The cops was just making it sound good. . . .'

'Goddamn!' Nelse said. He stuck his knuckle in his mouth, sucked the blood off and spit it on the floor. 'Ain't that just like cops? Always beating their gums. . .'

He held out his hand and Mason took a ring of keys from his pocket and laid them in it. Then Nelse walked to the rear, somewhere behind the cars.

Mason turned to Holiday. 'I'll worry about that stuff in the car,' he said. 'You worry about getting together with Cotter.'

'Keep your pants on, Vic – keep your pants on,' Holiday said. 'I'll call you as soon as I can,' she said again to me, walking away, toward the front, toward the glare of sunlight in the big door. It was the first time I had seen her walking, and seeing her move like this, in silhouette, excited me all over again. She had beautiful legs and a pleasant body and she rolled a little with each step, the effortless sensual roll that very few women can ever acquire, no matter how diligently they practice. She had talent all right, a fine and wondrous talent; but she was simply more than one man could handle and I knew it, but I also knew that I had been a long time waiting. . . .

'Make yourself at home . . .' Mason was saying.

I looked at him. His blue eyes were wide and bland but there was a wise frozen smile on his lips and I could tell what he had been thinking too. 'Thanks,' I said. 'Incidentally, you made a couple of cracks I didn't get. Mind clearing 'em up?'

'Yeah? What?'

'You said a couple of times that you had an interest in me. What exactly did that mean?'

'Don't you know this set-up?' he asked, a little surprise in his tone

'I'm afraid I don't,' I said.

27

'Holiday owes me a thousand dollars for this job. I did it on credit.'

'Wasn't that risky for you?' I said.

'Well, she's the kind of a dame it's hard to say no to,' he said. 'I've done things for her before. She always paid off. . . .'

'One way or the other?'

'One way or the other,' he said mildly. 'Of course, everything's gonna be great now that she's got you to help her,' he said.

That's what you think, that she's got me to help her, I thought. You won't be long finding out who's going to help who. 'I'm sure of that,' I said.

'Crawl in a car and take a nap,' he said. 'I'll wake you up when she calls.'

'I'll do that,' I said. 'But, first I got to have some milk.'

'Milk?'

'Milk. It's been two years since I had any milk.'

'I like milk myself,' he said.

'Good,' I said. 'We got something in common, anyway.'

He winked at me. 'Yeah. But it ain't milk,' he said.

'Yeah. But it ain't milk,' I said, walking out.

The sidewalks were full of people and the street was full of trucks. It was a dead-end street. Two blocks down, to the south, it ran into a big produce market and stopped. The market was a single mass of movement and noise. The other way, to the north, the direction from which we had come, was the business district, with many tall buildings. It was a big town and that was good.

I walked on up the street, looking for the retail market I had spotted on the way in. It was nice and comfortable being out in the open again, moving among people who paid no attention to you. The street noises were pleasant and the grind of the trucks was like spring music. The market turned out to be in the next block. HARTFORD'S, the signs said. It was a cheerful market, with a bakery on one side and an ice-cream booth on the other and the vegetable department in between, with its neat rows of vegetables and fruit. I went through the enamelled turnstile by the cashier's counter and on back to the icebox, passing along between tiers of canned goods and bottled goods and packaged bread and cookies. It was wonderful, like a fairy land.

The icebox was the biggest icebox I'd ever seen. It took up the whole back wall. The door I opened was man-sized, and the cool, moist air tumbled out, smelling of butter. I saw no bottles of milk. There were many packages of cheese and stacks of beer and soft-drink cases and piles of melons and enough butter to fill a freight car, but I didn't see any milk. As I stood there, holding the door open, telling myself that this was always the way, I heard a scraping sound behind me and I turned and there was a man in a white uniform dragging a wooden box which was filled with bottles of milk. He stopped beside me and when he raised up I saw that he was an old man and was wearing steel-rimmed spectacles.

'This is like rubbing Aladdin's Lamp,' I told him.

'Late getting away from the plant this morning,' he said. 'Danged bottle-washing machine busted.'

I smiled sympathetically and picked two quart bottles out of the wooden box. Just then a slender man wearing a neat double-breasted suit paused in the aisle.

'We're both a little late this morning, Joe,' he said to the milkman.

'Oh, hello, Mister Hartford,' Joe said. 'Yeah. Danged bottle-washing machine busted.'

Mr. Hartford nodded and went on. He had a bundle of currency in his hand, tied with a string, and a couple of bank books. I looked around to see where he had come from. A flight of steps led to an office directly above the big icebox. That was where he had come from. Yes, sir. . . .

'What time do you usually get here?' I asked Joe.

'Oh – around nine-thirty,' he replied, starting to empty the box, putting the bottles of milk on a metal shelf just inside the door.

'You deliver to that other market up the street too, don't you? That – er – what's the name. . .?'

'You mean the A-One. Sure. That's my last stop before coming here.

'I thought I'd seen you at the A-One,' I said. 'Well, so long. . . .'

'So long. . . .'

On the way out I picked up a package of Fig Newtons. I paid the cashier for the milk and the Fig Newtons, and walked back to the garage, taking my time, still feeling nice and comfortable, looking in the windows at electrical supplies and boats and fishing tackle and second-hand typewriters and adding machines, just like any other guy.

At the rear of the garage there was a station wagon with the hood off and the motor removed and I opened the door and crawled inside. I put one bottle of milk on the floor and shook the cream off the top of the other one, and then opened the box of Fig Newtons and settled down to my picnic. I didn't care if Holiday ever called. This was wonderful, being hemmed up in the station wagon nice and cosy and in the half-dark that felt vaguely familiar, vaguely reminded me of something and I sipped the milk experimentally, for the first taste of something you have craved for a long time is never what you have imagined it will be, but after the fourth or fifth sip I knew that this was finally the real thing, much too good for the common people. I ate some Fig Newtons, measuring them to last through the two bottles of milk and they came out almost to the last crumb.

I stretched out on the seat, taking the thirty-eight revolver out of my pocket and putting it on the floor beside the empty milk bottles, making myself comfortable again, thinking about the market up the street. Mr. Hartford had a bundle of currency in his hand and two bank books and I knew where he was going. He had said to the milkman that they were both a little late this morning, and since the milkman had told me that he usually arrived around nine-thirty that meant Mr. Hartford didn't start for the bank before nine-fifteen. That wasn't chicken feed he was carrying, either. Well, I thought, I'll meet that milkman at the A-One Market tomorrow between nine-five and nine-ten. I've got to make a start sometime. . . .

I was just on the edge of dozing off when I got a whiff of something, something burning. It didn't smell like fabric or anything familiar. But I sat up quickly, looking around, and then I got a good whiff of it. I still couldn't define it or tell where it was coming from, but it was pretty strong. I got out of the station wagon and looked around and under it but it wasn't here. Near by, in a corner, Nelse had the Zephyr on a hoist and was lubricating it. I picked up the pistol from the floor board, putting it in my coat pocket, going back to him.

'What's that smell?' I asked.

'The stuff Mason's burning, I guess. . . .'

'What stuff?'

'Your stuff – and hers. That prison suit.'

'Oh,' I said. I looked around. I still couldn't see anything.

'Where's he doing it?' I asked.

'Over there,' he said. 'In the battery room.'

I walked across the floor to the heavy tin door that was set in a side wall. The door was partly open. This was where the smell was coming from, all right. It was coming through the crack of the door like it had been shot out of a fire hose. I pulled the door open and went inside. It was a small, dark room with a single window that opened into the alley. Below this window, on the left, was a long bench on which there were several storage batteries and a charging plant and an assortment of electric cables. At the rear of the room was another bench, thicker, on

31

which were several steel tire forms and slender pipes and a lot
of vulcanizing and tire-patching equipment. On the right side of
the room was a big anvil and what looked like a forge. Mason
was standing there, wearing a pair of goggles and gloves and
holding a lighted acetylene torch which he was spraying over
something in the forge. His back was turned and because of the
hissing noise of the torch he didn't hear me cross the floor. I
stood there, looking over his shoulder. He was working on that
old prison-issue pair of shoes of mine, and there were a lot of
ashes that already had fallen through the grating. He held the
torch on the shoes and they actually melted before the flame.
They melted. I saw them melting.

Mason reached over to the tank to cut off the gas and saw me
and jerked, surprised, still holding in his hand the nozzle which
was spouting the blue-orange flame a foot long. His face
darkened a little, and he cut off the gas. The flame died, the noise
stopped, and it was unbelievably quiet.

'I smelled it all the way outside,' I said. 'I couldn't figure what
it was.'

He hooked the nozzle of the torch over the top of the gas
cylinder and took off his goggles.

'You're nosey, too, ain't you?' he said.

'I just wanted to know what it was,' I said.

'That's what it was,' he said, nodding at the ashes. 'You
oughtn't to look at a flame that hot without goggles. Twenty-
three hundred degree blue flame is nothing to let your eyes fool
around with.'

'I'll remember that,' I said, turning to go.

'One other thing to remember,' he said. 'I don't like nosey
people.'

Sometime later I felt somebody pulling at my arm and I waked
up and it was Mason.

32

'Holiday wants you on the telephone,' he said.

I backed out of the station wagon to the floor. He closed the door behind me, looking in over the rolled-down glass.

'I see you got your milk,' he said. 'You oughn't to leave them bottles laying around. Or maybe you're so clever you don't have to worry about fingerprints.'

'You're beginning to get a little tiresome,' I said. 'That fingerprint stuff's for kids. Where's the phone?'

'In the office. . . .'

I went to the office and picked the receiver off the desk. Holiday was at the apartment and everything was all right. She started telling me how to get to the apartment and I stopped her until I could get a pencil and piece of paper.

'. . . Maywood bus to Monteagle Street. Marakeesh Apartments. One, One, Four. Yeah, I got it. Where do I catch the bus? . . . Second and Front Streets.' I wrote it all down. 'Yeah – right away. . . Him? Oh, fine. We're getting along fine.' Mason came just inside the office, leaning against the door. 'No, he's not here,' I said into the telephone, looking straight at him. 'He's in the back somewhere. You can speak freely.' I continued to look at him, smiling. 'Yeah. I noticed that. . . . Sure – so long. . . .'

I hung up the receiver. 'She's got your number,' I said. 'She says you're a worrier. Are you a worrier, Mason?'

That burned him a little. He came all the way into the office.

'I'll be around when all you cocky guys are gone,' he said.

'See you later,' I said. 'And be sure and get my fingerprints off those milk bottles. You got an interest in me, you know. . . .'

... *chapter four*

I got a noon edition of one of the newspapers and read it on the bus. We were in the headlines in spite of the news that that same morning the Navy dirigible *Akron* was believed to be lost somewhere in the Atlantic. FOUR SLAIN IN PRISON FARM BREAK, they said. TWO GUARDS, TWO CONVICTS. Such ruthlessness was to be expected, the story said, when hardened criminals like Tokowanda, the slain prisoner, and Cotter, the prisoner who escaped, were worked in open fields as convict labor, always tempted by the near proximity of freedom and finally were made desperate by its nearness. Men with records such as these, it continued to editorialize, should be confined behind the walls of the state penitentiary. . . .

'Monteagle Street . . .' the driver was calling.

I folded the newspaper and got off the bus. This was a residential section but it wouldn't be for long. There were a few old houses still standing on Monteagle Street, two- and three-story gingerbread houses, eroding rococo rocks in a swelling ocean of business buildings. There was a lot of traffic, and filling stations and parking lots were all over the neighborhood. Down the street, half a block from the corner, there was an enormous excavation, and the smooth exhausts of the steam shovels floated in scrupulous unbroken lines of sound, each having the same content and each in precisely the same key. The Marakeesh Apartments were on the corner where the bus had stopped, a

34

two-story brick building that looked cheap and rundown, as if what went on inside was exactly what you suspected.

I went in. There was a small lobby and a desk and a switchboard. I went on down the hall to one, one, four and thumped on the door with my index finger. Holiday opened the door and I went inside. Before I had time to say anything, to look around, to even put down the newspaper I was carrying, she grabbed me around the neck, kicking the door shut with her foot, putting her face up to mine, baring her teeth. I kissed her, but not as hard as she kissed me, and then I saw that she was wearing only a light flannel wrapper, unbuttoned all the way down. I had the impression that her breasts were small and hard and firm, but they were not in focus; I was looking at that Eldorado again, and hearing all of Bach essenced into one single wondrous note. I quivered, holding her tightly; and she bared her teeth wider and started nipping at my ear, breathing loudly, like the early fall winds which used to roar down from the Great Smokies, through Vaughan's Gap and on to Knoxville, which was at the end of the world. I tilted my head a little, moving my ear away from her teeth, thinking above the moaning of the strings of the corpora cavernosa that this was the time to stop this, this was the time to stop this, this was the time to stop this, but they were only streaks of thought and moving much too rapidly to translate into action. And then I realized that she had me by the hand and was pulling me towards the bedroom . . .

I was asleep, of course, but even when you are asleep you possess a kind of propliopithecustian awareness that enables you to know and very acutely feel certain things. I knew that I was warm and comfortable and safe. Several times this awareness began to fade and I realized that waking was approaching, but I could do nothing about it because to rouse my will to fight it would surely have speeded consciousness. All I could do was try to slide back, but this was impossible and the world-noises crept through and slowly filled the room and when I finally was able to identify the dominant ones they were the damp-sounding exhausts of the steam shovel down the street and I opened my eyes and looked around. The shades were drawn but there was a small hole in one that the sunlight had found and was coming through, a thin golden wire, rich and alive and containing the quality of color that belongs only to the late afternoon. So it was late afternoon. I lay there listening for some movement that would tell me where Holiday was, but I heard nothing.

I got up, crawling under that living wire of sunlight, and opened the door, looking into the living-room. It was empty of everything except the cheap furniture. I went across the living-room to another door that was not quite closed and pushed it open. This was a small kitchen and it was empty too. As I started back to the bedroom the hall door opened and Holiday came in. She was wearing a grey woolen skirt, a white shirt and a green checkered coat and had a manila shopping bag in her hand. When she saw me she smiled.

'Aren't you afraid you'll catch cold?' she said.

I looked down at myself and discovered that I was naked.

'I just this minute got up,' I said. 'I was looking for you.'

'I been to market,' she said. 'Jinx phoned. He's coming for dinner.'

I was glad of that. I wanted to talk a little business with Jinx.

'How do you expect me to keep my mind on the dinner with you standing around like that?' she asked. 'Why don't you put on some clothes?'

'I will,' I said.

She went into the kitchen and I went into the bedroom and put on a pair of shorts and joined her. She was emptying the shopping bag, but she paused long enough to look at me and say, 'That's much better,' and went on emptying the bag.

36

'You like mushroom soup?' she asked, holding up a can of mushroom soup.

'I like anything,' I said. 'As my grandfather used to say, I'm so hungry I could eat the raw right rump of General Sherman.'

She laughed, taking some more cans out of the shopping bag, and an unwrapped loaf of bread in an open paper sack. I picked up the bread. It was still warm. I smelled it in long slow deep inhalations, packing them tightly into every corner of my lungs. Good God! By what mysterious alchemy had my grandmother's bread-baking secret been transmitted way out here? This had the same smell. The loaf was different and the color was different but this had the same smell. That thin little old lady humped over an oven . . .

'It seems,' Holiday was saying, 'that there's been a prison break.'

I looked around. She had spread a newspaper on the drainboard. I put down the loaf of bread and picked up the newspaper. We were still in the headlines, but this story contained more information. 'New facts have come to light,' it said. Toko had suddenly blossomed into a vicious criminal, a mad-dog killer, and was now ranked in the First Ten of public enemies. There was no longer any doubt about why he was trying to escape from the farm, the story went on. Two Illinois officers, properly and legally armed with extradition papers, were on their way to take him back to Illinois to face trial – and almost certain execution – for the hold-up murder of an aged shopkeeper.

Toko a murderer; that punk ranked in the First Ten, a mad-dog killer. I damn near laughed out loud.

'Looks like they're building him up for a personal appearance somewhere,' I said. 'I never read such a lot of junk in my life.'

'Didn't Toko ever tell you?'

'Tell me what?'

37

'That he was wanted for murder.'

Now I had to laugh. 'Who the hell did he ever kill?' I asked.

'Didn't he ever tell you who the hell he'd killed?' she said.

'Stop it,' I said. 'He was yellow. He had the heart of a humming bird. He quit cold on me. Half-way across the cantaloupe patch he quit cold. He was yellow. If he'd followed like I told him, he'd never been hit. He was yellow. That's what caused him to get conked. Mad-dog killer, my butt . . .'

'Why do you think he made his break with only ten months left to serve? They were coming to get him, that's why. Do you think I'd've let him take a chance unless he had everything to gain and nothing to lose? Do I look like that much of a chump?'

'All right,' I said. 'He was a killer. A very distinguished killer.'

'Go on, be jealous,' she said.

'Jealous? Of him? That bum? That popcorn thief?'

She took a step towards me and in a sudden flinging motion she clawed at my face. I closed my eyes to protect them and slipped my head, jerking my knee up, slamming her in the crotch. She uttered a groan that had no edge, and the thought of where I had hit her made me feel faint in the stomach and the color of it was a sharp-pointed painful yellow, and I hurried out going to the bathroom, turning on the water in the basin and filling my cupped hands with it and dousing my face in it, and washing the taste of what had happened out of my mouth with it – and when I straightened up, Holiday was sitting on the edge of the tub.

'Please, don't be sore,' she said.

I picked a hand towel off the wall rack and very carefully folded it into a wide strap and soaked it under the running water and then wrung it out and turned and slapped her across the face with it. I felt faint at the stomach again, but nothing like the faintness I had felt before.

'Please, don't be sore,' she said.

I threw the towel into the tub and went out into the bedroom, drying my hands on my shorts.

Holiday drifted in, standing by the bed.

'Please, don't be sore,' she said.

'I forgive you,' I said. 'Now, what do you intend to do about Toko's body?'

'Intend to do about his body? What do you mean?' she asked.

'I mean you ought to claim it. You're his next-of-kin. They got records of your visits to the farm. If they can't get in touch with you they're liable to think you're mixed up in this.'

'*Think* I'm mixed up in it?' she said. 'They know it. They know it already.' She turned and went out of the room and in a minute she was back with one of the newspapers. 'You better read this,' she said, handing it to me. 'Right there . . .'

I took the newspaper, looking where she was pointing. '*. . . Postal Inspectors have detained Bacon, the carrier who delivered mail to the Tokowanda girl's apartment. He has confessed that he warned her when a letter from her brother in the prison camp was intercepted by the police.*' I looked at her still holding the newspaper.

She said: 'The minute the postman told me the cops had intercepted the letter I knew Toko was a goner unless I moved fast. I had a friend who knew Mason, the guy out here. He telephoned him and when I got here everything was arranged. My only problem was to get Toko away from the farm before the cops showed up with the extradition papers.'

'You got nice friends,' I said, dropping the newspaper on the floor. 'The postman, the fellow in Chicago, Mason – Yes, sir. Not an enemy in the world.'

'There you go getting jealous again,' she said.

'You're nuts,' I said. 'I'm not jealous. I never saw you until two weeks ago and after tonight I'll probably never see you again. You're nuts.'

Her eyes narrowed a little and she took off the green-checkered coat and flung it over her shoulder with a cheap theatricality. Then with both hands she ripped off the shirt, pitching it, underhanded, into my face. I caught a fast faint flavor of woman-smell, and when I got the shirt from in front of my eyes she was unzippering her skirt, which she let fall to the floor. She wore no brassiere. She yanked at the top button of her shorts and kicked them clear over the bed. Then she moved a couple of steps in front of me, standing spreadlegged, her hands on her hips.

'Tell me that again,' she said. 'Tell me you won't be seeing me any more after tonight.'

I stood up slowly and slapped her across the face. Her mouth popped open and then it closed and she fell across the bed, sobbing. I trembled then and the color of it was pink turning to red, and I fell across the bed, having the thought as I fell that she was right, she was absolutely right.

'Look' – I said, reaching to turn her over. 'Look ...'

She swallowed the rest of what I was trying to say, banging her mouth against mine, gnawing at my lips and dragging her hands across my bare shoulders. I could feel my skin piling up under her nails, and in the bathroom I could hear the water still running in the wash basin ...

40

... *chapter five*

The bus was crowded with people going to work. I dropped my dime into the fare box, moving to the rear, holding my lunch in the brown paper sack so that everybody could see I was on my way to work, too. I noticed that we were still on the front page, but the headlines went to the Navy disaster. The *Akron* had been beaten down in a storm off Barnegat, New Jersey, and seventy-three persons had been drowned, including the Aviation Chief, Rear Admiral W. A. Moffett. That was what everybody was reading and talking about. I had no use for the lunch wrapped in the brown paper sack.

I picked a corner to get off the bus where six or seven others also were getting off, going out in the middle of them starting down the street towards the garage as if I had been doing the same thing for years.

Jinx was in the office with Mason, waiting for me.

'I'll say one thing for you,' Mason said. 'You sure don't waste a lot of time getting started.'

'I want to get Holiday out of hock,' I told him. I looked at Jinx. 'You got everything?'

'I'm set,' Jinx said. 'But I don't think Mason is.'

I looked at Mason. There was a wise smile on his face and he made a point of stroking an imaginary beard. 'I shaved 'em off last week,' he said.

'I don't get it,' I said.

'The whiskers,' he said. 'Who do you think I am – Santa Claus? Ten per cent and I furnish the car! You think this is a gravy train you're riding?'

'Is that what Jinx told you – ten per cent?' I asked, laughing. 'He misunderstood me . . .'

'I didn't misunderstand no such a damn thing,' Jinx said. 'You said ten per cent.'

'I said *twenty-five* per cent, Jinx,' I said, winking at him so that Mason could see, so that he would still think he had me over a barrel. 'I said one-fourth to Mason for the use of the car. . . .'

'That's more like it,' Mason said. 'Now, what's this about you not liking the color of the Zephyr?'

'I don't even like the Zephyr,' I said, dropping my lunch package into his wastebasket. 'It's too conspicuous. I want a black Ford sedan with a Mercury motor. Exactly like the cops use . . .'

'Well, now, ain't it just too bad that you got to ride around in a Zephyr. . . .!'

'I'll ride around in the Zephyr for this one job,' I said. 'For just this one job. But arrange to get me a black Ford sedan with a Mercury motor. And eight or nine sets of out-of-state license plates. . . .'

'Jesus,' he exclaimed, shaking his head. 'For a punk who's flat on his can you sure talk big.'

I ignored him, turning to Jinx. 'What about the guns?'

Jinx pointed to Mason. 'He's got' em.'

'I hear you don't like a revolver,' he said.

'You know what I like,' I said. 'Get 'em.' He stared at me for a moment, dubiously, and then opened the top drawer of the desk and picked up two blue-steel, bone-handled .380 Colt automatics. I took them, holding them in my hands, looking at them. I swung my hands up and down, feeling their weight, and then I put one down on the desk and sprung the clip from the other one, thumbing the cartridges into my palm, one by one. I tested the spring of the clip for tension. I put the cartridges back in, slipped the clip in the butt, and tested the other one. Then I looked at them again. They were flawless, precise, perfect as a circle is perfect.

'Jesus, that's a great act you put on,' Mason said with heavy sarcasm.

I drew back my leg and kicked him on the club foot as hard as I could. He grunted and doubled over, and when he straightened up his face was corrugated with pain.

'Don't you ever say that to me again,' I said.

'Jesus! Ralph,' Jinx said. 'What the hell . . .'

'You understand?' I said to Mason. 'Don't ever say that to me again.'

'You beat it,' Mason said. 'Beat it. Get out of here.'

I just looked at him. 'How much for these automatics?'

'Get out,' he said, with a little moan. 'Beat it. Put them pistols down and beat it.'

'How much?' I asked again.

He glared at me. Finally, he said: 'Two hundred dollars for the both of 'em.'

'It's a deal,' I said. I knew this was far too much, but I didn't want to argue with him. 'Come on,' I said to Jinx. 'Let's push . . .'

'Cash,' Mason said.

'I'll have the cash in an hour,' I told him. 'I'll settle for everything then. Including a Ford sedan with a Mercury motor.' I could see the wheels going around in his head. 'Stop worrying,' I said. 'I'll be back. You know that . . .'

He sat down in the chair, picking up his club foot and holding it as he would a baby. There was still a lot of pain in his face. I nodded to Jinx, and we went out into the garage and got in the Zephyr.

'Jesus. Ralph,' Jinx said, as we drove out. 'You shouldn't a done that. He's lame. . . .'

'So much more reason why he ought to be careful what he says to me,' I said.

We turned into the street, into the traffic.

'Yeah. But he's helping us a lot. . . .'

'If he didn't help us, somebody else would. All you need is dough. Christ look at Karpis and Dillinger and Pierpont and those guys. Dump all their brains together and you haven't got enough intelligence to get past the fourth grade. How the hell do you think they manage to get by? Dough, that's how. They want a guy like Mason, they buy him. They want a cop or a sheriff, they buy him. The answer is dough. . . .'

We were rolling down the street, in the traffic.

'No sense in throwing money away,' he said. 'You had a thirty-eight. Why buy another one?'

'I don't like a revolver. I told you that. I don't like any revolver. That's why I asked for automatics. Where'd he get these? These are brand new. . . .'

'Oh, he can get anything in that line you want. Pistols, rifles, machine-guns, tear gas masks . . .'

'How? That stuffs dynamite to handle.'

'Not the way he works it. His brother-in-law's chief of police out at the steel mills. They got rooms of the stuff at the steel mills. All the big plants around here've got that stuff.'

'Makes it nice.' I said.

'Especially for the little guy,' Jinx said. He turned into the parking space behind the A-One Market. 'Where?' he asked.

'Anywhere,' I said. The clock on the dashboard of the Zephyr said five minutes after nine. 'You set that clock?' I asked.

'Right on the nose at eight-thirty,' he said, easing the sedan into a parking place. 'There were a few cars on either side of us. 'He ought to be along any minute now if your figuring's right.'

'Unless the bottle-washing machine busted again,' I said.

'What?'

'It's a private joke,' I said. 'You get the tape?'

'Yeah.' He took two rolls of tape out of his pocket, showing them to me. They were white adhesive tape, two inches wide, the kind you can buy at any drug store. 'What about the pads?'

'I got it. And the masks, too.' I unbuttoned my coat, holding it open so he could see the masks pinned to my shirt. They were comic masks, the kind children wear on Hallowe'en Night. I unpinned one, handing it to him. It had dabs of black paint on the cheeks and under the nose was a handlebar moustache. The other one, mine, was a replica of a young girl's face; crimson cheeks and exaggerated eyelashes and an oversized mouth. He took his, not saying anything, putting it inside his coat.

'Holiday got 'em at the five-and-dime,' I told him.

'She got a lot of 'em. Hell of a gag, don't you think?'

'I'll say . . .'

'I'll have these cops crazy before I get through with 'em. A few nice jobs and west we go.'

He nudged me and I looked out. The milk truck was rolling up to the concrete railing in the rear of the market, by the unloading platform.

'That him?' Jinx asked.

'That's him. . . .'

Jinx leaned forward, looking past me at the milkman. It was Joe, all right. He had got out of the truck now and was filling the wooden box with bottles of milk.

'You think you can handle him all by yourself?' Jinx asked.

'I think so,' I replied.

A young boy wearing the greyish apron of a market helper came out the back door carrying a big wicker basket and walked to the truck.

'Hi, Joe . . .' he said.

'Hi, squirt . . .' Joe said.

The squirt climbed into the truck and began to fill the wicker basket with packages of butter and cheese and cartons of eggs, talking to Joe about an ice hockey team or something. I could not hear all of what was being said. He soon filled the basket and went back inside the market. Joe followed him in dragging the box of milk bottles on a piece of rope tied through the handle.

'You got this straight?' I asked Jinx.

'I slept on it. I follow you to Hartford's. I turn the car around and park outside. I go inside and wait by the icebox till everything checks.'

'Right:' I opened the door and got out.

'I'll keep my fingers crossed,' he said.

'You save that for next time,' I said.

He started the motor and backed out, heading the sedan for the street. I idled over to the milk truck. A fat, frowsy woman came out of the back door of the market eating a candy bar and carrying a manila shopping bag so full the paper sides were straining at the twine handles. When she passed I leaped into the milk truck, crouching down behind the front seat. I lifted the automatics from my coat pockets and laid them on the floor. Then I took off my hat and coat rolling them into a bundle which I pushed into a corner of the seat. I put one automatic in my left hip pocket and held the other one in my right hand, and then, over the top of the seat, I saw Joe emerge from the market, dragging the empty wooden box. When he reached the truck he picked up the box and tossed it over the seat, over my head, into the truck. He stepped into the truck and was about to crawl over the seat into the rear when he saw me.

'Come back here,' I said. My face was not more than two feet from his face. He was scared. He opened his mouth and I knew he was trying to scream; and I swung hard, left to right, laying the barrel of the automatic across the side of his head just above the ear. There was a sound like thumping a cantaloupe and the blood spurted. He fell forward and I grabbed him with my left

46

hand, hauling him over the seat, out of sight, thinking only one thing now: I had to keep his white jacket from getting bloody, I had to get it off him in a hurry. It was some mess back there in that narrow truck, with me trying to get his jacket off and milk bottles and butter and cheese packages spilling off the shelves and making so much racket that I expected at any moment to have somebody stick in his head to see what was going on. But I finally got the jacket off, and I hit him on the head again, straight down this time, feeling reasonably certain that this would hold him for awhile. I slipped into his jacket and put on his cap, which was a trifle small for me, and got under the wheel of the truck, rolling out into the street. Out of the corner of my eye I saw Jinx fall in behind me.

I turned the corner and drove down the street to Hartford's, stopping just inside the driveway, leaving room between the milk truck and the sidewalk for Jinx to put the Zephyr, making sure that there would be absolutely no way for the Zephyr to be hemmed up when the time came to get away. I cut the switch and sat there, watching Jinx turn the Zephyr around and back it into the slot I had made for him. Then he got out, moving to the rear entrance of the market. I crawled into the rear of the truck and started filling the wooden box with milk bottles. Joe was bleeding like a stuck hog. You wouldn't believe that an old man could bleed so much. The blood was running down a little drain in the center of the steel floor and I took a quarter-pound of butter from the rack and plugged the drain with it. Then I crawled over Joe's body, over the seat, out of the truck and went inside, dragging the box of milk behind. Nobody paid any attention to me. I opened the icebox door, and was stacking the bottles inside when Jinx came up and opened the other door, pretending to be a customer.

'Okay in front,' he said.

'Let's go then,' I said.

47

I closed the icebox door, shoved the empty wooden box over to one side, against a row of breakfast foods, and started up the steps to the office. I looked out to my left. There were about a dozen customers in the market; from up here, on the steps, it looked like a color advertisement of the interior of Any Market, U.S.A. There was a narrow landing at the head of the stairs, and I motioned to Jinx and we bent over and slipped on the masks. Then I opened the screened door of the office and went inside, taking the automatic from my pocket. Hartford was sitting at the desk nearest the door stacking cheques and silver and currency, and sitting at the next desk, her back to me, was a woman.

Hartford looked up when he heard the screened door open. He started to say something and then he saw the automatic in my hand and Jinx standing behind me, and his mouth snapped shut.

'Clasp your hands behind your neck,' I said.

He pushed himself back in the chair, clasping his hands behind his neck. Now the woman turned around, moving her body, and I saw that there was a small telephone switchboard on her desk.

'Get away from there and lay on the floor,' I said.

She got up slowly and stood by her desk hesitantly. She did not seem in the least frightened.

'Lay yourself down,' I said, hearing behind me the sound of adhesive tape being unrolled. She heard it too; there was a flicker of indecision in her face and I gestured with my automatic and she sat down on the floor. I took two pads from my pocket and handed them to Jinx as he moved towards her.

He said to the woman, 'All the way down,' pushing her over to the floor. Then he doubled on the Kotex pads, stuffing it into her mouth and taping it tightly.

Hartford turned his head, watching this operation. 'You're cute,' he said to me.

48

'Get down there with her,' I said.

He got up and lay down beside her on the floor and Jinx went to work on him. After he had been gagged and taped, Jinx pulled his ankles up behind him and taped them to his wrists.

'Now, you're cute,' I said. I put the automatic in my pocket and picked up all the currency and cheques in sight, stuffing them inside my shirt, not bothering with the silver. Then Jinx and I strolled out, taking off our masks, going down the steps. In the market, business was proceeding as usual . . .

We reached the ground floor and went outside. I retrieved the bundle from the milk truck that was my coat and hat, and when I got into the Zephyr Jinx let in the clutch and the car moved out into the street.

'You sure as hell knew what you were talking about,' Jinx said softly. 'We must've got twenty grand. . . .'

'Not that much,' I said. 'But for the first day's work it wasn't bad.'

'It was six thousand, one hundred and forty-two dollars, and Mason's eyes bugged out a foot. 'By God!' he exclaimed. 'You stick up that produce market?'

'What do you care?' I asked.

'What do I care?' he said. He turned to Jinx, his face dark. 'You ought to know better'n that, you crazy bastard!'

'Don't get yourself in such an uproar,' Jinx said quietly. 'It wasn't the produce market.'

Mason glared at him, not quite understanding, and then he suddenly reached over and picked up some of the cheques I had stacked beside the currency. He glanced at them, two or three of them, and his lips trembled angrily.

'Hartford's! Hartford's!' he said. 'That's just as bad! That's even worse! Right down the street! Whyn't you tell me where you were going?'

49

'I'm awfully sorry, old man,' I said. 'Truly. Your agitation distresses me very much. I would have been delighted to tell you what we had in mind except for one little thing – it never occurred to me that it was any of your goddamn business!'

The thin scream of a siren outside, down the street, reached our ears and Mason jumped as if a hot copper wire had been pushed into his urethra, all the way in.

'You crazy bastard!' he said to Jinx. 'Sticking up a place in this neighborhood!'

The siren, which had been growing thinner and more intense, now filled the office with its fragile ominousness as a squad car raced by in front. I saw Nelse run by the office door, going towards the street.

'No use bleeding now,' I picked up a handful of currency. 'One-fourth of sixty-one hundred and forty-two dollars is fifteen hundred and thirty-five dollars. Two hundred for the automatics makes it seventeen hundred and thirty-five. The thousand Holiday owes you makes it an even twenty-seven and thirty-five.'

'Just a minute,' Jinx said. 'What about my cut?'

'I'm coming to that,' I said.

'You're coming to it too late. . . .'

'Jesus!' Mason said. 'Do we have to stand here with all that money in plain sight and argue about it? Somebody might walk in here any minute. Let's go back in the battery room. . . .'

'You're a hemophiliac,' I said. 'Anybody walks in here, it'll be just too bad. . . .'

His eyes blazed and his lips whitened. 'Then hurry up and split the stuff and get the hell out of here and don't ever come back,' he said. 'You're a goddamn lunatic, that's what you are, and I don't want any part of you. If I'd known what I was getting into. . .'

'I got nothing to do with that thousand dollars Holiday owes,' Jinx was saying. 'Take out his seventeen thirty-five and you and me split what's left. It comes to forty-four hundred and seven dollars. I'll take two thousand. . . .'

I slapped the currency on the desk, looking at him. 'You cut it up.'

'Sure . . .' he said, moving to the desk, starting to cut up the money. Nelse came in and stopped, surprised by the sight of all the currency, staring at it.

'Is *that* what's the matter at Hartford's?' he asked.

'It's one of the things that's the matter,' I replied. 'What's more important, probably, is a body in the milk truck behind the market. It's the driver's body. I had to slug him a few times. He was an old man. I think maybe I killed him.'

Mason didn't say anything; he was in too much of a state already to react to this; he just raked his upper lip with his lower teeth. But Nelse was instantly concerned, and looked through the door of the office at the Zephyr.

'You got nothing to be alarmed about,' I said. 'This one was right off page seven.'

'So now it's murder,' Mason said slowly.

'It could very easily be,' I said.

Jinx turned, holding a stack of currency in each hand. 'Here,' he said, 'settle your back debts out of this.'

I counted off a thousand dollars and offered it to Mason, but he made no move to take it. 'Go on. Take it.' I said.

'In another hour every dick on the force'll be swarming in here,' he said in a slow, vexed, almost pitiable tone. 'They'll turn this place upside down.'

I held the money almost against his chin. 'The rest of it's on the desk,' I said. 'Take this . . .'

He finally took it.

'There're a couple of other trifling details to worry about,' I said. 'In the back of the Zephyr you'll find the milkman's coat and cap and two Hallowe'en masks. You'd better put the torch on 'em. And I'd get rid of those cheques too, if I were you. . . .'

'. . . Jesus,' he moaned.

I nodded to Jinx and we went out, pausing for a moment on the sidewalk, looking up the street at the widening confusion in front of Hartford's Market. People were converging from every direction, and the scream of another siren rounded the corner a few blocks away and soon it dragged into view an ambulance.

'You think you really killed that guy?' Jinx asked.

'Probably,' I said. 'An old man's skull is a pretty soft thing.'

When I got back to the apartment Holiday was still in bed. She was still in bed but she was not asleep. She was on her back, her hands clasped behind her head and as I approached the open door of the bedroom I saw her raise herself slightly and wiggle her body, shaking down the sheet, exposing her breasts, and when I got closer I saw that her face had been freshly made-up. She smiled, saying nothing, looking at me from under eyelids she tried to make very lazy.

'You damn well ought to make yourself alluring,' I said. 'I just paid a thousand dollars for you.'

'Then I'm out of hock?' she said.

'Temporarily,' I said. I unbuttoned my shirt, taking out the bills I had left there, that I had held out on Jinx and Mason. It was around twenty dollars, no more.

'Is that all we got left?' she asked.

'Are you kidding?' I said, taking the rest of the currency out of my pocket, showing it to her. 'I'm a hard-working man. And it seems to me that the very least a man's woman can do when he comes home all tired out is to have some hot coffee for him.'

She laughed, kicking off the sheet with both feet and turning her naked body towards me. 'What were you saying about hot coffee?' she asked.

One of these days I hope I can look at that thing and not hear

52

wonderful music, I thought, cramming the money back into my coat pockets. 'Why, you must be having hallucinations,' I said, taking off my coat and getting into bed with the rest of my clothes on. 'I didn't say anything about hot coffee. . . .'

... *chapter six*

I was sitting at the table in the kitchen sipping a cup of hot coffee, listening to the liquidy whooshwhooshwhoosh of the steam shovel down the street and telling Holiday what a panicky old woman Mason was, wondering how anybody as nervous and gutless as that ever started doing business with criminals in the first place, when there came a knocking at the hall door, sharp, impatient knocking. Holiday looked at me, startled. and my own heart skipped a beat or two, so unexpected it was.

'You stay here,' I said, going out of the kitchen into the living-room. The knocking came again, loud; loud as hell. I took a few more steps towards the door, easing the automatic out of my hip pocket. 'Who is it?' I asked.

'It's Mason, Ralph,' the voice said. 'Lemme in. . . .'

It was Mason's voice, all right. Puzzling as to what he wanted here, I put the automatic back into my pocket and unlocked the door, opening it and getting a fast flash of two men moving at me. I tried to slam the door and get the automatic out of my pocket, but before I could do either they had hit me with their shoulders, knocking me back into the room, piling in after me. They were stocky, medium-sized guys, one a little larger than the other, but both with guns in their hands. They had copper written all over them.

'Reach,' the little one said.

I straightened up and raised my hands. The second cop, the

54

larger one, stepped behind me and took the automatic out of my hip pocket and then Mason, who evidently had been watching all this through the door from the hall, came into the room, just inside the room and leaned against the door-facing.

'You son-of-a-bitch,' I said.

'Quiet,' the little one said to me. 'As long as you're in, close the door,' he said to Mason. 'Reece,' he said to the other guy, 'get the dame.'

'There's no dame here,' I said quickly.

'Nix . . .' he said, waving his gun for Reece to go ahead. 'We know this layout. By now, we got that other punk picked up, too.'

'You son-of-a-bitch,' I said to Mason.

'We had 'im by the short hair,' the little one said.

'I know who had who,' I said.

'Quiet,' he said.

'You faggot son-of-a-bitch,' I said to Mason.

'Shut up!' the little one said.

There was some noise in the kitchen and the sounds of a slight scuffle and the rising angry whine of Holiday's voice saying something I could not make out and then Reece led her in, holding her by the arm. She was still barefooted and wearing only the kimono and her face was furious.

'This babe's full of vinegar,' Reece said.

Holiday suddenly jerked loose from him and crossed to Mason and swiped at his face with her hand, the fingers arched like claws.

'I told you she was full of vinegar,' Reece said.

'Stop it . . .' the little one growled at Holiday. 'Behave yourself,' he said.

'I'll cut her goddamn heart out,' Mason said.

Holiday clawed at him again, and this time she scraped his cheek and three short welts sprung into sight, and Mason whipped out a knife and I heard the spring click as the blade flew open,

55

shiny and sinister, and he drew back his arm to slash at her and the little one hit him under the chin with the barrel of the gun, a quick sharp backhand lick, not vicious, just petulant. Mason blinked his eyes, patting his chin with the palm of his left hand, inspecting it, looking for blood.

'Make this dame sit down,' the little one said to Reece.

'I told you she was full of vinegar,' Reece said.

... I was thinking how nice it would be to stick that acetylene torch down Mason's throat and burn a hole in the back of his head big enough to push my foot through.

'Put that knife away and get outta here,' the little one said. 'Go on – beat it.'

Mason flipped the knife shut, wiping his face with his coat sleeve, and turned and opened the door going out. The little one leaned over and pushed on the door, making sure the latch was caught, and then came back to me.

'He ain't one of my pet people either,' he said; 'but I'll say one thing for him – he's got a heart as big as a Mack truck. You know what he did just before he came here? He took that whole twenty-seven hundred dollars you paid him and pitched it in the pot ...'

'I don't think he knows about the old lady,' Reece said.

'Is that a fact? You don't know about the old lady?' the little one said to me. 'She's got t.b.'

'What old lady?' I said.

'The one whose husband you beat to death in that milk truck,' he said in a mild tone. 'She's got t.b. We're sending her to Arizona. . . .'

'You mean Mason's sending her,' Reece put in.

'Oh, he's not doing the whole thing,' the little one said. 'We're putting in something, too. After all, how far will his twenty-seven hundred dollars go? She needs doctors and nurses and a place to live and something to eat for maybe years. Take six or seven gees for that ...'

All the fuzziness around the edges of my brain faded and the questions I had been asking myself about how they knew this and could start a collection for an old lady who had been a widow less than an hour, were answered – this was a shakedown, slick and workmanlike, the way things come out when they get done by professionals; and a tremor hit me in the middle of the stomach, red and twisting, because any cop who'll shake you down is a cop who'll kill you after he gets the money. Killed while resisting arrest, their reports read: it is a pattern that never varies and the reason it never varies is because it is perfect to begin with, absolutely fool-proof.

'Well, I guess we better get on downtown,' the little one was saying. 'You think we better put the cuffs on 'em, Reece?'

'I don't think so. He ain't packing nothing. . . .'

'Neither am I,' Holiday said, suddenly standing up, opening the kimono with both hands, holding it open, showing him she had nothing on under it. The Seven Cities of Cibola hit him in the face and he grunted softly, almost like a baby's grunt, and he stood there looking in fascination, utterly unselfconscious. . . .

'You can take your hands down now,' the little one said to me, putting his gun in the hip-pocket holster, making a ceremony of this, holding it in the palm of his hand, looking at it, then at me, pursing his lips thoughtfully as if weighing the risk, and then finally sliding it in the holster.

I lowered my hands.

'If we're going downtown,' Reece finally said to Holiday, 'I better help you get your things on . . .'

'Maybe you had, at that,' she said, turning loose her kimono but not tying it shut, leaving it open, the belt dangling, striding off, winking slyly at me, followed by this thickheaded hog.

'Maybe I better get my things on, too,' I said to the little one. I was not jealous; I only wanted to get my coat. It was on the foot of the bed. All the money was in the pockets. This is what I

wanted; the money. I did not want this pithecanthropus erectus
to find it. I was not jealous.

'. . . one at a time, one at a time,' he was saying.

'I'm sorry about the old lady,' I said. The minute he sees the
coat he'll feel it for a gun and find the money, I was thinking, and
that'll make everything very simple for them; they'll stash the
money away and turn us in and I can accuse them till I'm blue in
the face but nobody'll believe me. . . .

'She's got t.b.'

'I know. She's got to go to Arizona,' I said, trying to remember
if Holiday had kicked the sheet down far enough on the bed to
cover the coat. . . .

'. . . hell of a place, Arizona. Even if you ain't got t.b. Like to
go there myself someday. No trip at all now. Two or three buses
pull outta here every day headed for Arizona.'

'I know,' I said. If the sheet is covering only part of the coat
maybe he won't notice it. The last thing in the world he should
be interested in now is a coat. But I've got to hurry up; I've got
to get that coat first. If he finds the money and they turn us in
we're doomed, nothing can keep the ropes from around our
necks. If I can get the coat first and pay them off maybe they'll
kill us anyway, but there's a chance that all this talk about buses
to Arizona is on the level, and even if it isn't a lot more things
can happen in this room where only two cops have guns than can
happen in a steel-barred jail or a steel-barred death-house where
a hundred cops have a hundred guns . . .

'Any objection to me pitching something in the pot for the old
lady?' I asked.

'You don't have to do that,' he said. 'We'll manage. . . .'

'But I'd like to. I know what a person with t.b. goes through.
My old lady had t.b. I've got to give up the money anyway. I'd
rather the old lady got it than have it go back to the market. She
needs it a lot more than the market does . . .'

'No argument about that. Well,' he said, 'I suppose it'd be all right. How much did you have in mind?'

'I can raise about fourteen hundred. . . .'

That shocked him. He looked up at that, the right side of his mouth turned down. 'You got a goddamn nerve!' he said. 'You got six gees, didn't you? Fourteen hundred dollars . . .'

'That's all that was left,' I said. 'Mason got twenty-seven hundred and the other guy got two gees. That's four gees right there. I got fourteen hundred left. This is the first job we pulled here; we were just passing through on our way to Arizona. Jesus,' I said. 'Do you think I'd screw this thing up for a few hundred dollars? I know what a break we're getting and I'm grateful. But that's all we got – fourteen hundred dollars.'

'All right, all right,' he said. 'Where's the dough?'

'In my coat pocket, in there,' I said.

'Where in there is your coat?'

'On the foot of the bed. It may be covered up by the sheet. I'll get it,' I said. He moved a few steps toward the bedroom door, keeping his eyes on me all the while. 'Hey, Reece. Reece . . .'

'Yeah?'

'Get this guy's coat, will you? It's on the foot of the bed.

He drifted his eyes at me, his face vacuous, and in a moment my coat sailed through the door and landed at his feet, the gun in the pocket banging against the floor. He glared through the door and picked up the coat, taking out the gun and dropping it into his own pocket. Then he found the money and let the coat fall to the floor, kicking it against the davenport.

'We'll need a hundred to get to Arizona,' I said.

He paid no attention to me. He put the money in his other pocket, looking at the bedroom door again. 'Hey, Reece,' he called. 'Bring that dame out. . . .'

That scared me. That little red tremor started twisting again in the pit of my stomach. If he was going to let us get away with

59

this why have Holiday brought out? He was going to turn us in, the bastard, that's what he was going to do. All right, you son-of-a-bitch, I was thinking, I'll scream my head off about that dough even if nobody will listen, even if you do work me over...

Reece and Holiday came out of the bedroom. She had on her tweed coat and skirt and carried her hat and one shoe in her hand.

'Do you mind if I finish dressing?' she said.

'Why?' the little one said. 'You ain't going nowhere....'

'Ain't we taking 'em downtown?' Reece asked.

'It's better this way....'

'In that case,' Reece said, 'maybe I better help her get her clothes off....

The little one gave him a chastening look and said to Holiday: 'Stand over there with him.'

Holiday hesitated and Reece gestured with the gun he still held in his hand. 'You heard him. Stand over there...'

Here it comes, I was thinking; they're not going to turn us in, after all, they're going to kill us right here. Holiday moved beside me and I eased back just a little, getting her between me and the gun, watching Reece's hand, focusing my eyes on his forefinger curled around the trigger, turning my side toward him, slanting my head away from him, reducing the target as much as possible, figuring that when he fired the first bullet I'd dive for the little one...

'... Now, lissen,' the little one was saying: 'you get outta town on separate buses. Separate buses, I said. And don't come back....'

'Don't worry. Separate buses,' Holiday said. 'Don't worry. We won't come back....'

'Let's go ...' the little one said to Reece, starting out.

I didn't believe it, but there it was – Reece was following the little one across the floor to the hall door.

'Please, mister,' I heard myself saying, 'could I have my automatics?'

They both stopped and the little one looked around at Reece, who shrugged. The little one took my automatic from his pocket, thumbed the clip out and snapped the cartridge from the chamber. He pitched the gun onto the davenport and Reece handed him the other automatic and he did the same thing with this one. Then they went on out, saying nothing else, closing the door behind them.

I still didn't believe it; they were gone, but the feeling of danger still hung in the room, like a concrete cloud. It was like getting away from a ten-armed giant in a bad dream; you rounded a corner and shook him off but you knew that momentarily he would lean down over one of the buildings and grab you. I stood there trembling and then I heard myself breathing and I looked at Holiday and saw that she was staring at me. I sat down but did not have the strength to draw up my legs, letting the whole weight of them rest on my heels.

'I wouldn't go through that again for a million dollars, not for ten million dollars,' I said.

'Oh, it could've been worse,' she said.

'No,' I said.

'It wasn't too bad. . . .'

'For an imbecile it wasn't. For you it wasn't,' I said. 'You had a hell of a time, showing yourself to that swine. Whenever you can wave that thing in somebody's face you have a hell of a time. . . .'

'You're jealous, that's all. . . .'

'Nuts,' I said.

'Is that all you can think of? Never mind the wonderful break we just got, never mind that we're getting out of this town clean and free, never mind any of that. All you can think of is me showing myself to that cop. Whyn't you think about how lucky we are to get away with this?'

61

'I'm thinking about that, too,' I said, managing, finally, to get my legs up. I got on my feet and picked up the automatics from the davenport and my coat from the floor and went into the bedroom. I put on my coat, and from under a pile of lingerie in the bureau drawer I took two extra clips of cartridges, shoving a clip into each stock and snapping a cartridge into each barrel, in firing position. I dropped the guns into my pockets and put on my hat and started out. Holiday was standing in the door, watching me.

'Where are you going?' she asked.

'I'll be back inside of an hour,' I said.

'Forget it!' she said, sharply, blocking me. 'You start anything with Mason now and we're cooked. You stay away from him. . . .'

'I wasn't even thinking of him,' I said.

'Then what were you thinking of? Now, look,' she said swiftly. 'Jinx's got money of his own. If they've picked him up let him make his own deal.'

'I wasn't thinking of Jinx, either,' I said. 'We're broke. We need some money to get out of town.'

'No,' she said. 'It's too risky. I got a little dough left – enough for that. Enough to get us out of town.'

'How much you got?'

'Around twenty dollars . . .'

'How far will that take us?'

'Far enough . . .'

'Get out of the way,' I said.

She grabbed me with both hands, shaking me. 'Are you crazy?' she said. 'We *got* to get away from here! There's a murder rap staring us in the face! We can't press our luck too far. . . .'

'Stop shaking me . . .' I said.

She stopped shaking me, but kept her grip on the shoulders of my coat.

'They'd pull the switch on us in a minute . . .' she said, way back in her throat, a little slobber trickling over the edge of her lip.

'This is not the dame I saw handling a machine-gun yesterday,' I said. 'That must have been somebody else. That was some other dame. . . .'

'Somebody's got to shake you, you amateur, you punk' she said.

I hit her in the stomach with my left fist, knocking her back against the door facing. She wavered and then fell, pounding on the floor with both fists and sobbing and moaning.

'Shut up and listen,' I said, stooping down beside her. 'Will you please shut up and listen! Listen to me!'

She slowly stopped pounding on the floor and started to lift her head, but before she could look at me there was a knocking at the hall door. I was so dumbfounded that for a moment I was paralysed. Holiday had pushed herself up off the floor and was sitting on her shins beside me and I got a smell of fear from her, cinnamon-pungent and exciting. I rose carefully and crossed to the door, taking an automatic out of my pocket. The knocking came again, and then I realized that this was not a knocking but a rapping, impatient but not peremptory; tranquilizing me a little; surely, I was thinking, the bastards wouldn't be coming back as meekly as this, they wouldn't be thumping the door with one finger, which is what this noise is – and I opened the door, standing behind it, not taking any more chances, not being a punk this time, with my gun levelled and my finger around the trigger so tensely that the weight of one additional heartbeat would have caused it to squeeze fire.

It was Jinx. I closed the door with my shoulder. His face was drawn and his eyes were wrathful.

'Mason put the finger on us, the son-of-a-bitch, it was Mason,' he said.

'Goddamn you, Jinx, we know who put the finger on us,'

63

Holiday said, her voice throbbing, moving to him. 'If you got anything to settle with Mason, you settle it yourself and stop trying to suck Ralph into help you. We got a hell of a break here and I won't let you louse it up.'

'Who's trying to louse anything up?' he said, flaring. 'Why, for Christ's sake, I came out here to do you a favor and the minute I get inside the door you tear my head off. I came out here to try to tip you off to the cops and I get my head torn off.'

'She's been having hysterics,' I said. 'Leave him alone,' I said to Holiday.

'I'll take the chances I'm taking to do you another favor sometime,' he said to her. 'I was across the street in that second-hand lot,' he said to me. 'I saw him come out. The club-footed nance son-of-a-bitch. If I'd had a gun, I'd've popped him sitting there in that squad car . . .'

'If you want to get even with Mason, you get even by yourself,' Holiday said. 'Don't try to suck Ralph in. We got to get out of here, we got to get out of here fast. And not you, either. You don't go with us. You go in some other direction, not with us . . .'

Jinx stared at her for a second and then looked at me, frowning. 'What's the matter with her?' he asked.

'I told you. She's been having hysterics.'

'We got to get out of town,' she said. 'They told us to get out of town.'

'Would you believe this is the same dame we knew yesterday?' I asked him.

'I sure as hell wouldn't. . . .'

'You see?' I said to her. 'Relax for a minute, will you? Take it easy. Everything's under control. Let me handle this.'

'You've handled it fine so far. You punk.'

'Please . . .' I said.

'That club-footed nance son-of-a-bitch, he didn't even tip me off the plainclothes men were coming,' Jinx said. 'He lets 'em walk in on me cold. I look up and there they are.'

'I know exactly how you feel,' I said. 'They cleaned us, too.'

'They didn't clean me. I didn't know it was a shakedown then. I don't know these two cops and think it's a pinch. I didn't know it was a shakedown. I wouldn'ta minded a shakedown so much. That . . .'

'Wait a minute,' I said. 'What do you mean – they didn't clean you? You mean you didn't pay these guys off?'

'I didn't know it was a shakedown. I thought it was a pinch . . .'

Holiday lifted her eyes to mine and I dropped mine to hers. Both of us were thinking the same thing – if he didn't pay off the cops he still had the money.

'How'd you get loose then?' I asked.

'They never did have me. I'm working in the shop when they come in the back way and ask where Jinx Raynor is. I tell 'em he's in front, and then they go to the front I duck out the alley. I thought it was a pinch. I didn't know it was a shakedown till I got here, till I saw Reece and the Inspector come out without you. Then it figured.'

'Inspector?' I said. 'The little guy's an Inspector?'

'Yeah. Inspector Webber.'

Well, well, I was thinking. Cut yourself a piece of cake, Inspector. Cut yourself two pieces of cake.

'Then you still got the money?' Holiday asked.

'Sure, I still got it. Two gees. I got it right here,' he said, slapping the right-hand pocket of his trousers.

'That's wonderful!' Holiday said, and I knew she was thinking that now we could get out of town, that now I wouldn't have to pull another stick-up.

'That's wonderful,' I said, thinking about something else entirely.

'I'd rather've gave those guys half of it and stayed here than to keep all of it and have to leave. I was just getting started good in this town.'

65

You don't know how well you are started in this town, I wanted to tell him.

'You can get started good in some other town,' Holiday said. 'We can all meet somewhere. Denver. Dallas. Kansas City.'

'Now she wants to meet you somewhere,' I said. 'Now she likes you again.'

'Will you shut up, you punk, you amateur,' she said.

'I may not be the punk, the amateur, you think. I may surprise you,' I said to her. 'Maybe you won't have to leave town,' I said to Jinx. 'Maybe I can make a deal for you.'

'Look who's talking about making a deal for you.'

'Please,' I said.

'Big Stuff. Old Master,' she said. 'He knows all about how to handle cops. Yeah. You should of seen him handling 'em.' Her hysterics were getting better. The vinegar was rising once more. She knew she could have a helping of Jinx's two gees, and she was beginning to feel fine. ' "Maybe I can make a deal for you." Get him to tell you about the one he made for himself. Old Big Stuff. Why, for Christ's sake, he was so scared . . .'

'All right, I was scared. I admit it. I *was* scared. But not any more. Not, by God, any more.'

'You should've seen him five minutes ago,' she said.

'A lot can happen in five minutes,' I said. 'A lot has happened in five minutes. I got an idea now – a good one.'

'You ever hear such a lot of crap in your life?' she said to Jinx.

'Of course, you can't understand it,' I said. 'This is just one of the tragedies of a superior intellect – not being able to transpose his thoughts to a level low enough for an imbecile to understand.'

'Why don't you stop trying to act so important, for Christ's sake?' she said. 'Why don't you get wise to yourself? You're just a punk. . . .'

'But a punk with a few small distinctions,' I said slowly and quietly and clearly; 'including a Phi Beta Kappa key and a university degree and a collection of pyschoses for which Doctor Lombroso would have given his left arm, and a passion for the minor snobberies of life as symbolized by Charvet ties and Brooks Brothers shirts and Peal shoes . . .' You fools, you mere passers of food, I was thinking; I shall not be saddled with you for long, I shall not be saddled with you for longer than is absolutely necessary, and then, swiftly, exploding that, and the color of the fragments was mauve, came the image of Holiday naked in bed, in the tub, in the shower, on the floor, in the car, in the open, pulsing with a lust straight from the cave, and my navel fluttered, mocking me, and I knew that what I was thinking was indeed crap, truly crap, that if only for this she would always be absolutely necessary. . . .

'. . . Let's stop this squawking, let's start getting out of here,' she was saying, moving on into the bedroom.

Jinx was staring at me, frowning.

'You listen to her and she'll have you thinking I can't get in out of the rain,' I said. 'You're sure this guy's an Inspector?'

'Sure, I'm sure . . .'

'He's left himself wide open, pulling a shakedown like this,' I said. 'He's an Inspector, maybe we can do some business. Maybe I can fix this. Maybe you won't have to leave town. Maybe we can stick around here for awhile. Maybe we won't have to start running away as soon as we thought. Would that be all right with you?'

'Sure. That'd be fine. . . .' he said.

'Well, what can we lose?' I said.

Holiday came out of the bedroom wearing a hat and carrying a coat on her arm and a big purse in her hand.

'The thing now is to decide where we're going, where to send the suitcases,' she said.

'Leave this to me,' I said to Jinx. 'We've decided where we're going,' I said to her.

'Where?'

'Nowhere,' I said.

She looked at Jinx as if she thought I was joking, but when she looked back at me she saw that it was no joke. I handed Jinx one of the guns.

'We're staying right here,' I said. 'And this time I don't want any argument.'

'I won't argue. . . .' she said heavily. 'I won't argue with you any more. You're crazy man and I want to get just as far away from you as I can.' She looked at Jinx. 'Will you let me take a hundred dollars?'

'Sure,' he said. Then he took a couple of steps towards me. 'Look, Ralph, why can't we stay together? Why do we have to split up?'

'She's doing the splitting up,' I said. 'I'm not doing it; she's doing it. Give her a hundred dollars and let her split. Give her a hundred dollars and let her haul herself out of here. Let her go back to Chicago. She'll be happy in Chicago. In Chicago she's got a lot of influential friends. In Chicago she hasn't got a single enemy. . . .'

'Oh, God . . .' she said.

'The least you could do would be to listen to what I've got to say,' I said. 'That's the very least you could do.'

'Oh, God . . .' she moaned, putting down the coat and purse.

Early that afternoon the men from the music and appliance company delivered the portable recording set, a small phonograph, a dozen twelve-inch acetates, some extra cutting needles and a microphone with fifty feet of cable. Jinx paid them and from one of the men he bought a kit of used tools, and after they had left Holiday came out of the bedroom where I had been keeping her temporarily out of sight.

'It's a hell of a gamble,' she said. 'It's a hell of a gamble.'

'I don't see how you can say that,' I said patiently. 'You've just had a graphic example of the average cop's behavior when he locates easy money. If he hasn't changed in four or five lifetimes what makes you think he'll change in four or five hours?'

'Just the same . . .'

'Will you please not stand around dripping that awful doubt all over the rug? I like this idea. There's nothing elaborate or involved about it. It has the simplicity of a punk's, an amateur's brain. Please go lay down. Take a nap or something.'

'How do you expect to get 'em back here to make the recording? You've got to have 'em here to make the recording. How're you going to manage that?'

'By rustling, and very lightly at that, the remaining eighteen hundred dollars of Jinx's money,' I said. She frowned dumbly. Is this eternally to be my fate, I wondered, to always be over their heads, to always have to use diagrams to explain myself? 'The noise that eighteen hundred dollars makes when you rub it together is very faint,' I said. 'You hardly can hear it across the room – but a cop can hear it for miles and miles. It comes in on a wave-length to which only his ears are attuned.'

She shook her head dubiously, looking away from me to Jinx, who by now had taken the recorder out of the carton and was untying the recording and playback arms, paying no attention to us.

'Please go lay down,' I said to her. 'Take a nap or something. Is that the set you wanted?' I asked Jinx.

'Yeah. It's the best,' he said. He opened the back and took out the microphone. 'Got to find a place for this,' he said. He sat down on the davenport and dragged a small radio off the end-table into his lap, inspecting it. He turned the microphone sideways, holding it against the back of the radio, measuring. 'It'll fit in here,' he said. 'I'll take the speaker out of here and put in the mike.' He traced the radio cable with his eyes, leaning over

69

the back of the davenport and following it to the base plug. 'I think that'll do it,' he said.

'That's what I thought too. There's a clothes closet directly behind this wall. You can put the set in the closet. You can drill a hole in the baseboard behind the davenport. That way they can't see it. It'll be behind the davenport. The davenport'll hide it.'

'Look . . .' he said. 'Don't try to think for me. Think for her, but don't try to think for me.'

Once this is done, once this is in the bag, I'll show you who'll do the thinking, I thought. 'I was only trying to help,' I said.

'Well, this is one thing I don't need help with,' he said. 'Go lay down. Take a nap somewhere.'

He got up and went in to the bedroom, turning on the light and going into the closet. In a minute he was back.

'This'll do it,' he said. 'This'll work all right.'

I looked at Holiday.

'You heard him.' I said. 'Cheer up . . .'

. . . chapter seven

I got off the bus at the corner, feeling a small curious pleasure that I was able to do this in the easy habitual manner of a man who had been getting off the same bus at the same corner for years, a veteran; for there is nothing more inconspicuous than an expert, in any thing, even getting off a bus. The average stranger, riding in a bus to somewhere for only the second time, would not have been concerned with trying to act like an expert, it probably never would have occurred to him; if he had not known where to get off and from which end, he would have asked questions, the average stranger who is normal about such things. But I was not normal about such things. These were the minutiae I was so painstaking about, that I performed so perfectly, the very performances of which, since they are never mirrorized for the average man, convinced me that destiny had me by the tail. I walked down the street towards the produce market, towards Mason's garage, rising and falling on the swell of the noon-day crowd; girls and women with as many different shades of red gashes in their faces, through which teeth occasionally showed, as you have fingers and toes; and guys in linen coats and seersucker coats and shirt sleeves, all fetishists too, lip fetishes – cigars and cigarettes and pipes and toothpicks, these the fetishes that could be seen and God knows how many that couldn't, the most sinful of which was probably mediocrity: cheap, common, appalling people, the kind a war, happily, destroys. What is your immediate destiny, you loud little unweaned people? A two-dollar raise? A hamburger and a hump?

There was no excitement now in front of Hartford's. The boy tending the vegetable stalls was washing a bunch of chicory and a porter was sweeping the sidewalk with a long-handled pushbroom. The big blasting gap in the market's quiet casual day had been filled in with the heavy weight of routine.

And this is the way it looked at Mason's Garage too, but this I knew could not be true, and that is why I had come. The police had missed Jinx and by now the stake-outs had been set and one of the stake-outs had to be the garage, in case he tried, for any reason, to get to Mason. There probably would be a plainclothes man in the office by the phone and another lounging around the back door – and sure enough there was. Police procedure is as rigidly fixed as a geometrical problem – and the answer is always in the back of the book.

I paused in the doorway of the office and the plainclothes man standing beside the desk, by the telephone, looked at me stolidly. He was fifty or more and he had been a cop for a long time, for in his face was the flowered viciousness that only many years of petty police authority can properly mature.

'Yeah?' he said.

'Mason around?'

'What's it about?'

'It's about a car.'

'Yeah? What kind of car?'

'Any kind – just so it's transportation.'

'Where do you wanna go?'

Subtlety and caution now come to you in a brand-new handy-size package – a pot-belly and twelve triple-A shoe. When following the spoor of game in the open country be sure you move up-wind; and in heavily wooded sections exercise extreme caution, being careful not to step on twigs or rattle the leaves or bushes. Bear in mind that animals entrust their lives to sight, smell and hearing; and since the hunter cannot possibly conceive to what degree these instincts are developed, he must constantly be on the alert not to frighten the quarry. 'Mason around?' 'What's it about?' 'It's about a car.' 'Yeah? What kind of car?' 'Any kind – just so it's transportation.' 'Where do you wanno go?' Mr Big-foot was doing a beautiful job of moving up-wind, through the bush.

'I don't want to go anywhere,' I said. 'I really don't. I was planning to stay right here until Mason and Inspector Webber broke in on me. The Inspector wants me to get out of town. Maybe you better call Mason . . .'

He stared at me stupidly, frowning, and the frown twitched, vibrated by the ponderous machinery that was slowly turning over inside his capacious skull. He did not seem at all surprised that I had recognized him for a cop. A fact was trying to get through to his brain and its progress could be followed by the struggle on his face. It finally got through. The twitching of the frown stopped and the skin beside the lobes of his ears rose like the hackles of a suspicious dog.

'So the Inspector found you . . .' he said slowly.

'Yes,' I said.

The other plainclothes man, the one who had been lounging by the rear door, came in. He was about thirty, too young for his face to have flowered yet, but the bud was beginning to open.

'What's going on, Ray?' he asked.

'The same thing that's been going on for years. We're still sucking the hind tit. Inspector Webber wants this guy to get out of town,' he said, crossing to the doorway, beside me. He yelled into the garage: 'Mason!'

All this time the other cop kept his eyes on me. But both seemed disconsolate, discouraged.

73

'Where's Jinx Raynor?' he asked.

'I don't know,' I said.

'Maybe,' Ray said, turning back into the office, 'he's saving him for the Inspector, too.'

'If I knew where Raynor was, I'd tell you,' I said. 'You think I want to see the Inspector make a hog of himself?'

'What do you want?' Mason said, behind me.

'I want a car,' I said.

'A black Ford sedan with a Mercury motor, too, no doubt . . .'

I turned around and looked at him. There was a bold sneer on his face. The presence of the two cops had done wonders for his morale.

'I'm afraid I was too ambitious,' I said, with some penitence. 'The black Ford sedan with the Mercury motor'll have to wait. Just any kind'll have to do now. I thought maybe you or Nelse could drive Holiday and me out of town.'

'You oughta heard him this morning,' he said to the cops. 'He's changed his tune some. Sorry as hell I can't help you, Ralph, old pal, sorry as hell,' he said to me. 'Nothing I'd like better'n to drive you and the dame somewhere – and have one of you put a bullet in my back.'

'You got me all wrong,' I said. 'I don't hold a grudge. I'm not sore at you . . .'

'Take your business somewhere else . . .'

'But where?' I said. 'There's no time for that. I got to get out of town. Look,' I said pulling out Jinx's eighteen hundred dollars, folded neatly, 'I can pay. Eighteen hundred dollars.' All of them were surprised. 'You don't think I'd let the Inspector clean me, do you?'

'I don't care if you got eighteen thousand dollars,' Mason said. 'I don't care if you got eighteen million dollars. Now, get out of here . . .'

Ray looked fraternally at his younger partner, sniffing, trying to locate the wind. The hippopotamus was getting ready to move through the bush again.

'Ben,' he said, 'we ought to follow through on that other tip on Jinx Raynor. I know it's the hell and gone out on Highway Four, almost to the state line. We could give this fellow a lift that far...'

'No,' Ben said.

'Now, wait a minute,' Ray went on patiently. 'That's no way to co-operate. The Inspector wants this fellow to scram. Why don't we give a hand? We scratch the Inspector's back, he scratches ours...'

'No,' Ben said. 'This thing's off the track some place.' You can bet it's off the track some place, I wanted to tell him. Have a piece of cake Ben. It's not a big cake, not big enough for the whole department, but have a piece while it lasts. 'I'll not be getting gummed up with the Inspector...'

'That goddamn Inspector...' Ray muttered.

'Get out,' Ben said to me.

I got out. At the street entrance I turned and looked back over my shoulder. Mason was moving to the rear of the garage, bouncing up and down on his club foot. I knew where he was going. He was going to the other telephone. He was going to call the goddamn Inspector.

... the goddamn Inspector. He's so big he can get away with it. He's also so big that he can't get away with it. Well, all right *Lex talionis*. The big fish gobbles the little fish and the little fish gobbles the fingerling and the fingerling gobbles the mollusk and so on, R.I.P. Hello, there, Mother. The inauguration is all over and I am calling from the White House. Hello, there, Inspector. I'll need two or three plainclothes men tonight to help me knock over a joint.

If...

But there mustn't be any ifs. It's up to me to see that there are no ifs . . .

I rapped on the door of the apartment but there was no answer. Thinking that maybe I had rapped too softly, I rapped again, harder. There was still no answer, no movement, no sound at all from the inside. Sure. The minute I turn my back . . . I knocked on the door two or three times with my knuckles, and in a moment it slowly opened. I was surprised. I hadn't heard any footsteps crossing the floor. I went in. Jinx stepped from behind the door, closing it. No wonder I hadn't heard any footsteps. He was barefooted.

'I see that you belong to what we call the civilized school,' I said.

'What?' he said blankly.

'You have to take off your shoes and socks to do it,' I said. 'You disillusion me. I thought you were a catch-as-catch can man.'

'Oh . . .' he said awkwardly. 'I was just fixing to wash my feet.'

'Button up,' I said, but not too angrily; where Holiday was concerned you couldn't ever get too angry with the man.

She came out of the bedroom then, with not a wrinkle in her clothes, with not even a hair out of place, a gracious smile on her face, the vicar's wife coming in to pour. I could have cut her throat, but strangling this impulse, wrapped tightly around it in precise spacings as if it had been spun by a machine, was a strong cord of admiration, too. She had an armour-plated conscience. She knew that I knew that she'd just gotten out of bed with this poor stupid bastard but there was not the slightest suggestion of guilt or shame or even self-consciousness about her. She moved on into the room, bearing herself with a kind of necrophilic dignity, the vicar's wife now about to pour, and I told myself that she was tremendous, really tremendous, and my navel started fluttering again . . .

76

'You didn't take long,' she said pleasantly.

'An expert never takes long,' I said, also meaning it for a dig at Jinx, telling myself that I had to stop thinking how tremendous she was and get down to business; any minute now that goddamn Inspector would be showing up, and that there would be plenty of time later to think about how tremendous she was, plenty of time later to let my navel flutter, when I could enjoy it, when I could let it jump right through my belt buckle if . . .

If . . .

But there mustn't be any ifs. By God, there just mustn't be any ifs!

'Get in there, Get the machine set up,' I said to Jinx.

'It's set up. It's been set up and tested.'

'Well, get in there anyway,' I said.

'How do you know he'll come?' he asked.

'Goddamn it,' I said. 'This whole thing's designed to make him come. I arrange it to make him come. Where's that other gun?'

'In there – on top of the recording machine.'

'Take this one too,' I said, handing him my automatic. 'You keep 'em. I hope you got guts enough to use 'em in case anything goes wrong.'

'How can anything go wrong?' he said. 'You're an expert . . .'

'Get on the machine, will you?' I said.

'Sure,' he said agreeably. 'Just remember to keep him right on top that microphone all the time.'

'I'll remember,' I said. 'Get in there . . .'

'You think I got time to put on my shoes?'

'You got time to button up . . .'

He smirked at Holiday and walked out into the bedroom. Impassively, she watched him go.

'Please forgive me,' I said.

'For what?' she asked.

77

'For disturbing you at such an ecstatic moment. But try to appreciate the situation. There I was standing out there in the hall, unable to rouse anybody and momentarily expecting Inspector Webber to show up. That would have ruined everything. So you see, I had to get inside, I *simply* had to get inside. I'm the last person in the world who wants to interfere with your pleasure, but this time I couldn't help it. I hope you understand that . . .'

'I understand . . .' she said sweetly.

'You're tremendous,' I said. 'Truly tremendous.'

'Please don't be sarcastic,' she said.

'I'm not sarcastic,' I said. 'I'm trying to be very sincere. You're tremendous.'

'Please don't be sore,' she said.

'Then, goddamn it, keep your legs crossed,' I said. I took off my coat, stepping past her to the davenport. She shifted her base, turning, watching me go. I put my coat on the davenport and looked at her. All your taste is in your mouth, the one thing I don't want to get is the one thing you'll eventually give me if you don't stop laying up with every son-of-a-bitch you say hello to, I wanted to tell her, but I didn't; thinking that Jinx might overhear me through the microphone. I didn't want any rupture with him – yet. I needed him and his eighteen hundred dollars that I had in my pocket.

'What happened at Mason's?' she asked.

'Just what I told you would happen,' I said, and not too cordially. 'There were some cops there – and Mason. I gave him a flash of the eighteen hundred dollars and he went straight to the telephone.'

'Good,' she said, relaxing a little. 'I was worried about you.'

'Hereafter when you worry about me,' I said, 'don't narcotize yourself with sex.'

Her eyes flashed. She started to say something but she never

78

got the words out. There was a knock at the door. We both jumped a little.

'Remember everything I've told you now. Just follow my lead,' I said, as softly as I could and still make the words audible above the pounding of my heart. *Auto-da-fé*. Take it easy, my heart, slow down, slow down, I kept repeating, this is as safe as an old feather bed, otherwise he wouldn't have come, slow down, my heart.... I went past Holiday, getting that sharp-rising cinnamony puff again, striding to the door and opening it. The Inspector and Reece stood there, but this time almost apologetically, like door-to-door canvassers.

'Mind if we come in?' the Inspector said.

They came in and I closed the door.

'Sort of surprised to find you here,' the Inspector said. 'We thought you'd be on your way to Arizona by now...'

'I'm sure trying to get away, sir,' I said, 'I'm trying to locate a car.'

'Two or three buses pull out for Arizona every day, son. I told you that before....'

'Yes, sir, I know,' I said. Slow down, my heart, slow down. You're laboring my voice, you're making me aspirate. Nothing to be excited about now: we've got him, we've got him good. Just maneuver him over near the microphone, just ease him over.... 'I don't want you to think I'm a fresh guy, sir,' I said. 'I'm not one of those hard-headed punks who does just the opposite of what he is told,' I said, backing slowly to the davenport. 'I'm gonna do what you told me. I'm gonna get out of town. Aren't we gonna get out town?' I asked Holiday.

'Believe me,' she said, but she was talking straight to Reece, the other cop, smiling at him, and he was smiling back, thinking the same old thing – which was what she wanted him to think, goddamn her.

I finally felt the davenport with the calves of my legs, and sat down. The radio that concealed the microphone was on the end table beside me.

'When?' the Inspector asked. He took three or four steps towards me, a paternal frown on his face. 'Don't you appreciate it when people are nice to you? I gave you a break. Maybe that was a mistake in the first place . . .'

Well, now, copper, you just stick around and you'll find out whether or not it was a mistake. It was the goddamndest mistake you ever made, you thieving son-of-a-bitch. The pounding of my heart was less violent now and the excitement was dissolving and I was getting the feel of this.

'I certainly do appreciate it, sir,' I said. 'I wanted to take the Arizona bus like you said. Didn't we?' I said to Holiday. 'Didn't we want to take the Arizona bus like Inspector Webber said?' I had to identify him, I had to get his name on the record to nail him down.

'Yes, we did,' she replied. 'But we didn't have anything to use for money . . .'

She moved to the other end of the davenport and sat down, anti-charm school, spreading her knees, stretching her skirt tightly, while Reece laid his head on his shoulder, trying, blatantly, to see as far up under there as he could. You see what I mean? You couldn't blame him . . .

'That's where the trouble was,' I said to the Inspector. 'No money. You took all we had. There were only a few dollars left. I had to go find the fellow who helped me in the market job. He got two gees as his cut.'

'That's the fellow Pratt and Downey are after,' Reece said to the Inspector.

'Did you find him?' the Inspector asked.

'Yes, sir,' I said. 'He let me have a few hundred.'

'Quite a few,' he said dryly. 'Eighteen hundred, wasn't it?'

I pretended to be surprised that he knew. 'Well, sir,' I said, 'I can see that if I wanna keep any secrets from you, I got to stay away from Mason's Garage. I can see that – but it was the only place I knew to get a car. That's the only reason I went . . .' I took the currency out of my pocket and laid it across my knee, smoothing it down. 'Here it is, eighteen hundred in cash,' I said. 'How much of *this* can I keep?'

'Well, this time there's somebody else to be taken care of,' he said slowly.

'Who?' Reece asked.

'Pratt and Downey . . .'

'But why?' Reece asked.

'Don't be a chump,' the Inspector said sharply. 'They're wise to this. Why do you think they let this guy breeze in and out of their stake-out and not pick him up? There's enough goddamn jealousy in this department now . . .' He reached over and picked up the eighteen hundred dollars from under my fingers and riffled it. He held out two twenties and a ten.

'Here . . .' he said.

'Jesus, Inspector,' I said. 'Only fifty dollars for us?'

'It's your own goddamn fault, you go barging in that goddamn garage and give the whole thing away. I told you to get out of town. How do you think those guys feel? I been on the hind tit myself. Who do you think those guys are sore at – you or me?'

I took the fifty dollars. 'I never thought of that,' I said. 'Look, Inspector,' I said. 'This fellow who helped me pull the Hartfood Market job, this friend of mine. He lives here in town. He told me about a payroll that's a pushover. Now, we're going to Arizona, all right, but I was wondering. . . . If we just stay here in this apartment till the time comes to make the haul and then we make it and blow town right away, there wouldn't be any harm in that, would there? We're perfectly safe here, we wore masks on that other job and nobody could identify us – and this payroll's pretty big, Inspector. . . .'

'I wouldn't trust you,' he said.

'Naturally,' I said. 'But there must be somebody you can trust. We'll need at least a couple of men. You pick 'em. This is worth it, twenty thousand dollars is worth it. You pick a couple of guys you can trust to go in with us. Maybe you and Reece can go with us yourselves, to handle the getaway car or something. If anything goes wrong you can use the old stall, you know, that you were tipped off and just went there to grab us red-handed. You're an Inspector. You could get away with that . . .'

Using cops to actually help me in a hold-up had heretofore been only a thought, never specifically considered any more than the guy playing left field for Dallas specifically considers his participation in a World's Series; it had been only a vague ambition, a dream that had flashed through my mind and registered and passed on. But now I sensed that it might be attained without long years of bush-league apprenticeship. The Inspector's face was still hard and set, but his eyes widened, barely perceptibly, and he looked at Reece momentarily, telepathically, and then back at me.

'What the hell,' I said. 'Let's cut ourselves a real piece of cake.'

He fondled the knot of his cheap silk necktie, not taking his eyes off me, staring almost fiercely, as if the answer to the success or failure of the operation could be found in my face. After a minute he looked at Reece again and jerked his head towards the bedroom. Fine! I thought. You two gents step into the conference room and talk it over, and then I remembered that Jinx was in there, in the closet; and that maybe the Inspector was not taking Reece in there to talk things over at all, that maybe he was suspicious and was going to shake down the place, that maybe he knew there was something funny about this and how could he help but know, an itinerant punk doesn't make cold-blooded propositions like this to an Inspector of Police. Jesus, I told myself, you overplayed your hand this time, you didn't need this, you had him nailed with the pay-off, but no, you and your talent, you and your genius, you and your sadism, you had to screw it up, you punk, you child; and I could feel that tremor coming at my stomach and bang! it hit and the color of it was pale thermal-red, and it spun and twisted my intestines the way a rubber band is twisted when you wind up a toy aeroplane. From the other end of the davenport Holiday gasped and the sound of that was dripping of fear, too. I heard the bedroom door being opened and through the vortex I realized that Jinx had to be warned that it was not I or Holiday who was opening the door but the Inspector and Reece. 'Inspector, Inspector,' I said, turning around. That stopped him. 'You'll have to excuse the appearance of the bedroom,' I said, laughing. 'The maid hasn't come around yet.' They went on in, closing the door.

'Jinx!' Holiday exclaimed, shoving herself to her feet. She was trembling all over. I pantomimed vigorously for her to sit down, thinking: Jesus, I hope that stupid son-of-a-bitch understands, I hope he's got the closet door closed like I told him, I hope he'll be still and quiet as a creep-mouse. There was nothing I could do about it now, absolutely nothing. It's all right, it's all right, it's all right, I desperately pantomimed to Holiday, trying to get her to sit down, making up my mind that the instant I heard any voices, any noises, I would rush for the hall door. Jinx had two guns in there for just such an emergency and I hoped he had the nerve to use them. It's all right, it's all right, it's all right, I pantomimed to Holiday, goddamn it, sit down and wait. Still trembling, she looked wildly at the bedroom door and again I wondered how anybody could shoot at people with a machine gun, and hit them, could get so frightened. There wasn't one dame in a million who, her business suddenly interrupted could stroll out of the bedroom with the dignity and *savoir-faire* that she had exhibited. She was tremendous, all right, but at the wrong time and in the wrong places. This was the time and place for her to he tremendous; instead she was panicky. I was panicky too, but not that panicky. I could feel my intestines still being twisted, but, by God, I wasn't shaking all over. I didn't like to have these extraneous thoughts and I wished they wouldn't come: I wanted to concentrate on being scared. I didn't want anything to interfere with my listening for any kind of noise from the bedroom; I didn't want extraneous thoughts interfering with my dive for the door when the time came to dive for the door. I leaned forward, raising my heels, cocking the muscles in my legs, ready to go, gesturing to her that everything was all right, all right, but she knew that I was merely hoping . . .

'Oh, God, I knew this wouldn't work, I knew it,' she moaned.

I jumped up and grabbed her, hugging her tightly, putting my lips against her ear. 'Goddamn it, sit down!' I whispered. I turned her loose, giving her a light push towards the davenport, and sat right back down where I had been sitting, tilting my head, straining my ears. Nothing. The only sounds in the room were the faint febrile exhausts of the steam shovel in that excavation down the street. Holiday hadn't sat down yet, her eyes were on the bedroom door; and I kept trying to tell her with my lips and hands to please sit down, that we were in no danger now. I didn't believe this myself, but as the seconds passed and I heard nothing from the bedroom I slowly became aware that maybe this was so. If anything was going to happen in there it surely would have happened by now. If they were shaking down the room they surely would have found Jinx by now. It just wasn't possible that they could have found him and not made some sounds. It just wasn't possible. My intestines began to ease off and I began to feel better, heart-beat by heart-beat. I smiled and spread my hands at Holiday: You see? Now, please sit down.

She was just sitting down when the door opened and the Inspector and Reece came in.

'Where is this pay-roll job?' the Inspector asked.

I searched his face. He was not suspicious. He was on the level. My intestines finished easing off, sprawling into a luxurious heap. 'I don't know, sir,' I said. 'My friend knows . . .'

'Where is your friend now?'

'I don't know that either, sir. But I can get in touch with him . . .'

Reece moved around in front of me. He hadn't looked at Holiday since he had come out of the bedroom. He had his mind above his belt for a change. 'When'd you figure on pulling this?' he asked.

'We hadn't gone into that,' I replied. 'My friend's the one who spotted this. He just said it looked like a push-over. He didn't go into details.'

Reece looked at the Inspector and the Inspector looked at me.

'Well, I'll tell you what you do,' he said. 'You have your friend here at nine o'clock and we'll *go* into details.'

'I'll try, sir,' I said. 'I'll certainly try.'

'Whaddya mean – you'll try? You said you could get in touch with him.'

'Yes, sir, but whether or not I can get in touch with him in time to have him here by nine o'clock, I don't know. He's holed up somewhere. I'll have to get the word to him round-about. You can come back at nine, but if he's not here I don't want you to get sore at me.'

He stuck his left little finger in his ear and dug, grimacing, and then he looked at the nail to see what he had dug and wiped it off on his trousers. 'I'm not coming back till he's here,' he said. 'You think you can raise him by tomorrow?'

'Oh, I'm sure of that . . .'

'Call me at headquarters. If I'm not there say that Mister Baker called. I'll know what that means. Mister Baker.'

'Yes, sir, Mister Baker – Inspector, sir, what about those two plainclothes men at the garage, Pratt and Downey? What if

Mason brings them here? What if they come here?'

'All you got to worry about,' he said, 'is dragging that friend of yours out of his hole.'

'Yes, sir,' I said.

He turned and started to go and then stopped, glaring at Reece. Reece was paying no attention to what was being said now. He had his back turned to the Inspector, gazing at Holiday, his chin stuck out, nipping his teeth together in eloquent communication. He was not even aware that the conversation had stopped. He looked like a damn fool, standing there with his chin stuck out, nipping his teeth together, showing her what he'd like to do.

'Whenever you're ready, George,' the Inspector said quietly.

Reece whirled guiltily, startled. 'Oh – sure, sure,' he said. 'I'm finished, I'm finished . . .'

The Inspector nodded, moving to the hall door, followed by Reece. They went out without looking back. I got up and tiptoed to the hall door. I made sure the latch was caught and then I lay down on the floor with my ear near the crack at the bottom of the door, listening. I heard their footsteps moving down the hall. When the sounds faded I got up and crossed to the bedroom, motioning for Holiday to follow.

I went straight to the closet door.

'Jinx! Jinx!' I whispered.

Jinx opened the door.

'Did you get it? Did you get it?' I asked.

'I got it,' he said, 'but let's not make it that close again. If you hadn't tipped me off that they were coming in here . . .'

'You know me,' I said gaily. 'Always thinking.'

'Yeah – always thinking,' he said. 'What about that pay-roll hold up? I didn't tell you about a pay-roll hold-up. I don't even know where there is a pay-roll. Not that big, anyway . . .'

'That was just to keep 'em interested in us. Just to get 'em back here,' I said. 'Come on – I wanna hear that record.'

'No!' Holiday said suddenly. 'They might come back!'

'Relax,' I said.

She came over beside us. Her face was worried again. Her lips were trembling.

'What the hell kind of a dame are you, anyway?' I said. 'One minute you got all the guts in the world and the next minute you're scared to death. One minute you're mowing people down with a machine gun and the next minute you're shaking like a leaf. Up and down, up and down . . . The nervous system of a human being is a delicate thing. You can't bang it around like that. It won't stand the shocks. You'll have a breakdown. Relax.'

'Oh, God . . .' she said.

'Please, Holiday,' I said patiently. 'I wanna hear what's on that record. We can go in the closet and listen. Jinx can keep it down low. Please. Go ahead.' I said to Jinx.

She shrugged her shoulders, finally; and the three of us crowded into the tiny closet. Jinx picked up the recording and brushed the cuttings off and then put it on the turntable and started the motor, but I couldn't hear anything. 'Turn it up a little,' I said.

He turned up the volume. '. . . to find you here,' the Inspector's voice was saying. 'We thought you'd be on your way to Arizona by now.'

'I'm sure trying to get away, sir,' my voice was saying. 'I'm trying to locate a car.'

'Jesus, that doesn't sound like me,' I said.

'It's you all right,' Jinx said.

'That's way over by the door,' I said. 'I thought you had to be close to the microphone . . .'

'I'm surprised myself,' Jinx said.

'Start it over,' I said.

Jinx lifted the arm and started it over. *(Two knocks at the hall door.)* I: Remember everything I've told you now. Just follow my lead. *(That'll have to come out, I thought.)* (PAUSE – one, two, three, four, five, six) *(Sound of door opening.)* INSPECTOR: Mind if we come in? I: Why – why, of course not, *(Sound of hall door closing.)* INSPECTOR: Sort of surprised to find you here. We thought you'd be on your way to Arizona by now. I: I'm sure trying to get away, sir. I'm trying to locate a car. INSPECTOR: Two or three buses pull out every day for Arizona, son. I told you that before. I: Yes, sir, I know. (PAUSE – one, two, three) I don't want you to think I'm a fresh guy, sir. I'm not one of those hard-headed punks who does just the opposite of what he is told. I'm gonna do what you told me. I'm gonna get out of town. Aren't we gonna get out of town? HOLIDAY: Believe me. INSPECTOR: When? (PAUSE – one, two) Don't you appreciate it when people are nice to you? I gave you a break. Maybe that was a mistake in the first place. (PAUSE – one, two, three, four, five six) I: I certainly do appreciate it, sir. I wanted to take the Arizona bus like you said. Didn't we? Didn't we want to take the Arizona bus like Inspector Webber said? HOLIDAY: Yes, we did. But we didn't have anything to use for money. I: That's where the trouble was. No money. You took all we had. *(Christ, I was thinking, glowing with pride. This is wonderful. Listen to me suck the guy along!)* There were only a few dollars left. I had to go find the fellow who helped me in the market job. He got two gees as his cut. REECE: That's the fellow Pratt and Downey are after. INSPECTOR: Did you find him? I: Yes, sir. He let me have a few hundred. INSPECTOR: Quite a few. Eighteen hundred, wasn't it? I: Well, sir, I can see that if I wanna keep any secrets from you I got to stay away from Mason's Garage. I can see that – but it was the only place I knew to get a car. That's the only reason I went – *(This is where I took out the cake, I was thinking, this is where I showed him the money, this is where I started nailing him.)* Here it is, eighteen hundred in cash. How much of *this* can I keep? INSPECTOR: Well, this time there's somebody else to be taken care of. REECE: Who? INSPECTOR: Pratt and Downey. REECE: But why? INSPECTOR: Don't be a chump. They're wise to this. Why do you think they let this guy breeze in and out of their stake-out and not pick him up? There's enough goddamn jealousy in this department now. (PAUSE – one, two, three. (*This is where he reached out and took the money from me.*) Here . . . I: Jesus, Inspector. Only fifty dollars for us? INSPECTOR: It's your own goddamn fault, you go barging in that goddamn garage and give the whole thing away. I told you to get out of town. I been on the hind tit myself. Who do you think these guys are sore at – you or me? I: I never thought of that. Look, Inspector. This fellow who helped me pull the Hartford Market job, this friend of mine. He lives here in town. He told me about a pay-roll that's a push-over. Now, we're going to Arizona, all right, but I was wondering. . . . If we just stay here in this apartment till the time comes to make the haul and then we make it and blow town right away, there wouldn't be any harm in that, would there? We're perfectly safe here, we wore masks on that other job and nobody could identify us – and this pay-roll's pretty big, Inspector. INSPECTOR: I wouldn't trust you. I: Naturally. But there must be somebody you can trust. We'll need at least a couple of men. You pick 'em. This is worth it, twenty thousand dollars is worth it. You pick a couple of guys you can trust to go in with us. Maybe you and Reece can go with us yourselves, to handle the getaway car or something. If anything goes wrong you can use the old stall, you know, that you were tipped off and went there to grab us red-handed. You're the Inspector. You could get away with that . . . (*There it was. Audaces fortuna Juvat.*) (PAUSE – one, two) What the hell. Let's cut ourselves a real piece of cake. (PAUSE – one, two, three, four, five, six, seven, eight, nine, ten, eleven, twelve, thirteen, fourteen, fifteen) (*Light sound of movement; they are going into the bedroom.*) Standing there in the gloom of the closet,

knowing that this had come out all right, I still felt in my
stomach a recurrence of the fear-agony I had suffered when
they started for the bedroom, a faint recurrence, the way it feels
when you touch a freshly healed scar. You are pleased and
happy that it is healed, but that does not keep it from being
sensitive. (Sound of door opening.) Inspector, Inspector. You'll
have to excuse the appearance of the bedroom. The maid hasn't
come around yet. (Sound of door closing.)

Jinx lifted the playback arm.

'That's where they came in,' he said. 'I didn't have time to cut
the motor off, I was afraid they'd hear the click of the switch, so
I just let it run . . .'

The motor was running now and it made a lot of noise. 'Jesus,'
I said. 'You can hear that thing pretty plain.'

'I did manage to get Holiday's coat over it. Like this,' he said,
lifting the coat and dropping it down over the set. Now the noise
of the motor running wasn't so plain, it was muffled. 'My trade
has some tricks, too,' he said, meaning: You see, Holiday, he's not
the only guy who can think fast.

'Go on. Play the rest of it,' I said. 'When they came back.'

He put the playback arm on the record. I: I don't know, sir.
My friend knows. . . .

'That's wrong,' I said. 'There's something missing. He asked
me where the pay-roll job was.'

'Well, I didn't get that,' Jinx said. 'By the time I got Holiday's
coat off the set he'd already said that.'

'Start it over,' I said.

He started it over. I: I don't know, sir. My friend knows. . . . .
INSPECTOR: Where is your friend now? I: I don't know that
either, sir. But I can get in touch with him. REECE: When'd you
figure on pulling this? I: We hadn't gone into that. My friend's
the one who spotted this. He just said it looked like a push-over.
He didn't go into details. INSPECTOR: Well, I'll tell you what

90

you do. You have your friend here at nine o'clock and we'll *go* into details. I: I'll try sir. I'll certainly try. INSPECTOR: Whaddya mean – you'll try? You said you could get in touch with him. I: Yes, sir, but whether or not I can get in touch with him in time to have him here by nine o'clock tonight, I don't know. I'll have to get the word to him roundabout. You can come back at nine, but if he's not here I don't want you to get sore at me. (PAUSE – one, two, three, four, five, six) INSPECTOR: I'm not coming back till he's here. You think you can raise him by tomorrow? I: Oh, I'm sure of that. INSPECTOR: Call me at headquarters. If I'm not there say that Mister Baker called. I'll know what that means. Mister Baker. I: Yes, sir, Mister Baker. Inspector, sir, what about those two plainclothes men at the garage, Pratt and Downey? What if Mason brings them here? What if they come here? INSPECTOR: All you got to worry about is dragging that friend of yours out of his hole. I: Yes, sir, (PAUSE – one, two, three, four, five, six, seven, eight, nine, ten. *This is where the Inspector and I are watching Reece make a fool of himself nipping his teeth at Holiday.*) INSPECTOR: Whenever you're ready, George. REECE: Oh, sure, sure, I'm finished, I'm finished – (PAUSE – one, two, three, four, five) *(Sound of hall door opening and closing.)*

Jinx lifted the playback arm and cut off the motor.

'It's wonderful,' I said. 'It's all there – every beautiful syllable of it.'

'Except the part when he asked where the pay-roll job was . . .'

'Wait'll he hears the record,' I said, laughing. 'That's *one* part he'll never miss.'

Holiday was moving out of the closet, taking with her the mood of pessimism and lugubriosity which had remained undented throughout the playing of the record. I followed her into the bedroom and offered her a cigarette. When I lighted it she did not lift her eyes, keeping them on the match.

I said: 'I was hoping that when you'd heard the record through, you'd feel better.' She did not say anything. 'Obviously, you're still not very much impressed.'

'I'm not,' she said.

'Goddamn it!' I said. 'Here we are sitting on top of the world. . . . What does it take to please you?'

'Let her run things,' Jinx said, at my elbow. 'That's what it takes to please her . . .'

She merely flicked her eyes to him.

'Are you jealous because this was my idea?' I asked.

'Don't be a damn fool,' she said.

'All right,' I said. 'From now on it was your idea. Take it. You hear, Jinx? From now on it was her idea . . .'

'What difference does it make?' Jinx said. 'We're all in this together. You don't hear me beefing about whose idea it was and I got eighteen hundred dollars in it.'

'Well, you can't expect a dame to know much about sportsmanship,' I said. 'Look,' I said to Holiday. 'I think you're a very bad sportsman to get sore just because I conceived this idea – because I *just happened* to conceive it.'

'Big Stuff. The Old Master,' she said.

'This is getting us nowhere,' Jinx said.

'She doesn't like me,' I said. 'She's never liked me from the first day she saw me. She only took me in on the crash-out because there was nobody else . . .'

Jinx stepped between us, shaking his head. 'This is getting us nowhere,' he said again.

'The hell it isn't getting us somewhere,' she said, moving around him. 'It's getting us to the morgue – and fast, too.'

'Who's scared now? Who's pants are wet now?' I said. 'And you want to do the thinking for us! As emotionally unstable as you are, you want to do the thinking for us! Up and down, up and down, immitigable movements of fear and panic – why, all we got to do to get ourselves into the morgue is to turn the thinking over to you . . .'

'My thinking was all right when it came to getting you off that stinking prison farm,' she said, flaring a little.

'You didn't want me in the first place,' I said. 'You wanted your brother. You got him killed. Fine thinking.'

She moved within arm-length of me. Her eyes were flashing and her face was full of storm.

'Now, lissen . . .' Jinx said, putting his hand on her arm.

She yanked her shoulder violently, freeing herself of his hand. 'You lissen,' she said. 'This son-of-a-bitch is crazy. Him and his superior intellect. Him and his Phi Beta Kappa key. Him and his goddamn university degree. They may give him the right to look down his nose at us, but it goddamn sure don't give him the right to risk our lives with his maniac ideas. If we stand for 'em. goddamn it, we *ought* to be killed . . .'

'Maniac ideas?' I said. 'What're you talking about? The recording?'

'That's exactly what I'm talking about . . .'

'There's nothing maniacal about that. Is there anything maniacal about that?' I asked Jinx.

'I put in eighteen hundred dollars, didn't I?'

'There's nothing maniacal about it,' I said to Holiday. 'It's not even original. It's not even clever. And it doesn't even approach brilliance. You don't shade your words properly. First, it would have to be original and then clever and then brilliant and then, maybe, it would approach an outer degree of mania. This has not *one* of those facets. It's really cheap and conventional and melodramatic . . .'

'You and your goddamn fake modesty,' she said. 'Who the hell do you think you're kdding?'

'You don't really believe that I'm proud of this, do you?' I asked.

'Crap,' she said.

'I'm not only *not* proud of it,' I said slowly, trying to keep the rage out of my voice, 'I'm ashamed of it. It's not the kind of a *coup* – and I may dignify it with such a classical term – that pleases me. To gratify my colossal ego a triumph must deliver rich rounded satisfactory nuances that contain intellectual as well as physical components. This merely was a matter of expediency; a piddling little material victory. I feel truly degraded having had anything at all to do with it. But it was too easy and convenient to pass up.'

'.... Just a lot of big words that don't take any of the dynamite out of it,' she said. 'This might work on a rookie cop, but you're fooling around with an Inspector.'

'Inspector, Chief, Mayor – what the hell is the difference? All these guys have their price. With Cobbett it was his semi-annual heat, with others it's money. We don't have enough money yet – so we have to have a substitute. This is it. How the hell do you think bums like Karpis and Floyd and Dillinger got to the top? With brains?'

I wished I'd never had her. I wished I'd kept the whole thing on a professional basis. I wished I'd never glimpsed the Seven Cities of Cibola, Eldorado, Jagersfontein. Then I could tell her to pull out and go back to Chicago where the cops were waiting for her. Or even better, I could pull out myself. If I hadn't ... But I had. 'Jesus Christ!' I said. 'Can't you get it through your head that because the guy is an Inspector is the only reason the idea was ever any good? What would it get us to nail a rookie cop? How can you blackmail a guy who's got nothing to lose? Don't you see – it had to be an executive, an Inspector or something.'

'Can't you get it through your head that that's also what makes it so risky?'

'How, for Christ's sake?'

'You made the record to play for him, didn't you? He's got to hear it, hasn't he?'

'Certainly.'

'What do you think he'll do then?'

'He'll follow orders.'

'What's to prevent him from killing us and taking the record? He's an Inspector. He can get away with it.'

I stared at her in surprise. Is this always to be my fate? I wondered. 'You tell her,' I said to Jinx. 'Jesus, you tell her...'

'The record he'll hear'll be a copy,' Jinx explained. 'We're making a couple of copies.'

'I thought you understood that was the only way it'd work,' I said. 'Whaddya think we got the phonograph for? To play Bach fugues? We're gonna take the record you heard and put it on the phonograph and start playing it and then put the microphone up close and record it over and then we'll do that once more...'

'Now, now,' Jinx said. 'Don't rub it in.'

'She ought to've known it,' I said. 'My God, this is an advanced class. This is not kindergarten.'

Holiday looked at me and her eyes were venomous. Then she very slowly and very deliberately laid her cigarette on the ball of her right thumb and triggered the index finger against it, raising her hand level with my face, tendons tensed, ready to flip it. I didn't budge a muscle, just stared at her. You turn that cigarette loose, I was thinking, and I'll kill you, by God, I'll kill you, I'll kill you by inches, El Dorado and all, Jagersfontein and all, Koh-i-Noor and all...

'Make some coffee, Holiday,' Jinx said quietly.

She hesitated for a moment, and put the cigarette in her mouth and walked out.

'Hadn't we better get going making the copies?' Jinx asked me.

'I guess so,' I said. '*Jesus!*'

Jinx went into the closet and lifted the recording set off the chair and brought it in the bedroom and put it on the bureau.

'You oughtn't rub it into her so hard,' he said.

'She oughtn't be so dumb,' I said.

He picked up the phonograph and took it into the closet and put it on the chair and came out again.

'All of us can't have Phi Beta Kappa keys,' he said.

'I wasn't thinking of you,' I said. 'Don't get me wrong.'

'*I'm* thinking of me,' he said. 'Could I ask a question without being dumb?'

'Don't be silly now, Jinx ...'

'Why'd you tell Webber you didn't know when you could get in touch with me?'

'I got to have time to get copies of that record to the right people, that's why. When that son-of-a-bitch hears it and I tell him that certain right people have a copy of it – just in case he tries anything funny with me – I don't want to be bluffing. I damn sure want to mean it. And he's got to know I mean it, too.'

'How do you know who the right people are?'

'That's why I stalled him. I got to find out. I figured you could help. You know this town. You ought to know somebody. Don't you know any lawyers? That's what we need, a lawyer. A damn good lawyer.'

'I don't know any. Mason might.'

'Well, we can't ask him, that's a cinch. Didn't you tell me that you once drove Baby-Face Nelson somewhere to get his eye sewed up?'

'That wasn't to a lawyer's. That was to a doctor's. Doc Green. He's no lawyer.'

'Where does he live?'

'The other side of town.'

'What's the address.'

'I don't know the address.'

'Do you remember the house?'

'I think so. Why?'

'We're going out there.'

'He's no lawyer. He's a doctor.'

'I got an idea, though,' I said.

His face darkened and he lifted it a little, wrinkling his nose. He didn't sniff, but he was ready to.

'What's the matter?' I asked. 'Have I got to worry about you getting panicky now?'

'Doc Green'll cross you up in a minute,' he said. 'Anybody he knows'll cross you up in a minute. He's bug-house.'

'He didn't cross Baby-Face Nelson. He wasn't too bug-house for him. Baby-Face trusted him.'

'That was different.'

'How was it different?'

'Well . . .'

'Don't hedge, goddamn it, say it. He was afraid to cross Baby-Face, is that what you mean? Baby-Face was a big shot, is that what you mean?'

'I mean Baby-Face had a lot of dough,' he said, hedging. 'That's what I mean. He had a lot of dough.'

'Well, one of these days we'll have a lot of dough, too,' I said.

'I don't wanna argue with you, but I'll tell you one thing,' he said flatly. 'Doc Green's bug-house. He's a nut. I wouldn't trust him and I wouldn't trust anybody he knows. And I'm not gonna let you trust him, either.'

'Please, Jinx,' I said. 'My intelligence has been insulted enough for one day. Do you think I'm so stupid I'd try to play this hand without an ace in the hole? I'm not going to trust Doc Green too far. There's only one human being that I really trust, the only honest man on the face of the earth: my brother. I'm sending him a record to New York – not to be opened till I say so. That's all the insurance I need. Meantime, we got to have somebody here in with us, somebody who knows the score in this town, bug-house or not.'

'Does your honest brother know what you're doing?'

'I took care of that a long time ago. Ralph Cotter's not my real name.'

'What is your real name?'

I laughed. 'You'd drop dead if you knew,' I said.

... *chapter eight*

There were light standards along both sides of the street, but there were no lights burning, and in the lumpy glow of a moon becoming gibbous all the little houses in the block, chequered with windows that were squares and rectangles of yellowish incandescence, stood with amiable correctness, built to toy-town scale, and with scaled-up toy automobiles parked along the street. The house we were looking for was in the middle of the block, one-story, a cottage. We had no trouble finding it; we couldn't have missed it. The two front rooms on either side of the door were lighted, but with the windows shaded, and on the nice lawn near the pavement was a wooden sign, flooded with bright light from a goose-neck fixture.

DR DARIUS GREEN
PHILOSOPHIC GUIDE
ORGANON
(Aristotle)
NOVUM ORGANUM
(Bacon)
TERTIUM ORGANUM
(Ouspensky)
THE KEY TO COSMIC CONSCIOUSNESS
THE SPATIAL UNDERSTANDING OF TIME
DO NOT BE LOST IN THE LABYRINTH OF
CONFUSED THOUGHT

* * *

'I told you he was bug-house, didn't I?' Jinx said.

'Are you sure this is the right place?'

'Sure, I'm sure. This is the place. That's his name right there. Doc Green. But that sign wasn't there last time. That's something new. . . .'

We walked on up the curving brick pathway to the steps and on to the porch. It was not until then that we saw through the discreetly angled slats of a very long venetian blind a room filled with people. They were men and women, further than that a nondescript group, sitting in chairs with their backs towards us, and now I heard the droning of a voice speaking words that were also nondescript.

Jinx looked at me. 'This joint's full of people,' he said in a whisper.

'Nothing wrong with that,' I said.

'I don't like it. . . .'

'We got no choice,' I said. 'We got to see the guy. Come on. . . .'

'Why can't we hang around out here till they break up?'

'Why can't we hang around in there till they break up? You think these people'll pay any attention to us? All we got to do is open the door and go in,' I said, pointing to another sign, much smaller, that was painted on a side panel in the front door. PLEASE DO NOT USE BELL DURING LECTURES. OPEN THE DOOR AND ENTER. YOU ARE WELCOME. 'Come on,' I said.

I moved to the door and opened it and we went in. We were in a boxlike entry hall that was completely bare of decorations or furnishings, and there was a second door, an inner, swinging door, just ahead on the panel of which was painted in the same-styled professional lettering: ENTER QUIETLY, PLEASE. The voice that had been a drone on the outside now became sporadically human as certain unobese words, slender enough to come through the crack of the door, could be heard: 'Truth . . . is not the . . . our . . . an . . . with . . . the . . .' I pushed this door open, a little surprised with the ease and noiselessness with which it swung, stepping inside, holding it until Jinx was also inside, and then I closed it so carefully that it squeezed my finger against the facing, not enough to hurt, just enough to make me know it had been caught. There were twenty-five or thirty persons sitting in a living-room that contained only them and the chairs, and in the dining-room which adjoined, against a table, stood a slender old man who could only have been Doc Green. He had a gaunt face in the Lincoln mould and wore a black string tie and a linen coat, and was reading with some briskness from a paper in his hand.

'. . . consciousness, therefore, is the sole basis of certainty. The Mind is its own witness. Reason sees in itself that which is above itself and its source: and again, that which is below itself as itself once more. There is a raying out of all orders of existence, an external emanation from . . .'

I felt a touch at my elbow and I turned and there stood a girl, the most attractive girl I had ever seen in my life, the girl of a million dreams, beckoning for us to follow, her lips pursed, patting them with a rigid forefinger, warning us not to make a sound. The words the old man had been speaking were now just a sound, a hum and I heard nothing intelligible. The girl led us into the room where the others were sitting and indicated several empty chairs in the last row, near the venetian blind. She pressed herself against the wall to let us pass, the way you do when the passage is narrow, and she and I were suddenly face to face, body to body, but touching only lightly, and I caught a fragment of her perfume, a fragment of a fragment of a fragment that I remembered from somewhere and then I saw that she wore no make-up and that her face seemed unbelievably white for the lack of it, and that her hair was black, a livid black, my God, you never saw hair so black, and then I realized it was not so much the lack of make-up which made her face white as it was the mighty compulsion of that black hair. For a moment we stood there looking at each other, body to body, for only the echo of a moment, but long enough to fill my world with a white face and black hair, oh, yes, quite long enough. Then she moved on and I went back and sat down with Jinx and when I looked around again she had gone. She had disappeared on the left, by the swinging door, but I could not see because of the jutting wall. She must have been a sort of usher, and I kept wondering who she was and trying to remember where I had smelled that perfume before, or what the perfume reminded me of; asking myself who she was and what she had to do with all this, but watching all the time to see if she would come back.

'. . . instead of going out into the manifold, to forsake it for the one, and to float upwards towards the divine fount of being whose stream flows from within him. You ask: how can we know the Infinitive? I answer: not by reason. It is the office of reason to distinguish and define. The finite, therefore, cannot be ranked among its objects. You can only apprehend the Infinite by a faculty superior to reason, by entering into a state in which you are your finite self no longer – in which the divine essence is communicated to you. This is ecstasy. It is the liberation of your mind from its finite consciousness. Like can only apprehend like, when you thus cease to be finite, you become one with the infinite. It is the reduction of your soul to its simplest self, its divine essence, you realize this union – this identity.

'But this sublime condition is not of permanent duration. It is only now and then that we can enjoy this elevation above the limit of the body and the world. I myself have realized it but three times as yet, and Porphyry hitherto not once.

'All that tends to purify and elevate the mind will assist you in this attainment, and facilitate the approach and the recurrence of these happy intervals. There are, then, different roads by which this end may be reached. The love of beauty, which exalts the poet; that devotion to the *One* and that ascent of science which makes the ambition of the philosopher, and that love and those prayers by which devout and ardent souls tend in their moral purity towards perfection – these are the great highways conducting to the height above the actual and the particular, where we stand in the Immediate presence of the *Infinite*, who shines out as from the depths of the soul.'

He finished reading the paper and put it on the table.

'Such was one of Plotinus' letters to Flaccus,' he said slowly. 'This one I especially wanted you to hear because it coincides, as you know, with my own theory of knowledge founded upon the idea of the expansion of receptivity. Shall we concentrate on this for perhaps a minute or two?'

He bowed his head and so did the others. Jinx looked at me out of the corner of his eye, moving his head slightly. I frowned and winked and bowed my head, showing him that we should do as the others were doing. He bowed his head. I raised mine a little, pulling my eyes up, trying to find the girl with the white face and the black hair. Doc Green lifted his head, gazing at the people, waiting for them to lift theirs too, which they did in surprising unison, and now, for the first time there were sounds of movement, deferential movement. The lecture was over.

'Now, my friends,' the old man said. 'There is some new literature which Miss Dobson will distribute as you leave. Do study it and meditate upon it. Incidentally, I wish you would not insist on leaving contributions with Miss Dobson. As I have repeatedly told you, we do not take up collections. If the time ever comes when we need money I shall not hesitate to ask for it. All I want is your sincere interest. And now, my friends, I am tired. You must excuse me. Goodnight, and thank you for coming. . . .'

He walked away from the table and went through a side door, somewhere to the rear. The people stood up and started moving towards the front door, by ones and twos and threes, middle-aged people, although I saw a couple of girls who couldn't have been more than twelve or thirteen years old. There still was very little noise and no talking at all. There was in the room an air of humility and respect, even awe. I rose, pulling Jinx up with me, and on the back edge of the crowd we drifted into the hall. The swinging door had been pushed outward and propped open, and the girl with the white face and the black hair was standing there holding a stack of pamphlets in her arm, handing them out one by one. There still was very little noise, just the light sounds of a few scuffling feet and the low-spoken good nights between the girl and the disciples. I loitered with Jinx at the rear of the crowd so we would be the last ones out, but inching towards the door so as not to be conspicuous. So far, nobody had paid any attention to us. Jinx and I finally reached the door, the last ones.

'Good night,' the girl said, handing me a pamphlet. 'Good night,' she said, handing Jinx a pamphlet.

'Good night . . .' I said, lingering for a moment, waiting for the man and woman just ahead to get through the outer door. When it was shut and the three of us were alone, I said to the girl: 'May I speak to Doctor Green for a moment?'

'Never after a reading does the Master give personal interviews,' she said politely. 'He is always very tired.'

'I realize that, of course,' I said. 'But this is very important.'

'Those are his orders,' she said. 'He is available for consultations and interviews every morning between ten and twelve.'

'Unfortunately, this matter won't keep,' I said. 'It is very vital. Otherwise, I would not think of disturbing him.' White face or not, black hair or not, I meant to see him. 'Won't you please ask him?'

'He knows me,' Jinx said shortly. 'Just tell him that I'm . . .'

'I'm sure it'll be all right,' I said cutting in swiftly, giving Jinx an admonishing look.

She hesitated asking: 'May I have your names?'

'I'm Paul Murphy,' I said. 'This is Joseph Stockton. Although I don't think they'll mean much to him. . . .'

'I shall speak with the Master,' she said, moving away and again I could smell her perfume, a microcosm now, four or five times removed from a fragment, but still smellable, and this time recognizable. Once, somewhere, I had smelled that perfume before ... She was attractive from the rear too; she wore rawhide moccasins and her long legs were bare and her buttocks were thin but rounded enough to fit nicely into the palms of your hands. Walking, this girl did not have the sensual roll that Holiday had, but then this girl did not need it.

'... This is something new,' Jinx was saying. 'It wasn't like this the last time.'

I winked at him to keep quiet and he shook his head uncertainly and handed me the pamphlet, shrugging that he did not understand it. It was a small, mimeographed pamphlet, and on the cover in mimeographed capitals was printed:

THE VOICE OF STONES
Stones from the walls of a Church and
stones from the walls of a prison are
completely different things.
(interpreting Ouspensky)

The Similarity between Christian Mysticism
and the Vedanta and the Upanishads.
(interpreting Prof. James)

'I told you, didn't I?' Jinx whispered.

I gestured for him to keep quiet, laying the pamphlets on a chair, and I heard a sound and looked around and the girl was leading in the Master. He had removed his coat and tie, and his collar was unbuttoned. He glimpsed us briefly but there was no sign in his face that he had ever seen Jinx before.

'Master,' the girl said, 'this is Paul Murphy and Joseph Stockton.'

'How do you do,' I said, putting out my hand. He made no move to take it. There was nothing impolite about this, it was just as if he had never heard of the custom.

'I do not wish to be rude, gentlemen,' he said in a weary tone, 'but I am very tired. Cannot this matter wait?'

'Believe me, sir,' I said, 'if it could have waited we would have kept it waiting. I am a stranger to you, but I think you know my friend. . . .'

He looked squarely at Jinx but there was not even a glimmer of recognition.

'I don't recall it,' he said calmly. 'Well, gentlemen, what is it?'

'Could we see you alone, sir?' I asked.

'You may speak freely,' he said. 'I have no secret from Miss Dobson.'

'This matter, sir, is not concerned with Cosmic Consciousness,' I said.

His eyes flashed a little and his jaw muscles tightened. 'There are no other matters on which I wish to be consulted,' he said.

The girl looked at him self-consciously and said: 'Excuse me, Master. I shall take my leave.'

'I have no secrets from you, Miss Dobson,' he said.

'Of course not, Master,' she said quietly. 'It is simply that I too am tired. May I be excused?'

'If you insist,' he said stiffly.

She nodded perfunctorialy to Jinx and me, bowed to the Master, and went out the front door, bareheaded and coatless.

She did not look back. I was disappointed. I could not hope that I had aroused in her what she had aroused in me, I could not hope that she was even interested in a transient disciple. I resolved then that before I got through with her she'd be interested. . . . The Master took two long strides to the swinging door and kicked loose the wedge, the prop that was holding it open. The door swung shut. When he turned around, facing Jinx, all the weariness was gone from his face and frame and his eyes were wide and irate.

'How dare you come here?' he said. 'How *dare* you!'

This was better. This was more like it.

'Wait a minute, Doc. . . .' I said.

'I refuse to have anything to do with it,' he said. 'That life for me is over. Over and done with. They all know it – all of them. I shall heal no more bodies. I shall heal only minds. . . .'

'Stop getting your bowels in such an uproar,' Jinx said.

'Shut up!' I said to him. 'Lissen, Doc – there's nobody to heal. All I want is advice – for which I'm willing to pay. We need a lawyer bad. We don't know who to go to.'

'How dare you disturb my meditations for such a childish reason?' he said. 'The classified section of the telephone book is filled with lawyers, thousands of them. . . .'

'Goddamn it!' Jinx said, irritably.

'Will you please shut up!' I said. 'Lissen, Doc – we can't pick a lawyer that way.'

'I don't know the kind you seek. . . .'

'Please, Doc.' I said, 'let's be reasonable about this. You couldn't do business with the guys you did business with and not know *somebody*. . . .'

'That was years ago.'

'Two,' Jinx said. 'Just two . . .'

'Now, look here, Doc . . .' I said. 'This is no skin off your nose. It so happens that we need a lawyer and we need him fast. I can

107

understand your apprehension at the thought of becoming involved with these guys again, I not only understand it, I sympathize with it. But you'll not be dragged into anything. We'll not come here again.' How can I see the girl without coming here again? I wondered. 'There must be *somebody* you've heard of. You don't want to be bothered with us any more, do you?'

'No,' he said.

'Then think of somebody,' I said.

He stared at me, biting his lip, and then stared at Jinx. Jinx's face was grim. He was sore and he was about ready to give up talking and try something else. That was plain.

'Try Keith Mandon, ' he said finally. 'Cherokee Mandon.'

'Where can I find him?'

'He has an office in town.'

'Where in town?'

'I don't know where. One of the buildings . . .'

'Get the telephone book,' I said.

He squinted at me, but moved down the hall to a taboret and picked up the telephone book.

'Mandon . . .' I said, taking the book. 'M-a-n-d-o-n?'

'Yes,' he said.

I found the M-a's. Mandle, Mandler, Mandon.

MANDON KEITH atty 424 Broad CU 9491
MANDON KEITH r 608 Iris BA I-9055

'Look,' I said to the old man, pointing with my finger, 'is this the one?'

'Yes,' he said.

'Thanks,' I said, handing him the book.

'The only way you can thank me is not to come here again,' he said.

Not until tomorrow night, I thought. Not until the girl comes again. I turned and walked out, followed by Jinx. As we reached the porch the light in the living-room, where all the chairs were, went off, and halfway to the street the light in the opposite room went off, and when we reached the pavement the light on the sign in the yard went off. We turned up the street towards town.

'You got to watch that temper of yours,' I said. 'You got to learn to get along with people.'

'He's bug-house. You can see now why the guys gave him up.'

'He may not be as bug-house as you think,' I said.

'I don't trust him. I wouldn't trust this Mandon, either.'

'We haven't got time to do any picking,' I said. 'We have to take what we can . . .'

'What do we do now?'

'We try to find Mandon, that's what we do now,' I said.

He touched my arm in a quick startled warning and I turned my head to see what it was, reaching for the automatic in my right-hand hip pocket. It was a roadster, a big, powerful roadster that had crept up from behind us with the headlights off, and was rolling slowly along next to the kerbing, keeping pace with us, five feet away. The top was down. The girl with the white face and the black hair was driving. I smiled to myself and let the automatic be. I'd been right about this babe, after all. . . .

'Would you like a lift?' she asked.

'Sure,' I said. 'Come on,' I said to Jinx.

She stopped the roadster, leaning over and opening the door, and I got in. Jinx stepped in beside me, sitting down, closing the door.

'Are you comfortable?' I asked him. 'Got plenty of room?'

'I'm all right,' he said.

The girl got it at once. 'The back seat's full of junk anyway,' she said. She stepped up the speed of the car, and turned on the headlights, smiling at me guiltily, realizing only then that turning on the headlights made the whole thing obvious.

'This is very nice of you,' I said.

'Not at all. Where can I drop you?'

'At the drug store, if you don't mind – we're going to pick up a taxi . . .' I said, looking at her, not full in the face, but along the line of her chin. She was peering straight ahead through the windshield, but she knew that I was looking at her. She was still hatless and coatless. 'This is some car you got here,' I said.

'I like it. . . .'

'Fast, too, I'll bet.'

'I suppose so. I've never had it open. . . .'

'What's the fastest you've ever done with it?'

'Oh, eighty . . . eighty-five.'

'It'll do better than that. Don't you think so, Joseph?'

'I think so,' Jinx said.

'Sure it will,' I said. 'Don't you ever wear a coat?' I asked the girl.

'Sometimes. When it rains.' She laughed. 'I haven't had the top up in months.'

I looked at Jinx. He stared at me grimly. As far as he was concerned, she was bug-house too.

'What did you think of the Master's paper?' she asked.

'What paper?'

'The one he read from . . .'

'Oh,' I said. 'I don't know. I'm afraid I'm not up on Cosmic Consciousness.'

'The paper wasn't on Cosmic Consciousness,' she said. 'It was on the Psychology of Knowledge.'

'Same thing . . .'

'Oh, no. Not at all.'

'What I meant was they're equally difficult to understand. For a layman . . .'

'Yes, I suppose you do need some training. Was your consultation with the Master satisfactory?'

'Very. Thanks to you . . .'

110

She slowed up near the drug store, moving the car out of the center of the street.

'How far are you going?' she asked.

'We go the other side of town,' I said.

'I'm going that way myself. Why not let me drive on till we find a taxi? I don't see any around here. There wouldn't be, anyway. Not in this neighborhood.'

'We don't want to bother you,' Jinx said, reaching for the door. The car hadn't stopped rolling yet, but he was opening the door.

'It's no bother,' she said.

'Well, thank you very much,' I said. 'Close the door,' I said to Jinx, nudging him. He slammed the door hard. You goddamn sorehead, I thought. You son-of-a-bitch. The girl speeded up the car, turning back into the center of the street, and we rolled on. The city was ahead. Beyond the city were the Marakeesh Apartments and Holiday. Holiday was tremendous. El Dorado. Tremendous. But, I asked myself, don't you think that solely because she was the first one in better than two years? Isn't she strictly jungle? Why, right this minute, how do you know it isn't the janitor or one of the guys from the second-hand lot even. But this girl beside you now: would she? You know she wouldn't. This one's class. This one's quality. This one's no push-over for every guy she says hello to. You wouldn't have to go around worrying about what she was going to give you.

'How long've you been interested in Cosmic Consciousness?' I asked.

'Well, a long time. Three or four years.'

'I don't like to seem thick, but what is it? A religion or something?'

'No. It's a philosophy. It goes into the Fourth Dimension. Or, I should say, it goes into the mathematical concept of the Fourth Dimension.'

'That properly screws me up,' I said.

She laughed. 'It's very interesting, though. I hope to see you at one of the Master's meditations.'

'I'd be a bad influence. My vibrations would be poisonous.'

'Maybe not.'

'Oh, but they would,' I said. 'I don't know anything about Cosmic Consciousness – but I do know a little something about the Dimensions. And I don't hold with the theory that the Fourth Dimension is either philosophical *or* mathematical. I think it's purely intuitional.'

She looked at me, surprised.

'I'm not trying to give you an argument,' I said; 'and I don't want to sound pretentious. But that's what I believe.'

'I've never heard that before,' she said thoughtfully.

'We'll have to go into it sometime soon – that and some other things,' I said, and I knew from the glance she gave me that she understood what other things I was talking about.

Jinx straightened up, leaning forward. 'There's a taxi,' he said.

'There'll be others . . .' the girl said.

'We don't want to impose on you too much,' I said, winking at her slyly, so Jinx wouldn't see, trying to tell her that the next time I met her I'd see to it that Jinx wasn't along.

She winked back, pulling the car over and stopping it.

Jinx opened the door and got out. As I started to get out I caught that perfume again and this time I knew what brand it was. It was *Huele de Noche*. 'I like your taste in scents,' I said.

'What?' she said.

'Your perfume. It's wonderful,' I said.

'Perfume?'

'*Huele de Noche*. I recognize it now. It tugged at me before, but I couldn't quite place it. Now I can. *Huele de Noche*.'

'I'm not wearing perfume,' she said, with a tentative smile.

'I smell it,' I said. 'I've smelled it several times tonight.'

112

'It's your imagination,' she said. 'I've never used perfume in my life.'

'Come on,' Jinx said.

I shrugged, getting out of the car, shutting the door. If she wanted to deny that she was wearing perfume, as if to admit it would degrade her somehow, it was all right with me.

'Good night,' she said.

'Good night,' I said.

'Come on,' Jinx said.

I nodded to her, and following Jinx into the taxi that was waiting by the kerbing; and she was gone, two red dots disappearing into the distance. He reached across me and slammed the door, shaking his head.

'I never heard such a lot of crap in my life,' he said. 'You're full of that stuff, you know that?'

'Shut up,' I said. 'I'm remembering something.'

I was remembering something, I was close to remembering something, something that I vaguely knew I did not want to remember, but remembering it I was: the smell of that perfume was getting stronger and stronger and stronger, and then every nerve and fiber in my body began to vibrate with music from an old-fashioned organ and like a clap of thunder there was a bright blinding light inside my head and through it I could feel the cold wind tunnelling from many, many years away and when it passed it left in focus only a white, white face, and black, black hair, and there was my grandmother stretched stiffly in her coffin in the parlour in the old place in the Gap, only her head visible, and that lighted by single tall candles at either end of the coffin, and the room was filled with the smell of the big *Huele de Noche* bushes which had grown around the house. . . .

Great Heavenly God! I thought, fighting to get my breath, this is what I smelled. It was not the perfume the girl was wearing; she was right, it was my imagination. Her face was of the same

113

whiteness as my grandmother's, and her hair of the same blackness, and there was a sameness in the cast of features, too, and this was what had done it, that sameness, that same goddamn sameness....

I couldn't turn it off, I did not want to remember it, I had been a lifetime learning to forget, but I could not turn it off.

...*chapter nine*

When the door opened and I saw Keith Mandon, Cherokee Mandon standing there (for it had to be he), I thought: No, this cannot be, this is a grotesque symbol that belongs to the infantile world I have just left, from the infantile world of shameless libidinous fantasy that I have just left. That is what I thought: No, this cannot be. He was a little guy, barely five feet tall, certainly no taller than five feet, with a mongoloid nose and heavy eyebrows that seemed to grow straight out like primigenous feelers, so heavy and thick that you had to look twice to see if he had eyes at all, and carefully the second time. He was wearing a heavy cotton wrapper that almost touched the floor, and a pair of wooden sandals, the kind you wear in a locker room.

'What do you want?' he asked in a harsh coercive tone.

'I'd like to talk to you, Mister Mandon. . . .'

'This is where I live, not where I work,' he said. 'See me at my office.'

'Please, Mister Mandon,' I said. 'It may be too late then. . . .' He growled displeasure in his throat and started to shut the door and I moved forward, saying, 'Please, Mister Mandon. This is very urgent and very important. Important to you, too . . .'

'Well, what is it?' he asked slowly.

'I can't very well talk about it standing here,' I said. 'Won't you let me come in?'

He raised his eyebrows two or three times, the middle of his forehead sagging under their weight. 'Come in, come in,' he said grudgingly. He stepped back and opened the door, and I went in.

The room suddenly swam before my eyes and my first flash thought was that I was still in the grip of that same fantasy, and then I thought that maybe the fantasy had gone and that this was a dream, and then I thought: No, this cannot be a dream because it is too absurd and crazy, a dream makes more sense, things are not this haphazard in a dream. I was just talking to the guy in the hall, I told myself (or did I imagine that too?) and I turned around and there he was, his back against the door, staring at me with no expression on his face, and I turned around again, looking at the room, and now the things began to have some definition. Heavy, massive furniture had been placed indiscriminately around; there were seven or eight throw rugs on top of the carpet itself, and there were pictures and prints and photographs covering the walls. An enormous marble mantel stood propped against a wall where there was no fireplace, and on the shelf-piece four clocks of different sizes and makes chattered at each other in different keys. In front of this was a long red plush davenport, so big and ugly it could only have been originally designed for an exclusive country club, and in front of the davenport was a folding card table which had been transformed into a coffee table by sawing the legs off, bearing the weight of a complete drummer's outfit: bass drum, snare drum, traps, cymbals, and a triangle, with the yellowed skin of the bass drum wearing a faded monogram, not his. The only light in the room was from a tall stand lamp with a yellow silk mansard shade. It stood beside a wooden high-chair, the kind you see in pool rooms, and on the chair was bolted a kidney-shaped piece of wood, just rough wood, which served as a desk and which now was swung open and held several law books and typewritten papers, and a half-folded golf towel. You could not walk straight into the room, you had to pick your way. This was exactly what would happen to a room full of furnishing if, after many years of absolute subjugation, each object were given one wish. No; this was no dream, and it was too crazy to be accidental. This guy, I told myself, threading my way through the junk, trying to find a place to sit down, has deliberately arranged all this. This guy is trying to be eccentric.

He let me reach a deep wing-chair before he spoke. He said: 'Now, what is it?'

I sat down in the chair. It had a brocaded altar cloth for an antimacassar. 'I need help, Mister Mandon,' I said.

'People who come to me generally do,' he said. 'I'm not the type who attracts people socially. What kind of help?'

'Legal help. Advice . . .'

'Advice on something that's already happened, or advice on something that is going to happen?'

'Both.'

'How much money've you got?'

'It's not how much I've got, Mister Mandon. It's how much I'm going to have.'

'I don't deal in futures,' he said.

'But these futures, sir,' I said, 'are not gambles. I mean they're not gambles in the sense that Baby-Face Nelson's futures were gambles. . . .'

He slanted his head, staring at me for two or three seconds, and then he picked up the golf towel from the desk and blew his nose, hard. He dropped the towel back on to the crude desk and from the top tier of a two-tiered pedestal table he picked up a round pasteboard carton, holding it out to me. I saw that they were stogies and shook my head. He took one for himself and put the carton back on the table and then he saw something which annoyed him very much. I could not tell what it was, but he made a sour face and took from his pocket a small silver whistle because I had seen his cheeks inflate and deflate, but

117

there was no sound. I didn't know what this was, but I leaned a little to the left to get the right side of my body away from the bulge of the chair's arm so that nothing would interfere with getting my automatic; and I heard the rattle of wooden rings on a portiere pole and turned around and saw standing in the curtains a black boy in white duck pants and a gray-black sweat shirt, a young and handsome black boy, six feet or more tall. 'Empty the goddamn ash trays,' Mandon said, and the black boy reached behind him and came in with a brown paper sack into which he dumped an ash tray filled with sloppily chewed cigar butts.

'Would you like a drink?' Mandon said to me.

'No, thanks,' I said.

'Make some coffee, Highness,' he said to the black boy.

The black boy never said a word. He didn't look at Mandon and he didn't look at me, going out with the paper bag, through the portieres. Again Mandon slanted his head, looking at me, and then he lighted his stogie from the torch of a lighter so big he used both hands to hold it. He sat down in the pool chair, swinging shut the kidney-shaped board, hemming himself in, and put the lighter back on the pedestal table.

'What do you mean, these futures are not like Baby-Face Nelson's?' he asked.

'I mean these are not a sucker's futures,' I said. 'Baby-Face Nelson was a sucker.'

'Any man who breaks the law is a sucker,' he said.

'Does that include the police?'

'Any policeman who breaks the law is twice the sucker,' he said.

'There's a lot of suckers then . . .'

'Do you know one?'

'I know several,' I said.

'Can you prove it?'

118

'I got 'em nailed.'

'Then you should turn them in,' he said gravely.

'It's much more important to me not to turn them in,' I said. 'I got the evidence and I intend to use it in my own way. But it's dynamite. I've got to give it to somebody they're afraid of, somebody they know will turn it loose in case they try any monkey business.'

'What kind of evidence is it? What form is it in?'

'In the form of an actual recording of two plainclothes men taking money from me, eighteen hundred dollars, what was left of a market hold-up in which I killed a guy. And at the same time agreeing to be my partners in another hold-up which has not yet come off.'

He puffed on his stogie and frowned, pulling down his heavy eyebrows. They looked like the eaves of a house. 'Are you suggesting that I am the person to have custody of this evidence?' he asked.

'Yes,' I said.

'What do you mean when you say you intend to use this in your own way? As immunity from arrest after the commission of other crimes?'

'Something like that. I haven't got around to figuring out anything definite yet. I haven't had time. This just happened.'

'In other words, you're asking me to become a partner in your felonies?'

'It'd be worth your while,' I said. 'There'd be no danger. Look, Mister Mandon, when these guys shook me down, I was ready to laugh it off – just a couple of dumb cops grabbing a piece of change. I wasn't going to stay here. I was going to pull a fast hold-up and get enough money to get out of town. I fully intended to do that. But when I found out one of them was an Inspector, it changed everything. I figured he was high enough up to do me some good if I could nail him. . . .'

119

'So you nailed him?' he asked dryly.

'Yes . . .'

'With no trouble at all, you nailed him. Like pushing a button and turning on a light. Very simple and very easy. A rabbit nailing a wolf. You know his name, of course?'

'It was Webber,' I said, telling myself to take it easy now, take it easy now, don't get mad. 'Inspector Webber.'

'Charlie Webber of Homicide, no doubt?'

'Webber is all I know,' I said. 'Little guy. Stocky. About forty.'

He laughed and started to say something, but stopped when he saw the Negro, Highness, coming in with the coffee. The black boy balanced the tray on the flat of his left hand and poured with his right, awkwardly, and handed each of us a cup. Then he put the tray on the floor beside the pool chair and started out.

'Highness . . .' Mandon called. The Negro stopped and looked back, turning only his head. 'Don't go to bed yet,' Mandon said. 'Stand by . . .' The boy still had no reaction. He walked out.

Mandon sipped two or three spoons of coffee, alternately looking from the cup to me. I put my cup back on the tray without tasting it.

'Well, that just about makes it perfect,' he said. 'Charlie Webber splitting dough with a hijacker, and a punk at that . . .'

'He did,' I said. 'He certainly did.'

'You're overdoing it now,' he said. 'You should have had more rehearsing.'

'What?' I said.

'I'm surprised at 'em. They usually prepare their witnesses much better than this. . . .'

'What witnesses?' I said. 'What're you talking about?'

'I'm talking about the lawyers who sent you.'

'What lawyers? Nobody sent me. . . .'

He picked up his cup and drank from it and put it down. 'Well, young man,' he said, 'I'm not going to have my colored boy

120

throw you out of here on your ear, because I don't think you're to blame for this. But you go back and tell 'em I'm very disappointed. I thought they'd do better than this. Much better ...'

'I don't get this,' I said. 'Tell who?'

'The lawyers who sent you. If they want me disbarred why don't they file charges with the Bar Association? You tell 'em to do that, son....'

'Honest to God, I don't know what you're talking about,' I said. 'I really don't.'

'Please, my boy. Don't make me change my mind about having you thrown out. These traps they're setting for me get increasingly melodramatic, and their believability declines inversely. Charlie Webber. My God, Charlie Webber! What do they take me for – a bloody fool?'

'I didn't say his name was Charlie,' I said. 'I said his name was Webber.'

'There's only one Webber, and he's not one to have truck with common thieves and pimps. Why didn't they pick a cop I could believe was guilty of shaking you down? My God, Charlie Webber! The biggest cop in town....'

'Inspector Webber, goddamn it, that's who it was,' I said.

He laughed loudly and his hand went to his pocket and before I knew what he was doing he had blown the whistle that made no sound. 'I've changed my mind,' he said coldly. 'I'm going to have you thrown out, after all....'

The big handsome Negro was gliding into the room. I got up, pulling out my automatic, pointing it just above the bottom webbing of his gray-black sweat shirt, at the middle of his stomach. That stopped him.

'Put that gun away,' Mandon said.

'Tell him to get out, goddamn it, tell him to get out,' I said. The black boy stood there, tensed like a goddamn tiger, his eyes riveted on Mandon now, just waiting for the signal to spring. I was scared of him. I knew goddamn well that I could bring him down with a bullet, I knew what a bullet could do when it hit you in the middle of the stomach, but I was still scared of him. 'Tell him to get out,' I said again.

'Get out, Highness. . . .' Mandon said.

There still was no expression on the boy's face. He didn't even glance at me. He did not relax, but he straightened his head and walked out.

'Put that gun away,' Mandon said.

I half-turned so I could cover him and the back of the room at the same time, where the Negro had disappeared. I felt better with him out of sight. 'You son-of-a-bitch, you lissen,' I said to Mandon. 'You sarcastic son-of-a-bitch, you lissen. What I've told you is the truth. I crashed out of a prison farm the day before yesterday, and the only reason I came to this town in the first place is because this is where the getaway car was from and we had to bring it back. I used the same car in the market hold-up, just to get enough money to move on. But before I could move, the guy who owns the car brought these plainclothes men to my apartment, brought 'em, by God, himself. They shook down, I didn't know then that one of 'em was an Inspector. When I found out he was an Inspector, I made up my mind to nail him. And I did nail him. But that's no good unless you help me.' I lined the gun up with middle of his stomach, right over the coffee cup. 'Whistle for the boy. Tell him to bring your clothes. You're going to listen to that record.'

'May I finish my coffee?' he asked.

'Go ahead.'

He finished his coffee, putting the cup noiselessly into the saucer.

'If you're a stranger here, how'd you know about me?'

'Doc Green told me.'

'What Doc Green?'

'You know the Doc Green I mean. Baby-Face Nelson's friend.'

'What is the name of the man who owns the getaway car?'

'Vic Mason. Club-footed guy. A faggot.'

'Was there a girl mixed up in this?'

'Her name is Holiday Tokowanda.'

'Put that gun away,' he said.

I put the gun in my hip pocket.

He took the whistle out of his pocket and blew on it, and the black boy popped out from the portieres.

'Highness,' Mandon said, 'get my clothes. . . .'

Jinx set the machine up in the closet and played the record for him. He stood with his back against the door and listened, not moving a muscle, not even in his face. When the record was finished, he stepped into the bedroom and took off his loud green coat and came back and stood at the closet door. He loosened his brown necktie and rolled up the sleeves of his green shirt. 'I'd like to hear that again,' he said.

Jinx started the record again and Mandon put his back against the door and listened, but this time his interest was more clinical: he lifted and lowered his heavy eyebrows, he nodded his head, he pursed his lips, he bit his tongue, and occasionally he glanced at Holiday, who lay on her back on the bed, barefooted, her wrapper so snugly around her that all the monticules and concavities of her body were plainly outlined, as she intended they should be. But Mandon's glances were virtually unobserving. There were no sounds in the world now but the faint scratching of the needle and the voices from the record, rising at us from the gloom of the closet. Eventually, they were done, and Mandon moved away from the closet door, into the bedroom. I followed him and Jinx followed me.

'Is that the Webber you were talking about?' I asked Mandon.

'Yes. The same. Charlie Webber.'

'Are you convinced now?'

'I'm convinced, but I'm still dazed. You're a stranger here. You can't understand how inconceivable this is.'

'But it happened. . . .'

'It's still inconceivable. Charlie Webber. I can't explain it.'

'Do you have to worry about trying to explain it?' I said. 'All that matters is I got him. He's just another crooked cop who got caught in the wringer. . . .

'I won't argue with you,' I said. 'The evidence is on the record. I leave it to the record. . . .'

'Things like this just don't happen outside of books and movies,' he said. 'They don't happen in real life. . . .'

'The only place they do happen is in real life,' I said.

Holiday swung her feet off the bed, sitting up. 'I thought you weren't going to argue with him,' she said belligerently. I knew why she was belligerent; nobody had given her a tumble. She had put the rises and falls of her body on exhibit and nobody had paid the slightest attention, especially Mandon. That is why she was belligerent.

'All right, all right,' I said to Mandon. 'If you'll just try to get over your astonishment at a punk, at an amateur, at a minor offender, at a pimp, at a stranger accidentally locating the heel of the local Achilles, we'll talk business. Forget who he is and forget who I am and answer me one question. Have we got him?'

'Yes.'

'Then, goddamn it, all I want from you is yes or no. Do you or don't you want in on this?'

He dropped his heavy eyebrows and flattened his nose.

'I'm only trying to convince you that you can't go slambang into this. He's a big man. The slightest mistake here and we'll never know what hit us. . . .'

'Nuts,' I said. 'Answer the question. Are you in or out?'

124

He turned to Jinx and Holiday with a hurt expression on his face. 'Before he was begging,' he said. 'Now he's demanding. . . .'

'You got him wrong, Mister Mandon,' Jinx said.

'I haven't got him wrong,' Mandon said. 'He's the only thing I've got right.'

I didn't know what he meant by that and I didn't care. What the hell was going on with this guy? Was he scared to tackle Webber? 'I'm not demanding anything,' I said. 'All you've done is be amazed and talk about what a big guy he is. Well, Jesus, so much the better. If I've stumbled into something that good, so much the better. You heard the record. I got him nailed. . . .'

'*We* got him nailed,' Jinx said.

'Big Stuff. The Old Master,' Holiday said. ' "*I*".'

'Goddamn it, you know whose idea it was,' I said. 'I had to talk it into you. I had to slug it into you.'

'Cool down, cool down,' Mandon said. 'Nobody objects to you taking all the credit for thinking of it, But it now belongs to all of us. Her, him, me. Is that right?'

'Yes. Certainly,' I said.

'You're sure you don't mind if I include myself?'

'What the hell kind of a question is that?' I said. 'That's what I've been trying to get you to do.'

'Well, cool down then. Don't be so touchy. . . .'

I won't be touchy now, I was thinking, but later on, after we get rolling and I know my way around and can have my pick of lawyers, I'll be touchy. It's any old port in a storm now and I can't afford to be touchy, but later on I'll be touchy, you goddamn shyster, you yellow shyster. . . .

'Go in and sit down and get acquainted,' he was saying. 'There're a lot of things I've got to find out about you people before the Inspector comes tomorrow. . . .'

125

...*chapter*
ten

Reece arrived first. He was wearing the same suit, the same shirt and tie, the same two-ninety-eight shoes, and I was willing to bet that he was wearing the same socks too. The only thing different from yesterday was that he was now chewing on a toothpick. He came into the room and looked at Holiday who was sitting very demurely on the davenport. What the hell you got to be demure about after yesterday, after what you let this pig see, I don't know, I thought. Reece did not speak until I had closed the door and was halfway back into the room. Then he said: 'The boss'll be along in a minute.'

'That's fine,' I said. 'Would you like to go in the bathroom and use my dental floss?'

'What?' he said.

'Dental floss. You know...' I pantomimed, using a piece of dental floss. 'Wonderful for hard-to-get places. Some in the bathroom. Go in there and help yourself. Then you don't have to be embarrassed using a toothpick in front of people.'

'Oh, I'm not embarrassed,' he said. 'I had ham for breakfast....'

'I like ham myself,' I said. 'I come from a ham country. Hickory-smoked, country-cured. You don't get ham like that at any of the drug stores around here.... Sit down....' Holiday was looking daggers at me and I was looking daggers right back at her. This stupid, oestrual son-of-a-bitch. 'You're sure you won't have some dental floss?'

'Much obliged just the same,' he said. 'You locate that friend of yours?'

'I located him,' I said.

He grinned and looked at Holiday, shifting the toothpick expertly to the other side of his mouth. 'And how are you this morning?' he asked.

'I'm fine, very fine,' she replied, smiling warmly.

He hauled a chair around and sat down facing her. 'The Inspector'll be along in a minute,' he said.

'Don't be self-conscious,' I said. 'Make yourself at home,' I said, crossing behind him to the bedroom door. I opened it and motioned for Jinx to come out.

'This is Jinx Raynor, Mister Reece,' I said.

'Lieutenant Reece . . .' he said.

'I beg your pardon,' I said. 'Lieu-*tenant* Reece.'

Jinx went over to him and shook his hand briefly. Despite the fight-talks I had given him earlier, he was a little nervous. This was a brand-new experience for him, meeting the law socially with a crime hanging over him.

'I been hearing nice things about you, Jinx,' Reece said amiably.

'Yes, sir,' Jinx said, still nervous.

There was a knock at the door and they all looked at each other and Reece got up from the chair.

'I'll get it,' I said. I crossed the floor and opened the door. It was Inspector Webber: the Suzerain, the Nabob, the Maharajah, the Emperor, Colossus in person. Don't underrate him, Mandon had said, don't make that mistake; and of course he was right, so I looked at him with a new and eager interest, trying to feel some of the awe that Mandon had felt, truly hoping that I could. But – no awe. To me he was just another crooked cop, even if his shirt was clean. Well, Charlie, I was thinking, light and hitch. Come in and have a piece of cake. Come in and get yourself shamped. Come in and try to get those things of yours out of my wringer. . . .

'Sorry I'm late,' he said, coming in. 'I made it the back way.'

'I forgive you,' I said, shutting the door. 'Jinx,' I said, 'this is Inspector Webber. . . .'

The Inspector crossed to Jinx and stared at him, completely ignoring Holiday. Jinx raised his hand uncertainly to shake hands, but dropped it guiltily when the Inspector made no move to take it, and looked very apologetic.

'Does he know what this is all about?' the Inspector asked me.

'Ask him,' I said. 'He understands English. He doesn't need an interpreter.'

'What about this pay-roll you spotted?' the Inspector asked him.

'Yes, sir,' Jinx said. 'That's right.'

'How big a pay-roll?'

'Pretty big . . .'

'Well, how big . . . ?'

'Pretty big . . .' Jinx said again, looking at me for help. He was more nervous than ever. He had been awed by Reece and you can imagine how he was being awed by the Inspector. I was just going to let him dangle for a while. Maybe this experience would help season him. He needed seasoning very badly.

'Now, cut this out,' the Inspector said disagreeably. 'Where is the pay-roll? What place?'

'Well . . .' Jinx said.

The Inspector turned to me. 'Is this the bird you were talking about?'

'Yes, sir. That's the bird. . . .'

'I thought you told me he had this pay-roll spotted.' He turned back to Jinx. 'I thought you had this pay-roll spotted?'

'Tell 'im,' Jinx said to me, desperately. 'Tell 'im. . . .'

'Tell me what? What the hell is this?' the Inspector asked roughly.

Poor Jinx. There was torment in his face, and I knew that if I let him dangle any longer he would say the wrong thing and probably louse up the whole works. 'There's a friend of yours here, Inspector,' I said. 'Maybe I better let him tell you what this is. . . .'

'Morning, Inspector . . .' Mandon's voice said. The Inspector and Reece whirled. Mandon was standing in the bedroom door, smiling, his heavy eyebrows raised high, his forehead wrinkled. He looked all right to me. He didn't seem too awed now. 'Put your gun away, Lieutenant,' he said quietly. I looked and saw that Reece did have a gun in his hand, but I was more surprised to discover that the toothpick was missing.

'What the hell are you doing here, Cherokee?' the Inspector asked. 'What the hell is this?'

'It *was* a conference with my clients until you interrupted. . . .'

'Clients?'

'Clients,' Mandon said. 'But as long as you're here, let's put it on a friendly basis. Tell the Lieutenant to stash that gun. . . .' The Inspector nodded to Reece, who unwillingly put the gun back in his pocket. Mandon sounded all right too. He wasn't at all awed. 'It does sometimes happen, Inspector,' he continued, coming into the room, 'that I can have a conference with my clients without coming to your jail. Surprising as that is . . .'

'What the hell is this?' the Inspector growled.

Don't start making noises in your throat yet, you thieving son-of-a-bitch, I wanted to tell him. You're not hurt yet. I haven't even started turning the crank yet. You wait . . .

'We can save a lot of wear and tear and time if you'll sit down and listen,' Mandon said.

'I can listen from here,' the Inspector said. 'What the hell is this?' he asked, spreading his feet. 'Go on – start talking!'

'Later . . .' Mandon said, smiling. 'I'll talk later. First, I want to refresh your memory so that when the time does come to talk, we'll all be talking about the same thing. . . .' He moved to the end table where we had put the recording machine, and lifted the top and clicked the switch. The motor hummed and the turntable started revolving, spinning the record that already had been spindled. 'Come a little closer,' Mandon said, lifting the pick-up arm, waiting for the speaker tubes to get hot. 'No sense in making this too loud. . . .' I'm going to have to send this guy flowers and enclose a penitent note, I told myself. He's a hell of a workman. He's a real professional: sharp and icy. 'No sense in having the neighbors call the police. . . .'

The Inspector and Reece stared at each other. Reece's face was blank, but the Inspector's was grim and purposeful. Now he knew what the hell this was. Not exactly, not in detail, but he knew. He looked at me vindictively, but this time it was almost a pleasure, this time I was not frightened. There was nothing red and twisting in my stomach now, and it was hard for me to believe there ever had been. I tried to remember how I had felt then, so I could compare it with how I felt now, but I couldn't; it was like trying to remember last year's toothache, you not only couldn't remember the ache, you couldn't even remember the tooth.

'. . . And pay attention now,' Mandon was saying. He lowered the pick-up arm on to the record and there were a couple of revolutions of scratching and then the voices were heard, slightly distorted, and he gestured for Jinx to make the adjustment. Jinx moved quickly to the machine and tuned it, and now the voices came out of the speaker clearly and normally, a little softer than normal. The Inspector looked at Mandon, who was smiling peacefully, and then at Reece, whose eyes were wide in surprise, and then at me. I could see the hardness coming into his face, and the eyelids flickering as the venom damned up behind them. Pay attention to the record, I wanted to say to him. Listen to that sales talk you're giving me on Arizona. Listen to me paying you off, you thieving son-of-a-bitch. Listen to that crunching sound,

Inspector. You know what that is, don't you? Of course you know. It's your nose in the wringer. . . .

Suddenly his hand darted inside his coat and yanked out his service revolver. 'Get your hands up!' he barked. We raised our hands. Reece had his gun out again and was backing around to cover us. The Inspector charged at the recording machine and snatched at the pick-up arm with his left hand, trying to pull it off; but the only thing that came off was his hand, sliding down the arm, past the needle. He uttered an involuntary snort of pain and when he looked at his hand it was full of blood where the needle had laid the palm open, as neatly as if it had been done with a razor blade. He grabbed the record off the spindle with his bloody hand and banged it against the machine, trying to break it, and then realized it was non-breakable, and doubled it against his body and stuck it under his belt.

'You filthy bastards!' he said. 'Frisk 'em, Reece!'

Reece started frisking Jinx.

'You didn't hear the best part of the record,' Mandon said. 'The best part is where you conspire to hijack a pay-roll.'

'You filthy bastards,' he said, glancing at his bloody hand.

Reece started frisking me. 'We got no guns,' I said.

'They're clean,' Reece said.

'Where are the guns?' the Inspector said.

'In the bedroom,' I said. 'We got no use for guns now. . . .'

'I have,' he said. 'Get 'em,' he said to Reece.

'Whereabouts in the bedroom?' Reece asked me.

'Go find 'em,' I said.

He swung at my head with the barrel of his gun, but I threw up my arm and took the blow between my wrist and elbow. I could feel the pain in my ankles, but I was still not frightened, only mad.

'Lay off,' the Inspector said. 'We don't want the coroner to find any bruises on 'em. . . .'

Reece walked into the bedroom.

'Get over there against the wall,' the Inspector said.

'You crazy son-of-a-bitch. . . .' Holiday wailed at me.

'Move!' the Inspector said. 'This is what I should'a done in the first place. . . .'

This had gone far enough. I looked at Mandon. 'I wouldn't, Charlie, if I were you,' Mandon said. 'That record you got there is only one of several we have entrusted to reliable friends. If they don't hear from us within the hour that all is well, they have been instructed to play the records for certain groups in town that you might not be able to reach – the Lake Front Club, the Rotarians, the Lions, the Kiwanians – even the churches. . . .' The Inspector's jaw sagged a little. 'Now, Charlie,' Mandon continued persuasively, 'there's no sense in pulling this thing down on top of us. Everything's been all right for a long time, and it'll continue to be all right if you'll just be reasonable. All we want is a little co-operation.'

'We want a trifle more than that,' I said. 'Fourteen hundred dollars and eighteen hundred dollars make thirty-two hundred dollars,' I said to the Inspector. 'You got thirty-two hundred dollars of my money. I want it back.'

'Oh, God,' Mandon said. 'Can't you let well enough alone?'

'Goddamn it, it's my dough,' I said. 'I want it. . . .'

He jumped at me, grabbing me by the shoulders. 'Will you lay off?' he yelled. 'Later. Later.'

Reece came in with my two automatics. 'Here they are,' he said.

The Inspector didn't notice. He was looking at his hand. The blood was dripping on the carpet. 'I ought to get this tended to,' he said.

He wasn't roaring now. There wasn't so much venom damned up behind his eyes now. Colossus, eh? Well, what have you got when you castrate a Colossus?

132

'Go in the bathroom and get a towel for him,' I said to Reece. 'First thing you know, I'll have to buy a new carpet for this place. . . .'

*. . . part
two*

. . . *chapter* *one*

I was sitting in her car in front of the house, not quite in front of the house, down the street a little, under the limbs of a breadfruit tree which reached far out beyond the kerbing, listening to a Berigan record, waiting for her to come out. The meditation had been over for ten minutes more or less, and the disciples had left, some walking, some riding; but the lights were still on in the house and on the sign in the yard. There was no sight of the girl with the white face and the black hair. The Berigan record ended, and another one started, and after a subtle eight-bar introduction that whispered to my memory, an idiot announcer shouted that this was Mugsy Spanier's 'I've Found a New Baby', as if those trumpet inflections and great vibrato needed additional identification. But you simpleton, you loud fool, why call it Mugsy's record, peerless as he is? Can you not also hear the phrases of Tesch leaping at you, and the rattle of the incomparable Condon's banjo, and the wail of Mezz's tenor sax, inspired as always, and the piano of Sullivan, the King, graciously in the background? And who else, who else? Krupa for one and somebody else and somebody else – once I had known, but that was a long time ago, in '28. Pinky Lee had discovered that record, Pinky Lee who loved jazz and Spalding saddle shoes; and his room at the frat house, second floor rear, had shook and trembled to its beat until I, at last convinced of its aphrodisiacal magic, swiped it and traded it to the girl who waited on tables at the Mecca, the girl from Morgantown . . .

The lights in the front room went out and the light on the sign in the front yard went out. This was what I had been waiting for, and I leaned over and cut off the radio in the middle of that impeccable solo by Sullivan, and for the blink of an eye the echo of his rich piano harmony vibrated above the floorboards. Then I saw her coming out the front door, this is why I was here; I had to satisfy myself about the perfume. But the images in my mind were Pinky Lee and the other guys in his room and the phonograph we took turns winding and the girl from Morgantown: goddamn that radio, I wasn't listening for anything in particular, I just turned it on to kill time, and this was what I had heard. And this was what it had dug up. Get out of my mind, you ghosts, I told them, I'll remember you later. . . . She was coming across the porch, down the steps, down the walkway to the pavement, down the pavement to the car, hatless and coatless; and I got out and stood with the car door open. In the pale luminosity of the sky that came through the limbs and leaves of the bread-fruit tree I could see her white face and her black hair, and then the perfume got through, the smell of *Huele de Noche*, which was only in my imagination, which was only a hallucination, but which was more real because of that, and the ghosts of the campus curled and faded before the rush of a memory even more ancient. . . .

'Can I give you a lift?' I heard myself asking.

'I didn't know you were here,' she said. 'Why didn't you come in?'

'I didn't get here in time. I haven't been here very long,' I said.

'Is that the real reason?' she asked.

'You mean it isn't good enough?'

'Well, since you and the Master don't agree in principle . . .'

'That wouldn't keep me from coming in,' I said. 'I hope I'm not that narrow. I'll come some night. I'm willing to be convinced. I hope I'm not interfering with anything by coming...'

'You're not.'

'I'd have called you, but I didn't know where to call.'

'I'd have told you, but your friend was so anxious to tear you away....'

'That's why I came back alone.'

She smiled, inclining her head at the car. 'Would you like to drive?'

'You drive,' I said. I stepped back and she got in the car, sliding under the wheel. I got in and closed the door, and she started the motor.

'Where can I drop you tonight?' she asked.

'Anywhere,' I said. 'Tonight I got no place to go. Tonight, I'm all alone. I ditched the clunk – lucky me.'

She smiled at me again, putting the car in gear, sliding it away. 'I don't think he liked me....' she said.

'He had other things on his mind that night,' I said. 'It wasn't you. How was the meditation?'

'Good. I do wish you'd come with me sometime. We could have an interesting discussion, talking about your theory of the fourth dimension.'

I looked at her. 'I might as well tell you something right now,' I said. 'That was just conversation. I don't know anything about the fourth dimension....'

'Ah-h-h-h...' she said, meaning I should not be so modest.

'On the level,' I said. 'That was just something I'd read somewhere.'

'Well, you certainly sounded like an authority....'

'I take after my grandfather. He specialized on being an authority on things he knew nothing about. I inherited his inferiority complex. Talk big, pretend you know everything...I was only trying to seem different from the average guy you

139

meet. I thought that talking about anything as esoteric as the fourth dimension would sort of set me apart from the average guy.'

She was silent for a thoughtful moment and then asked: 'Was that just conversation about the perfume, too?'

'Yes,' I said, laughing. 'That was just conversation about the perfume, too. I didn't smell any perfume.' I was smelling it now. . . .

'You're a terrific actor,' she said. 'I'll have to watch my step around you. . . .'

'I was only trying to arouse your interest. . . .'

'You did – you most definitely did. I thought I'd heard all the approaches, but that one was brand new. . . .'

'Wonderful,' I said.

We passed the drug store where, the other time I was with her, Jinx had wanted to leave the car, and got into some traffic for the first time, from a three-way intersection, most of it moving toward town, towards the puff-cotton clouds whose lower edges were stained with the colored lights from the business district directly below them.

'You're sure you got nothing to do tonight?' I asked.

'I'm sure,' she said.

'What time do you have to be in?'

'I gave up punching the time clock a long time ago,' she said. 'I'm a big girl now – I have my own room and everything. Where do you want to go?'

'I'm a stranger here,' I said. 'I leave it to you.'

'Well, what would you like? A movie? A sandwich? Some music? Want to go hear some music and dance?'

'I've already had a small helping of music,' I said. 'On your radio. While I was waiting for you. Right there . . .' I laid the tip of my forefinger against the dial. 'Right there. Eleven hundred . . .'

140

'That's the record station. They play records.'

'I know. They played one. I'll go down there one of these days and get a copy of it, too.'

'What was the name of it?'

'I don't think you know it,' I said.

'I might. I listen a lot. . . .'

' "I've Found a New Baby." Chicago Rhythm Kings.'

'I don't know it,' she said, stopping at a traffic light. She looked at me with amused suspicion. 'Is this more conversation?' she asked.

'I'm afraid I got off on the wrong foot with you,' I said.

'There's no such record as that, is there?'

'No,' I said.

'You didn't listen to the radio, either, did you?'

'No. I never touched it.'

'You know why I know?'

'Because you got me pegged?'

'A much more infallible reason than that,' she said, laughing. 'My radio's out of whack. It won't play.' She reached over and turned it on. The honking of horns behind reminded her that the light had turned green, and she let the clutch in with her stockingless, moccasined foot. The little light was glowing on the radio dial, and there was a tiny humming sound, but nothing else. She turned the knob and the needle moved down the dial, but there was no reception. 'You see?'

'Yes, I see,' I replied, laughing. This was funny as hell. 'You ought to get that fixed. . . .'

'I will,' she said. 'You're prodigious,' she said. 'I don't know what to believe now. . . .'

'Well, we're sitting in this car together. That you can believe.'

'Yes. That I can believe.'

'And the top's down. That you can believe.'

'Yes.'

'And it's a hell of a night for a ride. That also you can believe.'

'Yes. That also I can believe.'

I shrugged. 'Well,' I said, 'why not save all the things you can't believe until tomorrow and lump 'em together and worry about 'em then?'

'That's a good idea,' she said. 'We'll take a ride then. Where . . . ?'

'I'm a stranger here,' I said. 'I leave that to you.'

'We have four directions here – a sort of local phenomena,' she said. 'North, south, east and west. Do you have a favorite?'

'My favorite's the one that's not so lousy with traffic,' I said.

She weaved over to the right. The radio was still humming and I turned it off before it suddenly popped on and she could catch me in a truth. She turned right at the next corner into a narrow residential street, both sides of which were so thick with trees that the foliage interlaced above the street, and it was like boring through a tunnel. There were restrained lights in some of the houses, and in one of the yards the sprinklers were going and in the rays of the headlights I could almost count the drops of water from one of them as they left the peak of the arc and started falling. They left a sliver of dampness in the air which was barely perceptible, only enough to make me realize that there was one other smell in the world than *Huele de Noche*.

'Nice,' I said.

'Yes,' she said, not knowing what I meant.

At the first block she turned right again, but this street was wide open above to the sky, and two or three blocks ahead I could see a red stop-light blinking, and cars passing. I looked at her, but did not say anything.

'I'm trying to get on the boulevard,' she said, 'where it isn't so lousy with traffic. . . .'

'Oh . . .' I said.

It was a boulevard, a big one, the one we had crossed on the other street, at the three-way intersection, and it was carrying a lot of traffic. She paused the car at the stop signal, and then shot on to the boulevard, turning left. There were stores and cut-rate filling stations along both sides of the boulevard, but a mile or so ahead the lights ended, and what looked like a wilderness began, and there was nothing beyond but space.

'We'll be out of the traffic soon,' she said. 'This is the highway west.'

The highway west? 'Is this the one the Greyhound buses use? The Arizona buses use?' I asked.

'It's the only one. Are you going to Arizona?'

'I was thinking about it once,' I said. 'I changed my mind.'

'Do you live here now?'

'Yes.'

'Where?'

'Downtown.'

'Downtown? In a hotel?'

'In an apartment.'

'What do you do?'

'Well, nothing just now. I got several irons in the fire. . . .'

She looked at me abruptly. 'What part of the South are you from?' she asked.

'What makes you think I'm from the South?'

'Your accent.'

'My accent?' I said. 'I got no accent.'

'I hadn't noticed it before. But I did then. When you said "iron".'

I laughed. 'That's one of the words that always gives me away,' I said. 'I'll have to be more careful. . . .'

'Are you ashamed of being from the South?'

'Not exactly. . . .'

'Then why try to hide it?'

'I don't know. . . .'

143

'You shouldn't try to hide it. Southern accents are cute.'

'Business reasons. Most people associate laziness and shiftlessness with Southern accents. I suppose that's why I keep trying to get away from it. . . .'

'Oh, I don't think that's true, at all.'

'Most business people do,' I said. 'I'd like to be a success one of these days. I don't want to put any hazards in my way.'

'That's a curious way to look at it,' she said.

'Well, maybe so. I guess it's a phobia, sort of . . .'

'But you should try to understand it. Phobias can be understood. Don't you know that?'

'I know that some of them can,' I said, looking at her full in the face, and seeing, again, the little old lady in the coffin. 'Some of them can,' I said.

She shuddered violently, and looked away, and I looked away too. The road raced straight west now, pearly black under a full moon, and almost emptied of traffic. The night whistled over the top of the windshield and whined off the wind-wings as the car drilled through, and I heard a quiet plop! and glanced down and saw that her foot was pressing the throttle against the floor rug. She had meant for me to hear that, she had slapped the throttle down to direct my attention to what she was doing. The whine of the night increased and I could hear the cylinders sucking furiously to take up the irruption of gasoline vapours. I knew what she was up to, but I didn't know why. Unless . . . But that was not possible. She was no mind reader and she couldn't have seen that in my face. But she had seen something or sensed something, because she still held the throttle open. She was trying to out-gut me. All right, sister, I thought, you go right ahead and out-gut me. You'll get fat trying to out-gut me. I settled back and dropped my eyes from the windshield to the floor rug, picking out a spot to concentrate on. The trick in not being out-gutted is to avoid looking at anything by which you can measure your speed. The whine of the night and the sucking hiss of the cylinders were my only gauges, but in a minute or two I was conditioned to the night whine, and the cylinders had at last caught up with the gas intake, and I told myself that as long as I could keep my eyes off the speedometer I could control my nerves. We hurtled past the other cars that were coming and going and there was a roar, roar as we hit the edges of their slipstreams, and the roadster shook and trembled under the impact of air already disturbed, and I heard the angry sounds of horns wailing at us from behind. This was a thunderbolt we were riding now, but she held it steady, both hands frozen to the wheel I noticed, out of the corners of my eyes, sliding them to her hands and back again to that spot on the floor rug, careful to keep them away from the speedometer. Three or four little thumps exploded somewhere in front of me and I looked up and saw blobs of viscous insect fluid on the glass. 'Look how fat they are!' she called. 'Good crops this year!' I said nothing, putting my eyes back on that spot on the floor rug, figuring we must be doing ninety at least, maybe ninety-five. Other squishy explosions sounded against the windshield, but this time I did not look up, and that disappointed her. I could tell, because she started the windshield wipers and their evil metronomic clicks filled the car: she was doing everything she could to call my attention to the speed. I still did not look up, but I was fighting to keep my eyes off the speedometer. In what seemed less than the passing of a second my equilibrium was suddenly disturbed and I slid across the leather seat against the door. Instinctively, I looked up. The road was still perfectly straight, she had merely swished the car a little. Jesus, I thought, this dame is insane. I looked out over the door. The flat, fallow field to my right was a strip of continuous undulation. We must be going a hundred miles an hour, I thought. At this speed anything can happen. I got out a cigarette, and she took her right hand off the wheel and

nonchalantly pushed in the dashboard lighter, holding it in. That
chilled me. You must be out of your mind, standing for this, I
told myself. You're no college boy now. You're no starving
musician making that wild jump from Rocky Mount to
Goldsboro in a Model T, ashamed to tell the hop-head at the
wheel to slow down. You're a guy with a future. But where the
hell is that future if you pile up in ditch?

I looked at the speedometer. The needle was just scant of one
hundred. I grabbed the cigarette out of my lips and flung it out
the door.

'This is too fast!' I yelled at her.

'The speedometer's not right,' she yelled back at me. 'It's
broken too.'

'Hell with the speedometer!' I yelled. 'This is too fast.
Goddamn it, *this is too fast.*'

She put her hand back on the steering wheel and feathered
her foot on the throttle and the speed of the roadster diminished.
The speedometer needle fell back slowly, ninety-five, ninety,
eighty-five, eighty, seventy-five, seventy, sixty-five, sixty, with the
whistle and whine of the night lowering, fifty-five . . .

'You know how fast you were going? A hundred miles an
hour. . . .'

'The speedometer's not right,' she said. 'It's out of whack. . . .'

'Well, speedometer or no speedometer, you got too goddamn
much power here,' I said.

She took her foot off the throttle now, pulling over on the
shoulder of the highway, using the compression as a brake.

'What are you stopping for?' I asked.

'So you can light a cigarette?' she replied calmly.

'Well, Jesus,' I said, 'you don't have to stop for that.'

'You drive,' she said.

I looked at her. 'What the hell are you trying to prove?' I
asked.

'Prove?' she said innocently. 'I'm not trying to prove anything. I just want you to drive.'

'All right, I will,' I said. I leaned across her and snatched on the hand brake and the car stopped and I got out and went around the front to her side. 'Move over,' I said. She slid over and I opened the door and got in under the wheel.

'Now,' she said. 'Feel better?'

'I do, indeed,' I said, closing the door. I took the brake off and put the car in gear and nosed it back on the highway.

'May I have a cigarette?'

I fished a cigarette out of the pack in my pocket and handed it to her. She lighted it with the dashboard lighter, and I could feel her looking at me.

'I think I like your driving better than I do mine,' she said.

'I like it better, too,' I said.

'It always makes me nervous when somebody else is driving. But I'm not nervous now.'

'Neither am I,' I said.

She suddenly put her hand on my leg, staring at me in wide-eyed surprise. 'Now I get it,' she said. 'You thought . . .' She broke off, laughing. 'Oh, no, you couldn't! The very idea! Do you think I was deliberately trying to scare you?'

'That's nice conversation from you, too,' I said.

'Why, it's too silly to even talk about,' she said.

I turned off into a side road that was narrow but surfaced and headed north. She had no reaction to this, none at all. In a minute or two I glided to a stop under an oak tree and cut off the lights. I turned the switch and the motor died and the world was suddenly quiet. I looked at her. The cigarette was in her mouth, twisted away from her nostrils, and she was fluffing her hair with both hands.

'Why'd you do it?' I asked.

'Do what?'

'You know what.'

'Speeding?'

'Yes.'

'Do I have to have a reason?'

'For that you do.'

'No, I don't. I don't, at all. I often feel like rolling . . .'

'That fast?'

'Sometimes faster.'

'Crap,' I said. 'What scared you?'

'What scared *me*? Now really . . .'

I took the cigarette from her lips and tossed it over her head, out of the car, and put my face close to hers.

'What scared you?' I asked again.

'Don't look at me that way,' she said.

I put my arms around her and kissed her on the half-parted lips and could feel her hot exhaling breaths against the roof of my mouth. She shuddered again, mumbling into my throat, twisting her head, but I had her lips anchored with my mouth, swimming in a balsamic sea of *Huele de Noche*. After a while she stopped struggling and moving and then I took my arms from around her.

'Get out,' I said.

She just looked at me with that white face. I reached over and opened the door on her side and twisted past her, stepping on to the ground.

'Get out,' I said.

She didn't move.

'Goddamn it, get out!' I said.

She got out and I took her by the hand. I slammed the door of the car and walked her to the base of the oak tree. The roots of the oak were exposed on the side of a grassy slope, and I sat down, pulling her down beside me. There was still no response from her, no excitement, no apprehension, no curiosity – nothing.

'Lie back,' I said.

She lay back against the slope of the ground, her arms folded across her breasts. I unfolded her arms and put them at her sides.

'Close your eyes,' I said.

'Don't move a muscle now,' I said. 'Don't even breathe.'

She stopped breathing and her chest stopped rising and falling. I moved my head backwards and forwards several times, trying to bring into focus in the gloom the whiteness of her face where it was whitest, and the blackness of her hair where it was blackest. I found the focus and held my head still, staring at her, surrendering completely to the ancient memory that was leading me back. . . . By Jesus Christ, it was true! This is what it was all the time. But this cannot be. I tried to tell myself, this simply cannot be! I did not know about such things then. I was only four years old. . . .

Beams of light suddenly bounced around us, and she sat up, alive now and startled, and I whirled on my knees and saw that the beams were from two headlights. Two motorcycles were idly rattling down the road towards us. She started to get to her feet, but I grabbed her and pulled her down, whispering: 'Sh-h-h!' They could only be motor-cops. I lay prone on the grassy slope, holding her beside me, having the feeling that she wanted to jump up and run away. I fluttered my hand in her face, warning her to keep quiet and remain still. The beams of lights now stopped bouncing around us and centered on the car, and I heard the motors being taken out of gear, but left idling, and the machines being racked. There was a brief pause and I knew they were standing beside the roadster, and I moved my right hand slowly along the ground to my hip pocket, reaching for my automatic.

One cop said: 'This is the buggy, all right. Last four plate numbers check.'

149

The second cop said: 'Radiator's hot as hell.'

'So are these tires. Somebody just parked this job.'

'You suppose . . .'

'I don't know. Let's have a look around. . . .'

'Damn lucky they're in one piece.'

'Hell. you know how people exaggerate. Hundred miles an hour!'

I heard the car door open and then one of them whistled.

'Hey, Nick . . .' the second cop said. 'Look. . . .'

Now Nick whistled too.

The girl grunted and sprang up before I could stop her and started towards the car, yelling: 'Stop it! Take your hands off my car!' God, I thought. I took my automatic out of my pocket and hunched up the slope and stooped down behind the oak tree.

'How dare you!' she yelled.

I peeked out from behind the tree and saw that she was walking into the glare of the pocket flashlights.

'Take those lights out of my face!' she said.

'Your name Margaret Dobson?' Nick asked.

'Let's see your driver's license,' the second cop said, turning his flashlights out of her face.

'I'll let you see nothing,' she snapped. 'Get on those machines and get away from here. . . .'

'Lissen,' Nick said, 'we don't want to have to run you in. . . .'

'What's the number of your badge?' she asked coldly.

'Please, lady – not that routine . . .' he said. He turned the light on his shield. 'Read it for yourself.'

She leaned in and read it. 'One-eight-two-two,' she said.

'I asked you a question, lady,' Nick said. 'Is your name Margaret Dobson?'

'Is this your car?' the second cop asked.

'Yes. Certainly. Of course it's mine. Whose do you think it is?'

'Now, lissen, Miss Dobson,' Nick said, 'we don't want to run you in. We're just checking up. Half a dozen people back there said you were travelling a hundred miles an hour. You might get yourself killed going that fast. We don't want Ezra Dobson's daughter killed on our beat. Do we, Damon?'

'No . . .' Damon said.

I almost fainted. The cops were apologizing. She was somebody they were afraid of. Now I knew why she had kept trying to get up when I was holding her down to hide.

'And something else, Miss Dobson,' Nick said. 'You oughtn't to be out here at night like this. You ought to be home. . . .'

'I'll get home when I please,' she said curtly.

'Well,' Nick said, 'you ought to get home just the same . . .' He flipped the light around the tree, looking for whoever she was with. I ducked back.

'I'm perfectly all right,' she said. 'Perfectly. Now, will you go?'

'Sure, Miss Dobson, sure,' Damon said. 'Remember me to your father. Name's Steer. Only one on the force. And my partner's badge number – forget it, will you, Miss Dobson?'

'That depends on how fast you get away from here,' she said.

'We're going. Good night,' Nick said.

She did not reply.

The flashlights went off, and they unracked their motors and got on them and rode away. She stood there watching them until they had turned off the surfaced road, back on to the highway. The sounds of their exhausts rose high and crackling as they went into high gear. I put the automatic back into my hip pocket, and moved from behind the tree as she walked to me.

'The next I come out with you, I'm going to bring along an extra set of nerves,' I said.

'I'm sorry . . .' she said.

'For what?' I said. 'That was wonderful. That's the way the bastards ought to be handled. Just who are you, anyway?'

'Don't worry about it,' she said.

151

'I'm curious,' I said. 'Who is your father? Commissioner of Police or something?'

'No . . .' she said. She looked around at the slope of the ground where she had been lying, and moved to it. What the hell is this, I asked myself, who is this dame, what goes on here? I looked around and she was on the ground again, on the slope.

I went over and sat down beside her. 'Who are you?' I asked.

'Stop thinking about it,' she said. 'Think about what you were thinking about before. Look . . .' she said. She placed her arms beside her and closed her eyes and stopped breathing, utterly inert, like a statue, like . . .

I just sat there staring at her.

'What's the matter?' she asked quietly.

'In a minute, in a minute,' I said, trying to think about what I had been thinking about before. But I couldn't. My mind was full of motorcycles and motor-cops and flashlights and one big question. 'Just give me a minute,' I said, struggling to recapture that most ancient memory . . .

. . . chapter two

The second I started waking up, before I had even got my eyes open, I knew something was wrong. The body in bed beside me was unyielding and displeasing, and the room was bitter with the feculence of imprisoned air that had been exhausted by a thousand usings. I at last came awake and saw that the window had been closed and that the door to the living-room had been shut, and I sat up, looking down, and discovered that it was Jinx who was in bed beside me. I got up and went over and unlatched the window and let the fresh warm morning come through the screen, and also the deep bass sounds of the steam shovel still digging away down the street, and the florid counter-point of city noises. I went back to the bed and snatched the covers off Jinx. This disturbed him, but did not wake him; he simply hunched up in the fetal position. I slapped him across the face with the back of my hand, and leaned down and shook him; and he raised his head, startled, and saliva drooled from the corner of his mouth.

'What – what . . .' he mumbled.

'How many times do I have to tell you not to shut windows?' I said.

He pushed himself up in bed, rubbing at his left eye to unglue the lids. 'It was open when I went to bed. I didn't shut it. It must've blown shut,' he said.

'The hell it did blow shut,' I said. 'It was latched. Somebody latched it.'

153

'Well, it wasn't me,' he said. 'It must've been Holiday.'

'Sure,' I said. 'This is just the kind of cheap petty stunt she'd pull. This is just the way her mind works. She told you to sleep in here too, didn't she?'

'Yeah. That's right. She was pretty mad about you staying away so long last night. . . .'

'That makes two of us that's mad then,' I said, going into the living-room. Holiday was on her back on the davenport under a blanket, smoking a cigarette; and one look at her and I wondered what was eating her and what she was up to. She wasn't mad now: she might have been mad last night – but not now. There was a bitchy smile on her face and it was evident that she had been awake for some time (if, indeed she had slept at all), waiting for me to discover the closed window and Jinx in bed with me, waiting for me to come to her as I was coming now. There was an air of almost eager anticipation about her, like a guy in a duck-blind at dawn, that was so obvious and so thick I could feel it, and when I felt it, I stopped, no longer certain of my ground. For her this kind of behavior was not characteristic, for that matter, I suddenly realized, neither was her behavior of last night – letting me sleep. I had left the apartment, telling her and Jinx I would be gone for only a few minutes, that I was just going to walk around the block, and instead I had gone out to Doc Green's to meet the girl, and had stayed away five hours. When I got back they were not here, but that didn't worry me; I went to bed, to sleep, fully expecting her, I now remembered, to wake me up when she came back, and raise hell. That was what I had expected and that is what I was prepared for and that would have been in character. But she hadn't. Why hadn't she? Why all this masquerade? I didn't know, but this I did know, this I could not escape: she was trying to force me to bring hell to her. All right, you son-of-a-bitch, I told her in my thoughts, here we go.

154

'Good morning. . . .' I said pleasantly.

'Good morning . . .' she replied, in a tone which the pleasantness of my own voice, and the hesitation I had suffered at the foot of the davenport, had forced her to make neutral, waiting to see if my genial manner were genuine, waiting to see which way I was going to jump.

'How do you feel?' she asked in the same sparring neutral tone.

'I feel wonderful. . . .' I replied, asking myself why I could not dispel the compulsion to play this neurotic game, why I was wasting my time, why I didn't save my energy for more important things, why I didn't just let this dame have it where it would hurt the most, and then I laughed inside. I wasn't kidding myself. I knew why, Perversity. *Dégéneré supérieur,* that was why. 'I thought I'd put on some coffee,' I said. 'Would you care for some?'

A flash of disappointment crossed her face, wiping off the bitchy smile, and she threw back the blanket and swung her feet to the floor, demurely pulling together the front of the wrapper she had slept in. 'Let me do that,' she said. 'Let me make the coffee . . .'

'I can do it. No trouble at all . . .' I said, going into the kitchen, leaving her standing there staring at me, light indecisive wrinkles on her forehead.

I put some water in the pot and was dipping the coffee with a glass measuring cup when I heard her come in. I turned around and she was standing just inside the door, smoking a fresh cigarette. She put her arms out full and arched her back, stretching lazily and elaborately.

'Did you sleep well?' she asked.

'I slept beautifully,' I said, putting the coffee pot on the stove, lighting a burner. 'I really did . . .' I said, adjusting the flame.

'No sign of a cold? No sign of a sore throat?'

'I?'

'Yes.'

'No.' I shook my head. 'No sign of a cold, no sign of a sore throat. Should there be?'

'I was hoping not, I guess I closed that window just in time. It got draughty around two o'clock. I didn't want you to catch cold.'

'I'm certainly due for a cold, all right,' I said. 'I haven't had one in ten or twelve years. . . .'

'Colds are very easy to get,' she said. 'They are very easy to get – *especially* when you're tired. You were very tired last night. You don't know how tired you were.'

'I can imagine. I didn't even hear you come in.'

She laughed quietly. 'You didn't even hear Jinx when he got in bed with you. You were dead to the world.'

'I must have been, not to hear that. I can't think of anything that would more conclusively prove how dead to the world I was.'

'Well, you see, that's when you catch things, when you get that way. And if you don't look out for yourself, somebody else has to. You catch a cold and it goes into pneumonia . . . I don't want you to catch pneumonia. Where would I be if you caught pneumonia?'

'Oh, I'm sure you'd manage somehow. . . .' I said.

'Well, I'm not so sure. . . .' she said. She flipped the cigarette into the sink and put that bitchy smile on her face again. 'You've got to be careful. The very idea of you walking for five or six hours when you're not used to it. I never would have let you out of here if I'd known that. You said you were only going to be gone for a few minutes. . . .'

'I was detained,' I said.

'Was it nice?' she asked, showing her teeth a little.

'Very nice,' I said. ' "Grand Hotel." First movie I've seen in three years.'

156

'Some movie,' she said. 'I hear she's got a Cadillac. . . .'

There! She couldn't carry the masquerade any further, the double-talk was ended and the silly pretence and spurious solicitude was finished and done with. So this was what was eating her – the other girl. Her information, of course, had come from Jinx, but what could he tell her other than the fact that I had met a girl who drove a Cadillac? If he had told her I was having a date with Margaret Dobson last night he had been guessing. I had been very careful not to mention her name around him, not even to refer to her, for this very reason. So now they couldn't prove a thing.

'She? Who? Cadillac? What're you talking about?' I asked.

'That queer you and Jinx met the other night. Hasn't she got a Cadillac?'

'I don't know what kind of a car she's got,' I said. 'I never saw her but once in my life. I don't know her name or where she lives or how to find her – even if I wanted to.'

'Finding her shouldn't be any trouble for a bright boy like you. For a master mind like you. I hear she's queer and classy . . .'

'What Jinx thinks is queer and classy and what I think is queer and classy are two entirely different things, I assure you,' I said. 'I told you I was at a movie last night. I didn't have a date with any girl. I dropped into a movie. ' Her lips were sneering now and her eyes were bulging with poison. 'If your berserk brain won't permit you to believe that, then you believe whatever the hell you want to believe. . . .'

'You crummy lying son-of-a-bitch!' she said, whirling, stepping over and pushing the coffee pot off the stove. It clattered to the floor, spilling over the linoleum, and she slapped off the burner, putting out the flame, but unaware of the sexual symbolism of this act. When she faced me, her lips were still sneering and her eyes were still bulging with poison. 'You out lumped up with some dame and me sitting here worrying myself sick about you, you crummy swell-headed son-of-a-bitch . . .' She picked up the tin can of coffee from the table and flung it at me, and it struck me in the chest, showering me with coffee. I leaped at her, grabbing her by the shoulders, and the impetus carried her against the drainboard of the sink. She fell back across it and her wrapper jumped open and her breasts popped out. I put my hands around her throat, with a thumb on either side of her Adam's apple, pressing hard.

'I went to a movie, you hear that, I went to a movie,' I said. She gurgled and tried to struggle, but I had her legs wedged between mine and her Adam's apple locked under my thumbs, and she could barely move. 'I went to a movie. Say it. Tell me I went to a movie. . . .' I released a little of the pressure on her Adam's apple so she could speak.

'You went to a movie. . . .' she spoke.

'That's better,' I said. Then I turned her loose and stepped back, and she straightened up, closing her wrapper, the sneer gone from her lips, but the poison still in her eyes, and I walked out. . . .

Jinx was emerging from the bathroom.

'From now on, keep that big mouth of yours shut,' I said. 'You told Holiday I was having a date with that dame last night.'

'No such goddamn thing,' he said.

'How'd she know about the Cadillac then?'

'I told her that, but nothing else. Mandon's the one who figured out the date business. . . .'

'Mandon?' I said, surprised.

'It was his idea, not mine.'

'Where'd you see Mandon?'

'Here. Right here.'

'What was he doing here?'

'She called him. . . .'

'Why?'

'She was worried. She thought maybe you'd been picked up . . .'

'That shows how stupid she is,' I said. 'The cops wouldn't dare to pick me up now.'

'Well, Mandon was worried too. We went out to get something to eat around twelve o'clock and he said if you didn't show up by the time we got back, he'd start looking around. But you showed up. . . .'

'Sure, I showed up,' I said. 'What else did they expect? I'll be a son-of-a-bitch! Every time I turn my back you all get panicky. I know what I'm doing. Jesus!'

'Sure, you do,' he said, walking out.

I turned on the cold-water spigot in the wash basin and then in the mirror I saw Holiday come in and motion to Jinx. She was holding my coat that she had taken from the back of a chair in the living-room, where I had draped it last night; and was indicating something to Jinx, not realizing that I could see the pantomime in the mirror. I shut off the spigot and went in.

'Look . . .' she said to me, turning the coat so I could see, pointing to some fox-tails and bits of dried grass that still clung in to the back. 'Some movie . . .' she said.

I went back into the bathroom, slamming the door. . . . I turned on the two spigots in the tub, full on, and the two spigots in the wash basin, full on, and pushed the flusher of the toilet, but not even all this noise inside the tiny, closed room could drown out her laughter – faint but triumphant.

... *chapter three*

When I said that I had come to see Mr Mandon, the younger of the two blondes asked me what my name was, not if I had an appointment, not what my business was, just what my name was, and she entered it in a ledger, and beside it the time which she got from a clock on the wall. 'He's expecting you, Mister Murphy,' she said, then, 'Right through the door there....'

She held open the gate in the wooden railing and I walked over to the door and went into Mandon's private office.

It seemed that everything in here, as in his apartment, had been arranged to create the impression of eccentricity too. In the middle of the floor there was a big circular bench, the kind they sometimes build around a post or column in a museum or a public place, only this had no post, in the center was the hole. Against the wall that formed the outside hall was a mahogany commode with a flowered china bowl and a big, flowered china pitcher, and towels on a rack at the side. Back where I had come from this was called a close-stool; and it was strictly utilitarian, no sleeping room was complete without one, and I remembered what a nuisance my grandfather had always thought they were. Next to this was a glass bookcase, filled with indiscriminate junk, and a few law books. The opposite wall was covered with photographs, framed and unframed, all of them forming an edging for a large print in the middle – a colored reproduction of Anneheuser-Busch's celebrated 'Custer's Last Stand.' These covered the whole top half of the wall. The bottom half was covered by a long, slanting, old-fashioned book-keeper's desk, in front of which, on a high stool, his feet hooked into the rungs by his insteps, sat Mandon. 'Well . . .' he said, unhooking his feet, twisting around on the stool, leaning backwards with his elbows on the desk, crossing his legs, making the whole operation seem as perilous as a high-wire act in a circus. 'The last time I saw you you were sleeping like a baby.'

'If I'd known you were with 'em, I'd've waited up for you.' I said.

'Don't be snotty,' he said.

'What'd you expect – bluebirds? You got me in a hell of a jam last night. How'd you know I was having a date with some other girl?'

'Were you.'

'Yes.'

He nodded vigorously. 'After hearing the facts, it was a logical deduction. . . .'

'Hereafter, if you don't mind,' I said, 'make your deductions for me instead of against me.'

He unfolded his legs and got down off the stool. 'I was only trying to reassure Holiday that nothing harmful had happened to you,' he said. 'She thought that maybe the police had picked you up. I felt it was safer that she be mad at you than worried and frightened. Don't you agree?'

'I agree,' I said. I had to agree. There was just enough logic in his argument to make it sound legitimate. But he wasn't fooling me. Make 'em squabble, make 'em fight, make 'em jealous, keep the dasher turning, keep it going up and down, be patient, be perservering, and pretty soon the butter'll be so thick that even a paralytic hand can scoop it up . . . He was looking at me, a sly smile on his face. Did he know what I was thinking? Probably, probably. He was a cunning son-of-a-bitch, all right.

'. . . However, I didn't come for that. I came because this is later.'

'Later?' he said, frowning.

'Webber's got thirty-two hundred dollars of my money. I tried to get it from him yesterday, but you said later. Well, this is later. . . .'

'Won't you please let me handle this?' he asked in a faintly grieved tone.

'Go ahead and handle it. All I want's the money. I need it to carry us over until I can lay out another job.'

'I asked you to please let me handle this,' he said again, but this time his tone contained a flavour of affability. He lifted his bushy eyebrows as high as he could, looking at me, his head angled. 'Please . . .' he said.

'I told you – go ahead and handle it,' I said, wondering why he was so suddenly coy.

He straightened his head, still looking at me, and pursed his lips, making little thoughtful sounds with them, wanting me to know that he was trying to make up his mind about something. Then he turned to the desk, lifting the lid with one hand and reaching inside with the other, bringing out a wide manila envelope. 'To a young man in your position there are some things more important than money,' he said, 'even if you don't realize it. This is one of them.' He handed me the envelope.

It felt empty and there was no writing on it, no marking of any kind. What could this contain that was so important it felt like nothing at all? I pressed up the flimsy metal catch that held the flap closed – and then I saw, before I even took it out, I saw. It was a fingerprint card, my fingerprint card, with the ugly but traditional profile and full-face photographs, my head measurements, and the location of my scars and all the other trifling physical imperfections which mug departments adore to amass. This was the master card from the files of the police in town from which I had been sent up. I was very surprised. How did this get here? I wondered. 'How did this get here?' I asked.

162

'You see what happens when you let me handle things,' he said gravely.

'You're a wizard. I take off my hat to you,' I said, and I meant it. Without this card the police had nothing to go on. My past was wiped clean. I had no past. Well, not quite; there was a copy of this card buried with five million other copies in the F.B.I. files in Washington, but now they couldn't dig that out without original fingerprints and I was very sure that I wouldn't be leaving them around again. That card in Washington I'd recover one of these days too, when I got bigger, much much bigger. 'I still don't know how this card got here,' I said. 'That town's a thousand miles from here. This is fast work.'

'As a matter of fact,' he said, 'Inspector Webber got it last night. I took the liberty of telling him to forget the thirty-two hundred dollars you mentioned, and suggested that he might get this card for us instead. It was no trouble for him – all he did was to pick up the phone. Just an exchange of professional courtesies. Shall we conclude the ritual?'

He took a cheap tin lighter out of his pocket and slashed at it, setting fire to the wick, which burned and smoked like a night-traffic construction torch. He held the flame out and I turned the fingerprint card over it. The heavy card curled and sooted and finally ignited, and the fire crept slowly upwards, over 'if apprehended, please notify,' over '. . . who was received at state's prison,' over 'Ralph Cotter,' over the profile photograph, over the index prints, over the classification, '9M 3U 000 12,' and I turned the card, catching the burned part in the palm of my left hand, guiding the flame over the physical description – and when it was consumed all but the corner I had been holding in my fingers, I rubbed the ashes briskly together between my hands and then swept them into a brass cuspidor. Mandon said nothing. I went to the commode and poured water into the basin and started washing my hands.

'I think you ought to forget about that thirty-two hundred dollars,' Mandon said.

'I think so too,' I said. I finished washing my hands and took a towel from the rack, and he came over and reached down, opening the little doors of the commode, and dragged out a lidded slop-jar, flowered to match the other pieces, knocking a roll of toilet paper to the floor, that rolled and unwound; and by God, looking at that slop-jar and the toilet paper like this, I suddenly remembered that it wasn't the commode or close-stool that my grandfather had called a nuisance. I was mistaken about that. This was what he objected to, the jar; devilish tortures he had called it, and he had said that he'd rather go outside in the weather and ease his buttocks into a bank of freshly-fallen snow than use one. He never did either. The whole thing came back to me now. . . . Mandon was lifting the lid and put the jar back into the commode. He retrieved the toilet paper and tore the length from it that was unrolled, and with the torn tissue he wiped the basin clean, the way you wipe a salad bowl. This was a careful procedure done with extreme fastidiousness. He put the pitcher back in the bowl and took the towel from me and hung it on the rack.

'Well,' he said. 'Now, how do you feel?'

'Fine. I feel fine,' I said.

'You ought to. It is not every man's privilege to be reborn. From this point on, you have nothing to worry about so long as you let me handle things.'

'Cherokee,' I said, 'the Homeric contempt which this frail body generates encompasses everybody in the world but you. I salute you as one who has proved himself worthy to share my frenetic genius. From now on, I shall respectfully and everlovingly let you manage things.'

'Of course,' he said, and smiled, 'you know that's a lot of crap.'

'Of course . . .' I said.

* * *

The City Hall was in the old town, three blocks from Mandon's office, but I didn't know that until we had started for lunch. They were three noisy blocks, filled with pawn-shops, second-hand stores, pool-rooms, bail-bond brokers, beer joints, sidewalk hamburger stands, flop-houses, oil stations and narrow, messy parking lots; ugly dirty buildings filled with ugly dirty people, the kind you have come to associate with the fringe of any City Hall that has jail attached. But this City Hall was neither ugly nor dirty. Dazzling white, covering an entire block, it leaped in symmetrical grandiosity thirty storys above the stink and squalor and obscenity of its vicinage, impressive and righteous, a mighty symbol, a shaft of thunder, mightier far than the world of the Lord God Jehovah which whined sing-song from the open doors of a nearby miasmatic mission. 'Nervous?' Mandon asked. 'Nervous? Why?' 'Take a look . . .' I looked and discovered that we were now approaching heavy pedestrian traffic – police in uniform, deputies in uniform, khaki, and coatless office workers wearing badges of various sizes and shapes pinned to their shirts, all of them with pistols swinging gaudily at their hips – a gamey dish of symbols themselves, seasoned with a few plain civilians. This was what he had meant. What did the little bastard think I had to be nervous about? I said, smiling at him. 'I've just been reborn. Remember?' 'Maybe nervous was the wrong word. A man's reflexes get conditioned to certain things – like the sight of police officers. There'll be quite a few cops where we're going. ' 'I got a reborn set of reflexes too,' I said. 'That's what comes of letting you manage things.' 'You may be only half-kidding about that,' he said. 'I'm not even half-kidding,' I said.

We stopped, waiting for the light to finish changing. He looked at me prudently and laughed quietly and then the light was green.

He took my arm, crossing the street. This was the block

165

directly opposite the City Hall, where most of the cops had
gathered, standing in little groups, moving in and out of a
sandwich parlour and a café which were next door to each other.
Mandon knew a lot of the cops and they knew him, but of the
eight or nine he spoke to, not one called him by either of his
names, Keith or Mandon, and only one called him Cherokee. The
others called him 'Shice'. I was curious about that. 'What's this
"Shice"? What is that?' I asked. 'It's just a nickname,' he said, but
I still did not understand and I looked at him and he saw from
the frown on my face that I did not understand, and said, 'It's
short for shyster,' and smiled a wan smile, plainly intended to
imply that they meant nothing derogatory or even disrespectful.
But that I knew from their tones. 'You certainly know a lot of
cops,' I remarked. 'Well, I've been around this neighborhood a
good many years now,' he said. 'I remember when there was a
livery stable right where the City Hall is standing. God, that goes
back to oh-two, oh-three.' He shook his head as if he couldn't
quite believe it had been that long ago, and still holding my arm
he steered me around a knot of cops and into a delicatessen.
Walking into the dimness of the delicatessen from the fierce
brightness of the outside, stepping directly in from the street, I
was blinded, but I heard a whirlpool of voices and smelled the
smells of food, fresh food, spiced food, and they were
wonderful. . . .

The delicatessen was packed with people, I could see now; it
was narrow but long, and looking over the heads of the crowd to
the rear it seemed endless. In the left corner there was a cashier's
cage and a cigar counter, using as little space as possible, and
against the wall to the right, stretching halfway from the front
window to the rear, was the serving counter. This was a cafeteria-
style delicatessen, you got your plates from one of the stacks on
the end of the counter ('No, no plate, it'll just be in the way,'
Mandon said.) and stepped in line and passed along the counter

behind which eight men wearing aprons and chef's bonnets of brown paper sacks, were slicing at the roast beef and corned beef and pastrami and tongues and sausages and dill pickles and loaves of rye bread, listening to the food orders and filling them more or less correctly (which nobody seemed to mind) and at last they handed you something and you moved out of line, past a squat curving bar where you also had to wait on yourself, and then you were ready to eat – if you could find a place to sit down; guys and cops were stacked two-deep around the tables, waiting, laughing and talking and hollering and slapping each other on the back. It was like a goddamn convention. Most of the men in here knew Mandon too, and called him 'Shice'.

Mandon finally found a vacant spot against the wall, between two tables, and backed into it, I behind him, each of us with a sandwich in one hand and a bottle of beer in the other.

'I see what you mean about the plate,' I said.

'Sure. A plate's all right if you come early enough – or late enough.'

'Why come at all?' I asked.

'What?'

'I said why come at all. You don't have to impress me with how many cops you know.'

He flicked his eyes at me. 'If this makes you nervous, we'll go. . . .'

'It doesn't. How's your sandwich?'

'Good. How's yours?'

'Good,' I said. 'If I can keep my eyes closed to these guys' table manners I'll probably be able to finish it. . . .'

Something touched the back of my neck and I turned my head. Standing beside me was a white-haired man in shirt sleeves, his forearms covered with black sateen elbow-cuffs, winking at me and pantomiming for me to keep quiet. He was trying to reach Mandon with the arm behind my neck, still chewing the last morsels of his food, his mouth opening wide with each chew, and I could see his tongue kneading the swill into a sodden bolus. Make a note of this, I was thinking, make a note of this and mark it with an asterisk to insure remembrance, because one of these days I shall jockey this carrion, this whoreson, this chawbacon into a nice safe corner where a pistol shot will be heard by nobody else.... The badge pinned to his shirt was not silver, like all the other badges in the delicatessen, this badge was gold and I knew he was no ordinary cop. I eased forward a little to give his arm sufficient play, and he slapped Mandon on the pate and snatched his arm back, ducking behind me, out of sight. Mandon turned thinking it was I who had slapped him, but I winked and indicated that it was the guy behind me, and he tilted his head, squinting his eyes, and then recognition came into his face. He sniffed loudly, saying, 'I smell a turnkey.'

The turnkey straightened up, coming out from behind me, laughing as if this was one of the funniest things he had ever heard. 'Hi, Cherokee, where you been keeping yourself?' he said, sticking out his hand. Mandon held his sandwich in his teeth to free one hand to shake with. 'What's happened to you lately?' the turnkey said. 'Don't your boys like my hotel no more?'

Mandon got his hand back and took the sandwich out of his mouth. 'How are you, Boo? Meet my helper, Paul Murphy. Boo Bedford, Head Jailer across the street....'

'Pleased to meet you, Mister Bedford,' I said. Hail and farewell, I was thinking....

'What do you help him do?'

'He's gonna take up law,' Mandon said.

'I'm gonna take up law,' I said.

'His father was an old friend of mine,' Mandon said. 'He turned him over to me to get practical experience.'

'Well, boy,' Boo said, 'you sure picked the right man.' He put his arm around my shoulder. 'Come to see me sometime and I'll give you the lowdown on the old bastard.' Learn to keep your mouth closed when you're eating, you pig, I thought. 'And as for you,' he said to Mandon, 'don't make yourself so scarce. I won't put you in High Five, much as you need it. . . .'

'I'll drop in when you least expect me, Boo,' Mandon said.

'Do that – and bring Paul. We'll show him what the inside of a jail looks like. . . .'

He patted me on the shoulder and left. Mandon watched him go.

'Contact, that's why I came here,' he said quietly. 'It's good business. That was the head jailer. Carries a lot of water, too. See the guy there at the middle table? In the linen coat. The one with the black horn-rimmed glasses . . .'

He was a slightly bald-headed man in shirt sleeves, sitting with three civilians. All of them looked a little superior to the others in the room – although not much superiority was needed for that. 'I see him,' I said.

'Judge Birdsong. Very good friend of mine. Him I met in here. . . .' he handed me the empty beer bottle, and sidled his way to the table. He leaned down and the judge saw him and smiled broadly and said something I could not hear. With all the noise that was being made I would have had to be right on top of them to hear. Mandon also knew two of the others and shook hands with them, but I could tell from the way he shook hands with the fourth man that he was meeting him for the first time. None of them got up and offered him a chair, none of them looked around for a waiter to ask for a chair. They just sat there, talking and chewing and drinking; everybody in the place was talking and chewing and drinking, and in my mind I saw in every mouth what I had seen in the turnkey's mouth a loathsome bolus: these swine, these offals, and I could not eat the sandwich. I half-turned my face to the wall to shut out some of the scene, thinking how nice it would be to wire the walls and the floor of this place with t.n.t. and set it off some day at noon, what a great public benefaction that would be . . .

'What's the matter with your sandwich?' Mandon asked at my elbow.

'Oh!' I said. I had not seen him come back. 'Nothing. Nothing at all. I'm just not hungry. . . .'

He looked at me quizzically. 'Don't be nervous. Go ahead and eat.'

'Goddamn it, I told you. I'm not hungry.'

'You wanna go?'

'Yes.'

'Come on then . . .'

I placed the sandwich and the two bottles on a nearby table, right under the nose of some surprised cops who were sitting there, and followed him to the front, bumping hard against a couple of the bastards, apologizing, pretending they were accidental. Mandon paid the check and we stepped into the brightness of the street, walking towards the corner. The crowds of cops had thinned out, they were inside one of the assortment of joints feeding their faces. 'Jesus – ' I said, glancing over my shoulder at the delicatessen we had just left. 'I never saw anything like that before in my life. Not among human beings. Not in jail, not in a road gang, not even in prison. I haven't seen anything like that since I was a kid. Not since I was a kid back in the mountains.' 'Well, they're cops,' he said. 'They like to make a lot of noise and let off steam. This is the only time of the day they can.' 'The noise didn't bother me,' I said. 'What did bother you?' 'We used to be in the ham business. We raised hogs. Did you ever see a thousand hogs feeding at the same time?' He did not reply, so I glanced at him and saw that he was staring at me, frowning, his heavy eyebrows raised, high. 'So that was it, so that was it,' he said slowly, and now the stare softened and a suggestion of understanding came into his face. 'I'm way ahead of you, Cherokee,' I said. 'Don't try to psychoanalyse me. I can do a much better job of that than you can. . . .'

We stopped at the corner.

'I apologize for subjecting you to an ordeal like that,' he said. 'But I had to find out . . .'

'Find out? Find what out?'

'I just wanted to see if you were a loud-talking punk, or a guy with the nerve to see this thing through.'

'How could you tell from what happened back there?' I asked.

'An accumulation of very vivid reactions. You'll do, Paul. . . .'

'That's fine. That only leaves one of us in doubt,' I said coldly.

He smiled at me, unruffled. 'As far as my courage and dependability are concerned, I'm afraid that you'll just have to take those for granted.'

'Will I?'

'I'm afraid so,' he said pleasantly.

He nodded to the City Hall across the street. 'Shall we go over and try it on for size?' he asked.

'Why not?' I asked.

Mandon stopped by the cigar stand at the corridor corner opposite the elevator. The clerk was at the far end of the counter giving a woman some change, but when he turned and saw Mandon he said in delight, 'Cherokee!' and came to him with his hand outstretched. He was a dark man and his right arm was off at the shoulder. 'Cherokee!' he said again, sticking his hand over the mints and cigarettes and magazines.

'Hello, Augie,' Mandon said warmly shaking hands.

'I don't see you around,' Augie said with a slight accent. 'You been gone?'

'No, I'm just busy, Augie. How are you? How's the family?'

'I'm good. The family's good. And – ' he grinned ' – business' good. You are good?'

171

'I'm good,' Mandon indicated me. 'Meet my helper, Paul Murphy . . .'

Augie put his hand out to me and I took. 'Hello, Augie,' I said.

'Yes, yes,' he said, nodding. 'Business is very good when Cherokee needs a helper. Many, many years he do the whole thing by himself.'

'No longer, Augie, no longer,' Mandon said, moving his fingers lazily, pointing at something on the rear shelf.

'I know . . .' Augie said. He took down a round pasteboard carton, like the one I had seen in Mandon's apartment, and removed the lid. Mandon reached in to take out some stogies and Augie said, 'His favorite . . .' and Mandon laughed, pleased, putting a handful of stogies into his inside pocket and handing Augie a one-dollar bill, waving for him to keep the change.

'See you soon, Augie . . .' Mandon said.

'Very soon, I hope,'Augie said. 'Please to meet you,' he said to me.

I nodded and followed Mandon away. 'You think that's wise to introduce me as your helper?' I asked. 'Nothing wrong with it,' he said. 'I can hire anybody I please. You've got to have some sort of connection. Gives us the right to be together whenever we want to. In here . . .' he said, nodding.

He stepped over to a big frosted glass door marked: MEN, and took out a key ring and found the key and unlocked the door. This was a charming bit of irony: the City Hall was open to the public but the toilets weren't. You had to have a key to get into one of them.

I went in behind him, through a bare hall, into the lavatory proper. It was shiny and clean with six stalls and six gleaming urinals, and a battery of wash basins all with foot-controls, like a hospital operating room, and a stack of linen towels. The doors of all the stalls were open, and there was a man in shirt-sleeves at the urinal, his back to us. Mandon moved in to one of the urinals and in a moment the other man shuddered his shoulders in a mild spasm and turned away, zippering his fly. He ignored the nice gleaming wash basins and the stack of linen towels and walked out.

Mandon turned quickly to me and said, 'Give me that gun!'

'Go away,' I said,

'I saw you switch it from your hip pocket to your coat pocket while you were standing at the cigar stand,' he said. 'You chump, give it to me, give it to me!'

I shrugged, taking the gun out of my coat pocket and handing it to him. He quickly moved to the stack of linen towels on the shelf above the wash basins and stuck the gun inside them, half-way down.

'What the hell is this?' I said, moving over to get back the gun. He grabbed my arm and there was anger in his face. I didn't want to hit him, so I shoved him backwards, and before I could reach for the stack of towels, I heard the click of the corridor door as it opened. I jumped into one of the stalls and as I closed the door I had a flash of Mandon moving back to the urinals. I held the door shut with my hand, not locking it, peering through the crack near the hinges, and the guy came in, going to the urinal. I pushed the flusher, waiting for him to finish, hoping that he too would go straight out, ignoring the wash basins and the towels, because I didn't want to run the risk of him finding the gun. But I knew that it would just be my luck for this guy to have very clean personal habits, and it was. He finally turned, moving to the wash basins, and I came out and took the one next to him. He was a stocky civilian. He inspected his face in the mirror, almost clinically, squeezing the skin, then he examined his eyes minutely, and when this was done he took a comb from his hip pocket and began to comb his hair. Hurry up, you son-of-a-bitch, I was thinking, but I confess that I felt some admiration for his poise. He seemed entirely unaware

173

that another man was standing beside him. How any man can go into a lavatory and be unaware of other men, impervious to them, fully at ease, untortured, I do not understand, but this one was. I couldn't stall any longer and I started washing my hands, and then he did too. I finished and took one of the towels, slowly drying my hands. He soaped his hands and rubbed them and cleaned the fingernails of each finger with the fingers of the opposite hand, and then soaped his hands again and washed them off. When he shook off the excess water, I reached for a towel for him, holding it out politely.

'Thanks . . .' he said.

I smiled at him.

He wiped his hands thoroughly and dumped the towel into a white metal container with a swinging top and went out.

I fished under the stack of towels and got the gun and Mandon stepped beside me. 'Goddamn it!' he said, popping out his hand for the gun. I gave it to him and he dropped it into his pocket, glaring at me. 'Did you use this crashing off that prison farm?' he asked tensely.

'No.'

'Have you killed anybody with it?'

'No . . .'

'Don't lie about this!'

'What the hell is this?' I said.

'Have you?'

'No!'

'All right, then. I'll keep it for you temporarily. I don't want to be carrying a gun that's killed somebody. This is no goddamn hick town. We got a ballistics department here.'

'Screw the ballistics department here,' I said.

He glared at me and went out.

In the corridor, he stopped just beyond the glass door marked:

174

MEN, and said softly, 'You're through with that strong-arm stuff. I'll get you a permit to carry this thing and then you'll be in no danger.'

'That'll be a novelty,' I said.

He eyed me flatly. 'You know what Holiday said about you last night?'

'I can imagine . . .'

'She said you were crazy. And I'm beginning to believe it. Bringing a gun to a place like this . . .'

'You forget one thing, Cherokee. When I started out I didn't know where I was going.'

'Would it have made any difference?'

'No.'

'I thought not,' he said, and resumed walking.

The entire corridor now, where we were walking, was used for police-department offices: *Administration, Traffic, Division Motorcycle Detail, Department of Personnel, Division of Robberies, Bureau of Homicides.* Mandon slowed up here, near this door. 'Is this another test?' I asked. 'No. Why? Shaky?' 'Not as long's Inspector Webber's on the force,' I said. Without stopping, he opened the door and we went in.

This was a small office, but it was bright and airy and from the ceiling hung a brass chandelier so enormous that its edges almost touched the walls. It didn't fit in here; it had been left over from some auditorium. There were two clerks, one a civilian, the other in uniform, sitting at desks, facing each other, and there were two desks temporarily vacated. At the counter was a paunchy cop wearing a sergeant's chevrons on his sleeves. 'Jesus, me beads! Cherokee Mandon!' he said.

'Hi, Truck . . .' Mandon said, moving to the counter and shaking hands. 'I thought you'd be out of that uniform by now, doing gumshoe work.'

'I thought so too. Every month I ask for a transfer outside and

175

every month I wind up right here. They think us old-timers ain't up on the new technique.'

'There's no technique like a piece of rubber hose and a high colonic,' Mandon said.

'Yeah. What brings you out in the heat of the day?'

'Just passing by. Webber in?'

'He's at lunch. Some little something I could do?'

'Nothing important. I'll drop back.'

The sergeant leaned across the counter. He seemed disappointed that Mandon wouldn't confide in him.

'Like you to meet Paul Murphy,' Mandon said. 'He's in my office now. Sergeant Satterfield . . .'

I took the sergeant's paw and shook it and he looked me over briefly. Then he said to Mandon: 'You figgering on retiring?'

'Eventually, eventually,' Mandon replied.

'How do you do, Sergeant Satterfield,' I said.

'The sergeant's a good man to know,' Mandon said. 'He practically runs the bureau. . . .'

'I wish to hell I did,' the sergeant said wistfully. 'Where you been hiding yourself?'

'Well, you know . . .'

'All your clients turned respectable?'

'I guess that's it.' He turned for the door. 'I'll drop back later, Truck. . . .'

'Good. Pleased to make your acquaintance, Paul. . . .'

'Thank you, Sergeant,' I said going out with Mandon.

'Nice old guy,' Mandon said to me in the hall. 'Been on the force for forty years. Used to be a bicycle cop . . .' We walked on down the corridor towards the entrance. Augie waved to us as we passed the cigar stand, and we waved back . . . We started down the broad steps to the street and Mandon suddenly touched my arm and stopped. Inspector Webber and Reece were coming up the steps. We moved near the stone balustrade, waiting. Both of them wore blue suits and I noticed that Reece had changed shirts, but that he still used a toothpick; and that there was a neat bandage on the Inspector's left hand, the one where the palm had been laid open by the phonograph needle.

'Charlie . . . Oliver. . .' Mandon said in a restrained voice.

They stopped. Reece glanced surreptitiously at the Inspector, who was looking, not at Mandon, but at me. His face was hard and his eyes were narrow.

'See you a minute, Charlie?' Mandon asked.

'Go ahead.'

I smiled, telling myself that right now was the time to take over. I hadn't forgotten what had happened in the apartment the first time I'd ever seen him, that red twisting tremor in the pit of my stomach, the fear that he was going to kill me; I would never forget. I would never let him forget, either. From now on, I'd give the orders. 'In your office,' I said.

His jaw squared and he pushed his lower lip out truculently, but he went, by God, he went, without a word, on up the steps, Reece beside him, Mandon and I behind him, with Mandon trying to signal me with his eyes to go slow and I pretending not to see; down the corridor beyond the Homicide Bureau where he stopped at a plain glass door. He unlocked it with a key and stepped aside, letting Mandon and me go in first. 'Thank you, Inspector,' I said.

This was his private office. It contained a small kneehole desk, four chairs and a brightly varnished bench. There was a carpet on the floor and four gaudy calendars on the wall, the near-pornographic kind that you find in some garages. The Inspector took off his coat and dropped it on a chair without folding it or hanging it, and put his hat on top of it and went behind the desk. He picked up some papers and looked at them hurriedly, playing the part of a big executive. He put the papers down and pressed the key of his dictograph.

'Yes, Inspector?' the dictograph said, and I recognized the voice of Sergeant Satterfield.

'Anything for me?'

'You're wife called. Cherokee Mandon was in. Said he'd be back. That's all. . . .'

What? I thought. No Commissioner raising hell about the unsolved murder of the old milk-truck driver. No newspapers putting the heat on about a crime wave? No big-wigs yelling for a clean-up? This couldn't be right. . . .

The Inspector let the dictograph key close and Reece moved in to stand beside him at the desk. Then the Great Man finally condescended to look at me.

'I haven't had a chance to thank you for that envelope you gave Cherokee this morning,' I said. 'I appreciate that very much. . . .'

'Don't mention it,' he said curtly.

'How's your hand?' I asked. 'I hope you got it treated in time to head off the infection. Those phonograph needles pick up a lot of dirt you know. . . .'

'My hand's all right. What've you got on your mind?'

I nodded for Mandon to tell him. 'I want a gun permit made out in the name of Paul Murphy,' he said.

'Who's Paul Murphy?'

'He is,' Mandon said, nodding at me. 'I thought it'd help if we changed the name.'

'Damned co-operative of you,' Webber said. 'But you know I can't issue a gun permit. . . .'

'Only the Chief of Police can issue a gun permit,' Reece said.

'We were hoping that the Inspector would speak to the Chief on our behalf,' Mandon said.

'The name is Paul Murphy,' I said.

'Well . . . I'll speak to him.' He opened the middle drawer of his desk and took out a printed form. 'Fill out this application and send it back to me and I'll see what I can do.'

'As long as I'm here,' I said, 'why don't I just wait?'

He looked at Reece, who started shredding the toothpick. with his incisors. This was a fascinating trick. I picked up the application blank, swinging the chair around and sitting down at the desk. I lifted the pen from its desk-stand and filled out the blank, using the name, Paul Murphy, and writing the address as Monticello Hotel, but making the personal description part very accurate. When I got to the bottom paragraph with its three blank lines, I stopped. 'Right here where it asks, "Reason for Requestion Permit," what do I put?' I asked.

'Put the reason you're requesting a permit,' Reece said.

'That's what I mean,' I said. 'There must be all sorts of reasons. Pick one for me.' Nobody said anything. 'How about 'always carry large sums of money?'

'That ought to do,' Mandon said.

'Yes . . .' Webber said.

I filled that in and signed the application and handed it to him. 'I should have made that, Always carry *very* large sums of money. But, then, I suppose that's understood, isn't it?'

'When do you think you'll begin carrying very large sums of money?' Webber asked.

'Soon. I'll give you plenty of warning,' I said. 'Did you say I could wait while you speak to the Chief?'

He grimaced and opened the middle desk drawer again, taking out a long book of blanks and an official City seal, not the big desk kind, but a small one, one you could carry in your pocket. He tore out one of the permits and sat down and started copying on it from the application. Then he stamped it with the seal and handed it to me. I saw that it had previously been signed by the Chief of Police, S. E. Tollgate.

'Thank the Chief for me,' I said, folding the permit and putting it in my pocket. 'I'm sorry to have taken up his time. . . .'

Mandon had been none to comfortable all through this, and now that it was finished, he made a move to go. 'I'll be in touch with you, Charlie,' he said.

'Just a minute, Cherokee,' Webber said. Mandon turned back to him. Webber said to me, 'You mind waiting outside for him?'

'Not at all,' I said.

Reece moved to the door to let me out, standing there, chewing on the splintered toothpick.

'I see that you still prefer a toothpick to dental floss,' I said. He glared at me but did not say anything. I went out into the corridor, wandering down to the big window at the end. Looking out the window, I saw police cars coming and going down the ramp, and the traffic in the street – and then Mandon called me. I went to him and we started out. As we neared the door marked: MEN, I jerked my head and said, 'In here . . .'

Mandon unlocked the door and we went in, all the way in. The place was empty.

'What'd he want?' I asked.

'Nothing . . .' Mandon said.

'Tell me.'

'It was about another matter entirely. . . .'

I got sore. 'I've had enough double-talk for one day. First him, now you. What'd he say?'

'He said you were crazy to come here. . . .'

'I didn't come here. You brought me. Did you tell him that?'

'He said I was crazy to stand for it. He also said for me to be goddamn sure you didn't fool with anything Federal, banks and things like that – that would bring in government agents. . . .'

'That, of course, is ridiculous. We'll not make the mistakes the others have made.'

'Not as long as I have anything to say. He insists that the minute we pick something out we tell him all about it – before we make a move. That was all.'

'That was enough,' I said. 'Now, give me my gun.'

He gave me the pistol and I put it in my pocket and we went out.

When we got back to Mandon's office, walking back the same way we had come, those few ugly dirty blocks, Highness, the handsome colored boy, was waiting. He was sitting in a chair in the outer office, outside the railing, reading a sports page, or looking at it. He was neatly dressed, certainly better dressed than anyone else I'd seen for some time, and had his hat in his lap. Mandon saw him as we went in, but neither of them offered any sign of recognition. One of the blondes was absent, the younger one, but the other rose and handed Mandon a slip of note paper. 'This was all, Mister Mandon,' she said.

Mandon stopped and looked at the slip of paper and raised his big eyebrows. 'When did he call?' he asked.

'Shortly after you had left. A little before twelve . . .'

'Did he leave a message?'

'Only his name, sir.'

'Try to get him on the phone. . . .'

He handed her the note paper and we went into his private office. He was suddenly worried about something. You couldn't tell this from the way he acted or the way he looked, but I knew he was suddenly worried. I sensed it. I could feel it.

'What's wrong?' I asked.

'Nothing,' he said.

'Was that call from Webber?'

'No . . .'

A buzzer sounded and he went to the long slanting desk and took the receiver of an old upright telephone. 'Hello, Roamer . . .' he said. He listened for a moment and said: 'It's no bother,' he said. He listened for a moment and said: 'No, I haven't forgotten. Are you going out there today?' He listened and said: 'I'll see you then. Right. At the bar? Right.' He listened some more and said:

'That won't be necessary. I got my boy here. He'll drive me.' He hung up and lifted the lid of the desk, taking out a big check book from which he tore two blank checks. He folded them and put them in his money-clip. 'How'd you like to go to the races?' he asked.

'What kind of races?' I asked, still wondering what he was worried about.

'Horse races.'

'I'm told they're not much fun when you're broke,' I said.

'I'll stake you to a few bets. . . .'

'Thanks just the same. I think I'll wander around and see what I can scare up.'

He suddenly lowered his eyebrows, gazing at me in severe thought, and then he smiled and his whole face lighted up and he wasn't worried any more. The process of getting rid of his worry was very visible. I hadn't any idea what had caused this, but I felt better too. He came to me and put his arm around my shoulders. 'You scare up nothing until tomorrow,' he said. 'You come here first thing in the morning.'

'But I'm broke,' I said. 'I need a few dollars for tonight. I'll pick a small place where there's only one guy. I'll be careful. . . .'

'You'll be careful!' he said with heavy sarcasm. 'Christ, with a set-up like this, that's perfect, you want to jeopardize it for a few lousy dollars! What're you doing tonight that needs money?'

'Never mind,' I said. 'You just don't let Holiday trap you on the phone any more. I'm supposed to be with you . . .'

'So that's it,' he said. 'Didn't you get enough last night?'

'I could never get enough of that,' I said.

'All right. I'll stay away from the telephone if you don't pull anything.'

'I won't pull anything. Just don't talk to Holiday, that's all.'

He took the money clip out of his pocket and handed me all the currency. 'Here's forty dollars. That ought to hold you until tomorrow. Things'll be different tomorrow.'

'How will things be different tomorrow?' I asked, taking the forty dollars.

'Wait and see. Be here early in the morning.' He slapped me on the back. He was feeling good. I looked at him and he was grinning. Shrugging, I walked out, putting the forty dollars in my pocket.

I was still hungry and, having got the images of those feeding swine out of my mind, I went into a drug store and had a sandwich and a glass of milk. Then I decided to do what I had been wanting to do all day, but hadn't had a chance: find out who Ezra Dobson was. I couldn't get over the demonstration of reverence and awe that the two motor-cops had put on last night when they had found out that Margaret Dobson was Ezra Dobson's daughter.

In the classified telephone directory in the booth I picked the name of a newspaper that was in the biggest type and called it and was connected with the city editor. 'I'm having an argument with a friend of mine and I wondered if you could settle it,' I said to him. 'Would you please tell me Ezra Dobson's title?'

'Well, he's got a lot of titles,' the guy at the other end said. 'Ex-Mayor, ex-Governor, ex-United States Senator – why don't you look in *Who's Who?*'

'I know those titles,' I said, hoping none of the amazement I was feeling could get through the telephone. 'I mean his title now. . . .'

'Well, he's President of Watco Steel. That what you mean?'

I didn't know what I meant, but this would do. 'Thank you,' I said. I hung up and stood staring at the telephone dial. Jesus! No wonder those motor-cops . . . I looked up Watco Steel in the book. There was half a page of listings of various plants and departments. I looked up Ezra Dobson. There were two telephones listed for him, but I was interested in the one that was indicated by the lower case 'r' meaning residence. 4100 Willow Creek Drive, it said.

I went out and flagged a cab and got in.

'You know where Willow Creek Drive is?' I asked.

'Sure . . .' the driver said, looking at me in the rear-view mirror. 'That where you wanna go?'

'Yeah. Just for a ride, just to see some of these big places I been hearing about. Somebody mentioned Willow Creek Drive. Is it nice out there?'

'They're all nice out there. That's the North Side. That where you wanna go?'

'Yeah. Just for a ride.'

The driver was right: they were all nice out there. On gently rolling hills and wide clean streets they stood, walled and iron-fenced, of mixed styles but triumphant miens, with fine green lawns and bright flowers and well-kept trees. It was a modern counterpart of a medieval duchy. 4100 Willow Creek Drive crowned the duchy, its eminence supreme. This gray fieldstone Renaissance house of many many rooms had been erected on the highest hill in the neighborhood, moated by a ten-foot grey fieldstone wall that surrounded it on all sides, thick enough to keep out an army. Near a corner of the wall was the entrance, but the big bronze gates were closed. Beside the gates, inside the wall, was a small gray fieldstone house – a private watchman's house.

'That place's a pip,' I said to the driver. 'Who lives there?'

'I don't know,' he said, 'but I'd like to have what it takes to run it.'

'So would I,' I said. I bet I could sure surprise you, I thought. I bet I could knock you right through that windshield if I told you I had a date tonight with the girl who lives there. And then I thought about the forty dollars. What the hell good was forty dollars when you had a date like this? How much caviar and champagne could you buy with forty dollars? 'Any time you're ready . . .' I said.

'Had enough?'

'I've seen what I came to see. Now I'm ready to go back to the common people.'

'Where I picked you up?'

'Downtown. Mason's Garage . . .'

'Where's that?'

'Downtown. Near the big produce market. I'll show you,' I said. I sat back and lighted a cigarette, feeling a tingling exhilaration.

Mason was in the back of the garage talking to one of the mechanics. My body, moving into the darkened entrance from the bright sun, disturbed the tight balance, attracting his attention, and he looked towards me and saw that somebody was there, but I could tell from his reaction that he had not recognized me. I walked on into the office and half-sat on the desk, and in a minute I heard him approaching, bouncing up and down. He saw me before he got through the doorway, and stopped outside the office. His eyes blinked with fear and his Adam's apple fluttered as he tried several times to swallow. He looked quickly over his shoulder to the rear of the garage and I thought he was going to scream. I pulled the .380 automatic out of my hip pocket and pointed it at his belly.

'Come on in,' I said.

'Now, lissen, Ralph . . .' he stammered.

'Come on in,' I said.

He came in, his eyes twitching. 'Lissen, Ralph . . .' he said. 'You got to hear my side of this. . . .'

'Stop shaking,' I said. 'I'm not going to hurt you.' I put the gun back in my pocket. 'See? I'm not going to hurt you. . . .'

He opened his mouth a little, letting go a sigh, and his eyes

185

stopped twitching. 'I know what you been thinking, Ralph,' he said. 'I been trying to get you on the phone. You ask Holiday, Ralph. . . .'

'You're confusing me with somebody else,' I said. 'My name's not Ralph. My name's Paul Murphy. Look at this . . .' I handed him the police permit to carry a pistol. 'Paul Murphy, that's me. . . .'

He looked at the permit, but there was still doubt in his face. 'On the level?' he asked.

'Sure. Ink's not dry yet. My pal, Charlie Webber. Inspector, Homicide. You remember . . .'

He did not say anything. I took the permit from his hand and put it back in my pocket. 'That was a nice thing you did, Vic – putting the Inspector in touch with me. We have a lot in common, and I have a feeling that he and I will be the best of friends. Of course, you didn't know that, but as long as it turned out all right. . . .'

'I'm glad it did, Ralph. I'm sure glad as hell it did.' He seemed more at ease now. 'It's mighty nice of you, Ralph, to come here to tell me that. . . .'

'Paul,' I said.

'Paul. I'm sorry about the deal I gave you, but a guy gets that kind of pressure put on him there's only one thing he can do. . . .'

'I know that, Vic. Forget it. Everything turned out all right. I'm not one to hold a grudge. Shake?'

'Sure . . .'

We shook hands. He smiled; he was positively jovial. 'Wanna go around the corner and have a drink?'

'It's a little early for me, Vic,' I said. 'I been on the wagon so damned long. Tell you what you can do for me though – '

'Anything, Ralph. You want the Zephyr?'

'Paul,' I said.

'Paul, I mean . . .'

'I'm short of cash until tomorrow. I was wondering . . . .'

'How much you want?'

'Oh, couple of hundred. Just till tomorrow. We got something lined up for then. . . .'

'Why, sure, sure,' he said, amenable but not too happy, pulling out a roll of bills. He flicked four fifty-dollar bills off the top and handed them to me.

'Thanks, Vic,' I said. 'This'll take care of the groceries. . . .'

'Any time, Paul. You think you'll be needing the Zephyr tomorrow?'

'I can't tell yet,' I said, putting the four fifty-dollar bills in my pocket. 'I don't know what the lay-out is. Maybe. I'll call you.'

'I'll have her ready – just in case.'

'Good. And, Vic, you don't know how much I appreciate the loan.'

'Ah!' he said modestly, putting his arm around me. 'Don't give it a thought. Your credit's always good with me.'

'Thanks . . .' I said, starting for the door with him still beside me, his arm still around my neck.

'If you get bored sitting in that apartment tonight, call me. I'll be here till late. I might be able to find some fun for you. . . .'

I won't be bored tonight, old boy, I won't be sitting in that apartment tonight, I wanted to tell him. This is one night that I won't be bored. 'I'll try to do that,' I said, stepping out from under his arm, turning towards the street.

When I opened the door of the apartment, Holiday got up from the davenport and advanced to me, her hands on her hips, her face blazing with anger that obviously had been a long time piling up.

'So you finally got here!' she said.

'Take it easy,' I said.

She grabbed me by the shoulders of my coat, clutching the

padding and poking her face almost against mine. 'What's the matter?' You run out of places to go?'

'Please . . .' I said. 'I've had enough melodrama for one day.'

'Me sitting here in this stinking apartment all day . . .'

'Please,' I said. 'I'm exhausted.'

'Oh, so you're exhausted! From what! Being lumped up in the sack with that bitch all afternoon?'

'Please,' I said. 'I'm hot and sweaty and in no mood to fight.' I tried to take her hands off my shoulder but she was holding too tightly. Her eyes were wide and rabid and her lips were thin. 'I haven't been with any bitch,' I said. 'I've been with Mandon. You're the only bitch I've seen today. Honest.'

She snorted and then without warning she clawed at my face. I caught this hand and knocked the other one from my shoulder and slapped her across the nose. But she wanted to be tough. She growled in her throat and raised both arms to grab me around the neck, and I slugged her on the side of the head, knocking her down. I reached over and lifted her dress and tugged at it between my hands and finally managed to tear off a hunk. She lay on her back, looking up at me, her eyes smoldering, fully conscious, but saying nothing. With the hunk of her dress, I wiped the spittle from my face, and then threw the rag at her and went into the bedroom, closing the door.

Goddamn it, I thought regretfully; but this clawing business had to stop and that was the only way to stop it, the only way. She's a goddamn savage, this dame is, a real primitive, and the only way to teach her something is to knock her on her ass. Well, she'd sure as hell come to the right place. . . . I separated the money, putting the thirty-odd dollars, all that was left of the money I'd gotten from Mandon, on the bureau, but folding the four fifty-dollar bills I'd gotten from Mason and poking them into my watch pocket. I took out my gun and started to lay it on the bureau when I thought, no, it'd be very dumb of me to tempt her like this, if she ever exploded in one of those violent passions and happens to see a gun handy – and then I thought that this kind of thinking was stupid because I couldn't keep her away from guns indefinitely, if she wanted a gun badly enough she'd certainly get one of her own, and changing my mind again, I left the gun on the bureau beside the money – in plain sight. I took off my clothes and went into the bathroom and started filling the tub. I got the water mixed and stepped in. I had to get myself nice and clean for Margaret Dobson, daughter of Ezra Dobson, Esq., of 4100 Willow Creek Drive, ex-Mayor, ex-Governor, ex-United States Senator, President of the Board of Watco Steel, the very mention of whose name caused little people, maybe big people too, but certainly little people, to tremble in their boots.

I was on my back in the tub when Holiday came in. She wore only silk shorts and stockings and her shoes and in her hand she held the torn dress. She stood in the doorway, looking at me almost calmly. The fury of the squall had passed, it should be approaching the North Carolina coast by now, and there was no smolder in her eyes. She leaned over and dropped the dress into the tub with me. 'There's a wash rag for you,' she said.

'The next time you spit in my face, you'll have a loose arm to drop in the tub with me,' I told her. 'I mean it. I don't like this spitting business. It's all over now, and I've forgiven you. Don't give the dress another thought. We'll get another one. We'll get a dozen more. Two dozen. All you want.'

She stepped back, closing the door, not saying anything. I wrung out the dress and put it on the back ledge of the tub, and finished my bathing. Then I wrapped a towel around myself and went into the bedroom.

She was standing at the bureau, looking down at the money and the gun. All she had to do to get the gun was to just pick it up, but I wasn't alarmed, for all the apprehension I felt she might just as well have been looking at a water color. 'Where's Jinx?' I asked.

'He went out.'

'Where?'

'He didn't say.'

'That's what you should have done, gone out.'

'We can't all be crazy,' she said. 'What's this?'

'What does it look like? It's a gun.'

'I don't mean the gun. I mean the money. Where'd it come from?'

I started to tell her that all during the time she thought I was lumped up in the sack with some other dame I was out hustling for her, trying to scrape enough together to buy the necessities of life, and really pour it on so she would feel guilty for accusing me falsely, and then I thought, the hell with her. 'From Mandon. I put the bite on him. It's enough to last until tomorrow.'

'What's happening tomorrow?'

'I'm not quite sure. He's got something up his sleeve, something big.' I threw back the sheet and blanket and got into bed, stretching out. 'He's got several prospects. We're going to decide on one of 'em tonight.'

'With Mandon . . .'

'Where?'

'I just got through telling you. I don't know.'

'Didn't he give you some idea?'

'Just look things over, he said. That's all I know.'

'Looking things over! That could mean a lot of things.'

'Well, that's what he said. Look things over.'

'When's he picking you up?'

She certainly was full of questions. Well, she'd been sitting here all afternoon biting her nails and conjuring up all sorts of fantasies, and now she was full of questions. That was perfectly natural, and since I wanted the leavetaking tonight to be peaceful and pleasant – which it wouldn't be if either of us provoked another eruption – I decided I'd better make myself a little more agreeable, a great deal more agreeable. 'Come on over and sit down,' I said.

She came over and sat down on the edge of the bed. 'He's not picking me up,' I said. 'I'm meeting him. . . .' She darted her eyes at me and I saw the suspiciousness coming into them, and I also saw, on the side of her head, the egg-size profile of the bump where I had hit her. I had the impulse to sit up and examine the swelling and kiss it and say that I was sorry and lay her down and get a cold towel and treat it, and then I realized that this would be carrying the act too far, that this was one dame whose suspicions could never be smothered by contrition. 'Look, Holiday, this is business,' I said placidly. This was the way to do it, be straightforward and agreeable. 'I'm going with Mandon on business. We've got to have some money. You need clothes, I need clothes, and we need a bigger place to live in. If you'll just have a little patience and trust me, we'll be in clover before you know it. We can't miss. This is an absolute cinch. This makes Dillinger and Nelson and Underhill and Floyd and Barker and those guys look like beginners. There never was a set-up like this in the history of the world. . . .'

Now she looked away from me and got up and walked slowly towards the living-room. Jesus, I thought, I just won't be able to get away from her tonight without a fight. I tell her a perfectly believable story . . .

'All afternoon I have been thinking,' she said, turning around. 'You talk about what a set-up this is. Have you ever thought about how easy it's been?'

'Easy? I don't get it.'

'This's been too easy. All of it. It's been just too goddamn easy.'

I laughed softly to myself, feeling better. This was what she was concerned about, not the other girl, she was suspicious of the set-up. I swung out of bed and went to her. This was going to be very simple now; it was going to be very simple because she was wrong and I genuinely knew it and I could prove it – once and for all. Yesterday I might have done some whistling in the dark, but not today. Today I had the facts, from personal observation and experience I had the facts, and the infallibility of my instincts had been corroborated.

'What's been easy about it?' I asked.

'Everything. The way it just *happened*. Can't you see that?'

'No, I can't see it,' I said. 'Your premise is wrong, that's what's throwing you off. Nothing just *happened*. It happened because we *made* it happen. We worked like hell to *make* it happen.' She shook her head, not argumentatively, still held by the original doubt. How could I make her understand that this was no casual fortuity, no happenstance, that this was conceptional volition, and the subservience of that volition to certain golden ends? 'Jesus, you know that,' I said. 'You know the chances we took to make this happen. . . .'

'All afternoon I been sitting here thinking. All afternoon . . .' she said.

'If you're going to do that every time I turn my back, if you're going to sit around and worry, you'll wind up in the bug-house. The danger's all over. The danger was when the cops shook us down and when I baited 'em back to hear the record. But there's no danger now. You got to realize that. You don't have to stay cooped up here any longer. Don't be afraid. Get out and go somewhere. You know where I been today? Police Headquarters. Yes, sir, Police Headquarters, right in the office of Inspector Webber. Mandon and I. And what about Mandon? Is he a dope? Did he come in with us or didn't he? There's your answer. He's a smart cookie. Do you think for one minute that he'd have touched this thing if there'd been any danger in it? Not on your life. He's got too much to lose. Before he pitched in with us, he checked all the angles – but *all* the angles . . .'

'That son-of-a-bitch,' she said. 'He'd double-cross us in a minute. . . .'

She was right, of course, but at that moment she wasn't thinking of his morals. She was thinking of the first time she'd seen him, when she'd put her body on display for him in that pleasant predatory way that women have, and he had disregarded it, showing no interest in the rises and falls and curves of her body. . . . This was what had burned her up, this would always burn her up, even if he became her sexual slave, she would still be burned up. 'Oh, for God's sake, of course he'd cross us up in a minute,' I said, 'but only if it's to his advantage. Loyalty's a matter of convenience and profit, and as long as we can offer him those, he's on our side. He's useful to us and we're useful to him, and between us, we've got this town in our pockets. You've got to believe that.'

She had stopped shaking her head, but I could tell from the doubt still in her face that none of this had made her feel any more confident. I didn't know what else to say. There she stood . . .

Yes, there she stands . . .

I went over and took her in my arms and she opened her mouth and I heard the hiss of air being sharply sucked through her teeth.

193

...*chapter four*

The name-plate on the radiator said, DELAGE, and it was a long, low automobile, black with red-disc wheels, and quilted red-leather upholstery, and parked on the street front of Dr Darius Green's cottage, lined up along the kerb with a lot of heaps and small cheap cars, its class and quality evident even in the dim light of the street standards. I knew it was hers before I read the registration certificate that was clamped around the steering post: Margaret Dobson, 4100 Willow Creek Drive. Jesus, I thought, this dame is loaded, she really is. This was a hell of a piece of equipment. It was a right-hand drive, with the individual front seats so low they were practically on the floorboards, and the instrument panel was full of dials and gauges and controls, all identified in French. There was a key still in the switch.

I eased through the opening between the front seats and sat down under the wheel, taking out the key. Now a lot of automobile keys are left in the switches. Most people just forget, but there are some who leave them out of sheer damned arrogance, and I knew that with her it was sheer damned arrogance. The hell with it, they figure, they don't give a damn, it's insured and if it's stolen it will be no inconvenience, they will simply have the Number Four boy pick another one out of the stable and bring it around. The butt of this key was gold and ornate with the initials M.D. forming a stencil, and it was with some other keys, all gold, on a big gold safety-pin that served as a key-ring. There were two objects on the key-ring that were not keys. One was a gold St. Christopher, the back engraved with her name, and the other was a gadget, the like of which I had not seen before. It was slightly bigger than a silver dollar and I finally discovered that it was a folding magnifying glass. I opened it and looked at the keys: 14c. gold. They were the real things, and so was the big safety-pin: on the bottom bar in very small letters was stamped: Cartier. Yes, sir, not a false note . . .

I put the key back in the switch and turned it and heard a faint click. I turned if off and looked at Doc Green's cottage. The disciples were still in there groping with cosmic consciousness. They were due out now, it was after 9:30, I noticed by the clock on the panel, the time she had told me to come. But from where I sat there was no sign of an adjournment, there was no noise; everything inside was quiet and spellbound. Maybe I had time to take one turn about the block. What the hell, why not? I asked myself, turning on the switch. I located the starter button and checked the gears and shoved the clutch out and pushed the button. The motor caught on the first spin, so quickly that I barely heard the starter gears mesh, and the exhaust exploded with a roar and a clatter that caught me wholly off-guard. Frightened and shaky, I quickly turned off the switch and jumped out of the car and started walking down the street. I walked a hundred feet or more, listening intently for the sounds of alarm and excitement that I thought must follow the racket I had kicked up, but there was no sound except my own footsteps. I stopped, stepping behind a bread-fruit tree, and looked back. It was quiet and peaceful, deserted; and then I suddenly realized that Mandon had been right: a man's reflexes do get conditioned. Mine had been conditioned by an almost identical situation that had occurred long ago – only the automobile was not a Delage and I had been caught (this was before I had perfected the art of

195

Tampering). This reaction was stupid, this was strictly lower animal response, and knowing that, and also knowing why, I told myself that now it could never happen again.

I started back to the Delage to drive it around the block, the hell with the racket it made, this time I hoped it would make ten times as much.

I had just reached the car when the front door of Doc Green's cottage was opened and the disciples began to emerge. Well, no matter: I didn't need to prove it . . . Some of the disciples got into their modest automobiles and drove away, and some walked, and the street was full of sombre and serious 'Good nights', and the clash and rattle of gears, and then it slowly grew still again, and Margaret Dobson came out the door and walked across the lawn towards me, the silhouette of her swinging against the paleness of the cottage, and it was not until she stood directly in front of me and I saw her face still white and her hair still black that the ache in my lungs told me I had been holding my breath.

'Well,' she said. 'What's the matter? That perfume again?'

'That's very cruel of you,' I said, inhaling deeply.

She laughed. 'Or are you afraid my car will bite you? Why did you cut off the motor so quickly?'

'You heard it . . .'

'*I* heard it? Everybody for miles around heard it. It's quite noisy. To tell you the truth, I never use it at night except to annoy people I don't like. I just ride up and down their street racing the motor. . . .'

'Is that what we're doing tonight – annoying your friends?'

'I've already done it,' she said.

'It's a hell of a piece of machinery, all right,' I said, helping her into the front seat. 'Is it fast?'

'Very . . .'

'You won't have it very long if you aren't more careful of your switch key,' I said, closing the door. I went around the rear and got in beside her and slammed my door. 'It's people like you who keep car thieves in business. . . .'

'I never lock anything . . . .'

'What do you do – change cars every day?'

'Just about . . .' She turned the switch and started the motor and the exhaust exploded again. She looked at me, smiling, and shifted gears and we rolled away. I never heard an exhaust like this one; it made as much noise rolling as it did when it was started. It couldn't have been any louder if it had come directly out of the cylinders.

'How was the meeting?' I asked.

'The usual. How was yours?'

'Profitable. Nothing definite, but great prospects.'

'I'm very glad,' she said.

'Thank you,' I said, leaning towards her, trying to smell the *Huele de Noche* again, but not being able to. I looked at the side of her white face and the black hair, trying to force the odor, but it simply wouldn't come. I wondered why that was. . . .

She turned her head and caught me staring at her, and smiled softly.

'I was just wondering . . .' I said. 'Why don't you wear make-up?'

'Because I don't like it,' she said. 'Incidentally, have you any plans for tonight?'

'Only to be with you,' I replied.

'I'd like to go somewhere and just talk. There are many things I want to talk to you about. Many. Where will we go?'

'Anywhere at all – except the country.'

'I thought you liked the country.'

'I did – until I got home last night and took a look at my clothes. I had a hell of time cleaning my clothes. . . .'

She slowed to a stop at a traffic signal and looked at me mischievously. 'Next time,' she said, 'I'll bring a blanket. . . .'

197

* * *

It all happened so fast I didn't have time to ask questions. One minute we were rolling along the street in moderately light traffic, in front of a row of high-class apartment buildings, with me sitting there on that quilted red-leather seat thinking how far I had come from the Great Smokies and how much farther I would go before I got finished, and the next minute she had turned the car across the pavement and we were going down a ramp into a basement garage. My heart leaped. I thought this was the ramp down into the basement of City Hall, where I had seen the police cars and that she had sucked me into some sort of trick: and then the nose of the Delage lowered going down the ramp and below I could see two lines of expensive automobiles against opposite walls and I knew then that this was no police garage, not with big, rich cars like these. Two uniformed attendants were springing to attention, and she stopped the Delage between them.

'Good evening, sir,' said the one on the left. 'Good evening, Miss Dobson,' said the one on the right.

'Good evening,' said Miss Dobson, with the proper aloofness in her tone.

The one on her side opened the door and she got out, and he promptly moved to the elevator; but the one on my side, whose chore it evidently was to rack the Delage, stood there his hand on the open door, looking at me; and now that I was undoubled, unseated, out of the car and could properly be seen, surprise came into his face. I thought it was the surprise of recognition until I saw that he was not actually looking at me, but at my clothes, and I was suddenly reminded of how cheap and disreputable they were, in what particular and in what detail I could not recall, just cheap and disreputable, and then I realized that it was not surprise in his face at all, but shock of seeing a bum like me in a place like this with a girl like this. I flushed and tingled all over, moving to the elevator, keeping my eyes off the other attendant who was there waiting for it to descend, but knowing that he was not keeping his eyes off me. The outer doors of the elevator opened and the inner doors opened and we stepped in.

'Good night, Miss Dobson,' said the attendant. 'Good evening, Miss Dobson,' said the elevator operator, and as the doors closed I dared to lift my eyes and I had a flash of this garage attendant's face and sure enough it had shock in it too.

I moved around, trying to get behind the elevator operator, trying to hide from his eyes, feeling that I was very conspicuous. He was middle-aged and wore white livery; and I had the impression that the rug on the floor was white and that the walls of the cage were white.... With no direction from her, he stopped the elevator at the fifth floor and opened the doors, and as she started out, he said, 'Good night, Miss Dobson.'

'Good night,' said she, and I went out behind her, swiftly, still not giving him a chance to be shocked, and I heard the doors close and the elevator start down, going straight to the garage where the three flunkies could gossip about that bum the Dobson girl had dragged in. . . .

There was no need for me to ask questions now. I knew where we were; this was where she lived. 'I thought you lived at Forty-One Hundred Willow Creek Drive,' I said. 'What made you think that?' she asked. 'The registration certificate in your car,' I said. 'I read it while I was waiting.' 'Oh . . .' she said. 'Well, once in a while I live there and once in a while I live here.' 'This is nice,' I said. 'Very high-class. I can always tell a high-class place from the degree of shock the flunkies get into their faces when they see me come in. The more high-class the place the greater the shock.' She laughed merrily, pausing in front of a door.

She turned the knob and we went in. It was a small entrance hall, with the walls painted dark green.

'Put your hat there . . .' she said.

I put my hat on the console table, taking a look at myself in the girandole that hung from the wall, and now I could see in what particular and in what detail my clothes were cheap and disreputable; the second-hand suit didn't fit and was unpressed, the white cotton shirt was almost dirty and the collar sagged and the dime store necktie into which you couldn't get a decent knot was already cracked from only three or four tyings. I needed a haircut and my face was gaunt and undernourished. No wonder the flunkies were shocked. I was shocked myself. I looked like a bum, all right, and in a place like this, as high-class as this, I looked ten times a bum. That a girl of her background could be unaware of this was inconceivable. What the hell was this anyway?

There was a white chenille rug in the living-room and the walls were green and the drapes were white with red fringe, now drawn closed. Thank God, the neighbors couldn't see me. All the furniture was covered with red and green chintz, and along the mantel a copper pan had been inserted from which a species of ivy grew and trailed: the table lights were big-shaded and improvised from green vases. It was all soft and opulent, spotless and shiny, in keeping with Delages and Cadillacs and gold keys and key-rings from Cartier's and obsequiousness from flunkies. The only thing it wasn't in keeping with was I. . . .

'The chief charm of this apartment for me,' she said, 'is its convenience. It's close in. The other place is out from town.'

'This is nice. Very high-class,' I said.

'Miss Dobson . . .' a woman's voice said.

She turned and I turned, jumping a little. A woman of about thirty-five or forty was standing in the doorway that led off to the rest of the apartment, a nice-looking woman who wore a black dress and a small white maid's apron. 'Your father called,' she said.

'Thank you, Julia. Is there ice in the bar?'

'Yes, Miss Dobson. He said would you please call him back this time?'

'Very well, Julia. That'll be all for tonight. . . .'

'Yes, Miss Dobson. Good night,' Julia said, and now with no message to interfere with her looking, she looked. There being no place to hide, I had braced myself for this. The expression that came into her face was just what I had expected, and she turned at once and went out.

'Would you like a drink?'

'Would you?' I asked.

'Yes, I think I would. Let's go in the bar. . . .'

The bar was next to the living-room. It was a small bar and the walls were were done in the same shade of green, and the furniture and the stools and the bar itself were done in red leather. Behind the bar were four rows of mirrored shelves, stacked with bottles.

'This used to be a closet,' she said. 'I turned it into a saloon.' She lifted the hinged end of the bar, going behind it. 'Now all I need is to have my liquor license renewed,' she said, laughing. 'Scotch?'

'Cognac . . .'

'Any preference?'

'Well . . .'

'Half a dozen kinds here. Might as well have what you've been used to. . . .'

'I've been used to Delamain,' I said.

'Delamain?' She looked on the shelf. 'No Delamain . . .'

'Remy Martin's all right.'

She looked again, 'No Remy Martin . . .'

'Anything. Doesn't matter,' I said indifferently.

'Otard?'

'Otard's fine,' I said.

She put a bottle of Otard and a brandy glass on the bar and I poured some cognac while she fixed a drink for herself. 'Me, I like Cuttysark,' she said. She dropped ice cubes in the glass and raised it to toast. 'What'll we drink to?'

'Flunkies,' I said.

'Flunkies,' she said.

We drank, and she came out from behind the bar, moving to the wall seat opposite, and I slid around on the stool to face her. She sat down and sipped her drink, studiously looking at me over the rim of her glass. It was almost a stare. I looked around the walls, taking another taste of cognac, giving her a chance to take the stare off her face and put on something more polite, but when I brought my eyes back to her I saw that the expression had not changed.

'Well,' I said, 'I guess you'll miss this place. . . .'

'Miss it?' she said.

'When you move . . .'

'I'm not moving. . . .'

'You don't know it, baby, but you're moving. Not for long, probably, but you're moving. She'll tell you about it tomorrow.'

'*She'll* tell me? Who'll tell me?'

'That woman, that maid. Julia. Didn't you see that look in her face when she saw me? She's having the place fumigated first thing in the morning. She'll probably burn all your clothes, too.'

She laughed and took a sip of her drink. 'You've got quite a sense of humor,' she said.

'Yes, haven't I?' I took a swallow of cognac and looked at her. 'What is this – a social experiment? More cosmic consciousness?'

'What're you talking about?'

'I'm talking about us,' I said evenly. 'Why bring a bum like me to place like this?'

'This is were I live. I wanted you to come here,' she said, with some spirit.

202

'Doesn't what your flunkies think of the kind of guests you have concern you?'

'Certainly not! They're *my guests* . . .'

'Well, I suppose the record now belongs to me. I'm sure you've never entertained a more disreputable-looking guy.'

'What's the matter with the way you look?'

'You ought to know,' I said. 'You've been sitting there staring at me. . . .'

'Was I staring?'

'That's perfectly all right,' I said. 'Go ahead and stare. Scientists stare. That's what specimens are for. It's not considered rude.'

She got up and came to the bar, standing beside me. 'I didn't mean to stare,' she said. 'I apologize if I've hurt your feelings. I was just looking at you. Do you realize that this is the first time I've had a good look at you? After all that's happened between us, don't you think I'm entitled to know what you look like?'

'Well, by God, you ought to know by now, you and your flunkies,' I said. 'You've done everything but put a microscope on me.'

Her jaw muscles tightened. 'You're too self-conscious,' she said.

'I told you last night. Inferiority. Now you see it working.' I took a swallow of cognac. 'Frightful things . . .'

'If you know what it is you should be able to correct it,' she said.

'I'll get it corrected when I can get out of these clothes,' I said. 'Cheap shoddy clothes for cheap shoddy people. Typical American stuff. Two ninety-eight shoes and production-line suits. I'll get it corrected when I can get some Peals and Izods and Milbank and Howse. Mead gabardines and John Hardy flannels and some Godchaux linens.'

'And some Delamain cognac . . .' she said thinly.

'And some Delamain cognac,' I said. 'Tell you what you do' – I said in cold anger – 'you get all the goddamn connoisseurs you know, for whom you have any respect – connoisseurs isn't the right word, it isn't properly shaded, degustateurs is the right word – you get 'em all with me some night and blindfold us and put ten brands of cognac in front of us and see who's faking. . . .'

'I didn't say you were faking.'

'Dames like you don't have the guts to say what they think. Dames like you have to be content with implying what they think.'

'It seems to me that you're being very disagreeable,' she said. She moved slightly to the side of me. 'Can't we just talk and be friends? There's so much I want to talk to you about. There's so much I have to talk to you about. If you'll stop being so rough and tough, maybe we can find out why you like being disagreeable.'

'Nuts,' I said. I took another swallow of cognac, turning away from her.

'Are you *that* uncomfortable?' she asked.

'Yeah,' I said.

'Would you like to leave now?'

'Yeah, I'd like to leave now,' I said. I put down the cognac glass and pushed myself off the stool.

'I'm sorry . . .' she said.

'Forget it . . .' I said.

'I'm sorry it couldn't have been like last night. . . .'

'So am I . . .' I said.

'But it obviously couldn't,' she said quietly. 'The kind of ecstasy that came last night can only come from Brahmanada, and Brahmanada can only be arranged by Fate. Fate arranged last night. Tonight, I – a mere nothing – tried to arrange it.' She laughed unhappily. 'A ritual like that cannot be arranged by a nothing, by an amateur, by a dabbler, That's what I am – just a dabbler.' She held up her drink. 'This last one's to me,' she said. 'To the Sorcerer's Apprentice . . .'

I was thinking, when she first had started talking like that, that she was just spouting the same nonsense other girls did, other girls who had more leisure time than anything else, and sat around before and after rehearsals on the gloomy stages of Little Theatres drinking bad gin and speculating on Kismet and Fate and the true meaning of Leonardo's loveless life and the importance of Carl Van Vechten and the rightful place in American letters of E. Pettit; girls who were pushovers for smart boys like me – it sounded like the old stuff. But by the time she had finished it dawned on me that this wasn't the old stuff at all; this was real. She was utterly sincere. Last night on the grassy slope, under that oak tree, she had submitted to me not from desire but because she read into my plainly curious behavior some sort of totemic significance. What followed had not been for her a physical experience, it had been an intellectual experience, a cabalistic adventure. She was a dabbler; a dabbler in the esoteric philosophy of Dr Green, and God knew who else, and once they get off the deep end of this, it is but a short breast-stroke (if they can swim) to the occult and voodoo and black magic and diabolism. . . . Get out of here, you bastard, I told myself, get out of here fast; and then I became aware of one other thing – I was trembling. Trembling not with fear, but trembling with the sudden realization that last night had not been a true physical experience for me either, for me too it had been a ceremony, ritual-cloaked . . .

I went to the wall and snapped off the lights and went back to her. There was just enough light reflecting from the hall for me to see the outline of her body and the whiskey glass she had put on the bar. I went close to her. Her eyes were closed and she was standing rigidly, almost cataleptically, her fists clenched, not breathing – exactly as I had asked her to do the last time, trying desperately to summon from her own private Infinite whatever it was that had come last night and prepared her for ectasy.

My eyes were full of her white-white face and her black-black hair, and then the smell of the *Heule de Noche* rolled over me . . .

That awareness from the Miocene was moving in on me, that infallible awareness that serves the purpose of preserving man's existence, and was waking fast. Then I caught an enemy scent and heard body movement and in the flash that my eyes were opening I spun my brain trying to remember where in that strange dark room was the chair that held my coat and gun, and the light on her night table snapped on and I saw a man standing there. He was big and baldheaded and aristocratic, a man of about sixty, wearing a blue suit and a bow tie, and he was shaking Margaret, trying to waken her, paying no attention to me. My heart flopped and that red flash hit me in the stomach and, I saw my coat on the back of a chair and I swung my feet from under the sheet, to get my gun. 'Hold it, son,' I heard a voice say, not the big man's voice, but another voice somewhere in the room.

Two other men were standing just inside the door, both of them still wearing their hats. There was nothing aristocratic about them. They were cops. They were in street clothes but I knew they were cops. They just stood there.

'Midge, dear, Midge, dear . . .' the baldheaded man was saying, and it dawned on me that this could only be her father. 'Midge, dear . . .' he was saying.

Margaret muttered some sleepy unintelligible something and then her eyes opened and she saw him. She quickly sat up, holding the sheet under her arms to cover her nakedness, looking at me wildly. But only for a moment was there wildness in her face, and then she got her bearings. 'You shouldn't do things like this, Father . . .' she said.

'I thought this was probably why you didn't return my call,' he said tensely. He picked up her wrapper and and held it over the bed, screening her against the brocaded headboard. 'Put this on,' he said. 'Take this man out of here,' he said to the cops.

They started towards me . . .

'You'd better stop them, Father,' she said calmly.

They kept coming, but they glanced cautiously at the old man.

'Take this man out of here,' he said.

They stopped beside me. I started to get out of bed.

'Wait a minute!' Margaret said to the cops. 'This is ridiculous! Father,' she said to the old man, 'I want you to meet my husband, Paul Murphy. This is my father, Paul . . .'

Jesus, I thought. Holy Jesus!

Ezra Dobson's jaw dropped and he looked at me with narrow eyes. 'Husband? Married? Married! When?' he asked indignantly.

'Tonight. Earlier . . .' she said. 'We were going to tell you all about it at breakfast, but . . .'

'My God, my God,' the old man murmured in a lifeless whisperation, and I knew then that she'd stopped him. I felt better. I didn't know where we were going from here, but at least she'd given me time to think.

'Will you please ask your private policemen to leave?' she asked.

He looked at them and waved them out. They shrugged and moved to the door.

'Really, Father,' Margaret said. 'You make things so awkward sometimes. I'm sure Paul must be wondering what kind of family he's gotten into . . .'

She smiled at me, knowing that he was looking at her, intending it as an apology for him. She was doing great. She was a dame who kept her head and thought fast and also knew where to place the bullet. She had placed it just in time. Those cops looked like tough customers. I didn't know what they had intended doing with me, but I was very glad to have missed it, not because I was afraid of what they might do to me, but because I was afraid of what I might do to them. This was no time to be killing cops, not hemmed up like this, not with the

City Hall fitting so nicely into my pocket.

'Of course, we were wrong,' Margaret was saying. 'We should have waited. It was impulsive and insane and I'm very sorry, but you can raise all the hell you like and it won't change things.'

Ezra Dobson slowly lowered the wrapper that was screening her, and dropped it on the bed. 'I don't understand you, I don't understand you,' he slumped and he walked to the foot of the bed and stood looking at me.

'Don't blame Paul,' she said. 'It's all my fault.'

'It's mine too,' I said.

'Who else knows about this? the old man asked.

'The clerk, the justice of the peace . . .' she said.

'The justice's wife too,' I said. 'She was the witness.'

'Nobody else?'

'No,' she said.

'When'd it happen?'

'A few hours ago.'

'Where?'

'Across the state line.'

'Did they know who you were?'

'I don't think so.'

'That's why you signed the license "M. Dobson",' I said in feigned surprise. 'You didn't want them to know who you were.'

'Yes . . .' she said.

'I wondered about that . . .' I said. I was doing great, too. . . .

The old man looked at the ceiling, taking his eyes off us, and in that instant she nudged me to go on talking, wanting me to help her out. But what the hell else could I say? All I could do was to sit there like a dummy, following her lead, and wishing I'd never got mixed up in this and trying to figure a way out.

'Why in God's name did you have to cross the state line to get married?' the old man asked.

'Because we couldn't wait the customary three days in this state,' she said.

'What's three days if you're going to get married? What's three days? How long have you known this man?'

'Please, Father. This is very embarrassing to Paul. I've told you it was an insane impulse and I'm sorry. Can't we talk about it in the morning? We'll explain everything in the morning.'

He nodded grimly. 'Yes, we can talk about it in the morning. Meantime, you're going home with me. Put your clothes on.'

'You're mistaken,' she said. 'I'm not going with you.'

'You're going with me if I have to get Zumbro and Scott back in here to carry you out. Now, put your clothes on!'

'You'd better not. Believe me, you'd better not.'

I looked at her in amazement. This was the easy way out. Didn't she know that? What a hell of a time to be obstinate. If she started a fight now, no telling where it would end. 'I think your father's right,' I said. 'Go on home with him. We can talk about this tomorrow.'

She swept her eyes at me contemptuously. Well, screw the way you feel, I thought. I'm the one who's got his things caught in this wringer, not you, and all I want is loose. Goddamn it, I thought. 'A few hours out of our lives is not that important,' I said. 'We can talk this over tomorrow.'

'Margaret,' the old man said, 'are you going to put your clothes on?'

'No!' she said, almost shouting. 'Now, look here, Father. We've had these conflicts of will before, and it's no good having another one. I've said all I intend to say. Either you take those men and leave, or you have them carry me out bodily and live to regret it for the rest of your life. You know how you hate scenes, Father. I'll wake up this whole building. . . .'

His eyes were beady and his cheeks were puffed in rage.

'I shall expect you in the morning,' he said shortly. He

209

wheeled and started to the door and then stopped and turned. 'Will you please do me the small courtesy of not saying anything about this until after we've talked?' he asked acidly.

'Yes, Father. . . .' she said.

He went out. She jumped from the bed, putting on her wrapper, going out after him. I couldn't figure this move and I didn't even try to. . . I got up and grabbed my clothes, all of them, and went into the bathroom and locked the door. I started dressing as fast as I could, telling myself that if I got out of this, I never again would venture among the dead, never again; and in a minute there was a light rap at the door.

'You in there?' she said.

'It's all right now. They're gone.'

I picked up the rest of my clothes, draping the coat over my left arm, making the pocket that held my gun instantly accessible, and opened the door. She laughed. I had on a pair of shorts, two socks and one shoe. 'What's your hurry?' she asked.

'I'm getting out of here,' I said.

'We both are.'

'Thank God!' I said. 'But it sure looked rocky for a while.'

'The only time it looked rocky was when you jumped on his side. When you suggested that I go home with him. That damn near fixed it good.'

'*That* fixed it? Jesus, how can you say that? All I wanted was to get out of here without a fight. I didn't know he was gonna give in to you.'

'I did,' she said. 'Don't think I haven't learned how to handle my father. . . .'

'I can see that now,' I said.

'Well, I'll dress. We'd better be starting.'

'*We'd* better be starting?' I'd had enough of her. 'Where?'

'To get married. I told Father we were married. You remember.'

'Yeah. I remember. It was fast thinking too.'

210

'And now we'll have to do it.'

'Do what?'

'Get married.'

I looked at her. She was serious. She really meant it. 'Like hell we'll get married,' I said. 'All I want is out. From now on, I'll take mine in the country. I love the country. Never again will I squawk about my clothes getting dirty.'

'And what happens to me when I show up before my father without my husband?'

'That's your problem. You got plenty of time to figure that one. Fast as you think you'll probably have a lot of time left over. . . .'

'We've *got* to be married,' she said.

I laughed. 'Pardon me,' I said, going past her into the bedroom. I dropped my clothes on the floor and sat down in a chair and put on my other shoe.

She came out and stood beside me. 'Won't you please try to understand this?' she asked.

'You talk like a lunatic,' I said. 'You don't know anything about me – who I am, where I came from, where I'm going, what I do – you just don't know anything at all about me.'

'That's not important to me now,' she said.

'It'll be important to your father. Rich men are very particular about such things. . . .' What could I answer to his questions? Not the truth; I'd have to answer with lies. And how long would lies stand up? For only as long as it took his bloodhounds to find out they were lies. And what would happen then, with those bloodhounds loose? I'd have to start running again. . . .

'It's got to be done,' she was saying. 'Otherwise, he'll think I'm a common little tart, sleeping with any man I can get my hands on. That's a matter of morals he would *never* forgive.'

'What he forgives and what he doesn't forgive is no worry of mine,' I said.

'It will be when I tell him that you seduced me under promise of marriage and then changed your mind – and then ran out on me. You might discover that the consequences of that would be much more unpleasant than the consequences of actually marrying me – especially if you intend to stay in this town. . . .'

I laughed to myself. Why was this such a surprise? Why had I expected anything different from her? Cadillacs and Delages and gold gadgets from Cartier couldn't change the story; it was the same on both sides of the track. A tail in a crack was a tail in a crack . . . 'Yes,' I said, 'I suppose in this town your father could make it pretty rough on somebody he didn't like.'

'As a *great* many people have found out,' she said.

So she had me; marriage or not, she had me – either way the bloodhounds would be turned loose. I had an ache in my stomach, the thought of running again gave me an ache in my stomach, but I knew this served me right, it goddamn well served me right for digging into those ancient memories, for stirring those ghosts for trying to find out, for being so curious. . . . Well, now I had to take the City Hall out of my pocket and put it back in its squalid frame and take a farewell look at that shining tower. There'd be other towns with City Halls, all towns had City Halls you could put in your pocket once you found the gimmick, but finding the gimmick was what counted. Well, what the hell: I had found the gimmick in one town, I could find it in another. I was young, I had my whole life ahead of me. By dawn I could be well on my way to Arizona. Dillinger and Clark and Makley were down there somewhere – cooling off. Maybe I could get in with them till I could start my own business again. Maybe I'd go on to California, Nelson and Van Meter were out there somewhere punks; but at least they could give me some quick contacts with the cops. I could use Holiday for bait, she was a hell of a piece of bait, *she* was physical. . . .

'Why risk my father getting down on you?' Margaret was

saying. 'A marriage will save all of us: you, me, and Father. That's what he thinks this is – a silly impetuous marriage, with both of us slightly drunk. There's nothing immoral about that; it simply is a mistake of judgement. *That* he will forgive. He'll have it annulled and that's all there is to it.'

'Annulled? . . .' I said.

She looked at me. 'Certainly. It's quite easy for him.'

'I don't want any part of this,' I said.

'Please don't think you'd be required to live with me. You wouldn't. Father could have it annulled in a few seconds. And at a profit to you. My father's a very rich man. All those wonderful things you could buy. . . . You could use some money, couldn't you?'

I hadn't known about annulments. The possibility of collecting money for an annulment had not occurred to me. 'I can always use money,' I said.

'And then I have some money of my own. A little . . .'

'How much to you is a little?'

'Oh, ten thousand. Twenty-five thousand from Father . . .'

'Thirty-five thousand,' I said.

'Can you afford that every night of the week?'

She suddenly slapped me across my face. My eyes fuzzed and my right arm tensed and I started to hit her. But I didn't hit her. I saw the white whiteness of her face just in time to stop. 'Where's this place you get married? How far?' I asked.

She bit her lip. 'About seventy-five miles.'

'Get your clothes on. . . .' I said.

... *chapter*
five

Mandon looked up from the marriage certificate. 'Why did she sign this *M.* Dobson?' he asked.

'I had to make it match the story I told her father,' I said.

He folded the marriage certificate in its original creases and handed it back to me. 'Why don't you let me handle these things?' he said. 'I'm your lawyer. Why don't you consult with me?'

'What was there to consult about? I just got through telling you all I wanted was out, to get rid of her. The quickest way was to marry her.'

'Well, your great haste has just cost you sixty-five thousand dollars,' he said. 'Sixty-five grand – that's what you've lost. For that document I could have gotten one hundred thousand dollars. And you agreed to thirty-five. Jesus. Thirty-five...'

'If it'll make you feel any better, I'm not even taking that,' I said.

'What?' he said.

'I said, I'm not even taking the thirty-five. He can have the annulment.'

'Have it?'

'For free. I'm not taking one penny from him.'

'Stop needling me,' he growled.

'I'm not needling you,' I said. 'I mean it. Not one penny am I taking, not one goddamn penny. I figure I'm a lucky guy to get off this cheap....'

'Cheap?' he said. Slowly his big eyebrows went up, and slowly wrath came into his face. 'You bloody fool!' he said. 'You goddamn poor bloody fool! Do you know who Ezra Dobson is? He's got so many millions ... Why, there're men who spend their whole lives looking for a soft touch like this, and you have it dumped in your lap – right in your lap – and you won't take it. Why, this is worth a fortune!'

'Think some more about it,' I said. 'Go on – I'll wait. I got time.'

'I don't have to think any more. You've something he wants. Thirty-five thousand is cigarette money to him. . . .'

'That's what I thought too, at first – a soft touch,' I said. 'That's what you think when you think only for five minutes, which is all the long you've been thinking. But I've been thinking about it all night – all the way up to that hick marriage town and all the way back. I've been thinking. And it's not so soft after you think about it for more than five minutes. . . .'

He spread his hands, shaking his head slowly. 'Jesus, you *are* crazy,' he said. 'Holiday was right. Webber was right. You *are* crazy.'

'I've been crazy ever since that day a fox bit me in the ass,' I said. 'Dobson's just too big for me to tangle with, that's all.'

'How can you tangle with him? You've got something to sell and he wants to buy it. The price has been agreed on – and a goddamn cheap price, at that.'

'She agreed to it, not he. . . .'

'Well, what's the difference?'

'Maybe none, maybe a lot. I'm in no position to take the risk, not with what I've got hanging over me – enough to gas or fry me six times over. I've got some other reasons too, but they're too abstract even for me to grasp yet. Use your bean, Cherokee. I haven't been outraged, I haven't been victimized, I'm not fighting a rich man for justice. I'm the protagonist in a shake-

215

down. He knows that, he's got to know it.'

'I tell you he'll pay off,' he said.

'What if he does? What then? Will it stop there? You think a guy as big as he is will let a ragged stranger make a sucker out of him? You know very well he won't. He'll turn his bloodhounds loose and I'll have to start running again. I've spent most of my life running. I'm tired of sleeping in river bottoms and drinking polluted water and washing my teeth with the end of my forefinger and wearing rags and eating out of garbage cans and having my goddamn heart tear loose from its muscles every time I see a cop. No, sir, by God, absolutely not. I'll lay this down nice and easy and not disturb one penny of his big high stack. I've got one bone in my mouth. That reflection in the water doesn't fool me a bit. . . .'

He got down from the desk and went to the commode, the close-stool, and got a drink of water, drinking from the lip of the big flowered pitcher. Sure, he thought I was crazy, and I wasn't going to argue with him any more. He was a lawyer; all he was after was the dough. This would be duck soup for him; but it would be my ears that would ring with the yelp of his bloodhounds . . .

'You're a tornado,' he said. 'You're a cyclone. You're a ball of fire. How in the name of the good and holy God did you ever get yourself into a bloody mess like this? With a whole town full of girls how'd you happen to pick on this one?'

'I've wondered about that myself,' I said. 'I've wondered about it a lot.'

'Well,' he said gruffly, 'go on and get it over with and put it out of your mind and let's settle down to business. What's the matter with you?' he said suddenly. 'What are you shaking about?'

'Shaking?'

I was. I hadn't been aware of it, but I was. I was shaking all over.

216

'Jesus,' he said. 'You *must* be scared of the Old Man.'

The Old Man?

How could I tell him, how could I put it into words that he would understand ... ?'

There was a private switchboard in the big reception room of Golightly and Gackel's office. The girl announced me to somebody, and a heavy glass door popped open and a prim woman came out, a woman of about forty-five, and led me down a narrow sacred corridor to Mr. Golightly's office.

The office looked more like a library than an office. Mr. Golightly was tall and slender and wore a high linen collar and looked very antiseptic. 'Come in, Mister Murphy,' he said crisply. 'Mister Dobson and his daughter will join us in a moment. Smoke?'

He picked up a crystal humidor on his desk and held it open. 'Thank you,' I said, taking a cigarette.

He picked up a crystal lighter and flicked it several times, but the sparks wouldn't ignite the wick, and he laughed a little nervously and put it down and took a gold Dunhill lighter from his pocket and lighted my cigarette with that. Then an inner door opened and Ezra Dobson and Margaret came in.

Ezra Dobson looked very stern. He wore a gray suit and a blue bow tie, Margaret wore a tailored suit and brogue walking shoes. He said nothing. She said, 'Good morning, Paul. . . .'

'Good morning,' I said, holding myself steady, telling myself it would all be over in a minute, the sepulchre would be sealed again and I would be finally free. . . .

'Smoke?' Mr. Golightly said to them.

Neither of them took a cigarette. Mr. Golightly put down the crystal humidor and looked at me. 'I understand, Mister Murphy, that you have expressed a desire to rectify this unfortunate situation?' he said.

217

'Yes,' I said.

'You have agreed to sign a petition to have this marriage annulled?'

'Yes,' I said.

'You are – er – willing to swear' – he cleared his throat – 'that you and Miss Dobson have not lived together as man and wife?'

I glanced at her. She was looking straight at me, making no effort to avoid my eyes. 'Yes,' I said.

He nodded and pressed a button. Another inner door opened and the prim secretary came in, holding something in her hand.

'You will please sign here,' he said to me.

He moved a sheet of paper on the desk and handed me a pen. 'There . . .' he said, indicating the line. I signed it. The prim secretary put the thing on the desk that she had been holding in her hand and I now saw that it was a notary's seal. 'Now you, Margaret. . . .' he said.

Margaret came over and signed it. and Mr. Golightly handed it to the secretary, and she moved around to the other edge of the desk, out of the way, and stamped it with a rubber stamp and started signing it too. Mr. Golightly picked up a check from the desk and handed it to me. 'I believe that was the sum agreed on,' he said.

It was Ezra Dobson's personal check for $35,000.00. I unfolded it. The detachable voucher read:

Remittance from Ezra Dobson

Description	Account	Amount
Annulment of marriage to Margaret Dobson	401	$35,000.00

Detach statement before depositing

Mr. Golightly now handed me a neat-looking legal paper in a light blue backing. 'This is a waiver,' he said. 'It merely states that

218

from now and henceforth you renounce all further claims to the estates of Ezra and Margaret Dobson. Would you like for *me* to read it?'

'No,' I said.

'Before you sign it you have a legal right to know exactly what the instrument contains,' he said.

I looked from Mr. Golightly to Ezra Dobson. His face was dark with the ordeal. I looked at Margaret. Her face was impassive.

'I'll sign it,' I said.

I signed it.

'Is that all I have to sign?' I asked.

'Yes. . . .' Mr. Golightly said.

I put the check on the desk and looked at Ezra Dobson. 'I don't want this money, Mister Dobson,' I said. 'I regret this just as much as you do, just as much as Margaret does. It was thoughtless and childish of both of us. For my part, I'm very sorry – as I know Margaret is. Good day, sir, good-bye, Margaret. . . .'

I took the marriage certificate out of my pocket and put it on top of the check and walked out.

. . . part three

... *chapter* *one*

One guy was little and the other two were medium-sized, built like middleweights. They came out of the beauty parlor, the little one carrying the satchel, and got into a black Buick sedan that was parked in a loading zone five buildings away, the little one seating himself in front with the driver, who had been waiting under the wheel, and the two middleweights getting into the back. They pulled out and leisurely moved away down the street.

One, two, three, four, five, six times this was repeated in different parts of town – in one tobacco shop, one beer joint and four more beauty parlors – and the procedure was the same: the entrance, the length of time they stayed in each place, the exit, with the little one always carrying the satchel. The only things that varied were the satchels. Some were black and some were tan; he made seven stops and he evidently had seven satchels.

Down the street, in Mandon's car, we waited until the Buick was half a block ahead and then I told Jinx to keep on tailing it.

'We been tailing for two hours already,' Jinx said, starting the car. 'We keep this up much longer we're a cinch to give 'em the office ...'

'You heard Cherokee, didn't you?' I said. 'They been doing this so long and with such safety that they're fat, cocky and careless. They're not concentrating any more. We couldn't give 'em the office even if we moved right in behind 'em. They got this sewed up. Fat, cocky and careless ...'

'. . . Seven satchels, all filled with money,' Mandon said.

'What's your guess on how much money?' I asked.

'Plenty. Roamer'll take a bet on any track in the country and pay track odds. You know how people bet on the horses . . .'

'Make a guess . . .'

'It's hard to say. Fifteen thousand, maybe fifty. He's got the bookie business cornered.'

'He's got you cornered too, hasn't he?' I asked. 'How much you in to him for?'

'Not a dime, not a thin dime. Nobody gets into Roamer. That's why those satchels are stuffed with money.'

I knew he was a goddamn liar. He was in to him – for a hunk. That's what that telephone call in his office yesterday was about. When he saw this guy's name, Roamer, on that telephone message he got worried. He was worried all the time he was talking to him too, for the simple reason that Roamer was putting the squeeze on him. Then I remembered how he had all of a sudden brightened – that would be when he thought of this. But I didn't say anything. I was keeping my eyes on the black Buick, trying to figure a way to take it in all this traffic. There didn't seem to be any way – not without attracting too much attention. Every stop it made was on a busy street and it never once got off a busy street.

'What do you think, Jinx?' I asked.

'Looks like murder,' he said.

'That's what I think too,' I said. 'You see that, don't you?' I said to Mandon. 'You see how hopeless this is – why don't we have a look at the guy's headquarters, the place where this dough winds up. Maybe that's where the trigger is.'

'It's not there,' Mandon said. 'There're more people there than there are around here. . . . Of course,' he said, 'if you'd done what I suggested earlier this morning . . .'

'But I didn't. . . .' I said.

'What was it?' Jinx asked.

'Nothing,' I said. 'It was a worse idea than this one.'

Three cars ahead of us, getting into heavier traffic all the time, approaching the shopping district, the Buick turned a corner.

'Want me to hang on?' Jinx asked.

'Forget it,' I said. 'We've wasted damn near the whole day now – I'm tired. I want to get to bed.'

Jinx went on, straight across the intersection, pulling up behind a police cruiser, a traffic-control car, that was parked double, the rear bumper almost in the pedestrian lane, blocking us. A coupe was parked in a red zone and one of the cops was writing out a ticket.

Mandon and I saw this at the same time and from the smile on his face I knew that he was thinking the same thing I was. But I beat him to it.

'There's no sense in having a gimmick if you don't use it,' I said. 'I keep forgetting that the cops're on our side.'

'That's the answer, right there,' he said.

'That's the answer,' I said. 'Call Webber...'

'Let's go back to my place, Jinx,' he said.

'Why your place?' I asked. 'There's a drug store over there. Jinx, stick this thing in the first lot you can find and meet us in the drug store. At the soda fountain.'

I opened the door. 'Come on,' I said to Mandon.

He got out and we crossed the street.

'Webber won't like this,' Mandon said.

'The hell with what he likes,' I said.

'Too much chance for a kickback...'

'Call him,' I said. 'Make it right away...'

He went into a telephone booth and I went to the soda fountain. A soda jerk was mixing a drink as I sat down in front of the pumps. It looked familiar. 'What's that?' I asked.

'Cherry phosphate...' he said.

'I'll have one,' I said. My God, cherry phosphate! The first soft drink I ever had was a cherry phosphate. It was in Knoxville. I had gone with my grandfather to the East Tennessee Fair. He had five hogs entered. Cherry phosphate...

'He's not there,' Mandon said.

'When's he expected?'

'They don't know. I left word for him to call me at the office.'

'We can't budge till we see him,' I said.

'Well, he'll call sometime...'

The soda jerk put down my cherry phosphate. 'Want a drink?' I asked Mandon.

'What's that you're having?'

'Just some slop. I'm a sentimentalist....'

'Coke...' Mandon said to the soda jerk.

Jinx came up to us.

'He's not in,' I told him. 'Cherokee left a call.'

'You think he'll call back?' Jinx asked.

'You tell him,' I said to Mandon.

'He'll call,' Mandon said.

'Want a drink?' I asked Jinx.

'What's that you're having?'

'Just some slop. I'm a sentimentalist....'

'Coke...' Jinx said to the soda jerk.

I finished my cherry phosphate. My God, cherry phosphate... 'I'm going to run a few errands,' I said to them. 'I'll be back at the apartment in an hour. I got to explain why I didn't show last night. I got to think up a cute story about what you and I did last night, Cherokee....'

'Holiday's got to think up one too,' Jinx said. 'She didn't show either....'

'What?' I said.

'I had the whole place to myself last night,' he said.

'Where was she?'

226

'I dunno. She left around eleven and didn't come back.'

'Who was she with?'

'Reece, I think . . .'

'Reece, the cop?'

'I think so. She told me she was only going for a walk. I slipped out the back door and saw her get into a car at the corner. It looked like Reece.'

'I'll be a son-of-a-bitch,' I said.

'Fine thing,' Mandon said. 'You beating your brains out all last night trying to turn an honest dollar for her and she's off cheating on you. Fine thing . . .'

So who gives a damn, I kept asking myself all the time I was buying the stuff, who cares? I knew by now that she was the kind of a dame you couldn't turn your back on for five minutes without her having a body scissors on somebody, I knew that; I expected that and why pretend to be surprised? Who really gave a damn? Oh, sure, I had thought at one time that she was very valuable to me, but when a guy had been on a diet of saltpetre for as long as I had, and finally broke it, he was likely to think that the first woman he had was the woman to end all women, and that his life would be unlivable if she was ever more than a soft whisper away, if ever another man's eyes even strayed at her. A guy had a right to get emotional about that. But then gradually his own blood stream does to that narcotic what the Mississippi does to the Missouri; and he discovers that every other woman is possessed of the same fascinating equipment, all of them, so who gives a damn about any one of them?

I had to put the bundles on the floor of the hall so I could open the apartment door. I opened it and heard her voice coming from the bathroom, calling: 'Jinx?'

'It's I . . .' I said.

Scrub yourself hard, I wanted to say, scrub yourself very hard, that police stink is a tenacious stink. 'Good afternoon,' I said.

'What've you got there?' she asked.

'Just some crap . . .' I said.

'Something for me?'

'Next time . . .' I said.

I moved over to the bed and dumped the packages and was opening them when she came out of the bathroom, drying herself. Little beads of water clung to her body like drops of spring dew to a sugar-maple leaf. The body was beautiful and I looked at it full and frankly, waiting for the quiver within me, listening for the moaning of the strings of the corpora cavernosa; but no quiver came and no moaning was heard.

'I see you got that haircut you've been wanting,' she said.

'I got a shampoo too, but you can't see that,' I said.

'I can smell it,' she said. 'What's in the bundles?'

'Just some crap . . .'

'Must've cost a lot of money – all that,' she said. She was very friendly. Everything about her was very friendly. . . .

'This is only the beginning,' I said.

'Where'd the dough come from. Pull a job by yourself?'

'Nope.'

She sat down on the bed and picked up a box of shirts.

'Will you please not drip water all over my new shirts?' I asked.

She put the box down and looked at me. 'Please don't be sore at me,' she said.

'I'm not sore,' I said. 'Will you please fix some toast or soup or something? I'm hungry. Any milk here?'

'Yes,' she said slowly.

I went out and into the kitchen and got a bottle of milk from the icebox and poured some in a glass. I was drinking it, my back to the door, and I did not know she was there until I heard her speak. She said: 'Aren't you going to ask me any questions?'

'About what?' I said, turning around. She wore only the towel, knotted at her hips.

228

'About last night . . .'

I frowned as if I didn't know what she meant. 'Oh – you mean about where you were?'

'Yes.'

I couldn't help but think of how marvellous this was, yesterday's situation being reversed, even to the towel. Was she aware of this? Probably not. 'Why should I ask questions?' I said. 'That presupposes that I'm interested.'

'You would be if you knew who I was with. . . .'

'I know who you were with.'

'Who?'

'Reece.'

She did not seem surprised. 'Who told you? Jinx?'

'That's right.'

'He's a little sneak,' she said coldly.

'Not at all,' I said. 'You decided to take a walk and he decided to take a walk at the same time. Just a coincidence. He happened to see you. Just another coincidence. Will you please fix some soup or something?'

'Don't be sore, Ralph.'

'Paul,' I said.

'Will you not be sore?'

'Christ,' I said. 'I'm not sore. How can I be sore if I don't give a damn? With you it's just like hunger and you're a dame with a big appetite. You can't help it if you got a tapeworm. But of all people, a cop. And of all cops, that one . . .'

'I had to find out, I *had* to find out,' she said. 'What you were talking about yesterday – this set-up. I just couldn't make myself believe it was as good as you thought. As fool-proof . . .'

How could she find out by going with that pig? 'What does he know?' I said. 'He's a goddamn flunky. . . .'

'You're making a mistake to think that,' she said. 'He's a lot smarter than you give him credit for being. . . .'

'I know, I know,' I said. 'Mandon tells me how smart Webber is and now you tell me how smart the stooge is. Well, how smart do you have to be to know that you got caught in a wringer?'

'Well,' she said, 'he knows that now, and so do I. I want to tell you that I'm sorry I ever doubted you. I'll never worry about it again. . . .'

'That's fine,' I said. 'Now will you please fix something to eat?'

'I wish you wouldn't think that anything happened between us. Nothing did.'

'Oh, sure . . .' I said.

'I mean it. On my dead father.'

'Nuts,' I said.

She glanced at me grimly. 'I wish I'd done it now,' she said.

'You couldn't have found a guy with whom you've more in common,' I said.

Her eyes flashed. 'I'll remember that next time. . . .'

'You got more than that to remember,' I said. 'He chews toothpicks. Careful he doesn't poke one of your eyes out. . . .'

I went back into the bedroom and opened all the bundles. The shirts were not Brooks Brothers but they were a good imitation (until they were washed), and the ties were not Charvet's and the insteps of the shoes did not lace together (this way in every few pairs they save enough leather to make an extra pair, but most Americans don't know the difference anyway), and the socks were not Sulka's or Solly's, and the shorts stunk – but it was all new and clean, that much I had to say. The two suits I had bought off the rack had had to be altered slightly, but I had given the clerk a sawbuck and he had said they would be delivered this afternoon if the tailor could get through with them, and I had given the tailor a sawbuck and he had said he would.

'Your soup's on,' Holiday said from the bedroom door. 'You want it in here or in the kitchen?'

'You mean I've got a choice?' I said.

'You certainly have,' she said. She was very friendly again. 'Don't you think it's time you got some service around here?'

'I think it's past time,' I said. 'And just for that, I'll take it in the kitchen.'

'Good,' she said. 'That'll give me a chance to clear off the bed so you can take a nap. Did you get any sleep at all last night?'

'Not very much,' I said. 'Sleeping with Jinx is no way to sleep.'

'Well – you have your soup and I'll see that you get some sleep.'

'You overwhelm me,' I said.

She stepped aside, smiling at me as I passed her, going to the kitchen.

The soup, mushroom, was boiling around the edges and I stirred it and watched the boil come back to the edges and I stirred it again and then poured it into a bowl and sat down at the kitchen table. Holiday had placed a knife and a spoon there, with several slices of bread and a glass of milk she had poured. I spooned the soup, wondering what the hell Reece could have said to her that would restore her confidence in me, that would make her see that I did have the City Hall in my pocket . . .

'. . . that's a nice lot of stuff you bought,' she was saying.

'It's clean,' I said. 'I got a couple of suits too.'

'You did?'

'A brown one and a blue one. They're sending 'em. . . .'

'Today?'

'Yes.'

'Say, that's pretty fast . . . .'

'They didn't have to be altered much. I'm not hard to fit.'

'I guess you'll be glad to get out of that stuff you're wearing, all right.'

'I sure will. If I throw this stuff in the corner, it would stand up by itself. But – couple of days more, we can all have what we want. You can hold out for a couple of days, can't you?'

'That sounds like you and Mandon lined something up last night. . . .'

'It was a big night,' I said. 'But before we pull it, we have to talk to Webber.'

'When'll that be?'

'Right away, I hope. I'm waiting to hear from him now.'

She looked at me, smiling cosily, and I finished my soup.

'More?' she asked.

'No, thanks. That'll hold me till dinner.'

She took the plate and bowl and spoon and put them on the drainboard.

I drank some milk.

She came back and sat down. 'Can you tell me about it?'

'Webber has to okay it first. Nothing to tell till then.'

'He'll have to okay it if you want it okayed, won't he?'

'Naturally. But there's some angles I have to talk to him about.'

'Sounds big.'

'It is big.'

'When will it happen – if it happens?'

'Tomorrow, maybe.'

'More milk?'

'No, thanks.'

'Then you'd better try to get some sleep now. . . .'

'That's what I been looking forward to – a bath and some sleep.'

I got up and helped her out of her chair. It was nice, being well-mannered again. She smiled at me politely. 'This is just like being strangers again,' she said.

'I only hope we can keep it this way,' I said.

'*All* the time?'

'Not all the time. Just some of the time . . .'

I let her precede me into the bedroom.

'Would you like for me to fix your bath?' she asked.

'Thank you,' I said.

She went into the bathroom and let the water run into the tub and I started putting my shirts and shorts in a drawer of the bureau. This stuff was genuine crap, the kind they over-power you with in color advertisements in the magazines. Well, pretty soon now . . .

I turned to get the other stuff off the bed and almost bumped into her at my elbow, holding the packages I had not heard her get from the bed: the ties and socks. She put them on the bureau, but kept in her hand a small bundle.

'This feels like lead,' she said.

'Funny you'd say that,' I said. 'It is lead. They're cartridges. I got 'em at a hockshop, and half a dozen new clips. With new springs.'

'Springs?' she said. 'What do you mean – springs?'

'You shouldn't have asked that question,' I said. 'You give me a chance to show off my knowledge of criminal fundamentals.'

I took the package from her, opening it and taking out a new clip. 'You see this little platform here? That's the feeder. This keeps feeding a new cartridge into the firing chamber of an automatic whenever the blank shell is discharged. Now I'll show you something.' I loaded the clip. 'This spring's now compressed to its full limit, all the way down. There's a lot of tension on it. You understand that.'

'Yes.'

'Shove this clip in the gun and you're ready. Right?'

'Yes.'

'Well, suppose you don't use the gun now for a couple of weeks. All that time the tension's still on the spring. Now. All of a sudden you do want to use it. You shoot it two or three times and everything works well – except you discover that two or three times wasn't sufficient and you need some more shots. But after number three maybe they don't come out right. Maybe the feeder won't slam 'em into the chamber as fast as they're ejected. You're in trouble – and all because you kept that spring coiled at full tension all the time. That's what makes an automatic jam – weak spring. If you intend to use a gun a lot, the springs ought to be rested or you ought to get new clips. An automatic is the finest, safest gun in the world if you know how to use it. Most people don't.' I looked at her. 'Now, aren't you impressed?'

'I certainly am,' she said. 'I certainly am. But you told me once you didn't know much about guns.'

'Oh, you know I'm full of crap,' I said.

She smiled.

I leaned down and kissed her on the throat and started undressing, moving into the bathroom, feeling the water for comfort, just right, and turned off the spigot. I went back in the bedroom and finished undressing, and then went and got into the tub.

She came in, holding my trousers. 'Is this new too?' she asked, spreading a gold chain on her fingers.

'That's new,' I said.

'So is this little medal,' she said.

'That's no medal,' I said. 'That's a key.'

'Key?'

'Yes.'

'This?'

'Phi Beta Kappa key. I got it at the hockshop with the chain. I had the guy put it on for me.'

'Is it yours?'

'It's not my original key, no. But they're all the same.'

'Oh!' she said, 'so this is a Phi Beta Kappa key. . . .'

'Didn't you ever see one before?'

'I might have. But it didn't mean anything then.'

I stretched out in the tub and smiled at her modestly. I

wouldn't tell her what it meant or how good you had to be to get one or how the basis of my scholastic achievements recognition by Phi Beta Kappa was inevitable.

'So you're really Phi Beta Kappa. . . .' she said.

'Really. That was no crap,' I said.

'It's something very special, isn't it?'

'You could call it something very special, yes.'

'Did you go to Yale?'

'No.'

'Did you go to Harvard?'

'No. There are Phi Beta Kappa's who didn't go to Yale or Harvard, but it's pretty hard to make a Yale or Harvard man believe that. . . .'

She turned down the lid of the bowl and sat on it, holding my trousers in her lap. 'You know,' she said, 'I'm just finding out that I don't know anything at all about you. Where did you go to college?'

'Does it matter?'

'You're not ashamed of it, are you?'

'I think the college might be. I'm sure my career doesn't reflect too much credit on the school. It does prove one thing, though – it proves that I came into crime through choice and not through environment. I didn't grow up in the slums with a drunk for a father and a whore for a mother and come into crime that way. I hate society too, but I don't hate it because it mistreated me and warped my soul. Every other criminal I know – who's engaged in violent crime – is a two-bit coward who blames his career on society. I need no apologist or crusader to finally hold my lifeless body up to the world and shout for them to come and observe what they have wrought. Do you know one of the first things I'm going to do when I get some money? I'm going to have Cartier make me a little solid gold thing for my wrist, you know, that identification thing the army guys wear, on a solid gold chain and do you know what I'm going to have inscribed on it? Just this: "Use me not as a preachment in your literature or your movies. This I have wrought, I and I alone." '

'You seem to have yourself doped out pretty well,' she said thoughtfully.

'I have,' I said.

'Your name's not really Ralph Cotter, is it?'

'It's Paul Murphy.'

'You just made that up today.'

'Yesterday,' I said.

'You're *real* name, I'm talking about.'

'Would it make any difference?'

'But what about your folks. You got any folks?'

'No.'

'You said you had a brother in New York.'

'I have. I got a sister, too.'

'In New York?'

'I don't know where she is. I lost track of her.'

'Seems strange you'd lose track of your sister and not lose track of your brother. Seems it ought to be the other way around. . . .'

'You don't know my brother,' I said.

'I'd like to. I'd like to meet the most honest man in the world.'

'That was one other thing that wasn't crap too.'

'He'd have to be – for you to trust him with that recording. What does he do?'

'Why do you want to know?'

'No reason. Just curiosity . . .'

She took her eyes off me, looking at the wash basin.

I sat up in the tub. 'Why do you want to know?' I asked again.

She laughed, but the laugh sounded artificial. 'Well, I've got a small interest in that record myself,' she said. 'I face a murder rap too – or have you forgotten what happened at the prison farm? I just wanted to know who he was and what he did so in case anything happened to you I could get in touch with him. . . .'

'If anything happens to me you won't have to get in touch with him. This thing's rigged just like an alarm clock. . . .'

'Can't you even tell me what business he's in?' she asked.

'You're sweet,' I said. Do you want the soup in the kitchen or the bedroom, I'll see that you get some sleep, I'll fix your bath, I'll put away your new clothes, what was your school, what is your real name, what about your folks, what does your brother in New York do, to whom you sent the recording: so nice and affable and cosy, so goddamn nice and affable and cosy, so discreet and clever, building up, as they always do when they get in trouble or want something, the divine intimacy of domesticity, that or shaking The Last Resort in your face, the thing they always depend on to get you, which she'd been doing ever since I got here, and how long had she been sitting in the tub waiting for me to arrive, so that I could find her in a casual state of nakedness, how long? 'You need more coaching, baby,' I said. 'You went too fast.'

'What?' she said.

'Your new boy friend is certainly trying to find out who's got that record, isn't he?'

'What're you talking about?' she said.

'Reece and Webber,' I said. 'They cooked this up with you last night, didn't they?'

'Do you think . . . ?'

'Nuts,' I said.

'Oh, you couldn't think that I would . . .'

'Turn down the bed for me, will you?' I said.

'Lissen, Ralph . . .'

'Paul,' I said.

'I swear, Paul. On my dead father . . .'

'Fix the bed, will you?'

She got up from the bowl and stepped beside the tub. 'Do you actually believe that I would ... ?'

I pulled a bath towel off the rack and slapped her across the face with it. 'I asked you to fix the bed,' I said.

'Oh, God, why are you so suspicious?' she moaned, going out ...

...chapter
two

Mandon picked Jinx and me up on the corner near the apartment, a little after eight o'clock. He was sitting in the front seat and the handsome colored boy, Highness, was driving. The car barely paused at the curb and Mandon swung the door open and we got in.

'I hardly knew you,' he said to me. 'All those new clothes...'

'This is only the beginning,' I said. 'How are you, Highness?' I said. I thought: You gonna drive for a man, you ought to learn your job. You ought to learn how to get out and open the door.

Highness turned his head and looked at me impersonally, but did not say anything. There was nothing in his eyes either, but I had the old feeling that he was ready to spring. He gave me a chill every time I saw him. You son-of-a-bitch, I thought, I got a spot picked out right in the middle of your black stomach, you ever spring at me ...

'Where're we meeting Webber?' I said to Mandon.

'At his office...'

'Did you tell him the idea?'

'I should say not. You couldn't sell him that on the telephone. I don't know that you can even sell it to him in person.'

'I'll sell him,' I said.

'Well – he might come around....'

'He can come around or be brought around. He can take his choice.'

'Now, for Christ's sake, don't start getting tough with him,' Mandon said. 'You take it easy. You let me handle things.'

'You hear that, Jinx? That goes for you too.'

'I hear,' he said.

Mandon turned all the way in his seat, looking at him. 'What's the matter with you?' he asked.

Jinx didn't say anything.

'You heard the man,' I said. 'He wants to know what's the matter with you.'

'Nothing,' Jinx said to Mandon.

'I never saw such a collection of sore-heads in all my life,' Mandon said. 'What the hell is he mad about?' he asked me.

'You heard the man,' I said to Jinx. 'He wants to know what you're mad about.'

Jinx looked out the window.

'He's jealous of my new wardrobe,' I said.

'Well, he can have one, too,' Mandon said. 'Can't he wait? Does he have to have it tonight?'

'The man wants to know can you wait,' I said.

'Goddamn it,' Jinx said. 'I don't care how many clothes he buys with his own dough. The dough he used to trap Webber and that guy belonged to me. Any other dough coming in, I want my split.'

I leaned forward to Mandon. 'I've been trying to explain to him that the dough that bought these clothes was not corporation income,' I said. 'It was a loan. I borrowed the money.'

'That's right, Jinx,' Mandon said.

'Joseph,' I said.

'I loaned him the money myself, Joseph. . . .' He turned and looked at me and I saw that he hadn't realized yet that all the stuff I had bought cost more than the forty dollars he had loaned me. I had bought the clothes with the two hundred dollars I had

240

borrowed from Vic Mason, the two hundred I had borrowed to have a date with Margaret Dobson, but it would have been a waste of time to try to explain that. It wouldn't have changed the way Jinx felt, and I didn't care how he felt, anyway. The hell with him. . . . I wouldn't be saddled with him too long. . . .

'This the way to the City Hall?' I asked.

'We're not going to the City Hall,' Mandon said.

'I thought we were going to his office.'

'We are – one of 'em.'

'How many offices has he got?'

'Several,' Mandon said.

This office was on the third floor of an eight-story building. We walked up, not using the elevator, as Mandon had suggested, but relaying, I was sure, a suggestion from Webber himself. It was an old building and the stairs were worn and dirty. There were several lights in various offices, and Mandon led us down the corridor, finally jerking his thumb at a door on which was lettered: COOPERATIVE BORROWERS, INC. Loans – winking, flipping his big eyebrows, trying to indicate that this is where we were going. He stopped before the next door on which was lettered: COOPERATIVE BORROWERS, INC. Loans. PRIVATE. Entrance 306. He knocked on the door normally, not using a code, just a normal knock, and it was opened by Reece and we went in.

Reece smiled but didn't speak, closing the door. He wore a white suit and the armpits were stained by sweat, but he had no toothpick in his mouth. Webber was standing by a flat desk. He wore a striped seersucker suit and was smoking a cigarette. There were several chairs around the desk, and overhead a wooden fan was revolving slowly.

'Hope I didn't put you out too much,' he said.

'No, you didn't put us out,' Mandon said.

241

Reece moved away from the door, joining us at the desk. 'Sit down,' he said.

He sat down in an office chair and I sat down in a chair that had arms.

'Sit down,' I said to Jinx.

He sat down beside me.

'I thought it'd be better if we talked here,' Webber said. 'What's the big idea, Cherokee, that you couldn't talk about on the phone?'

'I could have talked about it on the phone,' Mandon said quietly. 'You were the one who didn't want to talk about it.'

'Well, what is it?'

'Before I tell you, Charlie,' he said, 'I want you to know that we haven't gone off half-cocked on this. It's dangerous, but we can handle it.'

'If the Inspector'll co-operate,' I said.

He glanced at me but didn't get the pun. He looked back at Mandon and said: 'Is this a heist?'

'Yes,' Mandon said.

'Who?'

' Roamer's collectors.'

'Roamer's collectors?' he said. He looked at Reece. 'How'd you happen to pick them?'

Mandon shrugged. 'They carry a lot of money. . . .'

'They carry a hell of a lot of money. . . .'

'They carry a hell of a lot of money, but they've never been heisted yet. Don't you know why that is? You couldn't take them without gun play and even then I have my doubts.'

'You think you're the first guys that ever thought of this?' Reece asked.

'We're the first guys that're gonna do it,' I said.

'Guess again,' Webber said. 'You try anything like this the whole town'd get shot up.'

242

I smiled at Mandon. 'Maybe you'd better tell the gentlemen how we intend to avoid that,' I said.

'You tell him,' Mandon said.

'There'll be no shooting – as such,' I said. 'I guarantee it.'

'How're you gonna do it – hypnotize 'em?' Webber said.

'That's where the co-operation comes in, Inspector. With your help we can hypnotize 'em.'

'What kind of help?' Reece asked.

'With the help of some police uniforms and a squad car, a traffic control car ...'

Webber blew the ashes off his cigarette to the floor. 'Disguise yourselves as cops, you mean?'

'Yes.'

He looked at Mandon. 'He's a very funny boy,' he said.

'I guarantee there'll be no shooting,' I said. 'That way we can take 'em without a struggle.'

'Yes, sir,' Webber said. 'He's a comic.'

'We want a traffic control car and some uniforms and two other cops to help, real cops,' I said evenly.

'Oh, now, for Christ's sake, Cherokee, you know I've got a deal with Roamer,' Webber said crossly.

'If you're gonna put it on that basis, Inspector,' I said, 'we'll have a hard time finding a customer. You don't want us to touch a bank or a Federal job, and with everybody else you got a deal. Where does that leave us?'

'With Roamer I've got a deal,' Webber said. 'What happens when the collectors tell him they've been stuck up by cops? Who do you think they'll come to? He won't be satisfied unless I put every cop on the force in the show-up for him. Jesus, Cherokee,' he said, 'maybe it's too much to expect this kid to use his head, but there's no damned excuse for you not using yours. . . .'

'Inspector,' I said, 'what makes you think his collectors'll tell him anything?'

243

He didn't get this, either. 'Of course, they will,' he said. 'They'll have to tell him something. You might buy one guy and you might put the fix in for two, but not four. . . .'

'Four of them. We'll keep 'em quiet without a fix,' I said.

Now they all got it. Webber and Reece looked at each other and for a moment there was silence.

'And how can that be arranged?' Webber asked.

'That's very simple,' I said. 'The part that isn't simple is arranging things so that the four bodies and the car cannot be found or identified. That'll take some thinking, but by tomorrow I'll have the answer to that too.' I heard Reece exhale heavily, but I was watching Webber. A little white showed around his lips. 'I promise you, Inspector, that unless this can be done cleanly and without even an echo, I won't touch it.'

'Four guys disappearing all of a sudden . . .' he said. 'Seems to me that'll leave an echo.'

'An echo,' Mandon said, 'is not evidence.'

Reece said: 'If it's as clean as that, Inspector, nobody can prove anything.'

I looked at him, nodding in surprised approval. I had begun to think that he never volunteered an opinion. Webber was staring at the desk. I knew what he was thinking. 'I realize, Inspector, that in this case suspicion against you is just as damaging as evidence against you. But nobody will ever suspect anything. They just disappear. As far as Roamer is concerned, they blew with the dough.'

'He'll never believe they blew with the dough . . .'

'Why shouldn't he believe it? It's happened before – probably to him too. Who is he that these guys won't blow on? Saint Francis of Assisi?'

'How much do you think they're carrying?'

'Mandon knows more about that than I do,' I said.

'A minimum of fifteen grand,' Mandon said.

244

'Jesus,' Webber said. 'Four guys for fifteen grand. . . .'

'If you're going to pro-rate this,' I said, a little annoyed, 'don't leave out the Buick. That's got to disappear too. A second-hand Buick on today's market is worth more than all four of these mugs put together.'

Webber looked at Mandon and shuddered a little.

'What kind of a job do you think we came here to tell you about?' I asked. 'A neighborhood drug store? An oil station? Snatching some old woman's purse?'

'That'd be more in your line,' he snapped. 'A swell-headed punk with all this talk about killing people . . .'

'Where the hell do you get off to be so goddamn scrupulous?' I said.

'Take it easy . . .' Jinx said.

'Now, now, now . . .' Mandon said.

'You shut up!' I said. 'A swell-headed punk, am I?' I said to Webber. 'You just won't learn, will you? That was your original mistake – thinking that. That's how you happened to get caught in the wringer in the first place. I'm no goddamn dilettante playing around the edges of the underworld for a vicarious thrill; I'm just as much a professional as you are. What do these mugs mean to me? I don't worry about them any more than you do about shaking a guy down and then shooting him in the back to keep him from singing . . .'

Fierce resentment was in Webber's face and manner, and Reece saw it and stepped back and reached for his hip pocket.

Jinx slid out of his chair, crouching behind the side of the desk and there was blank astonishment in Mandon's face.

I laughed, looking at Reece. 'Stop acting, stupid,' I said. 'The boss sees you. You're a hero . . .'

'You get this wild man out of here, Cherokee,' Webber said. 'Talk some sense into him.'

'Come on, Ralph,' Mandon said nervously.

245

'Paul,' I said.

'All right, Paul. Goddamn it, come on . . .'

'Wait a minute,' I said. 'You can come out now, Joseph,' I said to Jinx. He crawled back into his chair. 'Sit down, Cherokee, and relax,' I said. 'Why do we have to yell and scream and insult each other every time we get together? Hating my guts shouldn't make you act like that . . .'

'It'll do for the time being,' he said.

'Well, I hate yours too,' I said complacently, 'but that shouldn't be any particular hardship on either one of us, because we're not social friends. We're professional friends – and we surely can put up with each other if there's a profit involved. Of course, with your varied interests, a profit is not as great an inducement to you as it is to me. Consequently, it means more to me than it does to you. If you will try to understand that, then you can understand my behaviour. For which I apologize.' He stared at me, not blinking an eye. Reece had taken his hand off his hip. 'I don't want to jeopardize your deal with Roamer,' I said. 'I know the story about the goose and the golden eggs as well as you do. This job is proposed on the basis of a complete and perfect disappearance . . .'

'We got a happy town here,' he said. 'We all get along: the D.A., my office, all the boys around. The newspapers don't bother us, we got no reform element – we wanna keep it that way. We don't want none of the boys suspicious. We don't want none of the boys cutting each other's throats . . .'

'Please, Inspector,' I said. 'Such loyalty is very touching, but what you're really worried about is making Roamer's four collectors and his automobile disappear completely. Isn't that it?'

'Somebody'll find 'em sometime. They'll find something.'

'If there's the slightest chance of that, I won't pull it. If there's the slightest chance. And you can be the sole judge.'

246

'How're you gonna do it?' Reece asked.

'I haven't worked it out yet. Give me till tomorrow. That's fair enough, isn't it?' I looked at Webber. 'That's fair enough, isn't it?'

'I suppose so,' he said. 'You be goddamn sure you check with me first.'

'I will,' I said.

'You see to that, Cherokee,' he said to Mandon.

'I will,' Mandon said.

I got up, lighting a cigarette. 'Good night,' I said.

Reece moved to the door to let us out.

'You have a nice time with Holiday last night?' I asked him at the door. He said nothing. 'You ought to call her up. She's got some information for you. Names and addresses and stuff. . . .'

We went out, down the hall. Mandon started to speak to me several times on the way out, but didn't. We walked back down the stairs and into the lobby and into the street.

Highness was waiting for us in the car, and saw us approaching, but made no move to get out, made no move to even open the door without getting out.

'Why don't you teach that boy to get out and open the door?' I said to Mandon.

'Oh, for God's sake, why don't you stop making speeches?' he said. He opened the door himself and Jinx and I got in the back seat and this time he got in with us. Highness looked at him, waiting for orders.

'Where do you want to go?' Mandon asked me.

'Back to the apartment. To get Holiday,' I said.

'Holiday? For what?'

'To celebrate. Some music. To celebrate her loyalty. Her great loyalty. . . .'

'Back where we picked 'em up,' Mandon said to Highness.

The black boy started the car and rolled it away.

'You oughtn't to be wasting your time on a party,' Mandon

said sarcastically. 'You have some thinking to do.'

'I'm in a cold sweat about it,' I said. 'I'm just worried sick about it. Whatevereverever shall I do?'

'Let me tell you something, my friend. Webber's no man to push around. . . .'

'The castrated Colossus,' I said.

'One of these days you're going to lay it on too thick.'

'Am I?' I said. 'Cheer up.' I said to Jinx, who was looking out of the window. 'You didn't know the guy wasn't gonna shoot.'

'You son-of-a-bitch . . .' he said.

I laughed. 'One of these days you're gonna lay it on too thick,' I said.

'Am I?' he said.

It was Henry Halstead's orchestra. The music was sweet and not for my taste, but the tempo was fine for dancing. It was a dance orchestra, a hotel orchestra, and eight bars were all I needed to hear to know that it was better than most hotel orchestras. It used good harmonies and had a rhythm that fitted the rhythm of the human body. As we went in it was playing, 'I'm Dancing with Tears in My Eyes,' and the dance floor was crowded and the lights were low.

A captain took us to a table near the bandstand. It was too near. 'Haven't you got anything not quite so close to the music?' I asked.

'No, sir,' he said. 'I'm very sorry. Later, perhaps . . .'

'What about the loges up there?' I asked. 'What about a table up there?'

'Sorry, sir,' he said.

'This'll do,' Mandon said.

The captain helped Holiday into her chair and Mandon and I sat down and the captain put big oversized menus in front of each of us as a bus boy crept in and started arranging the table.

'We've had dinner,' I said to the captain.

The bus boy started to pick up the napkins.

'Leave the napkins,' I said.

The bus boy looked at the captain, who nodded once, and then he put the napkins back and started pouring the water. The captain beckoned to a waiter and walked away.

'I think I'll have a club sandwich,' Holiday said.

'Club sandwich for the lady,' I said to the waiter.

'. . . and bourbon and Coca-cola,' she said.

'Bourbon and Coca-Cola?' I said. 'That's the most depraved thing I ever heard of . . .'

'It's what I want,' she said.

'And tonight it's what you'll get too,' I said. 'Bourbon and Coca-cola for the lady,' I said to the waiter.

'What for you, sir?' the waiter asked me.

'Cognac,' I said. 'Would you like food?' I said to Mandon.

'Coffee,' Mandon said.

The waiter nodded.

'Try to make that cognac Delamain,' I said.

'Delamain, yes, sir,' the waiter said.

Mandon looked around. 'That's good music,' he said.

'Cherokee's a musician himself,' I said to Holiday.

'Are you?' she asked.

'Not exactly . . .'

'He is too,' I said. 'He's a drummer. You ought to see the drummer's outfit he's got in his room.'

'That was a fee,' Mandon said, smiling. 'Chap gave me that as a fee . . .'

I looked at Holiday. In the glow of the little table light she had a nice quality in her face, the kind of quality that went with gingham aprons and market baskets and general stores and streets lined with elms: a sweet thing, a one-man girl. Well . . . Margaret Dobson was pretty far in the past now, only a laceration on my memory, and only Holiday was left. Holiday, the Loyal – at least when you were with her . . .

'Would you like to dance?' I asked.

She nodded.

'Excuse us, Cherokee?'

'Go ahead,' he said.

I got up and helped her up and followed her to the dance floor. We began dancing, keeping to the edge of the dance floor, near the ringside tables. She was a good dancer. She vibrated sympathetically.

'You're a good dancer,' I said.

'Thank you,' she said in a pleased voice. 'So are you.'

'I used to . . .' I said, and then I caught myself and stopped. I was about to say that I used to play in an orchestra.

She took her head off my shoulder and looked at me. 'You used to what?' she said.

'I used to go to a lot of dances,' I said.

'Oh,' she said. 'So did I.'

We moved around to the edge of the crowd, picking our spots. She was better than good. She was an excellent dancer.

'This is swell . . .' she said.

'It's only the beginning,' I said.

'Too bad Jinx couldn't come,' she said.

'Why is it too bad?'

'Well – him staying there in that apartment. I know what that's like . . .'

'It's his own fault. Don't squander your sympathy on him.'

'I'm not.'

'Don't worry about him then.'

'I'm not worried about him.'

I'm worried about him, I thought. I'm worried about you too. 'He's still sore about the money I spent for these clothes. He thinks I'm holding out on him. He's a sore-head. Don't spoil the party by talking about him . . .'

'What happened with Webber? Is everything all right?'

'With me handling it? Don't be silly.'

'I'm Dancing with Tears in my Eyes' ended, and there was a riff, and a lot of applause and the orchestra wound up that set of numbers and the dancers started back to their tables.

I took Holiday's arm and threaded her through the people. She was happy and gay. She laughed softly, patting the back of my hand which held her arm. I smiled at her and squeezed her arm a little. But she wasn't fooling me this time . . .

The drinks were on the table. Mandon already had drunk some of his coffee.

'I'm glad to see you didn't let your coffee get cold,' I said. 'Nothing worse than cold coffee . . .'

'I didn't know how long you'd be,' he said, making no effort to rise and assist Holiday, not even thinking about it. How could I expect the black boy to have manners when the master himself had none?

I helped Holiday into the chair and sat down myself and picked up the cognac.

'Happy days . . .' I said.

Mandon only nodded sourly, but Holiday toasted with me. I took a sip of the cognac and looked around for the waiter, beckoning with my hand.

'Isn't it the proper vintage?' Mandon asked.

'It isn't even the proper cognac,' I said.

'Yes, sir,' said the waiter.

'I asked for Delamain cognac,' I said.

'That *is* Delamain, sir . . .'

'It's Martell,' I said. 'Bring me Delamain.'

'Begging your pardon, sir . . .'

'Please, let's not argue about it . . .'

'Yes, sir, I'll change it,' he said stiffly, moving away with the glass.

251

Mandon looked at me superciliously. He wasn't annoyed now; he was amused.

'What the hell . . .' I said. 'I'm all dressed up and in a first-class place. Why can't I have what I'm paying for?'

'You're sure you know what you want?'

'That, I am sure of,' I said. 'How's that fantastic thing you're drinking?' I asked Holiday.

'Good. Taste it . . .'

I tasted it. It was treacly and sickening. 'It's pretty ugh,' I said. 'Where'd you learn to drink that stuff?'

'In Texas. I lived down there for a couple of years. We used to drink this at ball games. We'd pour half the coke out of the bottles and fill 'em with bourbon and take 'em to the ball games with us. And along about the sixth inning we wouldn't be sure whether we were at a ball game or out flying a kite . . .'

'I should think not,' I said. 'How'd you ever happen to wind up in Texas?'

'I fell in love with a sports writer. I went down there to marry him.'

'I didn't know you were ever married,' I said.

'I wasn't. Between working and sleeping with every woman in town, he never had time to marry me. All he used me for was a crying towel. Funny guy, but – wonderful. A genius.'

'Whatever happened to him?'

'He went to Hollywood, I think. He's a movie extra or something.'

'Does this bore you?' I asked Mandon.

'I'm hanging on every last word,' he said.

The waiter came with another glass of cognac. 'I'm sorry, sir,' he said. 'The other *was* Martell.' He seemed more respectful now. The change in his manner was plainly noticeable. 'This is Delamain, sir,' he said.

I looked at Mandon and smiled, inhaling the cognac. I took a sip. This was Delamain.

'Is that all right, sir?' the waiter asked.

'It's better than that,' I said. 'It's perfect. Thank you.'

'Thank *you*, sir,' he said, moving away.

'Forgive my smugness,' I said to Mandon.

'So . . .' he said. 'In addition to other things, you're also a connoisseur . . .'

'Please, Cherokee,' I said. 'I'm trying very hard to be modest. Don't start flattering me. I'll unfold like a rose.'

He grunted and took a swallow of coffee, and I sipped my cognac, smiling at Holiday, who was sipping her bourbon and Coca-cola, and then the idea hit me: it rolled right out of nowhere, over the heads of the people sitting at the tables and hit me, and I knew that the question of what to do with those four bodies and the second-hand Buick was solved.

'Excuse me,' I said, putting down the drink, getting up. Holiday and Mandon were too surprised to say anything.

I went into the lobby and asked a bellboy where the telephone was. He pointed it out and I got five nickels from the clerk at the desk and went into the booth and looked up Mason's Garage. I dialled the number and a voice answered and I asked for Mason. 'He ain't here,' the guy at the other end said. 'You know where he is?' I asked. 'Naw, I don't. Who is this?' 'This is Paul Murphy,' I said. 'Who is this? Is this Nelse?' 'Yeah, this is Nelse.' 'Nelse, I'm the guy who had the Zephyr – remember?' 'Yeah, I remember.' 'You got any idea where Mason might be?' 'Naw, I haven't . . .' 'Can you let me have his home number?' 'Yeah. It's A-R six one eight one two – ' 'A-R six one eight one two,' I said. 'That's right . . .' 'Thanks, Nelse . . .'

I hung up and dialled AR 6-1812. There was no answer. I let it ring seven or eight times and there still was no answer.

I hung up and called the garage again. Nelse answered.

'Nelse,' I said, 'there was no answer at Mason's number. You got any idea where he might be?' 'Naw, I haven't,' he said. 'Do you ever hear from him at night? Does he ever call in?' I asked. 'Naw. Very seldom. There's a joint you might try. The Persian Cat. He might be there . . .' 'Thanks,' I said.

I hung up and looked in the book for the number of The Persian Cat and called that. They answered right away, a woman, and the noise of music and people talking came through the receiver. 'Is Mister Vic Mason there?' I asked. 'Who?' she said. 'Mister Vic Mason? You know him? Club-footed guy . . .' 'Yes, I know him, but I couldn't tell you whether he's here or not . . .' 'Will you ask the headwaiter?' 'We don't have a headwaiter. . . .' 'You got a doorman?' 'Yes.' 'Will you ask him?' 'Hold the phone . . .' she said wearily. I could hear her speaking to someone and in a minute a man's voice said: 'Yeah? This is the doorman . . .' 'I'm trying to locate Vic Mason,' I said. 'Do you know him?' 'Yeah,' he said. 'I know him.' 'Is he there.' 'Haven't seen him tonight . . .' 'Does he usually come there at nights?' I asked. 'Yeah, pretty often . . .' 'You think he'll come tonight?' 'I don't know. . . .' he said. 'Well, thanks,' I said.

I hung up and went back to the table. Holiday and Cherokee weren't there. The orchestra was back on the stand, playing 'Body and Soul,' and the floor was again filled with dancers, and, telling myself that they too were dancing, and not thinking any more about it, I sat down, picking up the cognac, waiting for them to return so we could leave for The Persian Cat.

The waiter eased his hand over my shoulder and laid a check in front of me on the table. 'The lady and the gentleman said to give you this, sir . . .' he said.

'Where are they?' I asked.

'They've gone, sir,'

'Gone where?'

'They didn't say, sir . . .'

'You mean gone for good?'

'That was my impression, sir. They left in quite a hurry. . . .'

'Well, I'll be goddamned,' I said.

'They said you would be happy to pay the check . . .'

'I'll not be happy to pay it, but I'll pay it,' I said.

I took a ten-dollar bill out of my pocket and laid it on the check. 'Will that handle it?'

'Oh, yes, sir. Thank you very much . . .'

I tossed off the rest of the cognac and got up and went out, through the lobby on to the pavement, up to the liveried doorman, a man who made a living opening doors.

'Did a middle-aged guy with a good-looking girl just come out? Little guy with big eyebrows? They were in a green Chrysler sedan with a colored boy driving?'

'The party you arrived with?' he asked.

'Yes.'

'They left a few minutes ago.'

'Did you hear where they were going?'

'No, sir.'

'Call me a cab will you?' I said.

He blew a whistle that made noise and gestured with a white-gloved hand and a taxi-cab glided to a stop by the marquee.

The doorman opened the door and I got in, handing him a quarter. The hell with Holiday and Cherokee, I was thinking . . .

'Where to, sir?' the cab driver asked.

'The Persian Cat,' I told him.

He turned in his seat and looked at me closely. I thought he had not understood. 'You know where The Persian Cat is?' I asked.

'Yes,' he said.

The Persian Cat was situated in the wholesale district (only a few blocks from Mason's Garage, I was to learn later), hemmed in by warehouses and big red-brick buildings that were now filled with darkness. The street was filled with darkness too, and empty; and when the faraway traffic noises finally reached here, through the lowered window of the cab, they sounded tired and forlorn and weak, as if they had come across vast spaces.

The cab driver swung open the door and I got out in front and paid him and then the only noises I heard were party noises from inside The Persian Cat; and I went directly across the pavement into a small box-like foyer hung with purple draperies and two life-size colored photographs of naked women, one upright, one reclining. Now I knew why the driver had looked at me so closely; The Persian Cat was a pansy joint. I went across the foyer to the entrance, where a chain that showed through purple velvet covering was hooked across the opening.

It was virtually dark inside and it stank with the fetidness of crawling things. A three- or four-piece combination was making music somewhere in the gloom, and the room was packed and jammed. I stood there for a moment, trying to decide whether to go in, I wanted very badly to see Mason; and finally telling myself that unless I saw him and got this thing settled I'd worry all night – and I reached for the velvet rope, intending to unhook it myself, when a man in a harem costume, with excessively mascaraed eyes, reached for the chain, saying through his veil: 'One?'

I recognized his voice. This was the doorman I had talked to on the phone a little earlier, but on the phone he hadn't sounded like a faggot.

'One?' he said again.

He didn't sound like a faggot now, either. 'One,' I said.

He lifted the chain and I stepped in. 'Let me see now...' he said, putting all the fingers of his right hand on his chin, trying to determine where to put me, but I knew he was sizing me up, friend or foe, visiting fireman or local talent, crank or explorer...

256

'I think I talked to you on the phone a little while ago,' I said. 'I called about Vic Mason. Has he shown up yet?'

'Oh, so you're the one,' he said. 'Are you a friend of Vic's?'

'Sort of a business associate,' I said. 'Is he here.'

'Yes, he's here,' he said, smiling at me, rehooking the velvet chain. 'Just follow me . . .'

I followed him. I never saw such a crowd of dikes and faggots. This was their joint, by God, and they were all over it – hanging over the tables, standing by the tables, sitting on the tables, blocking the aisle, filling the tiny dance space; all of them wearing a different kind of perfume that collected into a ball of debauched saccharinity and bounced off the walls and the ceiling and the floor. This was their joint, and here, by God, they could afford to be unrestrained. Here there were none of the daytime world's hostile faces to haunt them, none of the daytime world's cruel contemptuous eyes, none of the daytime world's merciless incompassion . . . This was their joint, by God, and around it and inside it they developed the innate defences which nature evolves in its weak: remoteness and repellence. Pushing my way through this laughing, shouting crowd, in which I now was the only inhibited one, over which the poor damned small combination was still trying to make its music heard, following the guy in the harem costume, I made a sudden and extraordinary discovery. The noxiousness and disgust I had felt a few moments earlier were gone, my own strength and virility, of which I was so proud when I entered, with which I could prove our difference, now served only to emphasize our sameness. We all had a touch of twilight in our souls; in every man there are homosexual tendencies, this is immutable, there is no variant, the only variant is the depth of the latency, but in me these tendencies were not being stirred, even faintly, they were there, but this was not stirring them. No. The sameness was of the species, of the psyche, of the . . . They were rebels too, rebels introverted; I was

257

a rebel extroverted – theirs was the force that did not kill, mine was the force that did kill . . .

'Well, I'll be a son-of-a-bitch,' I heard Mason's voice saying.'Look who's here . . .'

He was wedged into a corner booth with five others, but the space was only for four. A lighted candle was sticking in the neck of a rattan-ed wine bottle and there were glasses of drink on the bare table top.

'Can I see you a minute, Vic?' I asked.

'*Mais, oui, mais, oui,*' he said, laughing, and he lifted his head and yelled: 'Hey, Lorraine!' at the guy in the harem costume, the doorman who had led interference for me to his table. 'Sit down and have a drink,' he said, wiggling his hips in the seat, trying to push them over and make room for me.

'It's pretty important, Vic. . . .' I said.

'Oh, for goodness' sake, sit down!' he said, affecting a slight lisp.

'Sows,' he said to the others, 'this is Paul Murphy.'

'Hello,' I said, and they smiled and nodded, a little reserved. The three young boys sitting together on one side of the booth were flamers, with big Windsor knots in their gaudy ties and shirt collars four sizes too big, and their faces were cast in that pretty, pointed, aesthetic mould that indulgent doting mothers are so Cellini-like at shaping. With Mason on his side of the table was a woman of about thirty with hard masculine features and, in the corner, a man. This man was Ray Pratt, the plainclothes man, one of the cops who had been at Mason's Garage on the stake-out for Jinx.

'What do you want?' Lorraine said to Mason.

'We want a drink for my friend,' Mason said.

'For crying out loud . . .' Lorraine said. 'I'm the bouncer, not the waiter. If you want a drink, call the waiter.'

'Send me a waiter, will you?' Mason said.

258

Lorraine swished away.

'Thanks just the same, Vic,' I said. 'I hate to bust in on you like this, but it's very important. Could I please see you a minute?'

'Well. . . .' he said, pushing himself up from the table.

'So long . . .' I said to the people at the table.

I struggled my way back out to the foyer, pausing beside one of the photographs of the naked girls, the one reclining.

Mason stopped beside me.

'Vic,' I said quietly, 'we got something on fire. Something big.'

'We?'

'You know who,' I said. 'Here's what I want to find out. You think you could rent a truckaway for a day or two?'

'A truckaway?' he said. 'What do you want with a truckaway?'

'I got to have a truckaway,' I said. 'You know some place where you could rent one?'

'Maybe . . .'

'Without a driver. Just the truckaway. We don't want a driver. We'll drive it ourselves.'

'Are you gonna start draying automobiles?'

'One. One automobile,' I said. 'I'll see that you get something for your trouble. You think you can arrange it?'

'I think so . . .'

'What are the chances?'

'I think I can get one for you. I won't know till in the morning.'

'When in the morning? How soon can you find one out?'

'You're really hopped up about this, ain't you?' he said.

'Yes. Yes, I am. I'll sleep better if you think you can arrange to get a truckaway.'

'I think maybe I can. But I can't call 'em until eight-thirty in the morning.'

'You're pretty sure you can get it?'

'Yes.'

'Thanks, Vic. Thanks very much,' I said, patting him on the back. 'I feel better now.'

'Come in and have a drink,' he said.'

'I got to get some sleep, Vic. I haven't slept in so long, I haven't relaxed in so goddamn long – maybe tonight I can. I'll see you in the morning.'

I patted him on the back again and went out into the black street, walking towards the light reflections in the sky that marked the city, with the tentacles of the party noises in The Persian Cat clutching at me ...

In the hotel where the Halstead orchestra was still playing, the St. Cholet, I registered for a room and paid for it in advance and was shown up by a youthful bellboy.

He unlocked the door and switched on the light, went to the bathroom and switched on the light, came out and adjusted the window and the shade and then turned down the bed. He patted the bed and stood at attention.

'Will that be all, sir?' he asked.

'Yes, thank you,' I said, holding out half a dollar.

He came to me and took the half a dollar. 'You're *sure* that'll be all, sir?' he asked.

'I'm sure that'll be all,' I said.

He winked at me broadly.

'Not tonight, sonny,' I said.

He went out. He didn't know that this was the first time in years I had had the complete freedom and privacy of a sleeping room; that this was one night I didn't want a dame.

I went into the bathroom and started the water in the tub and came back and picked up the phone. 'Will you please call me at seven-thirty?' I said.

'Seven-thirty. Yes, sir,' the operator said.

I hung up and started undressing. I did not think about Holiday or Cherokee. The hell with them. I was thinking about tomorrow . . .

... *chapter three*

I was at Mason's Garage a little before eight o'clock.

'Did you find out about the truckaway?' I asked.

'I got hold of 'em,' he said. 'Only they won't rent one for one day. You can keep it for one day, but you have to pay three days' rent.'

'What about the driver? Do we have to take a driver?'

'Without the driver,' he said.

'That's wonderful!' I said. 'Jesus Christ, that's wonderful!'

He looked at me solemnly. 'Is this some kind of snatch?'

'What do you think I am – a chump? When can we get this truckaway?'

'I didn't ask them when. I asked them could.'

'Jesus, Vic,' I said. 'I told you this was important.'

'You didn't say nothing to me about when. You said could . . .'

'Well, can you call the place now? I'll take it today. Right away.'

He picked up the phone and dialled a number. 'Hullo,' he said 'Lemme talk to Rafferty.' He waited half a minute and said: 'Rafferty, this is Vic Mason again. About that truckaway. When can I have it?' He listened for a moment and said: 'This morning? That'll be fine. Deliver it here . . .' He listened again and said: 'Yeah, I understand about the rates. Seventy-five for three days, three-day minimum.' He said good-bye and hung up.

'That's wonderful,' I said.

'Will you please tell me what this is all about?'

'There're a few details to smooth out. I'll tell you then,' I said.

'I got the stuff to rent too, you know.'

'I know. I want to rent the Zephyr. Is it here?'

'Where'd you think it was – springing some guy off a prison farm?'

I smiled at him. 'Get it ready for me,' I said.

He went out.

I looked in the book for Mandon's home number, BA 1-9055, and dialled it. It rang a few times and then his harsh voice said: 'Hello!' 'Cherokee?' I said. 'Who is this?' he said. 'This is Paul,' I said. 'Paul – Paul . . .' he said vaguely. 'The guy you walked out on last night,' I said. 'The guy who paid the check . . .' 'Oh, the connoisseur,' he said. 'Where'd you go?' 'It's a long and bewitching story,' I said. 'Now, lissen, Cherokee. We're in. This thing's wrapped up, but we got to move fast. I want you to meet me in Webber's office at nine-thirty.' 'Wait a minute,' he said. 'I don't know what kind of office hours Webber keeps. He may not be there at nine-thirty . . .' 'You make it your business to see that he is,' I said. 'Well, all right,' he said grudgingly. 'I'll do my best.'

I looked up the number of the Marakeesh Apartment, WE 4-6247, and dialled it and asked for one, one, four. Jinx answered the phone. 'How are you, son?' I asked. 'Where the hell are you?' he said. 'Downtown. Holiday there?' 'She's still sleeping,' he said. 'Let her sleep,' I said. 'Meet me in front of the apartment in fifteen minutes.' 'What's up?' he asked. 'I'll tell you then,' I said. 'Look your best. And try to get out without waking Holiday,' I said, and hung up.

I went into the garage. Mason was standing behind the Zephyr.

'She's all right,' he said. He looked at me. 'You made quite a hit last night. Couple of the boys thought you were pretty nice.'

'They're a little young for me,' I said.

'Get 'em young and train 'em, that's my motto,' he said.

Don't get mad at him now, I told myself. Remember that he's a rebel too. You are of the same species, the same psyche. You understand all that now... 'I'll see you around,' I said.

I turned to go around the Zephyr to get in and a man came up to Mason from the next car, saying: 'That's all it was, Vic. Feed line stopped up.'

It was one of Ezra Dobson's policemen, one of the cops who had caught me in that bedroom. He stared at me. I trembled just a little inside. Mason saw us staring at each other.

'Paul,' he said, 'shake hands with my brother-in-law, Theo Zumbro. This is Paul Murphy, Theo...'

'Hello,' Zumbro said.

'Hello....' I said, shaking hands

'You ought to say thank you too,' Mason said. 'Wasn't for him you wouldn't be standing here....'

Now I got it. Brother-in-law. Zumbro had furnished the machine-gun for Holiday, the one she had used at the prison farm.

'Ralph Cotter,' Mason said to him.

'Oh!' Zumbro said in surprise.

Why the hell am I trembling inside, I asked myself? He's just another crooked cop. Zumbro was trying to connect the prison farm and that bedroom and Margaret Dobson and me together, but he couldn't.

'Well...' Zumbro said. 'You get around, don't you?'

'No telling where I'm liable to turn up,' I said. 'I'll see you,' I said.

I got into the Zephyr and started it and backed out. As I shifted gears, easing the sedan towards the front door, I waved at them.

They waved back. Zumbro was watching me.

Where the hell is this going to lead, I wondered.

264

Jinx was waiting for me in front of the apartment, looking his best.

I slid off the seat. 'You drive,' I said.

'What's up?' he asked, getting under the wheel.

'We're in,' I said. 'This thing's sacked.' I closed the door and he rolled the Zephyr away. 'Did you get out without waking Holiday?'

'Yeah.'

'Good. One more fight with her and I'm ready for the strait-jacket. Last night I found out what's wrong with her.'

'What?'

'She used to be in love with a sports writer.'

'Does that make something wrong with her?'

'A dame never gets over her love for a sports writer. She never forgets the memory. She wears the scar forever. Head for the City Hall, will you?'

'City Hall?'

'Webber's office. The sacrosanct cubicle of the Dalai Lama himself.'

'You finally figure something?'

'You know me, Jinx.'

'What is it you figured?'

'That can wait,' I said. 'Tell you what you think about. You try to remember some place around here where we can stash that Buick for six or seven hours, where there's no chance of anybody seeing it, where there's absolutely no chance of anybody seeing it.'

... *chapter four*

I didn't stop at the door marked BUREAU OF HOMICIDES. I went to the next door down the corridor, the door to Inspector Webber's private office, and rapped on it.

'Come in,' I heard Webber's voice say.

I opened it and Jinx and I went in.

Webber was behind the desk, looking displeased as always; and Mandon was sitting in a chair at the side of the desk. Reece was standing with his back to the window, his arms folded.

'Good morning,' I said, holding my voice down, not wanting to seem fresh or impertinent, what the hell, why rub it in, but the Dalai Lama's displeasure seemed only to increase.

I glanced at Mandon and I could tell from the way he looked that he already had been berated, and he was saying to me with his eyes, 'I hope this is good.' I smiled at him, reassuringly, and crossed to the desk.

'You feel better about this, Inspector?' I asked.

'You seem to,' he said in brief gruffness.

'I do,' I said. I leaned over the desk. 'I got the trigger to this thing now. I had Vic Mason rent a truckaway. We get it today – this morning.'

'What's a truckaway?' Webber asked.

'A truckaway is a truck that hauls automobiles,' I said. 'You've seen 'em. It loads three cars on the body of the truck and it has a track above, a platform, that loads some more on top, over the driver's cab. You drive 'em up on a metal ramp and then you disconnect the ramp and you're ready to go. You've seen 'em.'

He looked at Reece, and Mandon leaned forward in his chair, and I knew they had gotten the idea.

'We stick up the Buick and stash it somewhere till night, and then around midnight when there's not much traffic, we drive onto the truckaway and away we go.'

'Away we go where?' Reece asked, moving in closer.

'To one of the bridges across the river – the one that's most likely to be deserted. We may have to block off both sides for a few minutes, but that's only a detail. We back the truckaway up to the railing and roll the Buick off into the middle of the river. Clean and perfect . . .' Webber lowered his eyes to the desk, then raised them.

'And what about the four guys?' he asked.

'I thought we covered that last night,' I said.

'Just the same . . .'

'The balance in nature is always cold-blooded,' I said. 'Or did you ever for example see a goshawk wheel and dive at a partridge?'

They looked at each other, but nobody said anything. Webber turned but didn't move from behind the desk.

'I hate to say this, gentlemen,' I said, 'but I think this is a hell of an idea.'

Webber said ponderously: 'That means you'll have to kill these men right after the stick-up.'

'Naturally,' I said.

'When will that be? What time?'

'Three-thirty. Four o'clock. I got to let them finish with their collections. Otherwise, there's not much point to it.'

'And you figure to get rid of the Buick around midnight?'

'Yes.'

'Then you're gonna have a hot automobile full of dead men on your hands for eight or nine hours. Where you gonna stash the car?'

'That's what Joseph and I are going to decide when we leave here,' I said. 'He knows this country, don't you?'

Jinx nodded.

I went on: 'Findin' a place to stash the car is no problem. The problem is to find police uniforms to fit Joseph and me. That's the problem.'

'I don't like it,' Webber said. 'An automobile full of dead men is not something you can drive into a parking lot and forget. This is too risky. These guys disappear at four o'clock, the goddamn alarm'll be out by five.'

'Why will it?' I asked. 'Roamer'll come to you first. You don't have to put out the goddamn alarm.'

He hadn't thought of this, by God, he hadn't thought of it. I knew from the dumb look in his face that this had not occurred to him. Jesus, was I going to have to do all the thinking?

'Car full of dead men, blocking bridge,' he said, almost painfully.

'Hey, hold on!' Reece said. 'Why worry about stashing the car or using the bridge? I know where there's an abandoned quarry out here on the old Holt Turnpike that's three hundred goddamn feet deep. Why not use that?'

'What the hell good is an old abandoned quarry gonna do us?' I said.

'Well, for Christ's sake, it's got water in it same as the river,' he said. 'If anything, it's deeper. It's a hell of a lot safer than lugging an automobile full of dead men around town and dumping it off the bridge.'

Maybe Holiday had been right, maybe he was smarter than I gave him credit for being. This was something good. I grinned

268

at him. One more contribution like this and I'd have to put him
in Webber's job.

I looked at Webber. For the first time since I'd known him he
was beginning to smile. . . .

... *chapter five*

At three twenty-five Pratt eased the blue-and-white traffic-control car, a Ford sedan with a Mercury motor, into a parking space down the street from Harold's Beauty Shop. Downey was in the front seat with him, and Jinx and I were in the back. We all wore police uniforms. Racked on the bottom of the roof over Downey was a tommy gun, racked on the bottom of the roof over us was another tommy gun and an automatic rifle. On the floor between Jinx's feet and mine was the suitcase containing our civilian clothes. The clothes we would put on when the job was done and the suitcase then could be used to hold the contents of the little leather satchels – the money, a minimum of fifteen thousand dollars. The little leather satchels we would sink with the four collectors in the Buick.

Nobody said anything. Pratt lighted a cigarette and glanced at me a couple times, obviously still thinking about last night when I had seen him. Ever since I had got in the car in the police garage he had been self-conscious and shy with me, but I had been very careful not to do or say anything that might remind him of it. Downey half turned in his seat, looking back at me.

'Suppose those guys change the route?' he said. 'Suppose they don't stop here last?'

'Then I can't help it,' I said, 'and we'll have to try again. But I don't think they'll switch. Why should they? They're not looking for a heist. It's the last thing they are looking for. They've had things their own way so long they're fat, cocky and careless. That's what we're figuring on to carry this off without a hitch – their being fat, cocky and careless. Now, let's see if we got this. Jinx and I go over and give 'em a parking ticket. If they don't park in the loading zone, I fake a charge. There'll be a brief argument and we'll have to take the guys down.'

'These are not apple-stealers,' Pratt said. 'They're tough boys.'

'You sound just like Webber,' I said. 'I know all about how tough they are. When Jinx and I get in and start away with 'em, you guys follow. I'll make 'em drive to the quarry – the same way we just come from there.'

'They'll know something's wrong when they have to head away from the City Hall,' Downey said.

'I'll handle that,' I said. 'You just stick close. If anything at all goes wrong, the first guy I'll let have it is the driver. That'll put the Buick out of control, and in the excitement we'll get out and you come alongside and start using your tommy guns. Clear?'

They nodded.

'You got your orders from Webber. This has got to be absolutely clean. If you have to start shooting, be sure you wipe 'em out.'

I looked at Jinx. His face was a little drawn. I winked at him and offered him a cigarette. 'Take it easy,' I said, lighting the cigarette for him. 'Relax. This is the big league . . .'

I wasn't too worried about him, because I didn't anticipate any rough stuff from their end, from Roamer's men. He was along just to give the thing atmosphere and authority.

He took a few puffs of the cigarette and then touched my knee. I looked out the window. The black Buick was passing us, the four guys inside, it was slowing down, and I followed it with my eyes as it came to a stop in the loading zone down the street from Harold's. The same three guys, the little one and the two medium-sized ones, got out and walked back to the beauty shop.

Downey reached up and unracked the tommy gun and put it on the floor between his legs. I liked that. This fellow was concentrating. Pratt started the motor.

'Here we go,' I said to Jinx.

I got out behind him and Downey closed the door.

'Remember – all you got to do is act like a rookie cop,' I said.

'Yeah,' he said, dropping his cigarette.

I took another quick look at him. He looked at me. His face was strained, but otherwise he seemed all right . . .

We approached the Buick. He lingered behind, and I moved to the driver's window. The driver was about forty, with a cauliflower ear and a crooked nose and puffy cheeks. He hit me with his eyes, but not suspiciously.

'You know you're in a loading zone?' I asked.

'So what,' he said.

'Parking in a loading zone is a traffic violation,' I said.

'So what,' he said.

I moved a step closer. Now I could see into the car. On the floor in front were six leather satchels. My heart skipped a beat or two at the sight of them – minimum of fifteen thousand dollars; and I wondered what was wrong with the mentality of a man who could perfect a set-up like this, as Roamer had, and leave six satchels to be guarded by one frowzy punch-drunk chauffeur, while two men guarded the guy who only had one satchel. Fat, cocky and careless . . .

I took the book of traffic tickets and the pencil out of my pocket. 'Let's see your driver's license,' I said.

'I got no license,' he said.

'That's another violation of the law,' I said. 'Don't you know that?'

The three guys came back to the Buick. The little one got in front with the satchel, but he didn't see me until he had sat down.

He was thirty, with black eyes that instantly flared. 'Whadda you want?' he said.

'This man's name,' I said. 'I'm going to write him a ticket.'

'On your way, copper,' he said.

The other two guys were seated in the back row. One of them rolled down the window. 'What's the beef?' he asked.

'Parking in a loading zone, no driver's license . . .'

'That's a laugh,' the little one said.

'We park here every day, fellow,' the guy who had rolled down the window said.

'It's a violation of the traffic ordinance . . .'

'Yeah, yeah, yeah, yeah,' the little guy said.

'We work for Roamer, fellow,' the guy in the back said, in a reasonable tone.

'This is Roamer's car,' the other guy in the back said.

'I don't know Roamer,' I said. 'I'm new on the force. And it wouldn't make any difference if I did.'

'Look fellow,' the reasonable one said. 'You like your job? You wanna keep it? Then blow . . .'

Jinx strolled up to me. 'These boys are getting tough,' I said.

'Well,' he said, 'you know what the sergeant said. Anybody tries to get tough, run 'em in . . .'

'Lissen, for Christ's sake,' the guy in front said. 'Don't make a sucker outta yourself. Now, on your way . . .'

'Let's take 'em down,' I said.

'Sure,' Jinx said.

'Goddamn it!' the guy in front said.

'Shut up, Sid,' the reasonable one said. 'Lissen, bud,' he said to me, 'you don't wanna do that. They'll only turn us loose and you'll get your ass eaten out . . .'

I smiled at Jinx. 'The sergeant said they'd say that, didn't he?' I said. 'You get up front with the others,' I said to the reasonable guy. 'If the sergeant wants to turn you loose, that's his business.'

'You're only making it tough on yourself,' the reasonable one said.

'I'm just trying to do my job,' I said. 'Get up front.'

'Jesus!' he said. 'A rookie cop . . .'

'Screw these guys,' Sid said. 'Let's go, Rushy.'

Rushy turned the switch key. This was the first sign of interest he had shown since the three guys had got in the car.

'Hold it!' I snapped. 'Get up in front, you . . .'

Sid snarled something I couldn't understand but the reasonable guy cut him off, saying: 'Sid, don't start anything about a parking ticket . . .' and got out of the back into the front.

Jinx and I got in the back, flanking the other middle-weight, with him on my left. He was an average hoodlum, and thirty-five.

'You know where Police Headquarters is?' I said.

'We know, goddamn it,' Sid said.

'That's where we're going,' I said.

'Go ahead, Rushy,' the reasonable one said.

Rushy started the motor and put the car in gear and we moved away. I risked a quick look back. Pratt and Downey had pulled out from the kerb . . .

'You fellows take your jobs too seriously,' the reasonable one said.

'We got our orders, mister,' I said

'You're gonna get some new orders,' Sid snarled.

'If you're a friend of the sergeant's, that's fine,' I said.

'If you're a friend of the sergeant's,' Sid said. 'That's a scream for you. We don't fool with sergeants. Roamer even tells Webber where to get off . . .'

'Shut up, Sid,' the reasonable one said.

'We've got our orders,' I said.

Rushy kept the Buick going straight down the street, and turned the same corner he always did. There was a lot of traffic on this street too. We went to the next corner and turned left. In the middle of the block, on the other side of the street, between the street car tracks and the kerbing were some big wooden signs which read: MEN WORKING! BE CAREFUL! CONDUIT CONSTRUCTION! BE CAREFUL, and men were digging into the paving with compressed air-hammers that made so much noise you could hear nothing else. I looked at the quiet guy beside me, the quiet one who had spoken but once. His eyes were wide and his lips were parted slightly, and my spine tingled with that awareness. He wasn't sure, but he was wondering. ... I eased around and pulled my automatic from the holster, pushing it into his stomach, and shot him. His lips twitched and he fell against me, and I shot him again, a little higher up in his stomach.

The air-hammers were making so much noise that for a moment the guys in front could not separate these sounds from the pistol explosions.

Then Sid looked around. The stupefaction in his face was the stupefaction of a man who suddenly discovers in the space of an eye-blink that the mountain is no longer there.

'All right, you sons-a-bitches,' I said. 'Clasp your hands behind your heads.'

The reasonable guy slowly clasped his hands behind his head, but Sid tried to free himself and I knew he was reaching for his gun.

I hit him in the back of the head with my automatic. 'Clasp your hands behind your head,' I said.

He groaned slightly and clasped his hands behind his head.

'Keep your hands on the wheel,' Jinx said to the driver.

With my left hand, I shoved the guy I had shot. He rolled off my knees to the floor. The air-hammers were still making a terriffic racket. I shot him again, in the left temple, and with my foot I turned him over, facing the front seat, so he wouldn't bleed on my shoes.

'You'll never get away with this,' Sid was saying.

'That's a familiar chirp,' I said, thumbing the clip from my automatic, putting in a new one . . .

We pushed the Buick full of dead men and empty leather satchels over the shaly escarpment, and the front bumper struck a small jut and the car turned over and struck the water on its top, opening a concavity as smoothly as you scoop out a spoon of jelled dessert. For a few seconds it lay there in the concavity, an upended monster, its four paws turning and wabbling, its grotesque belly exposed, the belly and entrails which had been tooled to one one-hundred thousandth of an inch; and then the concavity filled and the car turned over slowly on its side and sank.

There were no tire tracks, no blood stains, no witnesses but us.

It was as clean as the Everest snow and as absolutely perfect as a circle.

Across the flat beyond the grove of poplars was the city, the tower of the City Hall rising, white and shining, a mighty symbol.

The only sound in the world was Pratt vomiting. . . .

. . . chapter six

The take was $51,304. We counted it behind locked doors in Webber's office at the City Hall: Webber, Reece, Pratt, Downey, Jinx and I – all of us working. Fifty-one-thousand, three hundred and four dollars.

We split it three ways: one for Webber, who would take care of his people, one for me, who would take care of my people, and one for Mandon: seventeen thousand, one hundred dollars apiece.

'Well, boys,' I said to Pratt and Downey, 'it looks like you have finally gotten off that hind tit.'

From my stack of money I took five one-hundred dollar bills and put them in my pocket for Mason – two hundred I had borrowed and the three hundred for the truckaway I had not used. I thought that should cover it. I wrapped the rest of my share in a newspaper and handed it to Jinx, who put it in my suitcase, and I then wrapped Mandon's share in a newspaper and put it under my arm.

'Drop me at Mandon's office and take the rest of the stuff home,' I said to Jinx.

He picked up the suitcase, and I turned to go.

'Gentlemen,' I said to the others, 'don't think it ain't been charming . . .'

Only one of the blondes, the younger one, was in Mandon's office.

'He's expecting you, Mister Murphy,' she said. 'Go right in ...'

I went in through the little gate to the door of his private office and knocked.

He opened the door. He was chewing an unlighted stogie. He saw the package under my arm and glanced nervously at the blonde, who was paying no attention to us, and I stepped past him to the inside.

'Relax,' I said.

He closed the door and came to me. 'Did everything go all right?' he asked.

'Sure. Fine.' I patted the package. 'Make a guess ...'

'I don't know.'

'Twenty thousand.'

I laughed. 'Hell, your cut alone is almost that much,' I said. 'Slightly over fifty thousand,' I said.

'My God,' he exclaimed.

'Seventen thousand and some small bills you can use as tips,' I said, handing him the package.

'That's unbelievable!' he said.

'It's only the beginning,' I said.

He unwrapped the package and looked at the money.

'And for your information,' I said, 'the dividing of the money was well audited. Webber, Reece, Jinx and I all helped count it.'

'I trust you,' he said, patting me on the shoulder.

'I know ...' I said.

'No hitches, eh?' He smiled. He had relaxed.

'It was well planned, well executed – and we were lucky,' I was thinking about the air-hammers and that quiet guy in the back. He would have started something for sure. I had got him just in time. 'Did you call Mason about the truckaway?' I asked.

'Yeah. I got him to cancel it.'

'Was he sore?'

'Not when I told him we'd pay for it. He was very curious though.'

'He's worse than an old woman,' I said. 'That was some idea Reece came up with – that quarry. I may've been wrong about him. I may have to put him in Webber's job before I get through.'

'Why not let things ride for a while? This came off all right . . .'

'Oh, I wasn't thinking of the future. I just don't want to have to go through these arguments with Webber every time we got something lined up. You saw how he was.'

'Well, now that you've shown him what you can do, I'm sure he'll be more amenable.'

'We'll see,' I said. 'Want to come down to the place? I promised Holiday a party if this thing came off to sort of make up for the one she didn't get last night. We're breaking open a bottle. Gancia. Lacrima Christa.'

'Champagne?'

'Champagne,' I said. 'The traditional victory drink.'

'You've earned it too, you have,' he said heartily. 'But you'll have to count me out tonight. I'll see you tomorrow.'

'I don't know about tomorrow. Tomorrow I got to get measured for some clothes and look for an apartment, a nice one, where I can have some freedom and privacy and have a few of my own things around.'

'Couple of more jobs like this and you can buy an apartment of your own,' he said.

'I got that in the back of my mind too,' I said.

He nodded his head with emphasis. 'We make a good team – you and I,' he said.

'Even if it did take a gun to get you into the line-up,' I said.

He laughed and patted me on the shoulder, moving with me to the door.

'See you around, Shice,' I said.

279

He seemed delighted to have me use his nickname. He simply beamed.

I smiled and went out.

Mason saw me get out of the cab in front of the garage entrance, and by the time I had walked to the office he had hobbled all the way from the rear. He was wearing welder's gloves, and around his neck were the dark goggles.

'What happened that you didn't use the truckaway?' he asked.

'A slight hitch,' I said. 'We postponed the job.'

'Postponed it?Mandon said it was cancelled.'

'Well, cancelled then. Temporarily. We'll use the truckaway sometime...'

'I don't get this,' he said. 'I never seen a guy so hot for anything as you was that truckaway. Then all of a sudden you don't want it.'

'One of the symptoms of the psychopathic super-ego is random behavior,' I said. 'I told you. A slight hitch...'

He looked at me with a wise look. 'Now tell me what really happened,' he said.

I took out the five hundred dollars. 'Here. What I borrowed from you and the rent on the truckaway that I was so hot for and didn't use because there was a slight hitch and which we cancelled but which we will get around to eventually,' I said. 'If there is anything left over, apply it on the Zephyr. I'm keeping it a few more days...'

He removed the gloves and took the money, squinting at me. 'So you pulled the job, after all,' he said.

'Oh, hell,' I said. 'This is a loan. You think you're the only friend I got who'll lend me dough?'

'A loan like hell,' he said. 'What job was it?'

'You're a regular old woman,' I said, smiling. 'You going to The Persian Cat tonight?'

'Probably...'

'I'm giving Holiday a whirl,' I said. 'We may see you there.'

There was plenty of Lacrima Christa in the liquor stores, splits, fifths, a few magnums, but no jeroboams. I wanted a jeroboam. In the third liquor store, called the Epigourmet (sic), I uncovered one. I had the clerk wrap it in white tissue paper and tie it up with a red ribbon, and I bought three goblets and had them wrapped the same way; and when I got back to the cab the driver looked at me in amusement. I had quite an armful.

'Whaddya got there?' he asked.

'A present for myself,' I said. 'My wife just had a baby.'

'A present for you?' he said. 'She had the baby, but you get the present?'

'Every time my wife has a baby, I buy myself a present,' I said.

'Well, say now,' he said, 'maybe you got something there...'

I had more here than he knew. I was a happy guy. I glowed a little in anticipation of seeing Holiday. The ghosts were gone, now and forever, and those ancient memories had been imprisoned again; the laceration was healing and the vision that had been a white-white face with black-black hair was now but a fragment of a secret nightmare in full and lonely flight, past impure idols, to the limitless abyss of yesterday... I was a happy guy.

I rode to the apartment in the soft warm dusk. A few store lights had come on early, like people who get to the depot an hour ahead of time, never quite trusting the schedule. The street cars and buses were filled with the little people going home after their day's work, and some of them had bundles too. What were they celebrating?

When I opened the door and went in, Holiday and Jinx were sitting on the davenport with the money stacked between them. She jumped up and came to me, smiling broadly.

'What's in the bundle?' she asked.

'Champagne,' I said.

'I never saw a bottle that big,' she said.

'A jeroboam,' I said. 'They come bigger than this. . . .'

I put the bottle on the table, and the goblets beside it.

'What're those?' she asked.

'Goblets,' I said. 'Glasses. To drink the wine . . .'

'You didn't have to buy special glasses,' she said. 'We got glasses in the kitchen.'

Good old Holiday. Nothing aesthetic about her. Pure animal, thank God. 'You don't drink champagne out of kitchen glasses,' I said. 'You're the most uncivilized drinker I ever saw,' I said with good humor. Good old Holiday. Nothing metaphysical about her. Pure animal, thank God.

I put my arms around her and kissed her on the mouth, and she kissed me back, burrowing into my coat. Jinx was watching me with dull flat eyes. There was a pencil behind his ear and a sheet of paper on his knee.

'I don't mind sitting in this apartment and waiting when you and Jinx bring back stuff like this,' she said. 'We've separated the money . . .'

Our arms around each other, we went to the davenport. The money had been stacked in piles, the 100s and 50s and 20s and 10s and 5s and 1s. The sheet of paper Jinx had on his knee listed the totals of each denomination.

'Did it come out okay?' I asked.

'Can't you open your mouth without being snott?' he said.

'Snotty?' I said. 'Am I snotty?'

'You're always snotty and you're always looking for a fight,' he said.

'Jesus, look who's talking,' I said to Holiday. 'What's the matter with you?' I said to Jinx.

'I got a right to count the dough,' he said.

'Of course you got a right to count the dough. I just asked if it came out okay.'

'I know what you meant.'

'I'll be a son-of-a-bitch,' I said. 'I come home happy as a lark, to have a party, a celebration – and this is what I run into: a sorehead who snaps and snarls. . . . I give up.'

Holiday turned me around by the arms and held me. 'You know how much we got?' she asked.

'Roughly,' I said.

'Roughly? Ha!' Jinx said. 'He knows to the penny.'

'Fifty-seven hundred apiece,' Holiday said.

'Lay off me, will you?' I said to Jinx. 'This is only the beginning,' I said to Holiday. I kissed her again, making much of it for Jinx's benefit. This is what the matter was with him. When I kissed her it was right out in the open. When he kissed her he had to sneak it. 'What about the champagne?' I said. 'Jinx, you know where there's an icehouse around here?'

'I know where there's a refrigerator. Will that help?'

'Hell, a refrigerator's no good,' I said. 'This takes ice. We need a sink full of ice. Fifty pounds, at least. We're gonna start the celebration here, but God knows where we'll wind up.'

'I'll tell you where I'm going to wind up,' Jinx said. 'I'm going to wind up at home.'

'Will you please get some ice first?' Holiday asked.

He looked at her making a weary face.

'The hell with him,' I said. 'I'll get the ice.'

I took myself out of Holiday's arms and picked up the phone. 'Hello,' I said to the operator. 'Can you tell me if there's an icehouse in the neighborhood?' 'We can send you some extra ice, sir,' she said. 'Fifty pounds?' I asked. She laughed. 'Oh, no, sir, not that much. But there's a package ice place at Truax and Withers Streets.' 'Is that near?' 'Only a few blocks, sir.' 'Thank you.' I said, hanging up.

283

All this time Jinx had been counting his share of the money. He saw that I had my eyes on him and he said, 'I'm taking my cut now.'

'So I see,' I said.

'Any objections?'

'Go ahead,' I said.

I stood there watching him. Behind me Holiday was tearing the tissue paper off the jeroboam. Jinx put the money in three stacks, 100s, 50s and 20s, counting the bills, consulting the sheet of paper on which he had already listed the amounts. He picked up the stack of 100s in his left hand. 'Thirty of these,' he said. He picked up the stack of 50s in his right hand. 'Forty of these,' he said. He put the two stacks down and picked up the 20s. 'And thirty-five of these. Fifty-seven hundred dollars. Wanna check it?'

'Oh, God, no – I don't want to check it,' I said.

He stood up, putting the money in his pockets with both hands. 'Now, I'll get the ice,' he said.

'Don't bother,' I said.

Holiday gurgled with delight and came past me, lugging the jeroboam, which she propped in a corner of the davenport like a doll. 'Why,' she said, 'there's enough champagne here to last a month.'

'You'd be surprised how fast it goes, once you get started,' I said.

'Fifty pounds, is that right?' Jinx said.

'Don't bother,' I said. 'That's not a sec champagne,' I said to Holiday. 'That's a trifle sweet, but I got it for you. Most women don't like very sec champagne.'

I turned to go. Jinx caught me by the arm.

'I'll get the ice,' he said.

Any other time I would have nailed him. I didn't want to hit him now. I didn't want to fight. I wanted everything to be nice and pleasant. This was a celebration, not only of a job damned well done, but of something else too – something much more important to *me*. 'Turn me loose,' I said.

He released my arm. 'All fight, if that's the way you feel about it,' he said.

'That's the way I feel about it, you son-of-a-bitch,' I said, going out. . . .

I dropped a dime and a nickel in the slot and a block of ice rattled down the chute, neatly wrapped in brown waxed paper. I dropped another dime and another nickel in the slot and got a second chuck, and loaded them into the Zephyr.

It was tentative night now, getting dark, and all the lights were on. The streetcars and the buses were not so crowded. Most of the day workers had gotten home. But I knew of four day workers who hadn't gotten home. Roamer, whoever he was, wherever he was, was now wondering what had happened to them. Had he gone to Webber yet? I hoped Webber could handle him . . .

I kicked on the door of the apartment with my foot, and Holiday opened it.

'Let me help you,' she said.

'I got it,' I said. 'Has Jinx gone?'

'Yes.'

'Fine. Glorious. Wonderful. Just you and me . . .'

I carried the ice into the kitchen and dumped it into the sink. I tore off the paper and wadded it up, and then I remembered the one thing I had forgotten. 'Jesus,' I said. 'I thought of everything but an ice pick.'

'Use a knife,' she said.

'I'll have to.'

I started chopping at the ice with a paring knife. It was slow work. The goddamn knife kept bending. I tried to hold it so it wouldn't break.

285

'How long'll it take to get the champagne cold?' she asked.

'Maybe an hour – who cares?Let's do it right.' I stopped chopping and flung the particles of ice off my hands and took her in my arms. 'This is one night when everything's got to be done right,' I told her. 'Slowly and easily and pleasantly, to the most trivial detail – like the tearing of a sheet of toilet paper so perfectly along the perforations that not one fiber will either be missing or added. That perfect, this has got to be. . . .'

I kissed her lightly, a flutter, only enough to know that I had touched her lips; and smiled and went back to the slow work of chopping the ice with the paring knife.

'This,' I said, 'is for me. Wouldn't it be nice to begin every night with a bottle of champagne and close it with a bottle of cognac?'

'Maybe we can,' she said; 'maybe we can.'

'Five'll get you ten,' I said. 'We're in. Tomorrow, we'll buy a case of each. Tomorrow, we'll buy some new clothes and look for some new apartments – maybe we both can find apartments in the same building. Something nice . . .'

'Separate apartments, you mean?'

'Yes.'

Her face darkened a little, and she frowned. 'So now it comes,' she said. 'I was wondering why you were acting so funny . . .'

'Funny?' I said.

'All this lovey-dovey crap. Wanting everything so perfect. I might've known this was the old brush-off.'

'Now why do you say that?'

'Separate apartments . . .'

'Well, Jesus, there's nothing in that to get mad about. There is such a thing as privacy, you know.'

'Haven't you got privacy here?'

'Oh, now, look. Don't you start getting touchy.'

'I'm not touchy.'

286

'Well, don't be. There's nothing personal in this. But we only got one bed, one bathroom. I'd like to be able to go in a bathroom sometime and not have to lock the door, that's all.'

'You don't have to lock the door. Have I ever bothered you when you were in the bathroom?'

'That's not the point. You're in the same apartment with me. That's enough.'

'You're giving me the air, is that it?'

'Jesus . . .' I said.

'I spring you off the prison farm and the minute you get some dough, you give me the air.'

'I'm sorry I mentioned it,' I said. 'Forget it. Pretend I never said it.'

'That's the way you want it, that's the way you get it,' she said flouncing out of the kitchen.

I threw the goddamn knife in the sink and followed her out. She went to the davenport and stood with her back to me and picked up some money and started counting it.

'What the hell are you doing?' I said.

She didn't look up or around. ' Fifty-seven hundred of this is mine. That's all I'm taking,' she said.

I stepped around in front of her, putting my hands on her shoulders. 'What goes on with you?' I said.

'Before I take my walk, I want what's mine,' she said.

'Oh, for Christ's sake,' I said, 'stop being so touchy. I thought I was neurotic, but I'm a son-of-a-bitch, I am an A-plus normal compared to you and Jinx. We got a party tonight, remember? Hey!' I said. 'I just thought of something else . . .'

I moved over and picked up the phone. 'This is that man again,' I said to the operator. 'Could you get me the Hotel St. Cholet?'

Holiday was still counting the money, her back to me. I put my hand over the mouthpiece and said to her, 'You won't need all that tonight. I promise to eat and drink very lightly.'

'Hotel St. Cholet,' a woman's voice said. 'What's the name of the room where the Halstead orchestra's playing?' I asked. 'Blossom Room, sir.' 'Connect me, please,' I said. 'Blossom Room,' a man's voice said. 'May I speak to the maitre d'?' I said. 'Maitre d' speaking, sir...' 'What is your name?' I asked. 'George, sir.' 'George,' I said, 'this is Paul Murphy. Could I have two for dinner around eight-thirty?' 'Yes, sir, Mister Murphy.' 'In that loge there – up above the dance floor. Could you manage that?' 'Yes, sir, Mister Murphy. Two on the dais at eight-thirty.' 'And could you have some flowers on the table – just a touch of something?' 'Yes, sir, Mister Murphy.' 'Thank you, George,' I said. 'I'll see you when I get there...'

Holiday was still counting the money. My sterling portrayal of the man-about-town had left her completely unmoved.

'Do you mind if I pick out something for you to wear tonight?' I asked.

She said nothing.

Whistling a casual tune, I sauntered into the bedroom and opened the closet. Her clothes were hanging from the center pole. She didn't have very many.

'Holiday!' I called.

There was no answer.

'Holiday!'

There was still no answer.

I went to the bedroom door. 'Holiday!' I said.

She moved a little, turning her back directly to me.

I crossed to her. She was still counting the money. She did not look up.

'Lissen,' I said.

'Shut up!' she said.

I grabbed her by both wrists. Her hands were full of money.

'Goddamn you!' she said, her face contorted, struggling to free herself.

I shook her wrists, poking my thumbnails into the palms of her hands, shaking her fingers loose from the money that fluttered to the floor. 'Lissen!' I said. 'I couldn't wait to get home to you tonight. I was a very happy guy. I had remembered what I had forgotten and I have now forgotten what I had remembered. Oedipus is dead, and the sepulchre is sealed. The road back to the womb is closed forever. You must burn the echoes of those memories, you must purify me in the crucible of your lust . . .'

The color was lacquer-white, there was no thought-motion; I did not remember picking her up and I did not remember walking, it was as effortless as the movement of a sun-shadow – but suddenly there she was in my arms, suddenly above the bed.

I dropped her on to it. She looked up at me with bright, glinty eyes and there was a miraculous silence, and I felt the sweat trickling down my stomach, clawing at me, and I whimpered and went down on my knees beside her and far far away I heard the sounds of solacing bells. . . .

'Holiday!' I called.

There was no answer.

'Holiday!'

There was still no answer. Hell, I thought, this is right back where we started from. I went to the bedroom door. She was down on her knees, retrieving the money.

'Come here,' I said.

She got up, putting the money under her arm, and picking up my share, what was left on the newspaper on the davenport.

'What do you want to do with this?' she asked.

'I'll take it,' I said.

I went to the bureau and put it in the drawer with my shorts, and when I got back to the closet door she was putting her money into a Gladstone. 'As I was saying thirty minutes ago,' I said, 'I'm trying to pick out something for you to wear tonight. You got very little here . . .'

'I'll manage,' she said, closing the Gladstone. She stood up and shoved it into the closet with her foot.

'Tomorrow, I'll help you pick out some stuff,' I said. 'Something sexy. If you and I are going to be habitués of the Blossom Room, you got to have something sexy. Which of these numbers are you going to wear tonight?'

'That one,' she said. She stepped into the closet and held up a flowered print. 'Is that all right?'

'It doesn't do you justice,' I said. 'But this time tomorrow night you'll have a rack full.'

There was knocking at the hall door.

'Jinx,' I said. 'He would have to come back . . .'

'We'll get rid of him,' she said. 'Don't lose your temper. Don't quarrel with him.'

'Quarrel – on this night?' I said. 'My first night of complete and utter freedom?'

The knocking came again and I went through the living-room and opened the door. It wasn't Jinx. It was Mandon.

'Come in, come in,' I said. 'We're about to pop a cork.'

He stepped in and I closed the door.

'Why don't you answer the telephone?' he said.

'What telephone? The telephone didn't ring.'

'Don't tell me. It *rang*. What're you so busy doing you don't hear the telephone ring?'

Those bells . . . 'Oh, for Christ's sake,' I said.

'Get your coat. I want to talk to you . . .'

'Talk to him here,' Holiday said.

He looked around. She was entering from the bedroom.

'You stay out of this,' he said. 'This doesn't concern you.'

'What concerns him concerns me,' she said.

'Beat it,' he said. 'Get his coat.'

290

She folded her arms and her eyes flashed. 'You shrimp son-of-a-bitch, don't you talk to me like that,' she said.

'Take it easy,' I said. 'Jesus, let's not louse up this night. Not this night . . .'

'Do as I tell you,' he said to her. 'Get his coat.' His tone was tense and his face had now taken on a dark worried look. 'We haven't much time,' he said to me. 'I'm warning you, we haven't much time.'

'What's happened?' I asked.

'Plenty,' he said.

He was a cold-blooded guy with virtually no imagination and he did not worry about nothing and now he was worried. I was suddenly worried because he was worried. This had something to do with the heist, or with Roamer or with Webber. Something had slipped . . .

I went in fast and got my coat.

'I'll be back in a few minutes,' I said to Holiday.

Mandon opened the door and we started out together, but on an impulse Holiday grabbed him saying: 'I'm going too. I'm tired of things happening behind my back . . .'

Mandon furiously shook loose from her, and pushed her a little and she fell back and began to work her mouth and lips, trying to collect enough saliva to spit at him.

I jumped between them. 'You do that and I'll break your neck, so help me, I'll break your goddamn neck,' I said. 'This spitting business has got to stop.'

She closed her mouth, looking daggers at me.

'You stay here,' I said. 'I'll be back in a few minutes.'

I followed Mandon out, almost running to catch up with him. I heard the apartment door slam loudly. The whole floor shook.

Mandon strode through the hall and out to his car in front. He jerked open the door. 'Get in,' he said.

291

I got in. He crawled in and shut the door. Highness looked over his shoulder.

'Pull in at an oil station somewhere,' Mandon said to him. 'That bitch,' he said to me. 'You'll have to get rid of her. I won't stand for her much longer.'

The car started.

'Never mind her,' I said. 'What's the matter with you? What went wrong?'

He crumpled himself into a corner of the back seat and cocked his head at me, screwing up his big eyebrows. 'So you're the guy with all the brains,' he said. 'You're the Phi Beta Kappa. You're the guy who knows it all . . .'

'What went wrong? What *happened?*'

'I'll tell you what happened. That girl came to see me.'

'Girl? What girl?'

'Margaret Dobson.'

'Margaret Dobson? Is *that* all?'

'Isn't that enough?'

'You mean to tell me you made all this uproar just because Margaret Dobson came to see you? Jesus Christ! I thought this was about the heist. I thought something had slipped. You promote a fight between Holiday and me just because that dame comes to see you? Jesus, I'm going to have to revise my opinion of you.'

'She was looking for you,' he said evenly.

'So let her look. She's got nothing on me. I didn't take the dough. Everything was strictly civilized. No hard feelings, no regrets . . .'

'Everything strictly civilized,' he said. 'And we'd both be a damn sight better off it it weren't. We'd be a damn sight better off if you'd taken the money like I wanted you to do. But no. You got brains. You know more than anybody else. Let it lay. You don't want his bloodhounds after you. Make it nice and quiet.

292

You made it nice and quiet, all right. The very thing you thought you'd avoid by not taking the dough is the very thing you've caused to happen. The bloodhounds are after both of us now.'

Bloodhounds? I didn't get this. 'Why?' I asked.

'She's looking for you, that's why.'

'But she's got nothing on me. Why should she be looking for me?'

'She's looking for you to offer you a job. She's got a job for you. Something very good – with a future. That's what you told her you wanted – didn't you? Some business connection with a future? Didn't you tell her that?'

'Probably I did. It sounds corny enough for me to have said. But it was just conversation. I'd just met her. I had to talk about something.'

'And you picked yourself, naturally.'

'Naturally. . . .' I said.

'And now you're making the distressing discovery that every man sooner or later makes when he goes around pushing over every dame he meets – eventually one of them gets stuck on him.'

'Stuck on me? She?'

'That's what I gathered.'

'Ah-h-h-h,' I said. 'You drag me out here to tell me a lot of crap like *this*? You break up a party and make Holiday sore at me to get me out here to tell me this? Why do you try to make it sound so goddamn ominous?'

He took a golf towel from his coat pocket and raucously blew his nose. Then he put the towel back in his pocket and crossed his short legs and scowled at me, putting his hand to his face, rubbing his lips with the palm and the lobes of his nose with the thumb and forefinger, giving an imitation of a man who was trying very hard to hold his temper. 'If you'll just keep your ego out of the way long enough, I'll tell you not what makes this

293

sound ominous, I'll tell you why it *is* ominous,' he said.

'Well, don't take too long,' I said. 'I got a girl and a jeroboam of champagne waiting. Neither is any good if it gets too cold. You'll pardon the epigram. Just happened to have one with me.'

'I'm afraid the girl and the champagne are just going to have to wait,' he said, looking at me. Not for long, old boy, not for long, I thought, looking right back at him. He said: 'When you didn't take that thirty-five thousand dollar check from Ezra Dobson, he was bowled over. Nothing like that had ever happened to him before. All his life he's been a target for people who wanted something – money, political favors, something – and *that* he couldn't understand, turning down thirty-five thousand dollars as a gift. But there it was. You'd turned it down. I infer from what the girl told me that it took him several minutes to recover, and when they tried to get you back, you'd disappeared. They talked about it – but the girl wasn't at all surprised that you'd refused the check. Not *she*. She knew all along that you had great pride and was a fine, noble character. She kept harping on that. She had to. Remember that she had her own ass in a sling and the more noble she made you out to be the more her own dereliction was mitigated. Oh, she's a shrewd bastard, that one ... Anyway, she convinced him. She sold him a bill of goods. So, they've both got guilty consciences now and they want to square themselves. They've got your future all planned. A nice, soft job ...'

'It's very flattering, I'm sure,' I said. 'But I don't want a job. Didn't you tell her that?'

'I told her you had a few excellent prospects, that's all I could tell her. She was suspicious of me anyway. She resented me. She knows my reputation. Christ, her own lawyer's been trying to crucify me for years. The less I have to do with this, the better for everybody. It's up to you now.'

'Just what am I supposed to do?'

'It's very simple. See her and tell her you don't want the job.'

'No,' I said.

'You have to.'

'The hell I do.'

'Of course you do. I promised her you'd call within the hour. It's damn near that now.'

'You're crazy,' I said.

'All you have to do is see her. Thank her and tell her no.'

'No,' I said.

'What's so tough about that?'

'I can't do it,' I said.

'What do you mean – you *can't* do it?'

'I mean I won't do it.'

'You've got no choice . . .' He leaned over, staring at me. 'What's the matter with you? What're you trembling about?'

'Nothing.'

'Are you sick?'

'No.'

'Then what is it? You're shaking all over? What's between this girl and you?'

'Nothing.'

'Every time I talk about her you get the shakes. What're you afraid of?'

How could I tell him? How can you talk about things like that? I never wanted to see her again. The road back to the womb was closed forever. Let it stay closed. He would not understand. 'I won't have anything more to do with her,' I said.

He straightened up, bringing his big eyebrows down, almost hiding the pupils. 'Now, goddamn it, you listen to me,' he said. 'I promised the girl that I'd produce you within the hour. It's either that or her father's bloodhounds'll turn you up. And his bloodhounds include the whole police department too. He snaps his fingers and the cops turn flips . . .'

'I can stop that,' I said.

'Don't try. Not with your ego. You'll get the surprise of your life. Do you know what she was going to do if I hadn't promised to produce you within the hour?She was going to have every downtown apartment and rooming house turned inside out. That's all she knows about you – that you live somewhere downtown.'

The car turned into an oil station and and stopped under the shed. An attendant moved from one of the pumps to Highness' window.

'Fill 'er up?' he said.

'Fill 'er up,' Mandon said. 'Roll up your window, Highness,' he said.

Highness rolled up the window.

Mandon waited until this was done and then looked back at me. 'Can't you get that through your head?' he said. 'She's made up her mind to find you. What's more ominous, the old man has made up *his* mind to find you. And he will – even if you start running. Why jeopardize our beautiful set-up when all you got to do is to say no to her. Can't you face her for that long?Jesus, is it a matter of life or death?' He took a sheet of notepaper from his pocket and held it out to me. 'This is her private number. She wants you to call her so she can put you straight on what she already has told the old man. Go on. Call here. . . .'

God!On this night, this night that I had thought was the night of *all* nights . . . . Why was I trembling?The sepulchre had been sealed. Then why was I trembling?

I snatched the sheet of paper from his hand and got out and went in to the telephone.

... *chapter*
seven

The taxi-cab stopped almost against the bronze gates, and the driver reached around to open the door and let me out.

'Wait a minute,' I said. It was a hell of a long walk up the hill to the house.

A door in the stone house beside the gate opened and a watchman in uniform came out. He was wearing a pistol. He came to the cab. 'Mister Murphy?' he said.

'That's right,' I said.

'Have you got some identification, please?'

'Miss Dobson's expecting me,' I said. 'Isn't that enough?'

'Don't you have a driver's license or something?'

'Well ...' I said, and then I thought of my gun permit and showed it to him.

He snapped on his flashlight and looked at the permit, nodding, and turned around, facing the little stone house. 'Okay, Chris,' he said, and now I saw in the door of the house another uniformed watchman, who pushed a button in the wall.

The guy who had done the checking got in the cab with me, and the bronze gates began to open slowly.

'Straight ahead,' he said to the driver. 'Then first turn to the right.'

We rolled through the gates. The driveway was wide and lined with cypress.

'Do you check all the Dobson guests?' I asked.

'Them we don't know we do,' he said. 'We don't usually ride up to the house with 'em though – that order was just started tonight.'

'Oh?' I said. 'Why tonight?'

'Trouble at the plant. Unions. Turn right,' he said.

We turned right. I could see the house on the hill now, its lights glowing.

'What kind of trouble?'

'That's all I know, sir.'

We stopped in front of the house and I got out and paid the driver. The watchman stayed in the cab.

'Good night,' he said.

'Good night,' I said.

I turned and looked at the house. It was a throwback to the Middle Ages, grim and foreboding on its hillsite, dominant and secure; but more than this I did not think about it; thinking instead of what awaited me on the inside. Something very formal and very official, of that I was certain. On the telephone I had tried to get her to meet me alone, somewhere else, anywhere but here. But she was adamant. Her father wanted to see me, he was going to somehow find time to see me in spite of the press of special meetings necessitated by an emergency situation at his plants. I *must* come here. Well, here I was, I thought, moving across the veranda to the front door. There was no escape and here I was. I would be very gracious and very appreciative and get it over with as soon as possible. This was the last instalment, by God, the very last....

I pushed a bronze button and the big door swung open. The conventional butler stood there. This one was about sixty.

'Mister Murphy?' he said. He had the conventional British accent too.

'Yes,' I said.

'Miss Dobson's expecting you, sir,' he said.

298

I went in. The hall was wide and creamy, mirrored and tapestried and chandeliered and the black and white marble floor was covered with Oriental rugs. A winding staircase was at the right and opposite this on the left wall was a cluster of portraits, all individually lighted. The butler had closed the door and was standing beside me, his hand half extended.

'I have no hat,' I said.

'This way, sir,' he said unperturbed, and started down the hall.

We walked past the drawing-room, and then a door in the wall ahead of me suddenly opened and Margaret got out of a small elevator. She wore a sweater and a skirt and, this time, stockings and new moccasins. But the color of her white face hadn't changed, nor the color of her black hair...

'Paul!' she said. 'I'm so glad to see you!'

Keep a tight rein, do not tremble, I told myself; after tonight the silhouette of horror will be gone, if there is to be a final instalment, this is it. 'Hello, Margaret,' I said.

We shook hands for the butler's benefit, and he bowed and resumed walking down the hall.

'Rushing,' she said, 'tell Father that Mister Murphy is here. We'll be in the tap-room.'

'Yes, Miss Margaret,' Rushing said, and came back past us.

'It was nice of you to come,' Margaret said to me, hooking her arm through mine, moving me down the hall. 'I do appreciate it – I had the deuce of a time trying to find you.' She put the palm of her other hand over the hand she had hooked through my arm, smiling as if we were seeing each other for the first time in a long time, a thousand years or so, and turned me into a very large room filled with tavern tables and benches and green and red leather-covered furniture. An enormous bar, as big as a saloon's, was built against one wall, and behind the bar in a white jacket and a wide grin was a Filipino boy. The lamps in here had been made from whiskey bottles and old coffee-mills and the humidors were tin cookie jars and the ash trays were old sugar scoops and little brass skillets. There was nothing grim or foreboding about this room. It was warm and cheerful and had a nice smell and I could not help thinking that this room belonged somewhere else, to some other house; it had just strayed from home and had been caught here by mistake.

'Cuttysark and soda, Rafael,' Margaret said to the Filipino boy. 'What for you? she asked me.

'Vodka martini,' I said.

'Vodka?' she said, frowning. She looked at the Filipino. 'Do we have vodka, Rafael?'

'Yes, Miss.'

She looked back at me. 'Any special way you want it made? I know how funny you are about your drinks.'

'Five to one,' I said. 'No lemon, no olive, no onion.'

'Rafael,' she said. 'Mister Murphy will have a vodka martini. Five to one. No lemon, no olive, no onion . . .'

This was unnecessary. The Filipino heard me, and I knew from the way he looked at me that he understood perfectly how I wanted the drink made. She was just being a bitch. You bitch, I thought, but I smiled the smile you smile for the hostess who insists on having everything just the way her guests want.

'Yes, Miss,' Rafael said.

'Sit down, Paul,' she said. 'Smoke?'

'No, thanks,' I said politely.

She sat down on the edge of the copper-covered coffee table, pushing back some magazines and a humidor of cigarettes and a couple of ash trays to make room for herself.

I sat down on a green leather sofa.

'I'm glad you didn't bring all that fire and brimstone with you,' she said. 'You sounded pretty ferocious over the phone. Did I do wrong in going to Mandon?'

'No. Of course not,' I said, very gracious.

'I didn't know what else to do. I didn't know where you lived. Where do you live?'

'Oh, in a hole in the wall,' I said, smiling.

'Is there some reason for all the mystery?' she asked. 'Doctor Green didn't want to tell me about Mandon and Mandon didn't want to tell me about you and you don't want to tell me where you live. . . .'

'You found me,' I said comfortingly.

'But what a price I paid in wear and tear! I was frantic. I thought that maybe you'd left town.'

'That's one thing you can be very sure of,' I said. 'I won't leave town.'

A serving maid came in with a silver tray of canapes and a stack of linen cocktail napkins. She offered the tray to Margaret who picked off one of the canapes and took a napkin; and then to me, and I also took a canape and a napkin. The maid put the tray on the coffee table and went out; and the Filipino boy arrived with the drinks.

'Try yours,' Margaret said to me.

I sipped it. 'It's fine,' I said. 'Very good, Rafael,' I said to the boy.

He smiled and backed away.

There was a little noise in the hall and a man came into the tap-room. He was about my own age, slender and tanned and attractive, and at once I saw he had the Dobson cast of countenance. He came towards us, smiling.

'Come in, Jonah,' Margaret said. 'This is Paul Murphy,' she said. 'My brother, Jonah. . .'

I got up.

'Hello,' he said, sticking out his hand cordially.

'How are you?' I said, shaking hands with him.

'Rafael,' he called, and made a measure with his hands. 'Sit down, sit down,' he said to me. 'God,' he said, waving me down, 'nobody has any manners in this house but the servants. . . .'

'*Toujours le* undergraduate,' Margaret said.

'Don't be bitter now, dear,' he said, with just a trace of bite in his tone. He picked up the tray of canapes and offered it to Margaret, who took two more and pushed them together and put them in her mouth, and then to me. I took one this time and he put the tray down and took one for himself.

I sat down and swept him with a glance. He had a hell of a flair for clothes. He wore a crew hair cut, and a tannish three-button Shetland coat, a Brooks Brothers polo model shirt with a foulard tie, gray flannel trousers, tan cashmere socks and white buck Peal shoes, with the red corrugated rubber soles, called by the English tennis shoes, and costing fifty dollars a pair. He was holding up his hands now as if he were afraid to touch anything with them, and Rafael came in with a bar towel and held it while he wiped his hands. Then Rafael handed him his drink and moved away.

Jonah held up his drink and said, 'Salute,' and we all drank, and I noticed now as he drank that he had practical button-holes on his coat sleeves and that just the right number, one, was unbuttoned. He was the best-dressed son-of-a-bitch I'd ever seen. I knew his school too. I could tell. You can always tell.

'Princeton?' I said.

'Yes', he said.

He did not seem surprised that I knew, but Margaret was.

'How'd you know that?' she asked.

'Just guessing,' I said.

'Do sit down, Jonah,' she said.

'I will indeed, I will indeed,' he said, sitting down, 'in spite of the fact that I'm late already. But this is one of our rarer occasions, Mister Murphy. . . .'

'Paul,' I said.

'I'm Jonah,' he said. I nodded thank you and he took a swig

of his drink and continued: 'Yes, sir. A very rare occasion it is when my sister brings home a date who can speak English. . . . .'

'Jonah!' she said sharply.

He laughed, not even looking at her. 'It's usually a Yogi or an East Indian with a practically hairless beard or some charlatan in a burnoose or. . .' He looked at her. 'What's the name of this latest craze of yours? Cosmic Philosophy?'

'Cosmic Consciousness,' I said, smiling. If everybody was going to play at being bitchy, I wanted to play too. I had a better reason than either of them had.

'That's it,' he said. Then his eyes widened. 'Good God!' he said. 'Don't tell me that you . . .'

'No, not what you're thinking,' I said. 'I read it on a sign in front while I was waiting for Margaret. And I must say, I feel the same way about it you do.'

He nodded vigorously and turned to Margaret. 'You know, this man may be able to do you some good. I've been trying to tell her,' he said to me, 'that this damned mystic stuff'll drive her crazy in the end. That's what happens when a woman has too much spare time on her hands. Why don't you get out and do something healthy?' he said to her. 'Get some sun. Get some color. You look like a ghost.'

'You mean get out the way you do?' she said. 'You mean do something healthy the way you do? You're a fine one to talk. Great hours you keep. Ten till twelve on the practice tee, twelve to one, lunch; one till five, golf; five till six, practice tee; six till eight, cocktails; eight till all hours more cocktails and parties . . .'

'I argue that it's healthy and that I'm in the sun,' he said. 'I leave it to Paul. And this month, incidentally, I've gone to plus one.'

'That only means you can lose more money,' she said.

'Well, I'd a damn sight rather do that with it than finance these weird institutions you're always finding. At least, I've got a chance to get mine back. . . .'

This could have been banter if there had been less sting in the words. She felt them too. She twisted on the coffee table, and flushed a little. He seemed to be pleased that he had stung her.

'Er, plus one's pretty good,' I said.

'Well,' he said, 'there's not too many guys who can give it the time I do. I work at it, I really do. That's all it takes. I've allotted myself five more years, and if I can't turn the trick by then, I'll give up and go to pouring steel. . . .'

'He wants to win the National Amateur,' she said.

'Who doesn't?' I said. 'That's a fine title. Next to the British Amateur, I'd like to win the National myself. . . .'

'It's no cinch,' he said. 'The minute Bob Jones quits, Lawson Little comes in. There's always a hell of a golfer at the top. Do you play?'

'Not in years,' I said. 'And not even good then. Most of the time I spent on the golf course was caddying. I used to caddy for Jack Hutchinson.'

'Did you?' he exclaimed. 'He was good, wasn't he?'

'One of the best,' I said.

'Are you new in town?'

'About a week . . .'

'What business are you in?'

'Well – I haven't made up my mind. I've been flirting with insurance.'

He gave Margaret a quick look. 'Don't be too hasty about picking a line,' he said. 'There's a lot of good things around. . . .'

'Most anything can be made good if you worked hard enough at it,' she said, trying to sting him. He just laughed. She stood up, motioning to Rafael that everybody would have another of the same.

'Not for me,' Jonah said. 'Not for me,' he called to Rafael. He got up, finishing his drink as he rose. 'I promised to pick up Martha early. Well,' he said, pleasantly, 'I'll clear out before the brother-sister act loses its subtlety. I've got to change and pick up Martha . . . By the way,' he said to her, 'you're not having dinner here, are you?'

'No,' she said.

'I thought not. Then why not join us at the club? Might do you good to get out with normal people.'

'You call your drunken friends normal people?' she asked.

'Catch them before they get drunk. At least, you can let them see that you have a date with a guy who speaks English and gets his hair cut once in a while. . . .' He stuck out his hand to me. 'Nice to have seen you, Paul – if I don't see you later. Let's have lunch sometime. . . .'

'Even if I go into insurance?'

'Even if you go into insurance . . .'

'Thanks, Jonah,' I said.

He took a step and paused beside Margaret.'Do try to make it,' he said. He smiled at her almost sympathetically and went out.

'I didn't know you had a brother,' I said.

'I don't brag about it,' she said.

'He seemed very nice.'

'Yes, he's nice. A little one-dimensional, but nice.'

'I wouldn't mind being one-dimensional myself if I could wear clothes that well,' I said.

She looked at me, at my clothes. 'You do all right,' she said. She got up from the coffee table and moved around to the green davenport. She looked at me again. 'Tell me about Mandon,' she said. 'How long have you known him?'

'Mandon?' I said. 'Oh, not too long . . .'

'Just since you've been in town?'

'That's right.'

'He is your lawyer, isn't he?'

I didn't know what he had told her, probably that he was my lawyer, but the circumstances proved that there was some association, and there was no use denying it. 'Yes,' I said.

'That's why you came to Doctor Green's that night. You were looking for him?'

'Yes.'

'Do you know what kind of a reputation he has?'

'What kind?'

'Very, very bad . . .'

I took a sip of my martini. 'I don't quite know what you mean by bad,' I said. 'Bad how?'

'He makes a business of dealing with the underworld. . . .'

'Who told you that?'

'Well, he does,' she said. 'When one lawyer talks about another lawyer, something's wrong. . . .'

'You mean Golightly?'

'This is strictly confidential. . . .'

'Of course,' I said.

'He's almost an underworld character himself.'

'You amaze me!' I said.

'It's true. I wouldn't say it unless I knew it to be true. Do you know something else? This afternoon when I'd told him my story and begged him to help me find you and started to leave, I offered him some money for his trouble. Just as a gesture, I had only twenty dollars with me, but he took it. Imagine that!'

He hadn't told me about that. Ten of that was mine. The son-of-a-bitch, I was thinking. . . . 'Well,' I said, 'he probably regarded it as a fee. You know how lawyers are about fees. . . .'

'I don't want you to have anything else to do with him. If you have any more legal business, take it to Fred Golightly. That's what you should do now.'

'Now?' I said.

'Now that you're going to work for my father.'

'I thought I made it plain on the telephone that I didn't want to work for him.'

She pouted a little. 'You can't very well refuse us a chance to get out of your debt,' she said.

'You've never been in my debt.'

She pouted a little. 'Not very many people refuse a chance to work for my father,' she said.

'I know,' I said.

'Only with you it wouldn't be just any kind of work. He likes you. He's very impressed with you. . . .'

'Oh, sure,' I said.

'He has a personal interest in you. Once you're in the company, he'd move you along very fast.'

'Look, Margaret,' I said. 'I know you mean well and I appreciate it, but why don't you let this alone? I don't want to be in the company. I don't want his help. I've got some deals on. . . .'

'But whatever your deals are, father can help. Just the fact that he's taken a personal interest in you is all you need. He's a very big man around here. All over. Even in the whole country . . .'

Oh, yes, of course. The Titan. 'I know . . .' I said.

'Won't you stop resenting him for just a little while? Won't you be nice to him and listen to what he has to say? Won't you try to keep your complexes under control for a few minutes?' she asked. 'He's got as many complexes as you have, and it's easy to pick a fight with him too – maybe easier, after the strain he's been under all afternoon. Please be careful . . .'

Naturally, I wanted to say. If the man's been under a strain then I shall be extremely careful. He's the only man in the world who's been under a strain this afternoon. I've been under no strain. All I did was spend a lazy and reinvigorating afternoon eating pheasant sandwiches and listening to Crosby and Columbo records. It was all I could do to keep from laughing. 'I want you to be nice to him,' she was saying. 'I want you to be

307

very nice to him. The kind of niceness I know. You will, won't you?'

Rushing entered and spoke from the door: 'Mister Dobson is waiting, Miss Margaret.'

'Thank you, Rushing,' she said. 'Bring your drink,' she said to me.

Rushing bowed and left.

We picked up our drinks. 'Now, remember,' she said. 'I've told him how wonderful you are. Please don't fight with him.'

'I don't want to fight with him,' I said. 'I just want to be left alone.'

'Well, hear him out. He may have a surprise for you.'

We moved out into the hall. I had a glimpse of the big dining-room as we passed. Rushing was standing in the door, just closing it. The wall brackets were burning and I saw two other butlers arranging the table. There was an epergne on the table as big as a wash-tub, holding what must have been a dozen candles. The chairs were all tapestried. This, I thought, was a long way from the Great Smokies – or was it?

Margaret rapped once on a big oaken door and then opened it and we stepped in. This library was a big room, filled with books on two sides. Across the room at a heavy, over-sized desk, sat Ezra Dobson. He got up and came to meet us. He was wearing a rumpled double-breasted blue suit and a white shirt and a blue-and-yellow-figured bow tie.

'Well, I see you found him,' he said to Margaret. He extended his hand to me. 'So, Murphy, we meet again. . . .'

'It looks like it,' I said, shaking hands perfunctorily.

Margaret gave me a quick glance, but Ezra Dobson had paid no attention to the remark. He said: 'And much more pleasant than the last time, too. I'm sorry to have kept you waiting. Midge, dear,' he said, 'I think I'd prefer to talk to Murphy alone.'

'But, Father,' she said petulantly. 'I'm a big girl now.'

'Darling,' he said, with a trace of weariness, 'I want to talk with Paul.'

Now it was Paul . . .

'Father,' she said.

'Dear,' he said, almost pleading.

This is what's the matter with your daughter, I was thinking, this is why she got away from you. . . . She was looking at me with disconsolate eyes. She didn't want me to be alone with him. She was worried about my complexes.

'Forget it,' I said to her, a little curtly, showing off for his benefit. 'Do as your father says. It's all right.'

'Yes, Paul,' she said obediently. 'I'll change and wait for you in the tap-room.'

You do that, I was thinking. You get an eider-down sleeping bag and make yourself very comfortable in the tap-room. You'll be waiting for me a long time. . . .

She was moving to the door.

'Dear,' Ezra Dobson said, 'have the boy fix a shaker of whatever Paul is drinking and send it in.'

'Yes, Father,' she said.

She went on out and closed the door.

'You have quite a way with Midge,' he said.

'Pardon?' I said.

'I tell her to go and she argues. You tell her to go and she goes.'

'Well . . .' I said.

'Sit down, sit down,' he said. 'Sorry to have kept you waiting, but I've had trouble on my hands since three o'clock this afternoon. The bastards've pulled a strike on me.'

'That's too bad,' I said.

'Too bad for them,' he said. 'I'll have 'em in the bread line in a week. I've got a police department that's specially trained in breaking strikes and a National Guard that's specially trained in

309

picking up the pieces. And a few patriotic organizations that'll wave the flag while they do it....'

Thunder and lightning ... Yes, indeed, oh Khan, I can feel the earth tremble beneath your tread. You reveal your heart, oh Celestial One, and rain mourns on ten thousand roofs. From your silken pavilion on the Persian plains, oh Splendid One, falcon on wrist and jewelled dagger at hip, gaze you at the blue domes of Samarkand which soon will fall ...

'Have you ever had any experience with unions?' he was asking.

'No,' I said.

'How old are you?'

'Thirty.'

'That's Jonah's age – and he's never had experience with unions, either. You met Jonah?'

'I had a drink with him.'

'That,' he said, with a little harsh laugh, 'is a very easy thing to do with Jonah. . . .'

He put his drink on the silver tray on the desk and poured more whiskey into it from a cut-glass decanter.

'May I look at that?' I asked.

'Certainly,' he said.

The decanter was of clear glass, heavy, with a six-inch stopper, and as I turned it in my hand the flutings and incisions refracted the light and sparkled like a mass of diamonds. It was one of the most beautiful things I had ever seen. 'It's one of the most beautiful things I've ever seen,' I said, putting it down on the tray.

'Really? Well now, not many people notice it.'

'It's magnificent,' I said. 'It looks like a Steigel.'

He stared at me open-mouthed, his drink arrested half-way to his lips. 'You know that?' he said. 'Nobody ever recognized that before. Is glass your business?'

'No,' I said. 'We used to have one like that. It had the same big

310

pontil mark. . . . No, by God,' I said abruptly, 'we didn't have one like that at all. It was a vinegar cruet. It used to sit in a caster on my grandmother's table. I dropped it one day and broke it. . . .'

'And you wound up in the woodshed. . . .'

'I would have if it hadn't been for my grandmother,' I said.

He laughed softly, as if the thought was pleasantly nostalgic. 'Well, that's the proper function of a grandmother – to protect the grandson. I don't remember mine,' he said. 'You're fortunate to remember yours. . . .'

I looked away from the decanter and the multitudinous refractions that stabbed at my memory. . . .

'I'll see that you get the decanter,' he said. 'I want you to have it.'

'No!' I said, and when he snapped his head looking at me, surprise in his face, I realized that I had spoken involuntarily. I was sorry I had noticed the decanter, I was sorry I had mentioned it, I was sorry I had picked it up. I had not known then. It was that girl, that goddamn girl with the white face and the black hair who had broken into my sanctuary again and uncovered more of the fetishes. This had to be ended. I did not want the damned decanter. I was sorry I had noticed it. I had to get the hell out of here. 'Thank you,' I said. 'I couldn't take it. . . .'

There was a single rap at the door and it opened with no invitation from Ezra Dobson and Rushing came in with another silver tray that held a martini bowl and a martini glass.

'Put it there,' Ezra Dobson said.

Rushing put the tray on the desk and stirred the martini with a glass spoon as Ezra Dobson regarded me closely; and then Rushing poured and I reached for the glass. He picked up my half-empty glass and went out.

I toasted Ezra Dobson with my fresh drink and he toasted me with his and we drank and then he said: 'Well, we had a hard time finding you. . . .'

311

'I would have been glad to help if I had known,' I said. 'I thought this was all over.'

'So did I. I had just about given up hope that Midge would ever find a man who could interest her.'

'I assure you that I did nothing to encourage it,' I said.

He took a sip of his drink and gave me a paternal glance. 'Even if you were trying, you couldn't have picked a better way than to show a complete disregard for money,' he said. 'Until then, I frankly don't think she was very keen about you.'

'You've both got me wrong,' I said thinly. 'I don't have a disregard for money. I have a disregard only for your money.'

'Good tactics,' he said, nodding. 'Very good . . .'

The son-of-a-bitch. . . . 'They are obvious tactics to use on the daughter of a man who is as rich as you are,' I said. I took some of the martini and stood up. 'Unfortunately, I don't seem able to convince you that you've got nothing I want – daughter, money or a job. I'm very busy, Mister Dobson. If you'll excuse me now. . . .'

I put the glass on the martini tray and nodded good night and turned to leave.

'Keep your shirt on,' he said. 'I'm just as busy as you are.'

'You're probably busier. And you're much more important. You keep people waiting and they feel flattered. I keep them waiting and they get mad. I've got people waiting on me now.'

'Tell 'em you were with me,' he said.

The pomposity, the royal arrogance of the son-of-a-bitch. 'And you think that'll square me?'

'I know it,' he said. 'Now, look here, Murphy,' he said. 'I had you come here because I wanted to talk to you about Midge. I don't want to impose on you, but I would like for you to listen. These are the only free minutes I'm going to have until God knows when – and I won't have very many of them. I've got people on the way out here now. I'm up to me neck in a strike –

312

a big one . . .' He took another drink and put his glass on the big brown blotter and sat down. He put his hands on the solid arms of the chair and lowered himself slowly, like heavy cargo, letting his arms take the full weight of his body. He had now stopped working at the job of being Conqueror. The thunder and lightning had been turned off, the jewelled dagger and falcon had been put away. He was just a tired old man. . . . 'And I've also got a daughter I'm interested in saving. I thought she would be off my hands by now, I thought one of the dozen men she's known would have taken over the responsibility. But they only wanted the responsiblity of the money, not the responsiblity of the woman. That made them subservient. You cannot do that with Midge. The minute she dominates you, you are through. She's got to have a man she respects. . . .'

'She's young, she'll find one,' I said.

He took a drink and shook his head slowly, leaning back in his chair, holding his glass with both hands. 'I can't wait. I can't run the risk,' he said. 'She's too far overboard now. You must know that.'

'Know what?' I asked.

'You've had dates with her every night for two weeks,' he said. 'You know what. Her mania for fakirs and crackpots and new forms of religion and revelatory thought and all the rest of that junk. It's ruining her life – if it hasn't already ruined it. She keeps on this way and she'll wind up in an insane asylum. You think I want that to happen? I can't break her away from this stuff, psychiatrists can't because she won't co-operate – but I think maybe you can. I think maybe you can wake her up. . . .'

Jesus Christ, I thought. Jesus Christ . . . 'Are you proposing to turn Margaret over to me?' I managed to ask.

'Yes. Exactly.'

'Don't you think she should have something to say about this?'

'She had said it. That's why you are here now. . . .'

'But you don't know anything about me,' I said. 'I'm a total stranger to you. I might have a wife already. I might be a thief. I might be an embezzler. I might be a convict. I might be a murderer. . . .'

'When a drowning man reaches for a piece of driftwood, he does not worry about getting splinters in his hand. I don't care what you are or what you've been. I can find out all that later. And I'm not particularly concerned with how you feel about Midge. I'm only concerned with how she feels about you. . . .'

'I'm very honored,' I said. 'But I don't think I can help.'

He took a drink. 'I don't like to throw my weight around, Murphy, but may I point out that a personal relationship with me might have certain advantages to an ambitious man?'

'I'm sure of that. . . .'

'Then you must also know that I can hinder as well as help. . . .'

'I'm sure of that, too,' I said. I tried to keep the rage out of my face and my voice, but it was no use. This son-of-a-bitch . . . 'Goddamn it, by what right do you insert yourself into my own personal destiny? All I want from you is to be left alone!'

'You married her once,' he said.

'We were drunk,' I said. 'I didn't even know who she was.'

'You know now. . . .'

'You've got nothing I want,' I said, 'but to be left alone.'

He idly turned the glass in the palm of his hand. 'Just how high does your disregard for my money go?' he asked. 'Does it reach to a million dollars?'

I put my arms across the back of the chair and looked at him, incredulous. I had heard but I did not believe.

'I will start you off with a million dollars,' he said. 'Outright. One million dollars. No strings, no books to balance, no questions asked. All I want you to do is give me your word as a

314

man that you'll do everything you can to restore Margaret to a
normal and healthy mental and physical life. And if you
succeed . . .'

This was not real. This could not be real. This was the reading
of a newly discovered Gilbert and Sullivan manuscript.

'One million dollars in cash . . .'

He had said it again. I was staggered. One million dollars!
What I could do with one million dollars and his influence – but
I would have to take Margaret too, Margaret the symbol, the
bridge to the past, Margaret, who would always be jabbing at
those memories, weakening the regression more and more and
more until, until . . . 'No,' I said. 'Thank you very much, but no.
And now I must say good night. . . .'

I nodded politely, waiting for him to nod or say good night,
but he just looked at me, and I turned and walked towards the
door.

'Before you do,' he said, 'I think you should see this . . .'

I stopped and turned around. He was taking something out
of the desk drawer. I thought it was a check and then I saw that
it wasn't a check, but a piece of paper. I went back to the desk.
He handed me the paper.

It was the annulment petition I had signed.

'When I found out how Midge felt about you, I thought I'd
better hold that up,' he said. 'So, you see – you're still married.'

I felt a quick cold nocturnal wind on my face and I got a whiff
of the *Huele de Noche* and I saw again the undulating curtains
at the slightly raised windows in that old parlor, and I dropped
the paper and leaned on the desk to keep from falling, dimly
aware that he was watching me, but much more aware that I was
revealing to him a fatal weakness, but not being able to hide it . . .

'Think it over,' he was saying. 'Let me know tomorrow.'

The colored refractions from the decanter bombarded me,
taking me back – and I walked out on legs that were not mine.

315

... Coming down the hall towards me, from the front door, were three men. As they approached I saw that they were Rushing and two men in blue uniforms – and then I saw that these were police uniforms and then I saw the men in the uniforms. They were Webber and Reece.

I moved away from the library door, giving them room to enter. The only sign that Webber recognized me was the narrowing of his eyes, but Reece was very surprised. I had no reaction to the sight of them, no reaction to their uniforms, although I had not seen them in uniforms before.

'Mister Jonah would like to see you, sir,' Rushing said. 'If you will wait a moment ...'

He rapped on the library door and opened it, speaking to Ezra Dobson inside. 'You said directly the officers arrived, sir ...'

'Show them in,' Ezra Dobson's voice said.

Still watching me, Webber and Reece went into the library, and I heard Ezra Dobson's voice, saying, 'Hello, Charlie,' and then Rushing closed the heavy door and said to me: 'This way, sir.'

All this, his words to me, his words to Ezra Dobson, Ezra Dobson's words, the movement, the uniforms, were super-imposed on my eyes and ears like bas-relief; I heard and saw and understood, but my reflexes were still paralysed – and I followed the tall stiff butler up the stairs, down the hall, with as little volition as one horse follows another on a carousel, to a door which he opened for me.

'Rushing?' Jonah's voice called.

'Yes, sir.'

'Mister Murphy there?'

'Yes, sir.'

'Paul – come on back ...'

I'm sorry I ever crashed out of the prison farm, I was

thinking. That was torture too, but torture of a different sort, much easier to stand. When I was on the prison farm, what I remembered of a lifetime ago was pleasant, not like this. Would those foul memories never be expiated?

'Paul!'

I must not let him see me like this, I thought. I've got to snap out of it. I went across the room to the open window and put my nose against the screen and sucked hard at the weight of the night air. It was fresh and clean and had no death smell, only the smell of foliage ...

'Yes?' I said.

I looked around and saw that I was in the sitting-room, filled with books and photographs and dozens of silver and gold cups and other trophies; these objects registering as what they were, with no distortion. I sucked at the night air again and moved slightly away from the window. My legs felt a little more like my own legs now.

'Come on back ...' he called.

'I'm admiring your trophies,' I said.

'Oh! Well, make yourself at home....'

My God, I was thinking, now that I could get my mind out of that phantasmagoria, now that I could use it with some objectivity, what kind of idiocy was this, trying to force me to take his daughter? I couldn't possibly have heard the monster correctly. It was the refractions from the goddamn decanter that had sent my memory back and while my memory was hovering over the foothills of the Gap he had said something about a million dollars, but there was so much confusion in my thought processes then, and desperation too, seeing flashes of things I did not want to see, fighting desperately to keep from seeing the whole thing, which would engulf and destroy me, that I could not remember exactly how he had meant it ...

'Come on back here,' Jonah was saying.

317

He was standing in the doorway in shorts and lemon-colored cashmere socks.

'Oh, sure, sure . . .' I said.

He craned his neck, staring at me. 'Are you all right?' he asked.

'Sure. I'm fine,' I said.

'Stop shaking then. You want a drink?'

'No, thanks.'

'Rodney,' he called, 'get some benzedrine.'

He took me into the bedroom, an enormous bedroom, with an open fireplace and an over-sized bed, and Rodney came out of the bathroom with a bottle of tablets and a glass of water.

'Take a couple,' Jonah said. 'I'll finish dressing, Rodney,' he said.

Rodney bowed and went out.

'These'll pull you through,' Jonah said.

I took two of the benzedrine tablets and half the water, and he took the bottle and the glass and smiled at me.

'Sit down,' he said.

I sat down in a brocaded armchair.

'Hell of a shock, wasn't it?' he asked. He smiled again. 'A million dollars cash.'

There was that same phrase again. Just the mention of it and those light refractions went off in my head again. That goddamn decanter.

'. . . Then I did hear him right?' I asked.

'Yes.'

'You know about it?'

'Knew about it? I suggested it . . .'

He stepped into his dressing-room and came out with a blue Brooks Brothers shirt, polo style, and a pair of black shoes. He dropped the shoes on the carpet and pulled the shirt over his head.

318

'*You* suggested it?'

'Mildred held out for a half a million – I held out for a million.'

'Mildred?'

'Margaret. Midge. Her name is really Mildred. She changed it. Numerology. One of the earlier phases of her mystic life.'

'I didn't know that,' I said.

'We're quite a surprising family,' he said, sitting down on the bed, taking the shoe-trees out of his shoes. They were wing-tipped Peal's. 'I probably don't have to tell you that.'

'I can't get over it,' I said. 'I can't get over it. . . .'

'Why? What's a million to him? He's got a hundred or so – and she's the closest thing to his heart.' He stopped tying his black whaleskin shoe-lace and looked at me soberly. 'She is to mine, too, I guess – even if we do sometimes say unpleasant things to each other. She needs help – and she needs it in a hurry. Maybe you're the one to do it. I hope so.'

I shook my head. 'This is the goddamndest thing I ever heard of,' I said. 'You people don't know anything about me and yet you offer me a million dollars to take her over. How can I comprehend that? Things like this just don't happen. . . .'

'Well, it did happen. Midge wants you. What the hell – we've tried everything else.' He finished tying his shoes and picked up a pair of blue flannel trousers from the bed and slipped into them. 'Funny thing,' he said. 'I got a feeling you two will hit it off together. Of course, when we had the meeting this afternoon, I was talking in the dark. I hadn't even seen you. But now that I have met you, I think maybe she's right. You didn't get a chance to talk to the old man very long, did you?'

'Long enough. Some officers came in.'

'Yes. The strike. Well, he'd tell you. She doesn't know that you're supposed to break her away from the stuff. You'll have to be clever – take her away on a trip somewhere. But she mustn't know. . . .'

319

'The whole thing is crazy,' I said. 'It's idiotic.'

'Nothing idiotic about a million dollars. . . .'

'I'm dazed . . .'

'There's something else that's much more important,' he said. 'You bring a physical balance to Margaret that she's found in no other man.'

I looked at him.

'Do I have to be more graphic?' he asked.

'No,' I said. 'But how do you know this?'

'She told me. She told the old man. He didn't quite know how to put it to you. Now, do you understand what you've got that we want?'

Yes. Now I understood. I got up. 'You suppose I might have a drink?' I asked.

'I'd say you need one. Same thing?'

'Straight, this time.'

He grinned. 'Step into my office,' he said.

I went behind him into the bathroom. The bathroom was almost as big as the bedroom. It had ultra-violet and infra-red lamps suspended from cables over a tile rubbing table, and in an alcove opposite the glassed-in shower was the bar. He picked up a bottle of House of Lords gin and started to measure some into a jigger.

'Not gin,' I said.

'I thought you were drinking a martini. . . .'

'I was. Vodka.'

'Vodka!My God,' he said. 'Now, you've got me.' He put the bottle down. 'I'll have to ring the bar. . . .'

'It's all right,' I said. 'I'll take gin. . . .'

'I'll get some vodka. It'll only take a minute.'

'No,' I said. 'Gin is fine.'

'Well . . .'

'Really.'

320

He poured the gin into the jigger and poured water from a silver pitcher into a glass and handed them to me.

I tossed them off.

'Vodka, eh?' he said. 'Is that the answer?'

The gin was going down like a slowly turning live ember. 'Most curious thing,' I said. 'Nobody has yet asked me what I think of Margaret. Or does that matter?'

'What do you think?'

'I suppose not . . .'

'Another drink?'

'No, thanks.'

'I'll finish dressing then.'

He went out into his dressing-room. I went with him. He picked a lemon-colored knitted tie from a long rack of many ties, Charvet's and Sullka's, and tied it in a tight windsor knot and buttoned down his collar. The door to his shoe closet was open and on racks that reached from the floor to ceiling were at least fifty pairs, and on a shelf with a built-in ladder were his boots and bluchers and walkers, – all fine English leather, and all glossed and not shined. On the dressing-table was an open jewelry box of gold collar pins and money clips, and in another jewelry box were half a dozen gold watches, strap and pocket.

'You got a hell of a lot of stuff here,' I said.

'Moth's Paradise, I call it,' he said.

He took a blue-flannel jacket off a hanger, and slipped it on, and I saw now that his trousers had no belt loops, but little tabs at the hips. He buttoned his jacket and from the handkerchief drawer he took a handkerchief of sheerest linen, twenty-four inches square, and monogrammed J.D. in plain block letters, one letter blue, one letter yellow, opened it, punched a teat in the middle, took it by the teat, shook it, gathered it in the palm of his other hand and stuffed it into his upper pocket. Then he opened a big gold humidor that was lined with purple velvet and selected one of seven or eight gold lighters, flipped it to see if it would ignite, which it did; and picked up a gold cigarette-case damn near as big as a brief case. He snapped this open. It was filled with sixty cigarettes.

'I smoke a lot,' he said, almost self-consciously.

'I see you do,' I said.

In my whole life I had never seen anything that remotely approached his wardrobe. I had never even dreamed of anything like it. Here was the finest in everything, the ne plus ultra, and he fitted it perfectly. He knew, of course, that I was watching him, all eyes, and he also must have known that I was fascinated, but he did not show off, he was not affected, he was perfectly natural, perhaps a little embarrassed, which was also proper....

'I didn't mean to ogle,' I said.

'I don't mind....'

'It's beautiful – all of it.'

He seemed pleased. 'You like clothes?' he asked.

'Yes,' I said. 'Only I've never been able to afford anything like this.'

'Well, you will now,' he said. 'You've now got a million dollars.'

A million dollars . . . I fought off the memories, excited, asking myself: Can I? Can I? Can I fight my way out of this trap? Here is what I've always wanted, now created especially for me and offered to me alone – it never could be offered to anyone else, it would be too fantastic, it is being offered to me, this world, because the axis of it is the symbol of my guilt and the tempting God dares me to face it because He knows it is but a short cut to destruction. But why should it be? Myth and memory retreat before the intellect ...

'You know,' he was saying, 'I'm just beginning to realize that we're practically the same size. If my hair were a little darker, we might even be twins....'

'I'd noticed that,' I said.

'Tomorrow, if you'd care to, I'll take you down to see Piggott. He's in town.'

'Piggott?'

'The Peal man from London.'

'Oh!Shoes ...'

'Yes. He comes around once or twice a year.'

'I think I'd like that,' I said.

'Good. Shall we see if Midge is ready? We're all going out together....'

'Out where?' I asked.

'To the club. Midge said she'd like to go. Do her good. You may as well start meeting the gang.' He looked at me, frowning. 'She said you were free tonight....'

'I'm free,' I said. 'I'm free as a bird....'

. . . *chapter eight*

The club was only a few blocks from the Dobson house – a rectangle of almost solid light against the blackness of the thick fir trees. The friction hum of the tires of Jonah's car changed keys now as we turned off the paved street into the driveway of macadam, a driveway lined with Lombardy poplars through which I could see in the reflected light the contours of the golf course and the ghost-like spray from the greens sprinklers; and I could smell it too, the smell of foliage and damp grass that comes with night-time watering: and now sounds came in through the lowered window on my side of the car, from the funnel of poplars: sounds of people talking and sounds of music noises, gay and wonderful party noises ... The kind I used to hear at our old club on a fall Saturday night after the football team had won a game, any game: and one fall, my senior year, when there were no victories to celebrate, we celebrated touchdowns – and once even a safety. That was the best party of all, that one ... My heart went up with the rising euphony of elation and my spirit soared and touched ectasy, touching it lightly, in flight, as the tips of a kingfisher's wings touch a remote lake, no more than this – a flash, a single instant's release, and the color of it was blue. This is for me, I thought, son-of-a-bitch, this is for me. I'll make this work, he's got me, but I'll make it work. Myth and memory retreat before intellect. Oedipus is dead ...

We stopped in front, beside a white marquee on which was emblazoned in red the crest of the club (and which I remembered seeing on many of Jonah's trophies), and an attendant in a white jacket with red piping and the same red crest over his heart took the car, and an elderly man in an identical jacket swung open the screen door. 'Good evening, Miss Dobson, good evening, Mister Dobson,' he said. 'Miss West is waiting for you in the grill-room.'

'Thank you, William,' Jonah said. 'Sounds like the joint's jumping. . . .'

'A fine crowd, sir,' William said. 'Never saw people so happy. Nice to see you again, Miss Dobson. . . .'

'Thank you, William,' she said, almost cautiously.

I took her arm and followed half a step behind Jonah as he led us past the coat-room and down the stone steps to the grill-room, from which noise and music were now vortexing upwards.

The grill-room was like the grill-room in any country club, perhaps larger than most, the walls hung with caricatures of the members and mounted game fish and antlers and other trophies of the hunt. It was filled with people, nice-looking people, gay people, and before we had reached the bottom step a girl had seen us and was coming through the crowd towards us, waving her hand. She was a tall girl, with long legs, bareheaded, with blonde hair that fell to her shoulders, unribboned. She had obviously been watching for us to arrive. She had an old-fashioned in her hand. 'Hello, Margaret,' she said.

'Hello, Martha,' Margaret said.

'Fine thing,' Jonah said. 'I call for you like a dutiful date and you're not there. Come here, you . . .' He took her by the arm, warmly. 'I want you to know Martha West. . . .'

'Hello,' she said to me.

'How do you do,' I said.

She smiled at Jonah. 'I hope you're not too put out with me,' she said. 'I didn't even get home to change. I got caught in a

325

bridge game and I was trying to get even.'

'Did you?' Jonah asked.

'No.'

'Then I am put out with you.' He touched the old-fashioned glass in her hand. 'How many are you up on us?'

'Two – only . . .'

'Shall we catch up standing or sitting down?' Jonah asked.

'I have a table,' Martha said. 'I *did* have . . .'

Jonah held her arm, moving through the crowd that welled out from the bar like breakers off a rocky point. Everybody, men and women, knew him and greeted him with familiar affection; and a great many of them knew Margaret and greeted her too, but with less cordiality, with no cordiality at all, actually with some coldness; and I understood then what Jonah had meant when he had said she seldom got to the club. It was very evident from their looks and their attitudes that they regarded her not only as a stranger, but as a curiosity. She gave me a little grimace of annoyance.

'Is it that bad?' I asked.

'It's worse,' she said, quite loudly, I thought.

I smiled at her reassuringly, telling myself that there was a lot of work to be done with her, but that I'd do it, son-of-a-bitch, this was for me. I wanted to think of one million dollars, but I dared not, and then I thought: what the hell, I may as well start licking this thing right now, it is certainly audacious enough to appeal to me; and I moved my mind along to the thought of one million dollars, carefully and stealthily, to get a look at one little corner of it, and I saw one little corner and it stabbed me, but not too painfully, and I said to myself: See? Myth and memory retreat before intellect. . . .

Martha stopped us at a small round table in the corner and we sat down and ordered cocktails, all but Margaret. She ordered ginger ale. Here the music was predominant, we were sitting against the rear wall and opposite us was a wide corridor that led to the ballroom where the music was, where people were dancing. It was a well-rehearsed band for a local band, but it was talentless.

'Well, Margaret,' Martha said, 'it's nice to see you again.'

Margaret started to reply, she had it on the tip of her tongue, and I knew from her eyes that it would be something caustic and I gave her a frozen smile and she altered the thought, saying: 'I must say the place hasn't changed much. . . .'

Martha and Jonah both had observed my look, and Jonah nodded thankfully to me. Martha must have realized that she had had a narrow escape from a snotty remark, although I was sure that what she had said was not intended to be bitchy, because she turned to Jonah and said with some embarrassment: 'Speaking of changes, what is this petition you've started?'

'Oh,' he said, 'just a thing.'

'Don't they run the club well?'

'Yes,' he said, 'but I don't think this Board of Governors is the only board that can do that. I just got tired of coming around to the annual meetings year after year and being handed a slip of paper containing nine names and being asked to vote for nine men. Why don't we have twenty-one names or even fourteen and vote for nine of them? You know how long this Board's been in office? Ten years. A lot of damned old fossils who creak and groan their way around and never step on the golf course. They ought to go off somewhere and die. We need new blood . . .'

A waiter brought the drinks. I didn't look at Margaret. I knew what she'd have in her face by now. But Jonah knew that if he stopped talking, Margaret might louse up the works.

'And I'm not running for office, either,' Jonah said, laughing. He lifted his glass informally. 'Happy days . . .' he said.

'And a new Board,' Martha said.

'And a new Board,' Jonah said.

327

We all drank to that, and a man in a linen coat and gray flannel trousers, about thirty-five and bronzed, slapped Jonah on the back and held out his hand and said in a jovial voice: 'Gimme!Lay fifty fish right in the palm of that meat hook. . . .'

'Hi, Jack,' Jonah said. 'You know these people. . . .'

'Sure. Hi,' Jack said.

'This is Paul Murphy. Jack Casey. Toughest eight man in the world.'

'Hi,' Casey said to me, shaking hands. Then he turned back to Jonah. 'Fifty fish,' he said. 'You didn't show today.' To the rest of us, he said, 'I leave it to you. I take him for fifty clams a day. Today he doesn't show. Does he or doesn't he owe me?'

Jonah laughed again. 'I was very busy today. Conference with the old man. . . .'

'My God!' Casey said. 'Don't tell me you're going to have to go to work?'

'This was about something else. . . .'

'Well that's a relief,' Casey said. 'I count on you to pay the nurse and the gardener. And something else, just to prove that I don't love you exclusively for your money.' He pulled out a mimeographed petition. 'Sixty signatures already. . . .'

'That's swell, Jack,' Jonah said, taking the paper and looking at it. 'I hope you explained to all these men that signing this automatically makes them outlaws?'

'You're telling me. One of our arthritic directors passed me in the locker-room today. He was taking the only walk our directors ever take – you know, from the card-room to the – er – thing, the johnny. He didn't even speak to me.'

'We've got 'em worried. . . .'

'Yes, sir. I hear Ravenswood is going to resign.'

'Don't count on that,' Jonah said. 'When a nonenity gets in power he doesn't give it up until it's taken away from him.' He folded the paper and handed it back to him. 'Keep up the good work. . . .'

Casey put the paper in his pocket. 'See you later,' he said to Jonah. 'See you later,' he said to us.

'Not too soon, I hope,' Martha said quietly.

'I agree,' Margaret said. 'After all, Jonah, this is hardly the place or the time to hold a committee meeting. . . .'

'I'm sorry,' Jonah said. 'That's why I didn't invite him to have a drink. I was trying to get rid of him. . . .'

'And very hard you were trying, too,' Margaret said. She made a sound with her lips, a sound of irritation, and Jonah looked at her steadily and then to Martha: 'Why don't you and Paul dance?'

Martha took the cue, nodding. 'Would you?' she asked me.

'I'd love it,' I said, getting up.

I helped her out of her chair and we went down the corridor.

'Are you a schoolmate of Jonah's?' she asked.

'No. I'm a friend of Margaret's,' I said.

'Oh!' she said.

'I noted that,' I said. 'But you did your best . . . .'

'Thank you,' she said.

We started dancing. The number was 'Wrap Your Troubles in Dreams,' and a tenor was singing the chorus, trying to imitate Morton Downey. Martha was not too good a dancer, like all women athletes she was unrelaxed on the dance floor, but she was nice and pleasant and looked swell in her clothes and she knew everybody on the dance floor too, which helped put me at ease.

'You're a marvellous dancer,' she said,

'I'm rusty,' I said. 'I used to work at dancing the way Jonah works at golf.'

'Do you know how Jonah works at golf?'

'Well, maybe not that hard,' I said, smiling. 'But I did work at it.'

'It shows too. Are you Margaret's house guest?'

'Well sort of,' I said. 'My father was a friend of her father's – in the old days.'

'Here or in Washington?'

'In Washington.'

I had to start building a background sooner or later. . . .

'Are you staying long?' she asked.

'Permanently, I think. . . .'

She lifted her head and showed her teeth. She had had just enough to drink to put a flush in her cheeks and become aware that she had very attractive breasts. 'Good,' she said. 'We'll see more of you then. Was Washington your home?'

'Maryland,' I said.

'I knew it was the South. . . .'

'My damned accent.'

'It's nice.'

'Do you really think so?'

'Yes.'

Son-of-a-bitch, this is for me, I thought. Gay people, nice people, everybody friendly and charming – this was the world for me. Oedipus is dead. As the son-in-law of Ezra Dobson I would have instantaneous prestige, with none of that tedious struggle to rise above the level of mediocrity, at once I would be somebody. What did it matter if Margaret was regarded as a curiosity? I would cure that. Where was the risk then? As her husband there would be photographs and publicity, but with a mustache and Ezra Dobson for a father-in-law I would have enough disguises. What a jump this would be! Why, nobody in the history of the world had ever made such a jump. . . .

'. . . don't think too hard,' Martha was saying.

'I beg your pardon,' I said. 'That song reminds me . . .'

'Did she break your heart?'

'Nothing that romantic. It reminds me of Mississippi.'

'Mississippi? Where's Mississippi?'

'I know where it is,' I said. 'I can find it in the dark. I spent a summer down there doing some construction work. . . .'

Someone tapped me on the shoulder. It was Jonah. Martha and I stopped dancing.

'I thought I could snap her out of it,' he said. 'You'd better talk to her,' he said to me.

'Is anything serious the matter?' I asked.

'She's bored, that's all. Wants to go.'

'But I thought she wanted to come here,' I said.

'She did, but she's changed her mind. Talk to her.'

'Maybe I'd better speak to her,' Martha said.

'No,' Jonah said quickly. 'Let Paul.'

'Sure. . . .' I said.

I went back to the table. Margaret didn't look up. I sat down beside her.

'Let's have a drink,' I said.

Now she turned her head, looking at me. 'Don't try to cajole me,' she said.

'I'm not trying to cajole you,' I said. 'I'm just trying to give you an antidote for what you think is a dull party. Why don't you have a drink . . . ?'

'No,' she said.

'Well, let's dance then. This is a good party if you'll let yourself go. Listen . . .' The orchestra had just gone into 'I Surrender, Dear.'

' "I Surrender, Dear" ' I said. 'Good tune. Come on . . .'

I got up and pulled a little on her chair, gently, to coax her and she finally got up and I took her arm and we went back down the corridor to the ballroom.

'Do you realize that we haven't had a minute alone since we left the house?' she asked.

'I know that,' I said. 'But what's the rush? We've got left all the

331

moments from now till the end of time. . . .'

She looked at me expectantly. 'That's what I want to talk about,' she said. 'What did Father say?'

'I can't go into all of that now,' I said. 'Later . . .'

I took her in my arms and we stepped off and then I got a surprise that I could put right at the top of a long list of surprises that had happened to me in my life. She was a fine dancer, the finest I'd ever danced with. I could feel the beat coming through her, the beat from even this uninspired music, and she had a subtle mobility that was amazing. I had never associated her with dancing.

'You ever do any ballet?' I asked.

'Some . . .'

'I can tell,' I said. 'Do you still do it?'

'No.'

'You're going to take it up again,' I said.

I let it go at that. I didn't want to tell her how good she was. She wouldn't have believed that I was sincere anyway.

'What did Father say?'

'Not here . . .'

She slowed me down before an open French door and dropped the beat.

'Oh, let's dance,' I said. 'That was pretty good. . . .'

'I want to talk,' she said.

'But you're a good dancer,' I said. 'No crap. You're good.'

'The music'll be here all night,' she said.

I pushed the screen door open to the sky. Off in the distance I could see the lights of the city, far, far away – farther away than that and I had a quick thought of Holiday and the others who were waiting. . . . Yes, I could make this work. Holiday and Jinx, I would have to kill to eliminate the threat of blackmail, and perhaps Mason and his brother-in-law. Mandon, I could handle. Webber and Reece, I had nailed to the cross. If any of them wanted to play at being recalcitrant, there was always that fascinating acetylene torch and its twenty-three hundred degrees of blue flame that could melt you down into a little puddle of fat. There always is some debris when you move into a new house. . . .

We walked down the stone steps and across the floodlighted practise putting green where several men were putting, and down a gravelled walk, bordered with zinnias, and across the back of the first tee. There was a bench on the tee.

'There's a bench,' I said. 'We can talk there.'

'I know a better place,' she said.

'Before dinner, even?' I said.

'It's buffet, you know. The food'll be there all night, too. . . .'

The walk sloped downwards as it left the tee and the border of zinnias, and now a plumbago hedge began, drooping its tendrils so far out over the walk that we had to push them aside. The hedge badly needed trimming, but the greens chairman here, like greens chairmen at almost all other golf clubs probably knew more about selling cement than he did about being greens chairman.

'Where is this better place?' I asked.

'Down here. We've got time . . .'

Well, I thought . . .

She put her arm around my waist and we went on, down a grassy declivity flattened out, and she led me across a small footbridge into another fairway, a parallel fairway, separated from the one we had just left by a small dry ditch. This, I thought is a water hazard. You can lay out with a one-shot penalty. . . . It was getting darker as we moved away from the glow, and the music and the wonderful party sounds were barely audible. . . .

We walked on. . . .

There was very little glow left now, and I could hear the wonderful party noises only when a sound wave dipped. We had gone a long way. This must be a par five we were playing maybe a par six. Was there such a thing as a par six?Maybe in the old country... Somewhere ahead I heard the sounds of a sprinkler, the whining ph-z-z-z-z-z-z-z of the pressurized stream and then the jerky plop-plop-plop-plop-plop as a brass flange flipped up and oscillated in the path of the stream making a coarse spray, a very ingenious invention and then I was vaguely aware that something was wrong with this, and after a few more steps I realized what it was: there was no smell of wetness here. There should be a smell of wetness here and there was none. I told myself that this was impossible, this was contrary to natural law, there was a smell of wetness there all right, but I just didn't choose to smell it. I told myself that I had just been looking for a reason to scare myself into going back, and that this was it. But why should I try to scare myself into going back?What kind of intellect was that?

But there wasn't any smell of wetness here. I wasn't hypnotizing myself. I wasn't trying to scare myself, goddamn it, there just wasn't any smell of wetness.

I stopped.

'Let's go back,' I said.

'There's a lake just ahead – and an oak tree,' she said.

'Let's not get ourselves into another of those morbid moods tonight,' I said.

'Are you frightened?'

'Frightened?No, I'm not frightened.'

'Then why are you carrying a pistol?That is a pistol, isn't it?' She had her hand on the gun in my hip pocket.

'Yes,' I said. 'That's a pistol!'

'Why are you carrying it?'

'It's legal. I have a permit.'

'Why?'

'Protection.'

'Against what?'

'Hold-ups. I generally carry a lot of money with me.'

'That's not the only reason, is it?'

'Of course it is.'

'How long have you been carrying a pistol?'

'Only a couple of days . . .'

That was a lie – and it jolted me. Not the lie – the implication. Not the implication – the fact. I had been carrying pistols of some kind ever since I had been in school, and now, for the first time, I knew why. So that was why. The syllogism was very simple, but that meant nothing now. That was part of the dross that had been burned away.

She looked at me and I saw her eyes and her lips and the whiteness of her face and the blackness of her hair, which I had not seen inside, in the light, but which I saw now, out here, in the dark; I saw that and more. I had been seeing that and more ever since I had met her, a little more every time I had thought of her; and I smelled the *Huele de Noche* again and I knew this was why I had not smelled the wetness when there was wetness there – not smelled anything then: the house was being made ready for new occupants – digging, digging, this ceaseless digging; how far could you dig before you had to stop? What else was there to uncover?

She took my hand and led me on into the blackness, the somnambulistic blackness, into a grove of beeches: and this I had done before too, my hand in the little old lady's, trembling at every step with the ridiculous fear of a child, past the apple tree that, in the blustery wind of a winter night, swayed against the stormy sulphurous sky, looking like a trampling elephant; past the smokehouse from the roof of which my younger brother had accidentally fallen to his death (of not even that accident could I be sure now, we were playing on the slanting roof, playing . . .); past the chicken-house with its unearthly wing-rustling, and finally to the little cloaca with its open door in which the outlines of three stars had been cut through; and then I saw it, looming in front of me there in that grove of beeches, the cloaca with the open door and the three stars, and my heart dipped like a silken sail in a hurricane and spilled the old wind into my lungs; but my intellect and my logic told me that this could not be, this was like the wetness that was there but that I could not smell, this was not here, but I saw. This was a hallucination, an embryonic figment, I was too susceptible this night, the conscious and the unconscious were too parallel, like the fairways, there was no intersection of the two, no scission; this was a symbol, a dream phantasy and I put out my hand to touch it and it was wood *This was where the whole thing had started, at the cloaca. I was one and a half years old, maybe two years old, and I had gone with my grandmother, only then I thought she was my mother; I did not then know what had happened to my father and mother. My grandmother always wore a great and capacious black skirt that dragged the ground, the hem of which was always dirty (that skirt is my earliest memory): and this night, while waiting outside the cloaca for her, I heard a loud commotion in the stable near by, whinnying and bellowing and then the sudden splintering of the wooden railings and I screamed, falling to the ground in fright, and the next thing I knew I was covered completely with that great capacious black dress as she sought to protect me . . . this started innocently enough, but it got to be a game with us, and then I began to depend on it to hide from my grandfather when he tried to find me to punish me because never would he look for me here, never would he suspect her of concealing me . . . and all the time I was growing up and getting bigger and wondering about things, but I never found out until one day when I was six or seven years old why animals sometimes whinny and bellow and break down fences, and then I saw my grandfather and the animal doctor castrate a ram . . .*

336

and other things I began to see too and then that day, that awful day when my grandmother took me on a picnic, letting me ride on the other side of the side-saddle, and we had our picnic and when she got up to go to the spring I screamed, pretending that I was terrified. I started moving towards her on all fours, screaming all the time, and she ran back and I crawled under and hid and finally started exploring her legs and she snatched the dress from over me and said angrily: Your grandfather shall punish you for this; he will beat you, he will do to you what he did to the ram; and I was genuinely terrified now and when she kept threatening me, I pushed her and she fell down, and when she shouted at me that I would be fixed good, I picked up a big rock and hit her, not to kill her, just to keep her from telling my grandfather and having him do to me what he did to the ram . . . I ran all the way home. She is dead, I said, she is dead. She fell off the horse, I said, she fell off the horse. The horse bolted and she fell off, I said, and I stuck to that. And nobody ever knew but I and I felt it; it was wood and it was there.

It was there, the cloaca, as it most certainly had to be, as it inevitably had to be *aváykn'* this was what else there was to uncover; this girl, this ghost, Alecto, the unceasing pursuer, born of a single drop of the God-blood Uranus ripped upon the earth, had stripped my memory integument by integument by slow integument until now there was no layer at all, nothing at all between my eyes and the pool of horror that was spinning faster and faster, climbing the inside walls of my skull, flooding me; and I cried aloud in terror and the color of it was black and I fell to the ground, crawling towards her, trying to get under her dress . . .

'. . . don't be frightened,' I heard her saying.

'I was at the stables,' I said. 'Those horses. They're wild. They broke down the fence. I thought they were going to run over me.'

'Stables?Horses?' I heard her say.

Then I saw that this was Margaret, kneeling beside me, holding my head. I looked around at the cloaca; and now I saw that it was not the cloaca, but a shack, a greenskeeper's shack.

'You fainted,' she said. 'Something frightened you.'

'Yes,' I said.

She helped me up.

'I'm all right now,' I said. 'I'm sorry about the noise.'

'Noise?'

'The screaming. It's not very manly to scream. I apologize.'

'You didn't scream,' she said. 'You just reached out for that little house and fell. . . .'

She held my hand tightly.

'The bench is over there. There by the lake. See?'

'Yes,' I said. 'I see.'

'Can you walk?Are you all right?'

'I can walk. I'm all right,' I said.

'Are you positive?'

'I'm fine,' I said.

'Then you won't be needing this any more,' she said.

She flung something from her, and in a moment I heard a splash in the lake.

It was my automatic. No, I wouldn't be needing that any more . . .

I looked at her.

'I am going away,' I said. 'I am going away.'

'I am going with you,' she said.

'No . . .'

'Yes.'

'Turn loose my hand.'

She tightened her fingers around mine. 'Please, let me try to help you,' she said.

338

'I killed you once,' I said. 'Do not make me kill you again. . . .'
She turned loose my hand.
I walked away into the darkness. . . .

...part
four

...*chapter*
one

I unlocked the door of the apartment and went in.

The living-room was empty. The bedroom door was closed. The faint smell of champagne in the shattered jeroboam still hung in the room.

The bedroom door opened and Holiday came out. She was wearing a wrapper. She closed the door.

'Well ...' she said. 'So you've come back. ...'

'I came back to get my money. I left it in the drawer. I'm going away.'

'Are you?'

'I'm going away.'

'Are you? Why are you going away?'

'I'm just going,' I said.

'You and the rich girl,' she said. 'In her Cadillac ...'

'Alone,' I said. 'I'm going away alone. ...'

I went into the bedroom. The bed was mussed. The bathroom door was closed and I thought I heard somebody in there. Mandon? Jinx? Highness? What would be the color of the puddle of fat if the black boy were melted down? Wouldn't it be black, too? Well, now I'd never know ... I'd never know how it felt to kill all the people I didn't like. ...

I went to the drawer and took out my money.

She came in and moved to the head of the bed.

'Which direction are you heading?'

North, north by east, north, north-east, north-east by north, north-east, north-east by east, east, north-east, east by north-east, east by south, east, south-east, south-east by east, south-east, south-east by south, south, south-east, south by east; south, south by west, south, south-west, south-west by south, south-west, south-west by west, west, south-west, west by south; west, west by north, west, north-west, north-west by west, north-west, north-west by north, north, north-west, north by west – what did it matter now? 'Any direction,' I said.

'Take a souvenir with you,' she said.

She tossed something at me. I missed catching it and stopped to pick it up. It was a bullet that had been fired.

'What's this?'

'A bullet.'

'A bullet?'

'If you had a magnifying-glass you could see the brains on it. If you had a magnifying-glass you could see Toko's brains on it.'

Toko's brains? I looked at her. She was holding my old thirty-eight, pointing it at me, the thirty-eight I had used to kill her brother.

'They dug it out of his head before they buried him,' she said. 'Just routine.'

'What're you talking about?'

'This,' she said. 'Put 'em together...'

She tossed me another bullet, but this time I didn't try to catch this one. I wanted it to fall to the floor so I could have time to get out my automatic. I crammed the money in my pocket and stooped to pick it up, and reached for my automatic.

The automatic was not there ... Alecto had thrown it into the lake.

'Cobbett!' Holiday called.

The bathroom door opened and Cobbett came out. He was wearing long white underwear.

344

'Tell him,' she said.

'I brought the bullet down myself,' he said. 'It's the bullet that killed Toko. It came from that gun.'

'We tested them tonight,' Holiday said. 'Ballistics . . .'

So now she knew. 'It was a mistake. It was an accident,' I said. She lifted the thirty-eight.

'Get back in the bathroom, Cobbett,' she said.

Cobbett went back into the bathroom.

'You got a nice set-up here, you and Mandon and Jinx,' I said. 'I'm leaving it to you. You can have it.'

'Big stuff. Phi Beta Kappa. The Old Master,' she said.

'You know how this thing is rigged,' I said. 'My brother is the biggest minister in New York. My brother is the biggest minister in the United States. His name is the Rev. Stephen C. Apperson. He has that recording. Unless he hears from me once a week he will play it. Let me go and he will hear from me once a week. I swear he will. If he does not hear from me he will play the record. If he plays the record all this falls down. You know what will happen to Webber and Reece and Mandon and the others . . .'

She just smiled. She was Tisiphone. Tisiphone, Alecto . . . and where was the third? Wasn't there a third?

I knew she was going to shoot, and I leaped at her and the flame from the thirty-eight met me half-way.

I felt nothing. I had been hit, but I felt nothing. I had nothing left with which to feel.

I saw the fire again, but I did not feel it this time, either. I dropped across the foot of the bed and started falling, but I wanted to laugh: this was a fine joke on her. I had already fallen, out there, in that grove of beeches, by the cloaca, this that was falling dead now was not I, it was only the physical residue of me, it was nothing . . .

There was another flash of fire and my eyes went out and now

I could see nothing. I could see nothing and could feel nothing, but I had a vestige of awareness left that made me know that I was pulling my knees up and pushing my chin down to meet them, and that at last I was safe and secure in the blackness of the womb from which I had never emerged. . . .